In This Hospitable Land

Cover design by Christo Brock
Graphics by B.J. Hinshaw
Editor, Steven Samuels

Booksurge Publishing

BISAC Code: RICO14000/Fiction/Historical

To order additional copies, please contact us online.

Amazon.com
or
orders@Booksurge
1-866-308-6235

Visit www.booksurge.com to order additional copies.

LYNMAR BROCK, JR

*For Elizabeth Lutz
with appreciation for
great teaching of
Yannick Lyman Brock
Lyman Brock Jr 3/6/14*

In This
Hospitable Land

1940-1944

BASED ON A TRUE STORY

2008

In This Hospitable Land

Also by Lynmar Brock, Jr.

Must Thee Fight

For Claudie,

With Love And Admiration.

PREFACE

I n This Hospitable Land is a work of fiction based on a true story, the story of a family during the Second World War that experienced the events described. The family name and some first names for those still living have been changed. Most others are actual persons. In large part, they represent the courage and bravery of so many that sought to establish a free society where the rights of all are respected and the ideals of the French Revolution might again be realized.

Not every story of the Second World War involves incarceration and death. Many are the sorrowful tales of successful lives abandoned, new identities assumed, and the desperate struggle to survive in alien surroundings. I learned that it was what had happened to the Severins. They related to me of their upper class family's exile in a remote French farming community and shared photo albums provided dramatically different glimpses of family life before and during the war. André, the pacifist, and his brother were involved with the Resistance. How did they reconcile the demands of serving as part of the Maquis?

Visiting the Cévennes in the southwest of France, retracing the family's journey and meeting many of the French who played a crucial role in helping to preserve their lives was critically important in understanding the time and the people. The Cévenols, people of the Cévennes, remembered so much and shared their own stories so generously. I wanted to comprehend the family's daily existence throughout the war, to tell the stories, and to celebrate all these remarkable individuals. The Cévenols themselves, descendants of the Protestant Huguenots, struggled every day to survive. At risk to their own lives, they took in, hid, and protected so many including the Severins. These acts are testaments to their integrity and to their belief in and devotion to the value of their fellow men and women, Jews, Christians, Socialists, Spanish Republicans, and the like.

This then is the story of one family surviving the cataclysmic events of the Second World War.

Lynmar Brock, Jr.

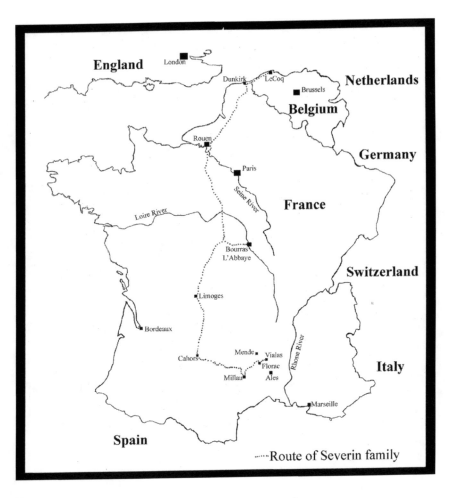

Map of France

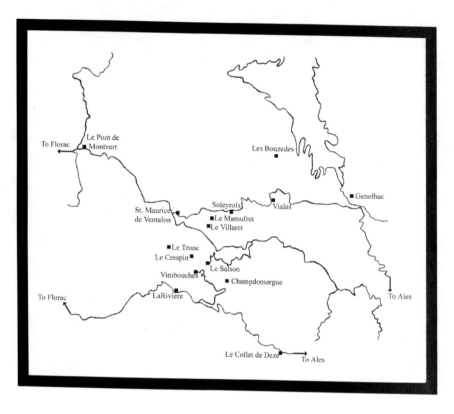

The Cévennes Region

PROLOGUE

It was a time of fear. It was a time of hope. It was a time of despair. It was a time for courage.

André Severin experienced the time. And, time was quickening as if it would run out. The more he thought, the more he feared: the future, his life, his family—wife and two little girls. And that of his brother, who had married his wife's sister, and who now had a little girl and baby boy? He also thought of all the great gathering of relatives and friends who lived in Brussels and Antwerp and other places in Belgium. A country that, through its own centuries of repression and power exercised by others, now was welcoming to almost all by almost everyone. Germany, so alien, yet so close, was reaching out to smother dissent, freedom, and independence. Hitler had become chancellor elected who then determined to rule. And, the German people followed—mostly, but not all. The crushing of spirit became more and more oppressive as it drifted across Europe, first as a haze of thought, then words, then pictures, and then with Armies. It was necessary to fear, for it offered a realization of an oncoming sweep of one man's power against those who disagreed and to those he buried emotionally, and with an ever-greater frequency, literally.

Chapter One

BRUSSELS

May 10, 1940

On what seemed like an ordinary spring day in Brussels, thirty-nine-year old Professor André Severin awoke, rose from his bed, stepped into his small kitchen to start a pot of coffee, then opened the single window of his rented room at 172 Chaussée Vleurgat. As usual, he stretched himself fully and took a deep breath. The skies were clear, the temperature was mild, and the sun shone brightly, low in the sky. André gazed east, feeling expansive and looking forward to his last day of teaching for the week and then his weekend on the coast with his family. Delightfully fresh air poured into the room, scattering dust motes and dispersing the stifling mustiness that had accumulated during the night. But as he relaxed his body, releasing his breath and savoring the scent of brewing coffee, he realized something was different this morning, something terribly wrong. No birds sang in the park across the way. The world seemed completely, preternaturally still. Wondering the cause, he leaned out the window and sensed, rather than saw, a vibration that disturbed his visual field. Listening, he heard a distant rumbling, soft at first, but steadily rising in volume from a low growl to a terrifying roar.

Squinting against the sun's glare, André couldn't be certain whether he was actually seeing clusters of dark spots or just floaters in his eyes, until the spots resolved into the shapes of aircrafts in formation and bearing down upon the suburbs and the city. As he watched—intellectually detached, but consumed physically with horror and dread—the planes, three to a squadron, kept coming and coming, first speckling the sun, then darkening the sky. Not until one group approached his apartment building and shot past overhead could André discern the German crosses on their tails.

Bombs began to drop through the clear sky as the sun glistened on the new green leaves of the trees lining august avenues and parks. Munitions fell as if weightless, in stepped ladder-like lines and odd arcs. Columns of smoke and debris rose from the ground like geysers before the concussion of explosions caught up with the frightening scene.

Air-raid sirens screamed an undulating wailing that mixed with the grumbling of engines and the slamming of bombs raining down and exploding on impact. André, transfixed, realized that the war he and his family had tried to prepare for—without ever really believing it would touch them—had actually, inescapably, come to Belgium.

He was thankful that the previous September, he had moved his wife and children to LeCoq, a non-strategic summer resort along the North Sea, the same weekend the Germans invaded Poland. His parents followed in January, and finally his brother Alin, and his family, had left Brussels for LeCoq at the beginning of May. Had he done enough to be ready for war? The question tormented André, and by the light of this day, his torment was much worse.

The banging of doors and yelling in the hallway snapped him out of his reverie. He couldn't understand the words his neighbors shouted, but their anxiety was palpable and the sound of their feet thumping rapidly down the stairs required no interpretation.

His instinct for self-preservation finally took hold. Striding into the bathroom, he opened the taps to fill the tub as a precaution against the disruption of the municipal water supply, conscientious to implement the government's much-publicized civil defense instructions.

Suddenly remembering the pan of water, he hurried into the kitchen to shut off the low flame, then reached for his gray raincoat—always a necessity in the steady drizzle of springtime Brussels. Buttoning the raincoat up to his neck, he grabbed a chocolate bar off the kitchen table and jammed it into a pocket. A nearby blast jarred him, shaking the building, just enough so that bits of ceiling plaster cracked and fell.

He hurriedly joined the rush of tenants tramping down into the basement.

In the crowded vaulted subterranean crypt, the apartment's makeshift bomb shelter, a single light bulb dangled from a thin cord swaying back and forth ever so slightly, casting an eerie shifting glow on the heavy dust layering the ledges of the cellar walls and on some two dozen faces. Working long hours during the week at the university, André hadn't had a chance to get to know his fellow residents. They held little interest for him anyway.

Everyone was hushed, listening to the muffled distant explosions. Being gathered together provided some comfort, but minute-by-minute, their collective fear grew.

André stood apart hardly looking at the others. He thought some knew him to be a professor, a profession admired and respected by Belgians. But these were all ordinary wage earners, reluctant to start a conversation with a person of his stature. It was fine since he had no wish to speak. He wanted to think.

His eyes may have appeared focused on the bare wood joist framing the underside of the ground-level apartment, but they were actually focused inward. He busily pictured bombs descending. Counting the seconds between successive blasts, he calculated—as he would from the intervals between lightning and thunder—the speed of the bombs' approach and how much time he and his neighbors might have until the storm of war broke upon them.

Meanwhile, Madame Uyttendaele lumbered into the basement. André had never found this overweight concierge pleasant, particularly compared with Madame Jaspart, who had cared for the Severins so well during their years at

36 Avenue Émile Duray in the more desirable section of Ixelles. An ugly scowl distended Madame Uyttendaele's fold-filled face. Decades of inactivity and overindulgence in the weight-inducing specialties of Belgian cuisine, and not a little of the Belgian ale favored by the Flemish, made her an unwelcome sight.

Madame Uyttendaele pushed her gray stringy hair away from her sweaty forehead and her weak watery eyes, and scanned the ashen faces of the tenants. "Professor Severin! I had to turn off the water running into your bath! You wanted the building flooded and more work for me?"

War has come, André thought. *Belgians are dying. Who cares about an overflowing bathtub?* But vowing not to lose his composure and to maintain his high standards of conduct and decency, he simply said, "Thank you for taking care of that," and turned away.

Nervous chatter and awkward bursts of laughter from the others came to an abrupt end as a bomb exploded near enough to disturb the supposedly safe underground chamber. In the silence that followed, all André could hear was choked breathing, rapid and dry and punctuated by the rattle of phlegm deep in his neighbors' throats.

Shuddering, he thought of his family again and wondered, *Have the Germans attacked along the coast too? They've been battling the British in the North Sea since fall...*

The awful buzzing of Luftwaffe warplanes and the booming of bombs receded into the distance. Would the all-clear siren sound soon?

André looked around, finally acclimated to the weak light. The others were so slovenly attired—some in nightclothes, most untucked and askew, one without shoes—André realized he too must appear peculiar.

Forced to remain in this uncomfortable cell, André cast about for a way to deploy his mind without edging back into anxiety-ridden territory. He would have tried to solve some equations in his head, but he was too rattled for the concentrated logic that such calculations demanded.

Bombs started falling again, seemingly with greater focus and ferocity. The bare bulb began to swing wildly, making their frightened faces, bathed successively in distorting shadow and light, grotesque masks standing out grimly against the rough whitewashed masonry of the dank cave-like walls.

Then the light went out. Even as the noise of the warplanes diminished, everyone in the darkness tensed for a third assault.

Finally, the light bulb flickered back on. The others slowly grinned in relief and even began to josh a little. Then a startling shriek violently erupted. Everyone jumped. But the sirens didn't signal another attack. It was the 'all clear', an invitation to come out and discover what remained of the city.

A stooped wizened fellow, with short white tufts of hair sticking out stiffly like the dried stalks of a harvested wheat field, called tremulously to Madame Uyttendaele, "Do your duty! March up those stairs and find out if it's truly safe for us to leave!"

Like every concierge, Madame Uyttendaele had been asked by the city fathers to act as a de facto air raid warden in the event of an attack. She grumbled as she hoisted her bulk slowly out of the basement, laboriously opening the cellar door. She was instantly forced back by an inflow of acrid smoke from a nearby fire, and by the screaming of ambulances and the groaning of fire trucks rushing through the streets.

Undeterred by the smell, the noise, or the heat, the huddled apartment-dwellers shielded their eyes and headed toward daylight. André led the way, taking the stairs quickly as was his custom. Thankful to have survived unharmed, he bounded up to his apartment as the others moved out onto the front steps. There they babbled excitedly and proudly of their experience, as if not being blown to bits had conferred honor upon them.

Have they nothing better to do at such a time? André wondered. He pushed open his unlocked door, unbuttoned his raincoat, dropped it onto a chair and considered what he had to attend to, knowing what he must do: resume his normal life, for as long as possible.

He shaved with the usual care not to nick his skin, then brushed his thinning brown hair with Roja tonic, an oil with a manly smell tinged with sweetness, sold with the promise of preventing hair loss. Back in his bedroom, he pulled on his familiar dark-charcoal trousers with the knife-edge crease, eased his undershirt over his thin body, shifted carefully into his starched white shirt, and fed his shoulders into the loops of his suspenders. At five feet eight inches, his slight build made him look taller, his manner of dress giving him an appearance of severity offset only by his gentle demeanor.

In the bedroom, he reached for a tie, ran it under his stiff collar, looped it repeatedly, and carefully centered the dimple of his newly made Windsor knot. He paused momentarily to admire the way the dark blue of the silk shone against the red triangles of a pattern descending to the perfectly matched ends, and then shot his French cuffs straight held by the silver cuff links inscribed with his initials, a cherished gift from his parents long ago. He considered with an involuntary shiver how little such precious metal meant compared with the iron and steel of guns, rifles, airplanes, and bombs.

Appraising his appearance in a mirror as he pulled on his vest and suit coat and adjusted the gold chain of his pocket watch, he finally felt fit to face the world and his students—at least those who could make it to the university, as he hoped he himself would be able to do.

He tramped down the stairs again, possessed by the perverse thought that the Nazis had been cruelly courteous in scheduling their attack early enough for him and his fellow Belgians to get to work almost on time. As he stepped outside, he was partially blinded by the smoke-smudged light. He began to worry about the Free University of Brussels. For the first time he considered the possibility that his beloved institution of higher learning—a bastion of Belgian freedom and a juggernaut of scientific and technological development—had been a target of the bombing.

Scanning left and right, through eyes half shut against the painfully bright sunlight that cut through wafting clouds of dust and smoke, André hurried toward the corner for the streetcar he hoped would come. He carefully skirted around a mound of rubble that spilled out into the street. Confused, and with his eyes tearing painfully, he finally realized the façade of the apartment building five doors down from his own had been completely blown away. Grit, ash, and lightweight debris swirled through the air above the disaster, slowly settling onto the accumulation of crumbled stone, wood, and plaster.

A half-dozen men frantically heaved bricks and timber aside. How awful if anyone was buried in that gigantic pile of debris! André felt a powerful impulse to lend a hand but couldn't, concerned not so much about encountering a dead body, but rather to become nauseated in seeing blood.

Relief workers shouted encouragement to each other and called down into the still-smoldering wreckage, seeking an answering cry. Then their shouting stopped.

André watched fearfully as several men cautiously shifted masonry to lift out a form and lay it gently on the adjacent pavement. The victim's grime-covered limbs had gone gray and were hideously distorted by death. The rescuers gazed wordlessly as the lifeless body grew cold. The poor man's hair, oiled and precisely parted down the middle mere minutes before, was now rudely, almost clownishly disarranged. His formerly immaculate white shirt was stained bright red with blood still seeping from the wound.

Glancing up and away from death, André saw that the façade's fall had left four stories of private rooms open to the sky. Disturbed furniture and sad-looking personal possessions jumbled by the force of the bomb's direct hit were plainly, painfully public.

On the third floor, the staring eyes of an elderly baldheaded man in an old-fashioned armchair seemed to take in the haphazard devastation casually. Why had he failed to evacuate the premises as all citizens had been instructed to do in the event of an air raid?

It doesn't matter anymore, André thought gloomily. The old man's eerie immobility stated clearly that he too was dead.

At last, the streetcar rounded the corner onto the Avenue Louise. Hastening up its steps, André was amazed that the public transport was still running as if the bombing were a temporary inconvenience rather than a death-dealing portent of still more horror to come. As André took a seat, a surge of thoughts and feelings washed over him as if a moment's relaxation allowed the flood to breach some protective dam.

Gazing out the window, traffic was lighter than usual, but cars still honked as street-corner crowds of stunned, disbelieving Belgians gathered, as if together they could dispel the attack's implications. Unusually large numbers of Army trucks, their military horns blaring relentlessly, raced along the broad avenues connecting Brussels' neighborhoods. Ambulances also appeared more frequently than ordinary, their singsong sirens sounding altered since the previous day—more urgent and desperate. Fat columns of smoke rose in the distance, filtering into the gray-orange haze, blanketing the city as munitions stored in bombed armories continued to explode.

"But Belgium is neutral!" one of André's fellow streetcar passengers lamented.

How naive that sounded. How could anyone believe the government's protestations of neutrality would protect Belgium any more today than they had during the "war to end all wars," when the country had been occupied? Hadn't these people noticed the military going onto full alert one month earlier? No. They believed what they wanted to believe.

André had taken no more comfort from the mobilization than from official assurances that Fort Eben-Emael was impregnable and would keep the Germans east of the great waterways of the Meuse River and the Albert Canal—natural lines of defense against invading foot soldiers. Self-satisfied bureaucrats and the parroting press insisted that the capital and the rest of Belgium would be safe, but André knew better.

Listening to others state that Luxembourg and Holland also had been invaded that morning, André clenched his teeth convulsively. So, the Germans had learned from their mistakes. In the last war, they had left the Dutch to their own devices, closing off a major avenue for attack and escape—but not this time. This time, the Severins wouldn't be able to seek safe haven as they had before in the Netherlands.

André could only suppose that the misery of the last war was about to happen again, except this time, it would be infinitely worse, especially for Jews, practicing or not. Anti-Semitism had played no part in the previous German hostilities. Now it seemed central, with an evil and unjust intensity.

Reaching with his long tapered fingers André gently removed his plain round horn-rimmed glasses and rubbed his clear gray eyes. Though secular, he was still part of a large Jewish family, a major concern that gnawed at his subconscious and occasionally surfaced, as now when he caught a glimpse of his reflection in the tram's window.

With his soft unmarked hand, he felt along an aquiline nose distinguished by just the hint of a Roman bump. Ordinarily that bump didn't bother him in the slightest, but today he couldn't help wondering, *Do others see it as Jewish?* Though he had never done anything to obscure his heritage, he had never done anything to call attention to it either. Could its concealment possibly prove a matter of life or death?

The tram passed the German embassy and André once more saw, parked in the compound, trucks marked "Bayer" and "Blaupunkt." He had first taken note of them immediately after April's attacks on Denmark and Norway, but did not understand then why the sight of the vehicles had disquieted him. Now he realized they might not have been delivering aspirin and radios. They may have contained war material—the first wave of the German invasion.

As he approached his stop, André rose and worked his way through the cluster of passengers. Oh, how he wished he could be with the rest of his family on this frightening morning! At least Alin was there to care for and comfort their two wives, four children, and aging parents. Alighting on the sidewalk, André saw people scurrying to shops, work, and school. Most were dressed and behaving as they customarily would. The university was open for education providing reassurance and reminding him that he had to get to his class. As he entered through the great gates, André knew he ought to make contact with his family soon. The news of Brussels' bombing must have reached Le Coq by then. But he had no time now. He would call later if the telephone service hadn't been disrupted.

Inside the university, professors and students proceeded at a fevered pace. André hastened to his laboratory-classroom, peered through the door's small glass pane, and was gratified to find his students hard at work. As he stepped inside, they stopped talking and eyed him unnervingly. Ritualistically, he slipped out of his suit jacket and into his long white lab coat.

Purpose and routine soothed him. As always, he marveled at the institution he had loved since his own student days, and now as an assistant professor and head of the analytical chemistry laboratory at the university, that had educated him. He was proud to have long embraced and been nourished by the Free University's tradition of unfettered intellectual pursuit, which dated back to its founding in 1834, three years after the nation's birth. Breaking with the educational paradigm of Belgium's older Catholic colleges, the Free University had played a significant role in the development of one of Europe's first democratic states, a parliamentary monarchy in which freedom of both expression and religion reigned.

Now focusing on his students, André realized fewer were in attendance than on most Fridays, even after the general mobilization of April when so many of the younger faculty members and older undergraduates had been called up for active duty. Only a half dozen were present today where recently there had been twice as many.

"Monsieur le professeur Severin?" his best student asked.

"Yes?"

"What are we to do?"

Suddenly the rules of chemistry seemed less important than the rules of war. Everything André could teach these fine young people would pale before the painful education they were about to receive in human frailty and cruelty.

From them, he learned the university had become a vast network of information and misinformation, with students slipping in and out to listen to radio broadcasts and report back what they heard. His class asked, "Would Fort Eben-Emael hold? Was the Army actually fighting? Where was the king? What was happening in France?"

"Be careful of rumors," André counseled calmly, taking on a role different from a chemistry professor. "Honor our school's heritage of free but responsible inquiry. As scientists, it's our job to determine facts, and only then to come to conclusions and generate further verifiable hypotheses. History should be treated as carefully, and so should current events."

"Professor Severin," a female student cried plaintively, "that doesn't tell us what to do!"

André pondered. "Usually I would say, 'Do your work!' And I still say that. But at a moment such as this, you must first look after yourselves and your families."

With his eyes ranging over this small rapt group, André wondered, very much against his will, how many of the young men in front of him would soon be drafted and then dead. He fell silent, providing an opening for still more questions, "Would classes be dismissed early today, perhaps for the summer? Would the rector implement emergency plans?"

"Why don't we break for lunch?" André suggested, as much at a loss as they. "I'll find out what I can."

Following his students into the corridor, he saw the stately figure of department chair Alexandre Pinkus hurry past, and called his name. Only a few years older than himself, Pinkus had mentored André at the university and had smoothed the way for his teaching career.

Now Pinkus waved him off, late for an emergency meeting with the rector.

Having dined and finally drained a cup of coffee in the faculty lounge, André found Pinkus in his cramped office, hunched over a desk covered with teetering stacks of books and papers. Corpulent and balding, with a small well-trimmed black moustache lining his upper lip and underlining his prominent nose, Alexandre Pinkus—whom André always addressed formally as Professor or Dr. Pinkus, the only manner appropriate and acceptable at such an august institution—was always as neatly and properly dressed as André. Permanently sporting a pince-nez that enhanced his somewhat affected air of importance and prestige, Pinkus, a prodigy, had risen steadily to tenured rank as head of the chemistry department, quickly settling into the comfortable life of an academic. A fine scholar and generous educator, he had failed to fulfill his early promise by banking the fires of his intellectual passion. A lifelong bachelor, he had banked all his other passions too. An openly observant Jew, the department chair had remained shockingly unperturbed by Hitler's ever-increasing oppression of Jews and opponents of the Nazi party and its fascist ideology, not to mention the Führer's now-demonstrated propensity for overrunning borders in pursuit of German territorial restitution and expansion.

But Professor Pinkus wasn't alone in this. In the face of lootings, beatings, burnings, and murders, many of André's scientific peers in Germany had remained mute. True, hundreds if not thousands of professors and scientists, particularly Jews, had escaped the pressing Nazi threat for less immediately endangered countries like France, England, America, and even Belgium, though Belgium was usually just a stopover. But the vast majority had remained without protest, many at the Free University.

Ever since the signing of the Munich Accords, André had been deeply troubled by the timidity with which the faculty had greeted the advancement of Nazism. What happened across Belgium's eastern border, they had declared, was "their problem." Even the invasion of Poland had not roused them or the Belgian people to action any more than it had truly roused the British and the French. They had honored their mutual defense pact with the Poles by declaring war on Germany, yes, but whose ineffectual troop maneuvers had thus far lent legitimacy only to the term most often used to describe that war: "phony."

Where was Belgian opposition? Was the university's glorious, much-ballyhooed ideal of free debate phony too? It all was too reminiscent of the university André had returned to, after his Army service, from the Ruhr Valley: frightfully conservative and closed-minded. Then, at age 27, he founded *Le Cercle du Libre Examen*—the Circle for Free Debate—an important vehicle for undergraduate inquiry that eventually reawakened the professors. Now, however, the faculty once more was sunk, like their counterparts in the German universities, into silence.

"Come in, come in, professeur Severin," the department chair called, rising to greet him. "How fare your students?"

"As well as they can under the circumstances, Professor Pinkus."

"Yes, yes," Pinkus replied halfheartedly, removing a snappy red handkerchief from the breast pocket of his gray herringbone suit jacket and dabbing at the droplets of sweat appearing on his brow. "I understand. But I have faith that life in Brussels will not prove as difficult as I know you expect. You plan to leave, but where would a man as set in his ways as I am go? And if everyone readied themselves to flee like you, where would Belgium be? What would happen to our dear university? What about our responsibilities?"

"As long as there is a free Belgium and a Free University," André informed his superior, "this is where you will find me. But once freedom is gone I shall be gone too, with my family."

"I spoke to the rector," Pinkus said blinking rapidly, his watery blue eyes magnified disturbingly by his pince-nez. "Were I you, I would assume the university will remain in session until further notice."

"What about my students?" André asked, resuming his polite tone. "It would be a kindness to allow them to return to their families."

"As you see fit professor," Pinkus said neutrally, turning back to his work.

André might have felt offended, but understood there were far larger forces affecting Alexandre Pinkus than himself.

Dismissing his class, André told them he expected to see them back as usual the next day. Then he exchanged his lab coat for his suit jacket, and also left the university.

The streets were more chaotic than before. Initially stunned, the populace now was panicked. André wasn't, yet he decided to return to Le Coq even though he usually didn't until after classes on Saturday. But this was no ordinary day. He had no idea whether the trains were running, but was determined to try to catch one.

Hurrying to the streetcar stop, clambering aboard the arriving tram, and struggling toward one of the last open seats, André realized he had forgotten to phone his family. Nothing he could do about that now. Besides, the only way his family would be fully reassured of his well-being would be to see for themselves that he was safe.

Involuntarily, he recalled the harsh, though well-intended, words of an old family friend who had fled for America in September, when the Severins had moved to Le Coq: "Don't kid yourself, André. The Belgian constitution forbids government archives from hinting at your 'historical affiliation,' but the Nazis will still be able to do their dirty work. It's your neighbors that you must worry about. They might prove deadly when the Brownshirts come with questions and demands. You believe they respect, and even love you; maybe that's so. But people say and do terrible things if they believe betraying others will keep them safe."

Heading toward the Gare du Midi, the crowded streetcar passed through the city's heart, where André was astounded to see a steady stream of refugees from the east, identifiable by the possessions on their backs. How had these unfortunates arrived in the capital so soon after the attack? How quickly might the Brussels André knew fade away as if a dream? Would Saint-Michel protect Brussels against the Nazi devil and his bombs? Or, would the Grand Place be reduced to rubble as had happened before? And would this be the end of Mannekin Pis? If only that fine famed little boy could urinate once more, putting out the flames threatening to engulf the world.

At the ever-impressive train terminal, André felt himself pulled into the great swirling crowd and the turmoil of a rapidly changing situation. Hundreds of men and women bustled about frantically, none really knowing what was going on. Even government officials seemed uncertain what was happening; they were as overwhelmed as everyone else was by the sudden German onslaught.

Some trains were still running. André battled the crowds, trying to see if his regular train to the towns along the North Sea was listed on the big board of arrivals and departures. His seaward train confirmed, André struggled out onto the crowded platform past excited newsboys, waving their newspapers overhead with the single headline, WAR!

The steam engine puffed smoke insistently from its shiny black stack, the smoke diffused as it drifted up against the roof of the great shed. The sky shone beyond, sunlight still bright against the darkening shadows of the spires and taller buildings of the central city. The deep green of the train's four carriages—new after the Great War but rather worn now—the gold lettering on them—faded but clean—proffered a reassuring familiarity.

Confirming the imminent departure for Ostend, the conductor stood by the last carriage, checking his pocket watch against the large clock above the station waiting room, his whistle at the ready. André clambered up the several steep black steel steps of the third car, pushed open the heavy metal door and hastened to one of the few available seats of plush green velvet in the center—a window seat, its view obscured by streaks of soot on the outside, dry after trailing down to the sill during a recent rain.

A rush of last-minute passengers crammed in as the conductor blew his departure-signaling blast, followed by a shrill piping from the engine. The car jerked and latecomers stumbled as the power of the steam thrusting into the pressure cylinders drove the train out of the station and across a switch, onto the rail line leading north and west, and toward Alost.

Suddenly André remembered that the next day was his sister-in-law's twenty-eighth birthday. He had meant to get her a present before returning to Le Coq, but perhaps, given the situation, Geneviève would understand and forgive.

Staring out the dirty window, André could discern through the darkening sky, smoke still rising from distant installations bombed many hours earlier. Was it possible that this was still the same impossible day?

At each station, as many got on as off, seated passengers shouted for the newcomers to reveal the latest news, though they had nothing better than new rumors to add to the incessant ill-informed chatter about German attacks. André did his best to block out the noise. Deep in his own thoughts, he watched automobiles racing along the roads. He peered over at the villages the train passed through, the lights coming on in the cozy-looking homes. It all seemed so normal, a Friday evening like any other. Yet he imagined the fevered, frantic fighting taking place in the eastern part of the country.

The train pulled out of Alost, a stop André hardly noticed and continued northwest toward Ghent. The land exuded a peaceful serenity, flat and green, with small farmhouses of weathered brick and red-tile roofs built alongside ditches cut into the rich dark soil to drain water from the fields. Willow trees were planted along the water courses, their tops cut off to allow the new growth to spring out from strong brown trunks as the weather warmed, stood thick and mottled with vertical ridges replicating, in nature's way, the classic columns of the Greeks and Romans. The sturdy browsing Charlerois cattle seemed so serene.

André again recalled the December day in 1930 during his American odyssey when, on a commuter train departing New York's Pennsylvania Station for Princeton, New Jersey, he had heard a gentleman ask politely in English as heavily accented as his own, "Is this seat taken?"

Looking up, André had been dumbfounded to see that wild gray hair framing the world's most famous face, Albert Einstein. André had previously run into the epochal figure at one of the famed Solvay conferences and had been profoundly affected watching the great man in action. That conference had brought André into direct contact with virtually all of the most important scientific minds of his intellectually tumultuous time, but none had impressed him as much as Einstein had.

"Herr Einstein," André had said humbly, switching to German, which was more comfortable for them both than English. "You wouldn't remember me but..."

"Of course I remember you! I refuse to forget you!"

"I was at the Solvay conference when you debated Bohr..."

"In October?"

14

"No, the fifth Solvay, three years ago."

Einstein chuckled, his devilish eyes sparkling with joy. "You would have loved it this time. I really gave it to Bohr. One of my thought experiments stumped him—poor man—which strengthened my faith that the theories of quantum mechanics are far from conclusive."

"I wish I could have been there."

"But you had important work to do at the Research Foundation, no?"

"You know I'm a Fellow there?"

"You think I would accept an invitation to this dinner without doing background research on guests of honor such as yourself?"

"Guests of honor," the phrase on Einstein's lips had made André's heart thump wildly. He couldn't believe he deserved to be in such company as Einstein's, let alone at the head of the table for that night's celebratory dinner at the brand-new Institute for Advanced Study. And to find himself discoursing privately with the most influential scientist since Newton...

Einstein had been neither stuffy nor proud. He had worn his greatness lightly and had seemed genuinely interested in the comparative youth he called "my dear colleague."

"All these ceremonies and honors," Einstein had sighed, "are not for me. I always feel like a trained monkey in my tuxedo. Imagine a Jewish pacifist monkey: Hitler's nightmare!"

Though many details of this decade-old conversation had faded away, the substance remained vivid to André. In addition to discussing the latest scientific advances, André had been anxious to learn firsthand whether Einstein believed Hitler a threat to the world generally and to scientists like Einstein in particular.

"You mean to a Jew?" Einstein had retorted chillingly with an odd twisted smile on his face. He had taken the Nazi threat seriously from the first, having fled Berlin for Leiden in the Netherlands as soon as he had learned about the Beer Hall Putsch. Subsequently he had returned to Germany only reluctantly, because Max Planck had urged him to and because Berlin was still the center of modern physics.

As the North Sea train entered the station in Bruges, André understood how Einstein had felt. Though he wasn't yet sure what the next hour, let alone the next day, would bring, it pained him to leave behind his much-loved Brussels, one of the world's great cities and arguably the best place for the pursuit of chemistry.

Einstein and André also had spoken of their mutual devotion to pacifism. What Einstein had to say about peaceful resistance to tyrants had been as much an encouragement to André as his scientific accomplishments. Einstein's thoughts had seemed altogether consonant with the *Peace Testimony* of William

Penn, which had had a formidable impact on André, reshaping his personal philosophy. André remained deeply interested in the Friends. But he had yet to meet a Quaker.

After another blast of whistles, the train moved slowly out of medieval Bruges, along the Boudewijn Canal and past low fields surrounded by ditches. Simple single-storied whitewashed farmhouses, their roofs pitched to shed the constant rain, stood forlorn along narrow roads. André could barely make out the carefully kept green pastures blending into the dark of the indistinct horizon as the train jogged a little south and then swung wide to the west, beginning the half-hour leg leading to the end of the line at the coast.

The train pulled into Ostend close to schedule. André rose reflexively and made his exhausted way onto the platform, then walked the short distance to the station for the tram that ran along the coast between the French and Dutch borders. It would be at least twenty minutes before he reached Le Coq. Yet seated almost alone on the electric transport, he felt oddly at ease. Physically and emotionally drained, lulled by the tram's rocking and clacking, André wondered whether Einstein hadn't been right. Maybe André needed to consider rejoining the Belgian Army to do battle with the Nazis. Then again, maybe not.

Though he felt too tired to be certain of anything, it occurred to André that the moment when one's ideals are most sorely tested is the moment one must cling to them most strongly.

Three hours after leaving Brussels, André struggled uphill on foot from the Flemish-style tram station to reach the villa and his family, and to rest.

What worried him most now was that which he did not intend to share with anyone, especially those he loved best. Recent arcane developments in the study of the elements had made an atomic bomb a distinct yet highly theoretical possibility. André suspected Hitler already had his best scientific minds and technicians hard at work making that potential actual. Fascists were splitting the world. Physicists were splitting the atom. It was hard to guess which was more dangerous. But nothing could be more fateful than the two combined.

Denise was standing by the door willing André's return. When he finally walked up out of the gloom, she ran to him and pressed her face against his, holding him tight.

"I'm home," he said simply.

"Thank goodness," Denise whispered with deep emotion.

She led him into the villa and through the gathered family. André greeted each in their special way. Then Denise guided him to their room where he collapsed gratefully onto the bed and instantly fell asleep.

Chapter Two

LE COQ

May 10, 1940

Friday started well for Denise, as she rose to the cheerful sounds of children playing.

Easing into the living room, she marveled again at her surroundings. Compared to her previous homes, this villa was cramped and threadbare, but with its low dunes and long smooth beach, Le Coq was a delightful retreat. At the height of summer, Belgians arrived there in astonishing numbers to swim, sunbathe, and play ball. The rest of the year, it was more desolate, but even in the continued cold of early May, Denise reveled in the resort's stark elemental nature.

"Tea!" her eldest daughter Ida called out gleefully, abandoning her composition book and racing to the antique toy chest jammed into the less-than-commodious space. At five and a half, Ida read constantly and worked hard at learning to write, frequently camping out in a corner of the couch, knees pulled up to brace her notebook as she traced and retraced her letters, the pale pink tip of her tongue protruding in concentration. Ida's younger sister Christel, who had turned two the previous Sunday, raced to join the sibling she idolized and adored. Small for her age, Christel shared the family's wavy chestnut-colored hair, clear white skin, and glow of good health. Smiling her cherubic smile by her sister's side, she clutched the well-hugged doll she took everywhere.

Their cousins Katie and Philippe had come across from their villa next door a little earlier than usual. Katie, who would turn six the next week, brushed her soft dark hair with her ever-present hairbrush, avoiding the clips holding the longest strands behind her small delicate ears. Adorable-looking fourteen-month-old Philippe, the only male Severin in the next generation, held his sister's hand and clutched one of the miniature lead cars and trucks that absorbed him. They were wonderful children whose faults—hers to whine when she didn't get her way, his to act the pampered prince—were due to their parents' indulgence.

Denise took pride in them all. How lovely the girls looked in the dresses she had sewn for them and how handsome Philippe was in his beloved sailor suit, which she had made by hand.

Overseeing this happy scene, Rose Severin, André and Alin's sixty-one-year-old mother, hardly looked her age, despite a few slight wrinkles at the corners of her eyes. Her dark eyebrows and long lashes surrounded ever-bright hazel eyes and her thin smiling lips were made up prettily with just a hint of red. Rose possessed an especially fine sense of style and retained much of the beauty attested by her wedding pictures.

Denise found her father-in-law, Louis, munching gaufrettes in the kitchen. Tickled as always to see him, she was shocked to discover Geneviève at the counter in her nightclothes, compulsively gobbling fresh strawberries—a rare, prized item.

"Geneviève! After all the trouble I went to get those for your birthday dinner tomorrow, why are you eating them now?"

Mouth half full, Geneviève answered flatly, "Ask him," nodding toward her husband.

Denise looked into Alin Severin's blazing eyes and stifled a cry.

Alin awoke that morning in the dark. After a week and a half in his rented villa, he still wasn't sleeping well. He was unable to adjust to the murmurous crash of the surf instead of Brussels' street noise that was ever present in his grand apartment on the fashionable Avenue Émile Duray and in the smaller place on the Rue du Magistrat that he and his family had moved to before coming here.

Annoyed, Alin got up and pulled the drapes aside, careful not to rouse Geneviève who, always sensitive and delicate, was still weak from a bout of scarlet fever. Running his fingers through strands of brown hair thinning less quickly than those of his two-year-older brother, Alin watched the sea wash against the beach, listened to the harsh winds buffet the stuccoed walls of the villa, and worried about the grievous international situation. What would this day bring? Anything? Nothing? No matter. Alin needed distraction, which he always found in work as a dealer in rare and fine stamps, particularly the French Empire and Swiss Canton issues in which his expertise was unsurpassed.

Focusing on his work improved his humor slightly, but Alin was constitutionally irritable. Alin couldn't help it if the world was mostly comprised of fools!

"Excuse me. Monsieur Alin?"

Speaking of fools: the temerity of the maid breaking his concentration by coming in from next door without even knocking, and speaking Flemish, a sound he recoiled from even though it was his father's native tongue. Not that Juli had a choice.

"I was about to start breakfast," she continued oblivious of Alin's anger. "Is there anything you would like?"

"Privacy and quiet!" Alin snarled.

The maid left with newly risen Katie and Philippe in tow, but Alin still couldn't concentrate. He turned on the radio hoping music would soothe him. But there wasn't any music, only very bad news.

His chest seemed to close in on his heart. Alin switched stations seeking confirmation and help in comprehending the extent and depth of the disaster.

One after another—in French, Flemish, and English—rapid-fire BBC announcers relayed accounts of German assaults on Belgian military installations. Armories had sustained the worst damage and there had been massive casualties. Obviously, the Germans had extremely accurate information, which could only mean spies...and that the Nazis had deliberately targeted civilians.

Unsurprised by this brutality, Alin worried about his brother. Suddenly he had the creepy feeling of being watched.

How long had Geneviève been standing there? How much had she heard?

Geneviève covered her mouth and raced across to the other villa.

Wiping perspiration from her forehead, Denise decided to devote the remainder of her day to willful blindness. It was important to keep the news from the children.

Alin said, "I need a breath of air," turned on his heel and walked out the back door.

Denise asked Juli to take the children out to the beach to play. Then she, her sister, and their in-laws sat around the radio fretting. They started and stopped talking about what they must do, knowing nothing could be decided without André and Alin.

If only André would call!

When Alin got back, the rest of the grown-up Severins were finishing a dispirited late lunch.

"Any word from André?"

Denise looked down and shook her head.

Alin went on. "I walked toward Zeebrugge and Knokke-Heist, to those wooded dunes dotted with pine trees—Wenduine I guess—at least five kilometers. I hardly saw a soul or any cars along the road. I suppose everyone's indoors, glued to their radios." He paused to see if his family had anything to say. They didn't, but he still did. "Peering out at the waves, I half expected to see a U-boat's periscope. Who called this war 'phony'?" Again, there was silence. "The prime minister claims Fort Eben-Emael will protect us. But the prime minister is wrong and we all know it. The Germans are too strong."

"The prime minister speaks for the government," Rose said gently, having long ago learned that her second son was quick to anger and an alarmist.

"I have never trusted the government," Alin barked, "and particularly not now!"

"But it is *our* government."

"Mother!" Alin retorted, not even trying to master his temper. "If you have such faith in the government, why did you change your name from Rachel to Rose? Why did father change his from Levie to Louis?"

Geneviève wept quietly. Rose's eyes filled with tears she was too disciplined to shed.

Every Severin knew the answer to Alin's question: in late 1935, after the German promulgation of the Nuremberg Laws on Citizenship and Race, Louis and Rose had tried to obscure their Jewish roots. The gesture had shocked their other relatives...except for Denise and Geneviève's father Josiah-Jacob Freedman, who had changed his name to Jack.

Alin turned up the radio. British Prime Minister Neville Chamberlain had announced his resignation and recommended Winston Churchill as his replacement. Denise translated for Louis and Rose, for though Louis spoke French, Flemish, and Dutch and Rose spoke French, German, and Polish, neither spoke English as their sons and daughters-in-law did.

As he listened, Louis' pale skin looked sallow and his gnarled hands knotted and unknotted convulsively. "What will we do?" he muttered. "What will we do?"

"Leave," Alin replied bluntly. "Isn't that why we came to Le Coq? To be ready?"

Denise focused on her role model, Rose—an exceptionally intelligent, knowledgeable, wise woman with an unshakable devotion to her loved ones. Rose's gentle personality belied the steely determination with which she would support any decision André and Alin reached.

Her sons would have to decide this because Louis—handsome and distinguished with his white hair, moustache and goatee and fine black suit— had never taken a firm stand on anything. In seventy years, his only show of independence was moving away from his birthplace and most of his family.

Those concerns and more filtered into Denise's dreams after her husband's return Friday night. When she awoke early Saturday next to still-sleeping André, she drifted mentally to thoughts of her father.

Late in the summer of 1939, gregarious, generous Jack Freedman had summoned his daughters and sons-in-law unexpectedly from Brussels to his house at 204 Avenue Jan Van Rijswijcklaan. They had happily ridden to Antwerp on the new clean electric train, knowing Jack loved to surround himself with family and friends, taking pride in seeing that a magnificent meal was served with a different correct wine for each course and that after dinner all retired to the library for coffee, cognac for the men and sherry for the women.

But all pleasure was replaced by anxiety when Jack announced he would not return from his annual visit to the south of France until the nasty business with the Nazis was finished. Poland hadn't been invaded yet, but Jack, like André and Alin, knew.

The men cut and lit fat cigars. André spoke of his plan to retreat to Le Coq—a plan Jack heartily approved. Though he would have felt easier if his children had chosen Great Britain, Jack Freedman believed Le Coq an excellent backup and insisted on giving them his large black 1938 Buick 57, in superb working order, to help them make the move and, when the time came, to move farther still.

"I'm going to take some diamonds with me," Jack said, referring to the immensely valuable cache he had kept after he and his father Samuel, the founder of the family diamond business, had retired very comfortably many years before. "The rest I'm giving to you." The announcement stunned the Severins, but Jack explained, "It's just a little security against the unknown. Hilde will take care of the house while I'm gone. That way she has a place to stay and the house will be ready for me when I come back."

Jack had cases of wine carried out to the car. "Wine may help you while away the hours on the shore. And I'd far rather you drink it than Hilde!" Then he reached through the open passenger-side window and handed Alin a velvet pouch containing some three dozen diamonds of various grades and sizes.

By August, Jack Freedman had decamped for the Bay of Biscay. On the first of September, Germany had invaded Poland, the very day André had rented a villa on the coast. On the third, André had driven Denise and their children to Le Coq, the small turn-of-the-century village with cottage-style dwellings rich in Belle Époque charm, where they had spent several summers, including part of that summer of 1939. The adults were glad to be well-positioned to escape in whichever direction might seem best: east toward the Netherlands, north toward England, and west toward France.

But it had been difficult for Denise not to spend much of each day with her sister. Geneviève had refused to leave her few good friends and her afternoon teas in Brussels for a shore so windy and cold in fall and winter. Even the invasion of Poland hadn't swayed her.

"Why are you all so worried?' Geneviève had asked. "Hasn't Hitler already gotten almost everything he wants? He won't come after Belgium. It's the British and French who've declared war on Germany!"

Two and a half years wasn't that great an age difference, but Denise had felt responsible for Geneviève since the beginning of their mother's long losing battle with breast cancer. Ida had been gone for a dozen years now.

Only sixteen, at their mother's demise, Geneviève had always been more fussed-over than Denise, and not just because she was the young one until their baby brother Francis came along. Geneviève was the more striking Freedman sister. Denise was attractive and nicely built too, with the muscular arms and legs as well as the confidence and ease in social circumstances developed by playing field hockey for Belgium's national ladies' team. But there could be no question which of the two was more stylish: Denise tended toward well-tailored serviceable clothes and practical low-heeled shoes; Geneviève affected Parisian fashions and steered clear of the homely arts of sewing, knitting, and needlepoint Denise had mastered at their mother's knee.

Denise loved her sister and had convinced their father to let her go to Saint-Cyr-l'Ecole, arguing that a finishing school was not college and that respectable nuns could be counted on to foster a proper appreciation of decorum.

Geneviève had returned from finishing school as spoiled as ever. Why not? After Ida's passing, Denise had taken charge of the household staff, but maids had always done all the cooking and cleaning for Geneviève and had even laid out her clothes. Geneviève simply expected to be served and actually enjoyed having their father's chauffeur drive her everywhere. Denise, on the other hand, wished she could learn to drive herself, but Jack Freedman believed a woman behind the wheel was as wrong as a woman doctor.

Whatever their differences, the empathy between Denise and Geneviève had remained deep and abiding and Denise had been unutterably pleased and relieved when, after Germany invaded Norway and Denmark in April, Geneviève had finally agreed to come to Le Coq.

Then Geneviève, Alin, Katie, and Philippe had come down with scarlet fever. Alin and the children, using one of the homeopathic remedies Alin favored, recovered quickly and moved to Le Coq at the beginning of May. Geneviève, who almost always sided with her husband, but derided his interest in homeopathy, was too sick to travel and had to stay with André on the Chaussée Vleurgat until this very week.

Even then, the warmth Denise could feel right through her clothes suggested Geneviève still wasn't well and probably should have stayed in Brussels a little longer. Denise now was glad that Geneviève hadn't waited one minute more!

Finally, feeling compelled to slip from the bed, Denise tiptoed into the living room. Shortly after, André woke with a start. The sun was barely above the horizon when he put on his maroon cotton bathrobe, found his slippers under the bed, and strode out to greet his already gathered family. Denise grasped his hands. Her forced smile masked nothing.

Seated close to the radio Alin looked up and said, "You look better than last night."

"What news?" André asked.

"None good."

Alin brought his brother out onto the deck overlooking the sea for a much-needed smoke.

"Are you all right?" Alin probed.

"Just tired," André assured him.

With the sky so clear and the sun shining brightly on glistening waves, it was hard to think of the previous day's horrors or consider clearly the troubles ahead. If only all of the Severins' worries could wash out to sea as easily as thoughts.

The brothers smoked without speaking, staring out across the North Sea in silent sympathy. André dropped his cigarette into the sand and watched it smolder, imagining it a miniature dropped bomb about to explode.

"Can she travel?" André asked Alin in a confidentially low tone.

"Geneviève? Of course. If necessary."

"If?"

The adults sat down to breakfast while the children, who had eaten earlier, played quietly nearby. Raising and lowering their cups of coffee and tea, the Severins listened carefully as André provided enough details of his experiences Friday to satisfy without upsetting them unnecessarily. Then he said what he knew would be badly received.

"I must return to Brussels now."

"What?" Denise erupted, leaping to her feet, voice trembling. "But there's no need! It's not safe!" She grabbed her husband's hand and held on tight.

Slowly and gently releasing himself André answered softly, but precisely, "It's my duty. To the university, my colleagues, and my students."

"What about your family?" Geneviève demanded hotly.

"It is my duty and I promised."

"Surely you don't think school will be in session!" Denise quailed.

André stirred and drank the last of his coffee. "We haven't heard that it won't."

"Let me drive you to the Ostend station," Alin said as he and the others realized the depth of André's determination.

Scant minutes later, Denise stopped André long enough to hug him tightly and straighten his tie.

"Must you go?" she asked warmly, longingly. "Won't it be terribly dangerous?"

André kissed her brow with fervor. "Nothing could stop me from coming home to you."

"Then why go at all?"

He kissed her again. "Because I'm the professor!"

Alin steered the big Buick out of the driveway. The usually quiet road west teemed with oversized Army transports heading the other way. André would have suggested turning back since taking the tram could have been faster, but once they had entered the stream of vehicles, reversing direction would have been as difficult as forging ahead. Besides, Alin wanted to talk.

"Don't worry about anything here." Alin braked for the stop-and-go traffic. "I'll convince them all to pack so we can be ready to leave at a moment's notice. After I drop you off I'm going to the bank to get as much cash as possible: Belgian and French francs of course, but also British pound notes just in case. By the way, where did you put the diamonds? I assume you brought them home last night."

The diamonds were still locked in the basement safe on the Avenue Émile Duray. Upon moving out, Alin had taken everything but the diamonds, which he felt would be safest there.

"Oh dear," André admitted, "I never gave the diamonds a thought."

"Then I guess it's good you're going back to Brussels."

André sighed. "I'll get them. But warn everyone I might not be back tonight. With all I've got to do, I'll probably have to stay on the Chaussée Vleurgat."

No one in his right mind would go to Brussels this morning without a rifle on his shoulder, Alin thought after dropping his brother at the station.

Alin did his business at the bank, filled the Buick's gas tank, and started back toward the villa. He turned on the car radio just in time to hear the announcer say that the "impregnable" fortress of Eben-Emael had been captured by a detachment of glider-borne German paratroopers.

Even after hearing of that disaster, the rest of the family remained indecisive about leaving. At this stage of her life, Rose said, she really didn't care who was in charge of the country as long as the street she lived on was quiet and safe. Louis questioned the French nation, their most accessible haven, as a way station, given its history of anti-Semitism.

"I know they're not as bad as the Germans," he acknowledged as lunch hour approached and his stomach rumbled, "but these problems run deep. The French have been known to turn on the Jews like that." He snapped his fingers.

The Severins had limited experience of anti-Semitism. In Belgium, there was far less stress between the Jews and the Christians than between the Walloons and the Flemish. But Alin Severin wasn't about to sit on his hands.

"I don't know about the rest of you. I'm going to pack."

What a dreadful Saturday. The children needed care and distraction, but so did the adults.

Rose and Louis agonized. Geneviève, spotting cars of escapees from the Ardennes, moped miserably through her unhappy birthday. Alin, in the other villa, packed frantically. The children, without understanding, became infected by the grown-ups' sour dispositions. Even Juli, overhearing a BBC broadcast in Flemish, became inconsolably upset.

On top of all that: no André. Alin had warned Denise not to expect him Saturday night but that hadn't stopped her from hoping or from feeling heartsick when he didn't show up.

Sunday was worse. Expected every minute, hour after hour, André failed to appear.

Well after dark, Denise, once more posted at the front window, finally saw him approaching—on a bicycle! His coat draped over the handlebar, his black tie loosened, his shirt open at the neck, his shirtsleeves rolled up, and a clip on each pant leg to keep them from getting caught in the bicycle chain, he somehow balanced a small suitcase on his lap.

"Oh André!" Denise called, racing through the door.

André pedaled doggedly. Sighting Denise hurrying down the front steps, he pumped as quickly as his exhausted legs and sore back would allow. Filthy, dehydrated and inexpressibly weak, he stumbled off the bicycle, leaving it and everything else to drop into the grass.

"It's been a long ride," he said in a daze, pulling his handkerchief from his back pocket to wipe sweat from his face and neck.

Denise embraced and gave him a long intense kiss. Ida and Christel careened down the steps to greet him.

"Oh, *Papy!*" Ida cried, burying her face in his side. "We were so worried!"

Clinging to his legs, all Christel could say was, "Pa...pa."

"What are you doing up so late my little ones?" André asked hoarsely.

"We couldn't sleep until we knew you were home!" Ida explained.

With a weary smile, André kissed each daughter on both cheeks in the Severin way.

"We thought you'd never get here," Denise sighed, leading her husband inside and, just as on Friday, putting him straight to bed.

Riddled with anxiety, everyone had difficulty sleeping that night. The rumble of trucks headed for the fighting didn't help—light ones followed by heavy ones then by tank carriers. Brief spells of silence were equally disquieting.

The government had issued orders for a total blackout; so all the shades were drawn in both villas. Only a small light was left on in each kitchen to provide the faintest glow.

At four-thirty a.m., Alin decided to step outside for a smoke on his villa's back deck. He only momentarily was startled to find André doing the same, and crossed the way to join him.

Side by side, they looked out to sea, listening, thinking, smoking. Apart from a half-moon, the coastline was devoid of light. Even the ships audibly steaming up and down the Channel were blacked out.

"The diamonds?" Alin asked.

"Got 'em."

A police officer bicycled along the beach, his civil defense helmet clapped on his head, as a red flashlight guided his way. He waved to the brothers and offered a quick quiet hello.

"Don't forget to keep the lights off," he warned as he rode off.

Monday morning, Juli took the children out to play on the beach again. Over breakfast, André told his latest stories.

Arriving in Brussels Saturday, on an almost-empty train, he had to struggle through the terminal to the street, bucking huge crowds hurrying into the station and scurrying toward the gates, everyone clamoring for a seat on westbound trains. The shock of the Germans' invasion and steady advance had given way to panic and hopelessness. A run on stores meant food would soon be impossible to come by.

The streetcars were still running and when André boarded his a well-dressed well-groomed young man climbed on behind him. As André moved to a seat, the young man attacked the conductor for no discernable reason. It took half a dozen passengers to pull him off his victim and eject him into the street.

The conductor recovered his composure and drove on. Everyone eyed everyone else warily. Even André had to wonder who among his fellow passengers might be a German sympathizer, a card-carrying fascist, or even a spy.

A man and a woman spoke together loudly, as if hard of hearing.

"That fellow over there comes from Germany, I know," the elderly gentleman said.

"There are those who admire Hitler and think his policies are right," his equally aged seatmate added. "And they might not be wrong."

"Of course they're right," a young fellow in ragged clothes declared unashamedly. Hanging on an overhead strap as the streetcar rumbled down the cobbled street, he leaned in and frightened the old couple. "Everyone knows there are too many Jews in power!"

"Did anyone answer that?" Alin demanded, disgusted.

"No, they just ignored him," André explained. "Everyone's afraid. No one wants to risk being reported for anything, to anyone."

At the Free University, controlled chaos reigned. Entering his laboratory André was caught off guard by a confusing tumult. As he reached for his lab coat, Dr. Pinkus appeared.

"Ah monsieur le professeur." Pinkus flushed. "I'm delighted to see you, especially considering our previous discussion."

"I don't understand," André said, watching his students frantically pack up the room.

"Word has come down from the administration," Pinkus explained. "We need to move everything out—equipment, notebooks, chemicals, all—so nothing can fall into German hands."

"Where will it go?"

"Various departments in the south of France have been reserved for Belgians. Army trucks already are lined up in the courtyard to take away the crates by tomorrow night. Our precious diagnostic equipment and chemicals may end up in an abandoned barn on some rural farm."

A tremor passed through Pinkus from head to toe. Taking off his pince-nez, he pulled out a handkerchief and wiped his beaded brow.

"André," he said, startlingly dropping his accustomed formality for the first time, approaching André confidentially, "it isn't official yet, but today or tomorrow the university will release professors who wish to go—the minute everything's out of here in fact." Lowering his voice further, Pinkus asked, "Where will you go? The south of France sounds good."

Interrupting, Geneviève wailed, "Why is everyone so anxious for us to go?"

"I only wish Pinkus would consider leaving too," André said. "'I'll be fine,' he told me. With all my heart, I hope he's right!"

"He's a good man," Denise put in quietly.

"Yes," André agreed. "'When you get to France,' he said, 'let us know where you are, if you can. When all this is over I hope we can work together again, contributing to the future instead of watching its destruction.'" André sat silently for several moments gathering the strength to go on. "After my students were gone and only the permanent fixtures remained, my lab felt spiritless. As I gathered my personal papers, one of the few remaining undergraduates came in and gave me a note from the rector that stated classes were suspended until further notice and I was free to leave. A few minutes later, I went to lock the door behind me by force of habit and stopped. What was left to protect? The Free University was no longer a center of learning, discovery, and scientific advancement; it's just a hollow shell. I placed the key into the lock and walked away. When I reached the courtyard, I saw a line of Army trucks slowly snaking out onto the street. Soon every last Army truck would be gone and with them, what remained of my beloved university."

"You mustn't despair," Rose consoled. "It will all come back and so will you!"

André sat silently once more then roused himself to say, "After that, I made my way back to the Avenue Émile Duray to retrieve our diamonds."

All the Severins felt sad recalling that location. Thanks to Jack Freedman, André, Denise, Alin and Geneviève had lived there in elegant twin apartments from their wedding day until…until things changed.

Denise was anxious to know about Madame Jaspart, the concierge who had been so attentive to them and especially good with the children.

"She's anxious, concerned, of course," André explained. "She told me, 'You are the lucky ones, who can get away.'"

"Even a concierge knows we need to flee," Alin said angrily.

André laughed. "It wasn't funny then, but when I got down to the basement I realized with a start that I didn't know the combination to the safe!"

"Oh no!" Denise exclaimed. "What did you do?"

"Besides panic and perspire? I tried to put myself in Alin's mind!"

"No small feat!" Denise teased.

"I thought the combination must be easy to remember, probably someone's name. There were several possibilities, but considering Alin's healthy ego…"

"No!" Denise cried out.

"I dialed the lock back and forth lining up the letters: 'A…L…I…N.' And voilà! The diamonds were saved!"

Everyone laughed except Alin. "I guess the joke's on me," he said, "but my ego got us back our diamonds."

"On my way out," André continued, "I noticed my old bicycle and carried it up to the courtyard. I knew I wouldn't need it, but someone else might."

"Then how did you end up…?" Denise began to ask.

"I'll come to that. Meantime I made my way back to the Chaussée Vleurgat, packed my little suitcase, and settled in for the night. The next morning, the streets seemed more crowded and chaotic every moment. I moved through them as quickly as I could, trying to get to the Masonic lodge. I thought someone there might know whether there are any affiliated lodges anywhere in France—because if we go there to hide, as I think we must, I know my fellow Freemasons could be counted on to provide welcome and support."

"Unfortunately the lodge was shuttered. So I started for the Gare du Midi. Every once in a while, I saw groups of men cornering and surrounding certain individuals. Everyone else glanced at these disturbing scenes briefly, but no one wanted to get close enough to find out who those individuals were or why they were being detained. Nervous-looking women crossed to the opposite side of the street to avoid these confrontations. Everybody seemed to walk much faster than usual, still trying to look normal, hoping not to attract attention to themselves."

"When I got to the train station, it was more of a madhouse than ever. At the newspaper kiosk, a radio blared the prime minister's voice assuring us the Belgian Army was fighting bravely. But you could hear the announcer's misery as he reported Stuka dive-bombers and two German Panzer divisions had torn a gap fifty miles long through French defenses."

"The effect was unbelievable, terrifying. I was forced this way and that as men and women ran heedlessly toward gates, trying to force their way onto trains already pulling out."

"On the great board listing arrivals and departures, I saw red flags next to the names of every train scheduled to the east and to the north along the coast. I fought my way to the information booth but it was true: trains to the shore had been cancelled. Then I caught the arm of a red-capped stationmaster rushing by and asked why. 'Because the Germans have bombed the railroad along the coast.'"

"And that's when you remembered the bicycle?" Denise asked breathlessly.

"Actually at first I thought I'd have to walk. But the idea of tramping more than a hundred kilometers spurred my memory."

"The whole way back to Avenue Émile Duray, I worried that someone might already have taken the bike. Imagine my relief to find it right where I'd left it. That's when Madame Jaspart gave me this."

André reached into his inside breast pocket and drew out a pale-yellow telegram envelope. To everyone's surprise, he handed it to Geneviève, who hesitated to touch it.

"I can't imagine," Geneviève said uneasily, using a thumbnail to open it methodically. "Oh!" she exclaimed excitedly. "It's from Lilla Tirouen, an old friend from finishing school days! She didn't know we moved."

While Geneviève read over the message, André decided there was no point in describing any of the scenes of horror he had witnessed on his seemingly endless bicycle ride to Le Coq. Luftwaffe bombs had twisted large sections of heavy iron railway tracks into knots, lifting and flattening railway cars. Burning fires revealed terrible glimpses of injury and death that André hoped, but doubted, he would soon forget. Neither did he wish to share the conversation he had overheard when he stopped at a café to restore himself with a bite of bread and cheese and a steaming cup of coffee.

"Soldiers are deserting."

"Cowards!"

"The Army is rapidly losing control."

"The situation is uncertain, possibly hopeless."

Suddenly Geneviève gasped.

"What is it?" Denise demanded. "Don't keep us in suspense!"

Geneviève took an astonished breath. "Lilla has invited us to her château south of Paris!"

"How nice!" Rose exclaimed, brightening.

"Better than nice!" Alin insisted.

"Maybe it's an answer," Louis offered tentatively, "to where we should go?"

"To begin with anyway," André agreed.

Rose got up, moved to the front window, and drew back the curtain.

"Look at that," she said, shaking her head.

Everyone gathered to watch a steady stream of refugees heading toward the French border, some forty kilometers west. The throng clogged the road, making it difficult for reinforcements to move east to the front.

"Shall we join them?" André asked.

"But we're still not ready!" Geneviève moaned.

"Maybe we should get ready," Denise suggested, gently touching her sister's back.

"Pack?" Geneviève wailed as Alin tried to hurry her along. "I haven't even unpacked! I thought we'd have plenty of time before we had to consider going away!"

She coughed convulsively. Denise ran to get water. After several sips, Geneviève waved a hand in front of her face as if to dispel an unbearable image.

"I don't even know what to take and what to leave!"

"Remember *cherie,*" Alin said sternly, "only the absolute necessities."

"But we've already put almost everything into storage!"

"After we leave here, possessions will be the least of our worries."

"I can think of lots of things we don't really need," Denise said comfortingly, "starting with clothes. Wherever we end up we'll probably have even fewer social occasions than here."

"Don't forget warm things for the cold," André cautioned.

"Cold?" Geneviève jumped as if slapped. "We're just coming into summer!"

"It may be a long time before we're able to return," André said sorrowfully.

"How long?" Geneviève demanded.

"My dear, we'll be back," Alin told his wife, showing more forbearance than usual. "You must believe that."

"How long?"

"Obviously no one can tell," Alin said sententiously, already losing patience. "Think how long the Great War lasted."

"Don't say that!"

Denise tried to appeal to panicked Geneviève's reason. "We have to accept the possibility dear."

"The likelihood," Alin snapped.

"All the more reason to prepare for all eventualities, to take everything we can!" Geneviève shouted, venting her unfocused rage on those she loved.

André polished his glasses with his handkerchief. "As big as the Buick is, even with the trailer we purchased, with six adults and four children, there are physical limitations."

Geneviève sank to the floor whimpering, "I'll need help, lots of help!"

"We'll all help," Denise assured her, falling to her knees to embrace and weep with her.

In the dining room, Geneviève ran her hands across the silver chest atop the sideboard as if in a trance. "All your flatware," she murmured to Denise. "Mine's in storage."

"We'll take this silver service," Denise said. "We'll need it wherever we end up."

"And the linen," Geneviève pleaded. She opened a sideboard drawer and clutched the fine fabric. "To give us a sense of civilization."

"Maybe something." Denise gently removed one of the Severins' oldest heirlooms from Geneviève's hands: an elegant tablecloth with an elaborate "S" embroidered on it. "This."

Alin and André came clattering through with two large unwieldy Army trunks, leftovers from the Great War that they had the foresight to acquire.

Everyone agreed they must bring the family Bible, not that anyone but André read it religiously.

"And I'm bringing my homeopathy text," Alin insisted. "I bet we'll need it."

"Please Alin," Rose demurred. "You know how I feel about 'old country' medicine. It didn't work then and it doesn't work now."

"Then how do you explain the children's and my quick recovery from scarlet fever?"

"I suppose there could be some wisdom in those old traditions," Denise said supportively.

Instinctively everyone turned to André for his expert scientific opinion. Ordinarily he would have put up a fight, but he had no wish to argue today. Besides, if he sought one kind of faith why couldn't his brother pursue another?

"I wouldn't dismiss it out of hand," he finally said diplomatically.

As Monday wore on, the main road became increasingly overwhelmed. French Army units and British Expeditionary Forces, which had disembarked at Dunkirk, rumbled towards the fighting in the east. The Severins continued to pack.

Just before dinnertime, the Severins gathered around the radio again only to learn that with massive artillery support and bombardment across northern France and Belgium, German Panzer columns had pushed out from the Ardennes, crossing the Yssel and the Meuse at several points. Peering out the front window André could still see hordes of refugees streaming west.

"It's just as well we didn't go today," he said. "We wouldn't have been able to get anywhere."

"But if we don't leave soon and the Germans aren't held back," Alin said testily, "we'll be trapped."

The following day, the children went back out to the beach while the adults returned to the radio and learned that the Germans had crossed the Scheldt—a nerve-shattering development.

"Well there you have it," André said. "We leave first thing tomorrow morning."

Geneviève grew paler and paler and burst into tears. Between sobs she choked out, "I wish we were in England right now. Oh, if only we'd gone when we had the chance!" She appealed to Denise. "It worked so well for us during the last war!"

Denise put a comforting arm around Geneviève's shoulders and said soothingly, "We've been through all this before. We couldn't go back to England because we would have had to leave André and Alin and Louis and Rose, and we weren't willing to do that."

"Come," Alin said to André. "We still have work to do."

The brothers hitched the trailer to the Buick. Then they carried out the double mattress Ida and Christel had been sharing and set it alongside the trailer, planning to put it on the car's roof. One after another, they brought out the metal Army trunks and lined them up next to the mattress. They needed to think through the best way to arrange everything to have easy access to daily necessities. Even in exile, they would have to keep up appearances.

Hours passed and progress was made, but Alin found himself increasingly concerned that the gray mattress was too light a color—too easy for German fighter pilots to spot from the sky. He rummaged around the garage until he found an old dark-blue tent to lash over the mattress, not that in and of itself it would protect against bullets or bombs.

Just before dinner, the adults again gathered around the radio. Ida and Katie raced in breathlessly from the beach, greatly agitated.

"Mommy," Ida blurted, "we saw soldiers on the road along the water's edge!"

"They had rifles," Katie added, anxiously fingering her mother's knee, "just like we used to see in parades near the royal palace!"

"Only the rifles weren't up on their shoulders!"

"They held them out, pointing!"

Ida climbed up into her mother's lap and Denise stroked her forehead distractedly. Her child looked far too thoughtful and sad for her age.

"It's not much fun playing in the sand with soldiers standing there with rifles," Ida moped. "Sometimes they stared at us. Sometimes they stared out to sea."

"They seemed nice to me," Katie, in Geneviève's lap, disagreed. "Some said hello!"

"I'm sure those soldiers have children of their own at home," Denise said sweetly. "That's who they were thinking of while they watched you play."

After a quiet meal, the adult Severins put the children to bed and assembled gloomily in the living room. Alin tuned the radio to the BBC. The announcer confirmed that the combined forces of Belgium, England, and France were being pushed back quickly toward Brussels.

"So," Alin said, "we go."

The silence spoke eloquently. No one could possibly disagree.

Chapter Three

ESCAPE

May 15, 1940

Denise awoke early Wednesday from another troubled sleep, uncertain she'd slept at all.

Today was the day. Pale streaks of dawn were just beginning to show in the far sky.

Alin was up too, sitting in an easy chair in his brother's villa, and listening to the radio.

"The Germans have turned west," he told Denise dolefully, "trying to cut off the Dutch and the Belgians, keep us from escaping into France."

A muffled explosion in the distance startled Denise.

"What's that?" she asked fearfully.

"A bomb," Alin answered matter-of-factly. "Hard to say how far away the front is now."

Soon every Severin was racing to get dressed and make final preparations. The children played with the toys they had to leave behind as if telling them good-bye.

When the adults had breakfasted—lightly since they all had nervous stomachs—they cast one last look around, then André called Juli aside.

"Here's some money," he said handing her a small roll of bills. "It's not much but perhaps it will help. And thank you for your service."

"But what am I to do?" she begged, tears welling in her eyes. "You're going. The Germans are coming. What about me?"

"Go to your family. Families must come together at times like these."

"But the trains have stopped running!"

"Stay here until they start again. The rent is paid through the month. Perhaps the landlord will keep you on to protect his villa." André took Juli's hand. "You must be brave. We all must be brave."

Outside, Louis called, "Come, little ones! Where's your sense of adventure?"

The four children raced out of the villa and piled into the car.

"It's so crowded in here!" Ida complained.

In the back of the Buick, she and Katie sat on the two jump seats and Christel and Philippe perched atop two small suitcases wedged into the space between. Denise, Geneviève, and Rose shared the backseat to watch, entertain, and quiet the little ones when they got rowdy or cranky. The three men crowded into the front, with Alin driving and Louis in the middle.

They started off slowly, as Alin learned to handle the big car with the trailer attached.

"Hard to see around that big thing," Alin growled.

The quiet two-lane road hugged the curve of the terrain, running parallel to the coast. The short side streets were mostly traffic-free, the sandy shoreline peeping out now and again between undulating dunes, green with grasses and dotted with marsh stalks. The salt sea scent pervading the atmosphere added tang but no relief to the anxious air inside the cramped car.

The road became more congested. Every family living along the North Sea seemed headed for the French border.

Stopping at one corner, Alin drummed his fingers on the steering wheel then impulsively rolled down his window and signaled to a newsboy. As the traffic began inching along again he handed the newspaper to André.

"'The Belgian government encourages all who can to go to the south of France,'" André read aloud. "'Belgian refugees will be reorganized to join the French in repelling the Germans.'"

"You see," Alin chuckled, glancing at his brother. "You may yet be called on to fight!"

André stared straight ahead. "Let's see if I answer that call."

When the shore road gave out, the Severins finally turned onto the main route along the coast. Farther on—near Middelkerke—they spotted a grocery store still open for business.

"We need to stop," Denise called to Alin. "We brought enough food for a meal or two, but we need to have more available. I never dreamed it would be so congested, or the people so desperate."

Alin let out a heavy sigh, unhappy to be further delayed. He pulled up past a clutch of cars clustered in front of the market. André and Denise climbed out and fought their way through the crowd, pushing and shoving like everyone else to get inside. The shopkeepers sold everything as quickly as they could, but not fast enough to satisfy their mostly new customers.

"Hurry!" an older man cried. "Before the Germans overtake this village and all these foodstuffs are destroyed in the fighting!"

"Or looted," someone else suggested, "by soldiers on either side."

André filled his basket indiscriminately. Denise struggled for lettuce and cucumbers. When she touched a tomato, another rougher hand grabbed for it too as she snatched it away.

It took fifteen minutes to reach the counter where a display of fruit had been pulled down, spreading bruised samples everywhere including underfoot. There was no bread but the Severins grabbed some crackers, a hunk of firm Belgian cheese, thick slices of ham, and a portion of the local pâté. Waiting to pay, they protected their goods from darting grasping hands.

Purchases made, André and Denise struggled and stumbled out of the shop. Meantime the road had become more jammed by refugees in and on cars, trucks, bicycles, buses, and even several tractors pulling farm wagons.

When they got back to the Buick, it was surrounded by a half dozen Belgian soldiers ordering Alin to step out to be questioned.

"Let's see your papers," the officer in charge demanded sternly, impatiently.

Alin reached back into the car and handed the family's passports to the lieutenant. The other Severins knew they had done nothing wrong, but worried about the response to their mix of nationalities. André and Rose were Belgian. Geneviève and Denise carried British passports. Alin and Louis retained Dutch citizenship.

"Remember how much freer and easier life used to be," Louis asked Rose nostalgically, "before the Great War, when we could cross borders as we pleased?"

"What's happening?" André asked approaching his brother closely.

"They think we stole the king's car," Alin replied quietly.

"What?"

"King Leopold sent Crown Prince Baudouin and his two other children with a governess to drive down through France to Spain. Now the Army fears their car—a big black Buick like ours—has been stolen with all of them in it."

Despite the soldiers with their rifles at the ready, Geneviève opened her door for more air. A soldier slammed it shut, frightening the children. But Geneviève would not be cowed.

"How dare you!" she said, rolling down her window, incensed. "We're Belgians!"

"So is the king," a sergeant replied brusquely.

The lieutenant showed his aide-de-camp the Severins' varicolored passports and car registration then consulted with him hurriedly. After walking around and scrutinizing the car, he handed Alin the family's papers and said, "Thank you Monsieur. Your passports reveal a complicated heritage but everything's in order. You may proceed."

Alin cautiously merged back into the slow-moving traffic. The soldiers who had intercepted the Severins stood on either side of the road looking in both directions in search of the king's missing Buick.

"We still need bread," André said as they crawled along.

"And something to drink," Denise added, "if we find another market."

"And if there's anything left in it," André sighed. "People have lost all reason. They're beginning to act like animals."

"Every man for himself!" Alin sang out cynically.

In the next town, shoppers were more civilized and the Severins succeeded in acquiring bread, water, wine, and a further supply of biscuits and cheese. As it was midday, they drove up and down the streets repeatedly, seeking and finally spotting an open restaurant in a small hotel.

Only two of the tables were seated. People were in too big a hurry to get away to waste time on a cooked meal.

The Severins appreciated the quiet reserved atmosphere as much as the food. At the end of the meal, the proprietor agreed to sell them a small quantity of ham—at a premium.

Late in the afternoon—after being stopped and released one more time by soldiers searching for the king's children—they approached the French border plainly visible several hundred meters ahead. But the traffic wouldn't budge. Military police frantically motioned all civilian vehicles off the road. Disgusted, Alin eased the car and trailer onto the shoulder.

"Why are we stopping?" Ida asked, twisting around on her jump seat to get a better view. The children had been good passengers until then, but now were running out of patience.

André stepped out of the car to peer about. Vehicles were stopped all along the side of the road, some with their motors running, others stalled. Disgruntled drivers and passengers wandered about aimlessly, dazed.

"The border must be closed," André leaned back in to report. "The barrier's down and no one's going through."

He walked toward the customs building straddling the border. Frenzied Belgians questioned French authorities to no avail. Rumors spread that German troops had broken into open country, and were headed toward the English Channel, which had panicked the people of Paris—not that it explained the border problem.

French and British soldiers were still pouring into Belgium, overwhelming the roads.

"Get out of the way you fools!" authorities bellowed at the milling, distressed, would-be exiles as a convoy of French Army trucks rolled glacially forward.

When André returned to the car, Denise suggested they might all stretch their legs.

The children jumped out eagerly. Lined up alongside the road, they watched with wide eyes the steady flow of warriors and war matériel passing by. French soldiers leaned out of their canvas-covered transports and waved. The Severin children waved back enthusiastically. Philippe even received a salute, which he manfully yet unsuccessfully returned.

The older Severins gazed at the canal running parallel to the road and at the hedgerows surrounding the fields where cows lazily grazed.

Denise, glad the children now considered the soldiers their friends, asked André, "Where should we go? We can't cross the border and we can't stay here."

"And we can't go back to Le Coq." André gestured at the impossibly congested road east.

"What's wrong with here?" Rose asked gamely. "It's a lovely spot and the weather's quite pleasant."

As if to demonstrate the practicality of the notion, Denise immediately brought a blanket and some food and drinks out of the car and laid them all out on the ground picnic-style. She cut bread and cheese into little sandwiches and shared them around.

Everyone sat down and ate hungrily.

"Thank you Denise," Louis said gravely. "But where will we sleep?" He tremulously remembered André's promise that they wouldn't have to sleep in the mud. "I can't stay out here all night." He put an arm protectively around his wife. "And neither can Rose."

"You and Mother can stay in the car," André suggested, "along with Denise, Geneviève and the children. There's room enough if you're willing to snuggle. Alin and I can stay outside to serve as lookouts. If anything happens, we'll hop in the car and race away."

The sun began to set. The family spread blankets on the car's front and back seats and on the floor in back after restoring the jump seats to their storage positions.

"Mother," Ida said softly, as Denise gave her a goodnight kiss, "this really is an adventure!"

"I'll say it's an adventure," Alin called testily, leaning against the Buick's hood.

"But mother, where will we do our business? I'm not like the little ones. I don't wear diapers anymore."

"Big girls like you sometimes have to make do. That's what the hedgerow is for."

"Oh!"

As the night wore on, it was only Christel who couldn't sleep—due to the unnatural angle that huddling required. She began to whimper.

"Stop being such a spoiled brat!" Alin exploded outside. "This is hard on everyone, and I don't hear the rest complaining!"

"Come here sweetheart," Denise called softly, picking up a blanket, placing Christel over her shoulder, and leaving the car to lie down on the least steep part of the slope.

Christel hugged her mother closely. "Maman, what if I roll into the canal?"

"You won't if you hold on to my skirt."

Christel clutched the fabric tightly through the night. Denise slept fitfully, unable to block out the intermittent drone from the constant stream of outmoded Berliet trucks slowly carrying military forces past the many stranded refugees. In an irregular progression, airplanes passed noisily overhead. But she was glad to have helped Christel slip into a long deep sleep, as if she had purged her darling's fears by adding them to countless fears of her own.

As the morning sun broke through the early mists, it was strangely quiet beside the canal. The military had largely passed far into Belgium while the Severins struggled to sleep.

Louis Severin, the earliest riser, felt impossibly stiff, scrunched up with his wife on the front seat of the car, the Buick's steering wheel pressed into his back. He listened as the children wriggled and talked in their sleep. Lying there quietly, so as not to disturb the others, he realized he'd been wrong to worry about staying in Adinkerke.

André and Alin stood up beside the car. The others grumbled and groaned into consciousness then emerged to stretch awkwardly and complain of the difficult night.

Alin climbed the ridge to see what he could learn from other stranded refugees.

"André!" he called suddenly as André marched his way. "Look!"

The striped wooden barrier at the border crossing had been raised. Large groups of fleeing Belgians came to life and revved their engines to cross into France.

"We'd better go," André said. "This might be our last chance."

"Everyone!" Alin shouted. "Back in the car! Hurry!"

The Severins joined the bumper-to-bumper traffic with André driving. It took an hour to reach the checkpoint. The little ones quickly grew restless.

"This is a bad sign," Alin said grumpily.

Belgian officials thoroughly checked passports before stamping them with exit visas. The prim mustachioed border guard of short stature and cold demeanor handed back the Severins passports. He had no difficulty with the Dutch and British citizens nor even with Rose's Belgium one. But he gave André a dubious glance.

"You prefer running away to staying and fighting?"

Blood drained from André's face.

"Don't even think about it," the border guard said, stamping and handing back the passports, smiling almost imperceptibly. "Take your family to France. The war in Belgium is already lost."

Flustered, André didn't hesitate. He eased his foot from the brake to the gas and rolled the Buick into the no-man's land adjoining French soil. The Severins clapped and cheered.

While they waited for the French authorities to approve their entry, André asked Alin anxiously, "Should I go back? Does my nation really need me?"

"Not if you're not willing to take up arms," Alin replied blithely.

"Is Papy afraid?" Ida asked her mother. "Is he a coward?"

"No," Denise declared instantly, definitively, startled to realize Ida knew such words and concepts. "Your father is very brave. He's a pacifist."

"What's a *pastafitz*?" little Christel asked.

"Someone who doesn't believe in killing," André said firmly. "Someone who thinks it's never right to take another person's life."

"Oh," Ida said very quietly.

"Relax, André," Alin told him, trying to do so himself. "Didn't you understand the border guard? Belgium's done for. Better to save your family than risk your own skin on a losing battle."

Watching and waiting, with some concern, for the uniformed French customs officials to determine the Severins' fate, André considered the two years he had spent in uniform himself as part of the combined Belgian and French forces occupying the Ruhr Valley. The heart of Germany's coal, iron, and steel industries had to be "overseen" to enforce compliance with the onerous reparations payments required by the Treaty of Versailles. But to what had André's service amounted? Observing Frenchmen and Belgians mistreat Germans so badly it had inevitably led to the present mess. Exercising the Belgium general's horse on the long rides through the countryside had exposed André to the misery and anger of the sorely put-upon German people. He had watched in horror as leading industrial and investment interests organized a campaign of passive resistance, grinding production to a veritable halt, leading to arrests and prison sentences, and ultimately the collapse of the German economy, complete with huge numbers of unemployed and inflation on a hitherto unknown scale.

A pall of gloom spread over the Severins. They looked a sorry sight to the French guards who examined their passports next. This time, Louis and Alin's nationality caused comment.

"Have you heard the latest?" one Frenchman asked, leaning in through the passenger-side window. "Yesterday Rotterdam fell and the government went into exile in London."

"Terrible," Louis said, shaking his head. Not that he was surprised.

Geneviève held her telegram from Lilla Tirouen at the ready should proof be needed that the Severins had a place to stay. However, the immigration officials handed back the passports, not even bothering to stamp them, and quickly sent the Severins on their way, with one caution. "Remember to register as soon as you reach your destination."

Moments later, André watched the border crossing recede into the distance.

"I suppose the French don't much care who enters the country," he speculated, "as long as the roads stay clear."

Smartly dressed auxiliary police directed the flow of Belgian vehicles. Strikingly, businesses all across the northern coast were open for customers as usual. How strange after the panic in Belgium to see French citizens sitting easily at outdoor cafés, drinking their *cafés au lait*, and eating *petites gateaux* as if they hadn't a care in the world.

Traffic was orderly and steady, allowing the Severins to make real progress. At Dunkirk, they turned south for the longest leg of the journey.

The children settled into a routine with Ida and Katie, reading books they had brought along, and Christel regaling Philippe with fairy stories she invented. The adults focused on the changing scene of low hills, green with long-tilled crops planted in narrow fields, speckled by grazing cows and sheep. Alongside the roadway, lining the hard surface of black macadam, scraggly weeds flitted between straight and ordered trees.

After traveling several hours, they found themselves just south of Abbeville, at Blangy-sur-Bresle. André signaled his intention to turn off for a road heading further west of Paris.

"Shouldn't we keep going straight?" Geneviève asked, pointing out a sign indicating the direction of the French capital. "Lilla lives south of Paris in the Loire Valley."

"I think we need to stay to the west," André explained. "It would be too easy to get delayed or lost in the confusion of the big city. And if what we heard yesterday about panic there is true..." André trailed off, focusing on merging onto the highway west. "This road seems better able to handle the traffic anyway."

Their progress continued and their pace picked up a bit. However, as the hours passed and road signs became scarce Louis asked, wearily and warily, "Where are we?"

"I'm not exactly sure," André admitted.

Concentrated quiet followed. The sun cast varying shadows on the road that ran straight for some distance and then twisted alongside a meandering stream, coming upon a village of neat orderly houses lining narrow sidewalks on either side—one house after another with little variation, shutters open to reveal white lace curtains framing clear clean glass windows. At night, the shutters would be closed tight securing each family within its own domain.

In the center of a village, an imposing church stood back from the road, its single spire reaching toward the sky as high as the faith and money of villagers of times past had allowed. Leaning forward to point out this landmark, Geneviève accidentally brushed against little Philippe, who pushed back and inadvertently hit his sister in the process.

"Ouch!" Katie squealed.

"Stop it!" Alin yelled.

"But he started it!" Katie whined.

"Now you're pushing me!" Ida complained, giving her female cousin a little shove.

"I'm warning you," Alin growled threateningly. "All of you!"

"Shouldn't we stop to let the children get some exercise?" Denise asked diplomatically.

"That might be best dear," Geneviève added, trying to appease her husband.

"We need to keep going," André cautioned, "to get far from the Germans as quickly as we possibly can."

The market town's houses abruptly came to an end. The fields again began spreading out into the distance.

Then Katie said, shamefaced, "I need to go pee-pee."

Exasperated, Alin demanded, "Are you sure?"

"Yes, Papy. Badly."

"I'll find a place," André sighed. "She's probably not the only one in need."

Short as their roadside stop was, it was long enough for the road to become congested.

"Anyone mind if I turn on the radio?" Alin asked.

Without waiting, he turned on the news. The previous day's rumors about the German breakthrough at Sedan, a few hours northeast of Paris, were true. Thousands of civilians were fleeing west and south, clogging highways and stranding Allied military transports, turning them into easy targets for Luftwaffe attacks.

They traveled on as the sun began to sink into the western horizon over the famous cathedral spires of the nearby city of Rouen.

"Maybe we should stop there for the night?" Louis suggested tentatively.

"Alin," Geneviève piped up, "didn't we spend a lovely time near here one night at that little inn along the river?"

"It's not very far," he said. "Les Andelys—a little east and upstream of Rouen."

"Why not just stay in the city?" tired Louis asked a little grumpily.

"You and Mother will really like this place," Alin replied, "especially after last night."

"Let's just hope they're open," André cautioned.

"And that you can find it again," Denise added.

They turned off the main road, striking out in a very different direction than the rest of the refugees they could see. Shortly they were all alone on a very small road. Only a few lights showed in the twilight.

"It's set in a garden," Alin said searching, "right beside the Seine..."

"There it is!" Geneviève cried out joyfully.

The little inn—a half-timbered building with brickwork at the entrance, constructed in the Norman style typical of the area's architecture—seemed perfect: a centuries-old structure that had been altered only enough to accede to the most pressing modern demands. Geneviève and Alin remarked on the warmth the place had retained. Everyone was charmed by the gardens surrounding the main building, with walkways set among flowers, bushes, and a few trees. A pergola here and benches there enhanced the lovely isolated setting.

The burly innkeeper, recognizing Alin and Geneviève, effusively welcomed the Severins. For the few minutes it took him to check them, in the war seemed mercifully distant.

After a fine filling family-style meal in a cozy dining room, the Severins settled down in adjoining rooms. It was wonderfully comfortable and Louis was especially grateful for the soft mattress, complete with fluffy pillows. He felt full, content, and secure.

During the night, he was awakened by the sound of bombs exploding. Tiptoeing to the window, he pulled back the shade. A nightmare landscape of bright flickering fires burned in and around Rouen. Hypnotized, Louis watched helplessly as flames licked at the uneven towers of the cathedral.

Dreadful. Horrendous. How glad he was not there.

As dawn broke, smoke hung over Rouen. The city was altered dramatically, the tall spires of its many churches and towers shortened to jagged stumps. Other buildings were reduced to unsteady walls without roofs to support.

The heartsick Severins sat in the inn's small breakfast room joylessly eating croissants.

"It's my birthday tomorrow," Katie said miserably. "Will I still get presents?"

"Tomorrow is tomorrow," her mother said sadly.

"Drink your milk," her father ordered dismissively.

A radio crackled in the kitchen. The innkeeper brought a fresh pot of coffee and news.

"Yesterday the Germans broke through the Dyle Line," he told them cheerlessly.

The Dyle Line was constructed between Antwerp and Namur after the Great War to protect the eastern border of Brussels. Without it, the Belgian capital was defenseless.

"And today the Belgian government removed itself to Ostend," the innkeeper continued grimly. "Also the French-Belgian border has been closed."

"It was only open for a day," André breathed incredulously.

"Lucky we made it through," Alin said, sounding more glum than grateful.

"We'd better be going," Denise said.

Silently, hurriedly, the Severins finished up, settled the bill, and checked out of Les Andelys. Squeezing themselves back into their big Buick they started south, having no idea what road conditions or how much refugee-bearing traffic they might meet.

"You think your friend will still have us?" Denise asked Geneviève. "You never answered her telegram."

"I didn't have a chance. But I'm sure it's all right. Lilla is a very good friend."

"She'd better be!" Alin groaned.

André, driving again, peeked furtively at Alin and asked, "Do you think there's another way to go? I can't help thinking it would be faster and safer to stay off the main road."

"There ought to be a country road close by, along the Eure," Alin said. Finding a narrow road running parallel to the river, André turned onto it.

Its serenity was a relief. The road wound up and down undulating hills, some higher than any they had seen since entering France. The sight of woods of chestnut and oak trees covering land too steep to cultivate, streams that ran down little valleys into the river coursing steadily toward the Seine, and the sea some two hundred kilometers west were a soothing contrast to the turmoil of war. Sweet-smelling fertile fields cleared of rocks in an earlier age bordered the river. The grasses were deep and wildflowers grew in pockets of abundance undisturbed by the numerous brown-and-white-speckled cows browsing the profusion of green shoots—source of the fat-rich milk that gave a unique savor to the soft flavorful cheeses the Severins had sampled at breakfast.

"Look," Louis said hoarsely after a while, weakly pointing through a line of trees to a far road, "flames."

"That must be the main refugee route," André guessed. "But what..."

A fighter plane, marked with the dreaded German cross, swooped low. Flying just above the traffic to the west, it began firing machine gun rounds. Then more fighters zoomed into view, shooting bursts at the highway below.

"Watch out!" Alin shouted.

A German fighter plane lined up dead ahead along the Severins' road, aiming straight at them. As it flew toward the Buick and dropped low, André swerved violently off the road and onto the grass shoulder. The big car and trailer bounced bone-jarringly under a row of trees, jostling the Severins against one another while André struggled fiercely to retain control as the trailer, dancing behind, jerked one way and the other.

The fighter plane disappeared into the distance. Shaking, André slowed the car to a stop. All the children cried.

"That was close," Alin said angrily.

André's voice quavered with shock. "I guess one car isn't worth that many bullets."

After the coast was clear, André managed to pull the Buick back out onto the road. The Severins slowly came back to themselves, aided by the distraction of the lush ever-changing landscape.

But André kept glancing up at the sky with trepidation.

Vineyards stretched down the hillsides toward the river. Louis pointed out the orderly staked lines of grapevines shooting out from the stalks, cut and pruned above the roots. The grown-ups spoke of the promise of the new growth and the vintage that might result—the distinctive smoky intense acidity of the wines for which this region was justly famous.   Passing through Orléans, they drove up the Loire River valley, finally arriving in the little town of Pouilly late in the afternoon. Farther on they came to a crossroads and a small sign they followed to an ancient abbey and the Tirouens' château, Bourras L'Abbaye, which dominated the small collection of farm buildings standing to one side.

André drove through the ornate gates of the sizable estate. The château was set in the heart of a well-tended park, itself in the midst of fields of wheat and vegetables, and orchards ripe with an abundance of fruit. Cattle ranged the pastures. Trees stood in small clumps as if guarding the quiet meandering streams that burbled throughout the property.

"At last," Denise sighed.

"Thank God," Louis said.

"What 'God?'" Alin demanded

Geneviève declared, "I won't feel right until I see Lilla."

Chapter Four

BOURRAS L'ABBAYE

May 17, 1940

T he long gravel drive of red and tan stones matched the elegant château looming around the bend that was built of shaped stones from the same quarry. An inviting terrace fronted great double doors framed by four large windows on either side, mirrored by matching windows on the upper floor. A steeply slanted roof made of soft red tiles completed the façade's perfect symmetry.

As the Severins stepped stiffly out of the Buick, Lilla Tirouen appeared at the top of the broad expanse of stone steps. "Welcome!" she gushed rushing down to Geneviève's outstretched arms and kissing her repeatedly. "How wonderful to see you! I've been so worried!"

Small, trim, vivacious, enthusiastic Lilla, like Geneviève, was in her mid-twenties. Her short, soft brown hair curled about her ears. Her cute little nose turned up. Her mouth was pert and full-lipped. Her dark eyes shone brightly against clear light skin.

"And which of these handsome gentlemen is your husband?" she asked charmingly.

Alin stepped forward; he was treated to the same affectionate reception as his wife. Then Lilla greeted each Severin, paying special attention to the littlest, who hid behind their mothers.

"What a beautiful family!" Lilla enthused. "And you all look so alike even these cousins could be siblings! Come meet my parents and refresh yourselves; food and drink await! I'll have our houseboy gather your bags and park your car and trailer by the garage." She started up the steps briskly then looked back at the stragglers sympathetically. "I want you to make yourselves at home. Bourras L'Abbaye will be what it has always been: a refuge."

The presence of the Severins was a relief. Even with her parents in residence, Lilla needed distraction. She couldn't stop thinking about her husband, Francis, who had been mobilized into the French Army after the Germans invaded Poland. It had been many months since Lilla had heard from him. She kept visualizing in ugly detail all possible causes for his silence.

Learning of Katie's sixth birthday, Lilla and the household staff improvised a small party for the displaced girl. Katie was very good about receiving no presents beyond some freshly cut flowers and a birthday cake everyone enjoyed. But the celebration was almost ruined by the news that the Germans had taken Antwerp, and that all the territory ceded to Belgium by the Treaty of Versailles had already been reincorporated into the Fatherland.

After the children bedded down for their second night, Lilla had a good long laugh with Geneviève who reported a conversation with Katie, who had unearthed one of the few flaws in this paradise.

"'*Maman,*'" my sweet child asked, "'are the French really poor?'"

"'Darling,' I replied, 'I only wish we were well enough off to live as they do at Bourras L'Abbaye!'"

"'But I like it better at home,' Katie whined, fighting back tears, 'where you just flush your business away. Here it drops down a hole!'"

"'Now Katie,' I replied struggling to keep a straight face and well aware the children will have to get used to many ways of life that seem strange to them, 'the customs here are different, that's all.'"

"Then she prayed, 'I hope they're not all so different like this!'"

Denise busied herself with the children. Louis and Rose kept company with Lilla's parents and the two older couples found enormous pleasure in watching the little ones frolic. Lilla and Geneviève took an extended "constitutional," overjoyed to have a chance to talk as they hadn't since they were schoolmates. André also strolled about the grounds, musing on the war and mulling actions his family shortly might have to take. Alin joined André when he was able to tear himself away from the radio.

The progress of German attempts to overrun France was seriously worrisome. In short order, German forces had reached Cambrai, vanquished Péronne, and occupied Amiens, about one hundred kilometers north of Paris. Rapidly advancing south, they might soon directly threaten Pouilly and Bourras L'Abbaye.

Changes in the French government seemed hopeful. Prime Minister Reynaud appointed the much-decorated General Weygand as chief of the general staff and commander-in-chief for all theaters of operations, and named Marshal Henri-Philippe Pétain, the celebrated hero of the Battle of Verdun, deputy prime minister. Everyone in the château interpreted these as good signs.

Monday morning, while everyone breakfasted at the table overlooking the park, the butler brought Lilla word that her brother-in-law—who like her husband served in the French Army—had been killed defending his country.

"I need air," Lilla gasped turning paper white.

Her parents and the Severins rose and stood silently as she rushed from the room.

"Excuse me," Geneviève said hurrying after her.

After several awkward moments, Monsieur Thiern invited them all to sit and finish their meal.

"I hope the south of France will serve to protect you," he told the Severins.

Geneviève spent hour after hour with Lilla. The two women had corresponded for a decade, but Lilla wanted more detail about Geneviève's life, particularly the way she and Alin courted and married.

"You lived in Antwerp, the Severins lived in Brussels," she said. "How did you meet?"

"Suzanne Freedman—the wife of father's younger brother Maurice—felt inspired to play matchmaker for the first and only time in her life. She alerted father to expect a call from André. To this, he readily agreed—as long as I went along as a chaperone. Then André decided to bring Alin for support."

"Were you all instantly smitten?"

"I wouldn't go that far," Geneviève said blushing slightly, "but Denise and I were impressed by the striking figure they cut, so well-dressed for the first of many evenings on the town."

"Then when did you fall in love?"

"It happened gradually, but there was a definite turning point when André announced he had given up his mistress to remove any possibility of embarrassment."

"*What?*"

"Lilla! Don't pretend to be shocked! You're French!"

"Yes, but..."

"It's commonplace in Belgian society for young men to keep mistresses they *see* once a week."

"André seems too elevated to engage in such a practice."

"But he is a man," Geneviève laughed. "And at least he had the good sense to end it!"

"What about Alin?"

"He never said anything and I never asked. I just assumed he didn't behave like that."

So in September 1932, André and Denise were engaged. Everyone was surprised when Beatrice Herz, our very proper grandmother, insisted on throwing an elaborate engagement party. In the midst of it, she hobbled over to Alin and myself on her ever-present cane and said, "You're obviously in love. Since all your friends and family are already gathered don't let me stop you from announcing your engagement too."

"Wait!" Lilla demanded. "You didn't say..."

"Alin and I were already betrothed, but to this day we don't know how Granny Beatrice guessed."

Then the double wedding—a civil ceremony as per Belgian law—was held at Antwerp's city hall on September 11, 1933. André and Alin were decked out in full formal dress, complete with tails, striped pants, spats, and top hats. Denise and I wore cream silk dresses and little flowered caps bordered with heirloom antique lace of the finest Belgian workmanship. The ushers were attired as formally and attractively as the grooms; the bridesmaids looked lovely in simple silk dresses; the little girls were darling in white dresses sashed with large bows; and the little boys charmed, decked out in sailor suits with hats to match. Afterwards, the entire wedding party proceeded in horse-drawn carriages to the grand *Salle du Centenaire*—the centerpiece of the 1931 celebration of Belgium's first hundred years of nationhood—for a Jewish religious ceremony.

"Wait, wait, wait!" Lilla interrupted. "A Jewish ceremony? But I thought..."

"Believe me," Geneviève said, "it was odd, but grandfather insisted even though he's hardly religious himself. As founder of the family fortune, he has certain rights and deserves our respect, and since many others in our large extended families are observant in varying degrees, he felt it was important that their feelings be acknowledged. In any event, it wasn't that bad for Denise and me; but imagine poor Alin and André, who had to don yarmulkes, march around the vine-twined *chuppah*, and stomp on and shatter a glass to cries of '*Mazel tov!*' Later Alin told me all he could think the whole time was, 'Don't any of you know what's going on in the world? Don't you realize that by publicly declaring our Judaism today we may have signed our own death warrants for tomorrow?'"

"What a horrible thought for a wedding day!"

"For any day. Happily we were distracted by immediately going on our honeymoon together to Majorca and then moving into brand-new twin apartments on the Avenue Émile Duray."

I can still see the façades of the four-story apartment houses down the way with the intricate swirls of their Belle Époque molding framing green lawns, the restful ease of their rooflines and the white-gloved doormen at each entrance. Then there were the formal *jardins* of L'Abbaye de la Cambre with stone paths between clipped hedges, their flower beds precise and stark in the late fall, and the uniformed man standing guard over all. In the years to come, we would stroll through those same gardens every day, weather permitting, with infants of our own.

I first realized I was pregnant—probably since our wedding night—in mid-October 1933, just after Germany withdrew from the League of Nations' international disarmament conference and just before it left the League itself. At the end of January 1934, Denise announced her own pregnancy. It was the same month that Germany signed a nonaggression pact with Poland and André asked, 'If aggression isn't intended who needs a pact?'"

The birth of Katie, on May 18, 1934, was a blissful occasion. Then late in September, Ida was born to Denise.

"The girls brought us such joy," Geneviève explained. "We pretty much sleepwalked through the next several years like all our fellow Belgians. If not, how could Denise have gotten pregnant again? How could I?"

With Katie and Ida and then the births of Christel and Philippe, we were distracted by happiness and proceeded as if all were well. The girls laughed and played on their walks in the gardens of L'Abbaye de la Cambre, skipping past the hedges, splashing in the shallow central pool to which all paths led. The spring bulbs flowering, poking up above the rich brown earth as the weather improved, lifted our spirits despite the growing troubles in the world. The yellow of the daffodils, the red, orange and purple of the tulips, and the pale pink and light blue of the hyacinths. All these brought such relief and release from the gray and damp, and fears of that last long winter."

Tears welled in Geneviève's eyes. Lilla thought it best to change the subject again.

"What news of your baby brother?"

"Oh that scamp!" Geneviève laughed as she wiped away tears. "Charming, charming, Francis, maybe too charming. After Poland was invaded," Geneviève continued somberly, "he went to England and enlisted in the Royal Air Force. Now we know as little of his fate as you do about *your* Francis."

All the adults now felt compelled to follow the war's progress closely on the radio. Commentators from Parisian radio stations offered up every scrap of good news they could find, but little they said could produce optimism. The war was being lost on all fronts.

On the second Saturday morning of the Severins' stay, Lilla tried to divert herself with one of her favorite pastimes: cutting fresh flowers and placing them in the wicker basket she carried on one arm to distribute later throughout the château. But she stopped clipping when she overheard a conversation coming from the other side of a hedge.

"Alin and I are deeply concerned about the increasing southward flow of refugees," André said. "The war is just beginning and we suspect it's going to get worse. Much worse."

Lilla started to cry as she had every day—sometimes every hour—since receiving the terrible news about the capture of her husband, Francis. Blinking and wiping away her soundlessly falling tears, she gazed across a lush green pasture. Cattle grazed by the far-distant fence, shaded by great oak trees.

André went on. "French authorities can force us to go back to Belgium anytime."

"They wouldn't. They couldn't!" Denise declared desperately.

"They can and they may. Their Army is disintegrating and the government is falling apart too. There is less and less logic to their actions."

"But what will we do?" Denise asked, her voice tinged with fear.

"I do not want to fight," André said slowly and firmly.

Peeking through the hedge, Lilla saw Denise glow as she squeezed her husband's hand.

"That's only one of the oh-so-many reasons I love you."

Lilla looked away discreetly. In the ensuing silence, she was struck by the contrast of the peaceful scene presenting itself to her eyes and the prison in which she vividly pictured her husband suffering that very moment. Now she knew she had to prepare herself for the loss of the Severins too.

At lunch that afternoon, Alin reported that Menen, Belgium had been taken, that the British garrison of Calais was under siege, and that the French had found their efforts faltering so completely that fifteen generals had been relieved of their commands. Rumor had it that Allied forces were being trapped at Dunkirk, freeing the Germans for their inevitable drive on Paris.

Clearly, Pouilly was no longer as safe as it had been just the week before. Everyone, including Lilla and the Thierns, agreed reluctantly that it would be best for the Severins to leave right away—but not Geneviève. Did they really need to go, she wanted to know—and if so where?

After lunch, Lilla took Geneviève aside. "My dear, dear friend," she said, trembling as she spoke, her eyes red, her face white, her hands folding over one another in a constant struggle of left with right, "you must go farther south, where you stand a better chance of remaining undetected and unmolested."

Within the hour, the Severins, Lilla, and the Thierns stood in the courtyard in front of the big black Buick and its trailer, smiling wanly while the women fought back tears.

"'Thank you so much' is such an inadequate way to express our appreciation for all your kindness," Geneviève said feelingly, clutching Lilla's hands and speaking for the whole Severin family, "especially when you are suffering your own concerns and losses."

"We all fear for the future," Monsieur Thiern said wistfully, but gallantly.

Geneviève gave Lilla a kiss on each cheek and then a warm embrace filled with such intensity that the two old friends instantly dissolved into uncontrollable weeping. They might have stood that way forever had not several members of the household staff appeared at the top of the steps to the château carrying out baskets of food.

"We still have plenty," Madame Thiern assured the Severins as André and Denise attempted politely to protest. "And the farm remains exceptionally productive."

"Maybe it's producing too much," Monsieur Thiern added anxiously. "I'm afraid we might prove a tempting target for any Army that happens along."

Too soon for all concerned, the Severins crammed themselves back into their car with a smoked ham, a roasted chicken, various cheeses, bread and marmalade, and fruit. Like the dining room at Bourras L'Abbaye, the Buick instantly became a redolent reminder of times past—of grand meals with family and friends in Brussels and Antwerp, and now Pouilly.

"We wish you well!" Lilla cried out. Then she leaned in through the car window to give Geneviève a final hug.

The Severins rolled slowly, gloomily, down the long driveway. When the Buick reached the gates of the estate, Geneviève turned back for one last glimpse of Lilla's château. Then she could see it no more.

The Severins were truly on their own, heading straight for the unknown.

Chapter Five

EN ROUTE

May 27, 1940

Skirting the highest points of the Massif Central, the road was substantial except when it passed through the narrow centers of medieval villages where the ways had been laid out in centuries past for animals and carriages, not cars and trucks. Alin was aggravated whenever he had to negotiate the Buick and trailer through one of the fearsomely sharp turns designed to accommodate the shifting boundary lines of earlier times. But the picturesque quality of those age-old villages remained remarkably intact despite years of diesel fumes spewed by passing trucks against the stucco fronts of close-laid houses—their walls turned first chocolate brown then gray.

Finally, in the late afternoon, a lengthy sweep of road led into Millau where the Tarn River rushed out of a dramatic gorge that cut through a limestone plateau rising high above this northernmost outpost of Aveyron.

As the family made its way toward the center of town and crossed the bridge under which the Tarn flowed, traffic became tighter and tighter until the Buick barely crawled. The farther into the city they went, the more chaotic, even dangerous, the crush of refugees became.

"Unbelievable," Alin breathed, feeling he'd burst a vessel in his brain if he didn't release his tension with speech. "Why would the French keep directing us here when there's already an impossible mass of people? I just hope there's a place to stay."

At every hotel, even the meanest, Alin hopped out to inquire about room availability. Each time he arrived too late: all rooms had been filled far earlier that day or week, often by as many as ten people. Alin couldn't imagine sharing a single room with his family even if he could bargain his way into one. But the alternative taken by other roomless refugees was more disagreeable: lying on the floor in lobbies and corridors.

André tried to project calm. "I thought we'd have missed these throngs after our stay at Bourras L'Abbaye."

Great crowds pressed back and forth, on and off side streets and the main thoroughfare. Exasperated, Alin angled into an open space: the small forecourt of a little church.

"Protestant," André said excitedly. "See? No Virgin Mary at the entrance. We have entered the territory of the Huguenots—the remote and demanding land they settled and in which they sheltered during their centuries of persecution at the hands of the Catholic majority."

Geneviève impulsively stepped out of the car. Buffeted by the horde of people, she grew concerned, and then alarmed by the mindlessness of its movement.

"I don't like this," she declared fearfully, reaching back to clutch Denise's arm as if to defend against being drawn into a whirlpool.

The unornamented church door swung open slowly, noiselessly, blinding the young man leaving the dark interior for the glare of day. With smooth fair skin, fine hair growing over his ears and deep-set eyes burning with earnest intensity, he was dressed in a somber suit and a white shirt buttoned at the neck without a tie, gray wrinkled collar points curling up. Dust clung stubbornly to his suit. Dirt from Millau's paved and cobbled ill-swept streets had worn the shine from the black leather of his brown-soled shoes.

Recovering his sight, the young man stared at the Severins who had emerged from the car in support of Geneviève. With neither surprise, concern, nor chagrin at the intrusion, he approached André and Alin who habitually stood side by side.

"May I help you?" he asked, thoughtfully taking their measure. "New arrivals?"

"Not the first you've seen I'd guess," André replied.

The young man smiled ruefully. "I'm the pastor of this church. Obviously we have many more people in town than normally, even at the height of market season."

"We're Belgians," André informed him.

"That much I surmised. Many of our recent arrivals are. Besides," he added nodding at their car, "your license plate advertises your origin."

"We were told to come here," Alin said heatedly. "We're looking for a place to stay. And we can pay."

"Even so," the pastor cautioned after counting the Severins, "it won't be easy." He nodded to André and Alin. "Follow me please." He led them into the crowded street. Out of earshot of the others he asked, "Twins?"

"Just brothers," Alin answered peevishly.

"Often mistaken for twins," André said more congenially.

Turning the nearest corner, they entered the town plaza where a fountain sparkled in the sun; gentle streams of water washed down the stone nymphs frolicking on its pedestal. The pastor led them to a small hotel they hadn't spotted themselves, the best in Millau. Potted flowers framed the elegant entranceway. The sign hanging above it spelled out the name in elaborate gold letters.

Alin went in and soon returned to announce, "It's all right. They have rooms for us."

"You are most fortunate," the pastor observed.

"That's the advantage of money," Alin said coldly. "They're happy to have customers who can afford their price."

The threesome pushed back toward the church through the ever-changing scene of refugees and the townspeople who came out to observe them as a curious entertainment.

"Few are as fortunate as you," the pastor said sadly. "I'm afraid I have to let some sleep on the floor of our church. All the houses of worship have been turned into temporary shelters. Even the schools have been shut down and turned over to the displaced." He shrugged his sagging shoulders with weariness and resignation. "We already have used every bed, pad, and pallet available. Yet you keep coming!"

Sitting alone at the window of his bedchamber on Tuesday morning, André enjoyed room service coffee and a croissant while looking down into the town square. With the struggle for life intensifying, it seemed longer than it had actually been since Germany's attack upended their lives—especially when André contemplated the depleted spirits of the refugees he had encountered throughout the hotel. Some of these guests and temporary lobby residents were Frenchmen from the north, but most were his fellow Belgians. He used to think he knew his people well. How little these individuals reminded him of those he had known all his life. Many were so testy they made Alin Severin appear a gentle, genial soul.

To them, nothing the French had done, were doing, or ever would do was sufficient, let alone right. They were particularly bitter that so little mercy and even less love was being shown by the citizens of Millau for the strangers in their midst.

André's experience had been different. The Protestant pastor had been kind and helpful. André would have enjoyed discussing spiritual matters with him, learning something of his church's history and its stance on war today.

Such a conversation could yet take place if the Severins stayed a while. Since the journey had already taken a toll on them all, especially Louis and Rose, André thought it best that they rest where they were another day or two.

Insistent knocking called him to the door. Alin entered like a whirlwind.

"Have you heard? King Leopold has capitulated and fled in the middle of the night. As of eleven a.m. our forces surrender unconditionally and Belgium will belong to 'the Fatherland!'"

"How do you know? How can that be?"

"The town is awash with the news!" Alin shouted. André gestured him to keep his voice down, hoping not to trouble the family members next door and across the hall. "If you thought the townspeople were angry at the Belgian refugees yesterday you should see them now."

André turned on the radio and the bad news was confirmed. Worse, as of that moment, Belgians in France were forbidden to move from wherever they were.

"How fortunate that we left Bourras L'Abbaye when we did," André sighed.

"Once again," Alin fumed, "one step ahead of disaster."

The brothers were further taken aback when the radio announcer proclaimed a single exception to the "stay-put" order. Every adult Belgian male below the age of forty-five was to report immediately to French police authorities to be sent to dig trenches in defense of Paris.

André and Alin faltered momentarily. André was thirty-nine and Alin thirty-seven. Duty in the Ruhr Valley no longer seemed so onerous.

"I heard from refugees in the square that the national gendarmes stationed here have a reputation for aggressiveness and vindictiveness," Alin said, "and the locals won't shield us since what little sympathy they had vanished overnight. They want retribution from anyone associated with the little country that gave up so abruptly while France struggles on."

The brothers drifted to the window. Across the square, three Belgian soldiers were being shouted at, poked, and spat upon by enraged Frenchmen.

"How can they blame the soldiers?" Alin asked angrily. "Leopold sold all of us down the river, surrendering without one word to his allies."

André agreed but said, "I can't blame the French either. With the evacuation of Dunkirk, they no longer have the British Expeditionary Force behind them and now can't even count on our little Belgian Army. They're on their own against the Luftwaffe and the Panzers and…"

Alin pressed a forefinger to his lips to silence André as the door handle to the adjoining room turned. Denise stepped in and André quickly apprised her of all—except the call to join a trench-digging brigade.

"Orders are orders, so I suppose we must stay," Denise said softly. "We're incredibly lucky to have three rooms when so many haven't any."

In the square, the crowd became more hostile, forcing the poor Belgian soldiers back and back and back.

Alin exploded. "We can't stay here, no matter what our orders may be!"

"With all this commotion," André said, pointing to the throng abusing the Belgian soldiers, "it might be possible to slip off unnoticed."

"We must leave immediately," Alin declared.

In a very few minutes, the ten Severins had packed up, settled the bill, and gone out the service door to the side of the hotel where they had parked their car and trailer. Unnerved by the engine noise, wincing at each squeak and creak of the awkward trailer, Alin maneuvered around to the front of the hotel and turned onto a street leading away from the square and the still-growing ever-growling crowd.

Looking back, André saw an elderly Frenchman who wore a Great War uniform festooned with medals interpose his person between the mob and the visibly terrified Belgians. The old warrior shouted and waved his arms, turning red in the face.

"What is he doing?" Denise asked André.

"Perhaps berating his fellow Gauls for their incivility and irrationality, telling them they ought to be ashamed of themselves for their herdlike behavior, that they must know no Belgian in Millau can be blamed for the actions of their king. I don't know. Whatever it is, it's working."

Gradually, the mob made way for the Belgian soldiers, giving them just enough space to escape rapidly down a side street and out of sight.

Alin made his way between parked trucks, shifted into second gear, then upshifted into third, heading toward the open road leading up the Gorge du Tarn. At the outskirts of town, several policemen stood alongside the road and Alin reflexively slowed.

"Here we go again. Where are our passports?"

"They're going to send us back," Geneviève predicted bitterly.

Everyone was astonished when the police waved them on without checking their papers.

"Keep going!" an officer shouted, waving vigorously. "Go ahead!"

Alin stamped down on the accelerator, speeding away from the dangers of Millau. "What was that about?" he asked querulously, rounding a bend. "As the Protestant minister pointed out, even our license plate gives us away as Belgians."

"Millau is at the far end of Aveyron," André said pondering. "Maybe it takes time for orders to reach there."

Alin barked a laugh. "Lucky for us they don't listen to the radio."

Puzzled and concerned, Louis asked, "Where are we headed now?"

"Into the Lozère," Alin announced. Everyone was startled by his certainty until he explained, "While I walked around the town square this morning I heard that the departments of Lot and Aveyron are filled to capacity with Belgians. The Lozère is the last department where the French have been instructed to make us welcome."

Digging into the store of religious history he had developed over the previous decade, André detailed that the Lozère was the stronghold of the Protestant Huguenots after the St. Bartholomew's Day massacre and its aftermath, when they were slaughtered by the thousands. Most of the survivors who hadn't fled to other countries moved up into the higher reaches of this remote region. Their life was almost unendurably hard and not just because of the stony soil. War against them raged for the next quarter century, until Henri

IV issued the Edict of Nantes granting freedom of religion for Protestants, and then again almost a century later, when Louis XIV revoked it.

"Hence the old rhyming adage," he concluded, 'Lozère, *pays de misère*—land of misery.'"

Sunlight played against the cliffs overlooking the constantly changing course of the mighty Tarn, casting shadows interwoven with bright spots of color. The growth along the river's edge stood out darkly green against the luminescent browns, tans, and rusts of the valley walls. Here and there, a little bridge connected the road to one of the small stone farmhouses perched against the far side of the river, structures built centuries before by rugged farmers who managed to scratch a meager living from the small plots of earth along the alluvial floodplains.

"Have we left Aveyron?" Denise asked.

"There are no signposts to mark the borders between départements but I would guess so," responded André. "Since we left Millau, there've been fewer and fewer gendarmes more and more widely scattered." They pored over the map, tracing the Tarn to its headwaters in the mountains of the Cévennes, as the Lozère also was known.

"What do you think about that?" Alin asked, finger pointing to a place called Florac.

"Florac must mean 'flowing water,'" André said, "if it's Latin as I suspect."

"The Romans certainly knew where to put a town," Denise said hopefully.

"I like the idea of an ever-flowing fountain splashing cheerfully in the center of town," Geneviève put in.

"At least we'd be still farther away from the authorities in Millau," André added.

Alin drummed his fingers on the dashboard then folded the map. As simply as that, the decision had been made.

A ribbon of road led the Severins through village after village of clustered black-roofed houses. They passed an old castle, what must once have been a battlemented monastery and vineyards, meadows and orchards thick with spring blossoms. They could hear the Tarn bubbling and rumbling, pummeling its way down the gorge.

Veering off along one branch of the river, they entered Florac, an aged city with an ancient castle and streets lined with plane trees. As Geneviève had hoped, a live fountain welled at the heart of the old *ville*.

There were only a few other refugees and a handful of cars with Belgian license plates on the streets. Rooms at the city's best hotel were available, for Florac also was a resort destination and it was still too cool this high in the mountains for casual visitors.

After a relatively relaxed and comfortable night, André felt agitated at breakfast Wednesday. He and Alin agreed they couldn't long afford such fancy accommodations. They needed a more permanent, less expensive place to stay.

Imagining official arrangements must have been made for accommodating refugees, they decided to pay a call on the mayor, even though that seemed risky. They could always hope the orders they had heard in Millau hadn't yet penetrated this far. And doing nothing was risky too.

"Why do you come here?" Florac's mayor demanded irritably. "Other departments are reserved for Belgians like you. We want nothing to do with refugees!"

Alin stepped forward aggressively, staring into the gaunt official's rapidly reddening face. "Lot and Aveyron are filled and this département is now open 'for Belgians like us,'" Alin asserted, biting off each word. "Understand, we don't want charity from you or anyone else. We need a place to stay and we can pay."

"We're not even allowed to let you pay." The spider web of blood vessels in the mayor's cheeks pulsed a sickly blue-green against his continuing flush. Rudely he pulled a great gray handkerchief out of his pants pocket and blew his nose loudly. Then he wiped his mouth disgustingly with the same handkerchief, balled it up, stuffed it back in his pants then slicked down the ends of his mustache with careful strokes of enormously long fat fingers. "Damn war," he growled, stepping back behind his desk. "How many of you are there?"

"Ten," André answered.

"Ten! Are you Jews?"

André paused to consider, but Alin demanded, "Why do you ask? No one anywhere else in France has."

The mayor glanced up from under an instantly furrowed brow. "Until now you've stayed in hotels and they're not required to obtain such information. But when you seek authorization for a more permanent situation, the law demands that we know a good deal more about you."

The brothers stood silently absorbing this discouraging information.

"Well are you?" the mayor badgered. "You must be or why flee Belgium?"

"We come from a Jewish family," André allowed, hoping this formulation skirted the complicated details.

"Many more like you," the gruff mayor huffed, "and there won't be room for the people who belong here." Turning his back on them, going to one of the shelves lining the walls of his small office, and pulling out a large black ledger, the mayor flipped through a number of heavily marked pages. "Such a large family," he whined. Then he stopped, stared, and let a little grin steal across his lips. "Yes," he hissed. "There is a small village not far from here— Bédouès—where the former governor of Djibouti has a large villa—a small château really. You're familiar with Djibouti, in Eritrea, on the Red Sea? A prestigious posting. And the ex-governor is a formidable personage. Space at his place has been reserved for the likes of you. Name?"

André gave it, praying the ex-governor of Djibouti was far more pleasant and less overtly prejudiced than this miserable man.

The mayor wrote "Severin" into his ledger laboriously and appended the term "Israelite." Then he went to the door, gestured dismissively in the general direction of "down the road," and could barely bring himself to say, "Bédouès."

Alin left abruptly, enraged.

"Thank you for your guidance," André said, mustering the last remnants of his manners to show that the Severins were superior to such rude treatment.

"Damn war," the mayor grumbled. Then he slammed the door behind them.

Chapter Six

BÉDOUÈS

June 5, 1940

lin felt so resentful he could spit. His respect and appreciation for the French had just descended several significant degrees. Nevertheless, he realized he and André had no choice but to explore the single option offered. What he really wanted was to go back and punch the mayor of Florac in the nose.

André drove slowly uphill, about four kilometers over the rocky terrain of a very narrow road. The tall spire of a Catholic church immediately ahead reached up to the heavens. The stone church sat prominently on a small bluff overlooking the single-lane road that bisected the little village of Bédouès and its small grouping of huddled homes.

One dwelling stood out dramatically. The grand villa, taller than any building besides the church, was constructed of massive brown corner-cut stones placed squarely up to the roofline. The walls in between had been freshly stuccoed a lighter color so that the whole contrasted with the gray slate of the roof. The front of the complex structure was anchored by a large square tower, rising three floors to its own pitched roof. Green vines straggled up the walls and tower, softening the severity of the design. Behind was a serene private park filled with ash, plane, fir, and oak trees.

All together, the château announced the importance of its owner. It was utterly incongruous with the other, much smaller homes and shops of the village discolored from long years of weathering and neglect.

As the Buick and trailer pulled up to the villa, the curtains in the front window shifted slightly. A featureless shadow appeared behind them.

Anxiously, the brothers walked up and tugged at the large round bell pull. After an unnerving few moments, the huge ornate hand-carved door opened very, very slowly. A woman, considerably past her graceful years, stood silent. Her severe face was lined and wrinkled. The straight gray hair, clinging tightly to her ears, emphasized the sharpness of her nose and lips drawn tightly across her narrow mouth and bespoke the reluctance of her manner. There was no smile or other indication of greeting or welcome.

André and Alin stated their business and the woman said shortly, "Wait here," retreating behind the door she closed partway.

From somewhere within, a harsh male voice called out, "Who is it?"

"Refugees from Belgium," the woman answered meekly.

A brief silence was followed by a heavy approaching tread.

The door swung back again and an imposing gentleman squinted at the brothers, formally inspecting them. Much taller than André and Alin, he had a broad cavernous chest, hands like meaty mitts, and a roughhewn face covered with a full carefully groomed white beard, disguising either a weak or too-pointy chin.

Stepping forward menacingly to within an uncomfortable distance, he declared, "I'm Claude de Montfort, former governor of Djibouti. What do you want?"

Alin thought de Montfort expected them to fall to their knees and salaam.

"We were told to come," André said forthrightly, "because you have room for us."

Unused to being challenged, the ex-governor spluttered, "He would do that to me," referring to the mayor of Florac. "We were told to anticipate people like you sooner or later."

There it is, Alin thought. *He doesn't like Belgians, he doesn't like Jews, and encountering both on his doorstep at once makes him apoplectic!*

"I'd prefer that it would have been later," de Montfort continued in so self-pitying a tone he sounded as if he had lost all stature with himself. "It's such an imposition. Why come here when plenty of other houses are available?"

"We have the means to pay," André said knowing he didn't have to, but doubting the Severins would find another place anywhere near as large as this.

The ex-governor exchanged a meaningful look with the woman who was his wife and then acknowledged, "We do have space on the top floor. That we don't use I mean."

"And it's out of the way," Madame de Montfort assured her husband, leaning into his shoulder and lowering her voice. "We won't even have to see them."

"Yes—right—okay then," de Montfort harrumphed, signaling he had made a great and beneficent concession.

Exasperated, Alin stepped aside while his brother completed the negotiations. The ex-governor knew full well that both moral responsibility and the law demanded that he welcome refugees from the German onslaught rent-free. Alin watched with revulsion as de Montfort ungraciously pocketed his first payment in cash.

The brothers were led to the attic by the rickety back stairs that kept the Severins away from the de Montforts' front door. The stairs did not inspire confidence, but both brothers held their tongues. Spacious rooms ran the length of the château. They were not only unused, but also shamefully filthy. Dust and cobwebs hung over windows, on doors and all over the beds, chairs and tables scattered haphazardly through out. The children didn't notice. They ran from room to room laughing and shrieking with glee. The de Montfort's attic was depressingly unkempt but also remote—a serviceable retreat in which the Severins could safely contemplate how to live out the war.

"Appalling," Geneviève spat.

Recovering from the initial shock Denise said, "We'd better straighten up right away."

Asked for some brushes, rags and soap, Madame de Montfort sneered, but offered the much-appreciated help of her cook. Removing the copious dirt took all day. It also exposed flaking paint, grayed and crumbling plaster and the tooth marks of mice and squirrels along the edges of doors and baseboards. Somehow, the space was made livable—barely.

André and Alin went to the general store most days for foodstuffs, supplies and the newspaper, so the villagers soon learned of the Severins' presence. The people of Bédouès expressed nothing resembling the hostility of the de Montforts and the mayor of Florac. Neither did they go out of their way to make any neighborly gesture, let alone extend friendship. Alin surmised they feared that harboring émigrés might eventually subject them to Nazi retribution.

Passing the time wasn't easy. The children frequently played outside the large windows, on the flat porch roof spanning the center of the château, where a small border around the edge kept them from tumbling to the ground. Rose kept a watchful eye out for them anyway. Louis kept her company.

Denise was occupied with cooking and cleaning for ten and engaging her ever-resentful sister in those domestic chores. How strange to see Geneviève wield a scrub brush!

The brothers concluded the family would have to remain in France for quite some time so they started thinking about providing food for themselves as a cost-saving measure and to guard against inevitable shortages. André jotted down in his notebook thoughts, plans, and information on local crops and farming techniques that he gleaned from talking to the mayor who ran the general store and farmers he met on daily outings. He had taken to stopping at small fields to admire the locals' efforts and politely ask questions. Most of the men were pleased to pass on knowledge handed down by previous generations.

With little to do besides review his homeopathy book and sit in the Buick listening to the radio, Alin was restless, distracted, and notably more short with the children than ever. "Stop running!" he cried. When they laughed he muttered, "Be quiet!"

De Montfort's original demands for his "hospitality" as landlord were outrageous, but when the Severin brothers inquired if he would accept British pounds so that they could conserve their supply of French francs they were alarmed when he swiftly and cheerfully agreed—and imposed an excessive exchange rate.

"He's hoarding it too," Alin exploded, "to conceal that he's charging rent at all!"

"Best not offer him our diamonds," André agreed. "That would increase his rapacity."

Word of the Germans' ongoing daily successes on the fields of battle filtered into Bédoués. The Severins' sense of isolation and peril increased. One bright spot was Nichette, the hard-bitten middle-aged maid at the château who felt for the family. Nichette didn't like her employers either and—careful not to let the de Montforts see—stole up to the Severins' rooms late afternoons cradling bread and leftover meats and vegetables. She always made sure to secret some sweets or fruit tarts in her apron for the children.

"I like it when you bring us these," Christel said with a two-year-old's enchanting guilelessness, sidling up to and hugging Nichette around her knees.

"Come look what I found," Alin called out one morning, bounding upstairs after a visit to the village. "Now you can take the children out for a stroll."

He had pushed a cart into the backyard. Though nothing like the wicker baby carriages of Brussels, its simplicity, coarse-grained handles, and iron wheels were perfect for Bédoués.

Immediately after lunch, Denise and Geneviève placed little Philippe into the cart. The three little girls walked, hopped, and ran around it as the mothers and children set off down the road.

The dirt road to Bédoués meandered through a gentle valley, passing between small fields crowded against the slope of a hill that curved up gently into the dominating mountain, which was rocky and spare with pine trees growing spottily on outcroppings and ledges. The fields were thick with tall grasses and lined with rocks long since piled into low borders.

The people who lived there plainly cherished their carefully tended gardens with vegetables, showing through waving stalks of cultivated wheat and rye, their sheaves already turning a rich coppery brown. Orchards were lush with the first fruits of the season just now ripening under the increasingly strong late-spring sun.

As they approached the first houses of the village, the mothers' pulses quickened. They had never walked into the heart of Bédoués and they worried about their reception.

The village was much smaller than they had realized. Strolling along they nodded their heads and smiled at each villager who happened by.

The women of Bédoués nodded back politely but never with a welcoming expression. One harrumphed. Another answered Denise's sprightly *"Bonjour!"* mutedly.

Some of this coldness was due to an age-old distrust of outsiders, but part was caused by the Severins' obvious "difference," apparent in their very clothes. The longstanding residents dressed in interchangeably shapeless dun-colored frocks. Denise and Geneviève owned nothing resembling these simple dresses. And though the children's outfits were mostly handmade, the fabrics, patterns, and sewing were so advanced stylistically that they seemed to mock and shame the village women's habitual dowdiness.

By the time the family reached the church at the end of the street, turned around, and started back again, Geneviève was incensed and Denise's strength had begun to falter. Then they heard disquieting news from people conversing heatedly on the sidewalks. The bad tidings were confirmed by a radio playing in the sole café.

Back in the attic, the mercifully oblivious children raced to Louis and Rose to share their excitement about visiting town. But Denise and Geneviève took their husbands aside to tell them Mussolini's Italy had declared war on France.

Events swiftly followed Il Duce's announcement, though his forces never actually deployed against the French. On Tuesday, June 11, Paris was declared an open city and the principals of the French government fled for Tours. Much of what remained of the population left amidst a pounding of the outskirts by the Luftwaffe. General Weygand ordered French forces to retreat. Three days later the Nazis captured Paris. The government left for Bordeaux.

Yet the Severins' lives improved slightly. Denise and Geneviève persisted in taking the children into town and one day the most talkative woman in the village—a short squat housewife in her fifties distinguished by a thick red gash of lipstick—made the first friendly overture. Soon other housewives became friendlier.

"Can you imagine?" Denise told André one night as they rested abed in each other's arms. "Madame de Montfort told everyone she couldn't take in refugees because we're relatives living here for free! When Nichette got wind of it, she was good enough to deny it. The villagers don't hold the ex-governor in high esteem. When they learned we actually pay a very high price they said, 'That's not right!' and began treating us as if we've lived here all our lives."

On Monday the seventeenth, André and Alin decided to experience the family's newfound popularity by joining the now-routine stroll to Bédouès. The weather was so agreeable that the family extended the walk all the way to Florac. Along the path, the brothers debated the implications of that morning's news. Prime Minister Reynaud had resigned and Marshal Pétain had been asked to form a new government. Would the old war hero rally his fellow countrymen to fight on to victory despite the long odds or was Pétain being positioned to sue for peace?

The Severins stopped to rest at Florac's central fountain. There was a sudden eruption across the way in a bustling café. Some patrons raced out. The rest sat stunned, silent.

The proprietor turned up the radio to so great a volume the fateful fearsome words could be heard over the pooling of water and the peals of laughter from the children's especially energetic game of tag: "France surrenders!"

The adult Severins looked at one another in horror and confusion. The war had lasted little more than five weeks.

"Can this really be happening?" Alin asked incredulously. "Did we abandon Belgium only to be trapped in another vanquished country?"

Alin spent much of the next melancholy day in the Buick listening to the BBC as if to an oracle. Churchill had made a great brave speech to the House of Commons, insisting that the British would "defend their island home and fight on until the curse of Hitler is removed." French General Charles de Gaulle, having fled to London immediately upon the installation of Pétain, broadcast an appeal to French soldiers to keep fighting despite anything their discredited subjugated government said or did.

This was cold comfort in Bédouès. The Severins now had no choice but to stay where they were and endure whatever the new circumstances brought.

André declared the time had come to find land to cultivate to grow food. It was the only positive step they could take.

Denise agreed enthusiastically. "That way we'll have fresher, better food to eat than we can buy. We'll save money too and prove we really care about Bédouès."

The brothers set off at once to see the mayor.

Lucien Mauriac ran the small shop where André and Alin had purchased lime for whitewash on their first day at the château, and almost everything else since. Lucien was thoughtful enough to always to put aside a newspaper for Alin so that he could get it even late in the day.

He reacted cautiously when the Severins revealed their present mission. A middle-aged man with a full head of hair that curled over his ears and neck and large hands with fingers roughened from sorting the stock and constantly cleaning the premises with strong soap, Lucien looked over the two brothers as if seeing and appraising them for the first time. Dressed as always in rough work clothes and the blue duster he wore in the store, he eyed the brothers' usual dark suits, clothes locals would only wear for church, weddings, and funerals. They were not typical farming outfits.

"So yours wasn't just idle curiosity," Lucien said to André and gently asked, "Are you sure you can handle farm work even in a small way? I'd guess you haven't done any before."

"We don't have much choice," André explained.

"If we don't learn now," Alin added, "I bet we'll end up hungry."

The mayor peered at them as if trying to divine their souls. Then he slapped his meaty hands onto the counter. "I have a little land that might get you started. Hasn't been worked for some years, but it's good earth."

No cash changed hands. Instead, the mayor and the Severins agreed to the region's traditional arrangement: he provided the land and they would give him half their crop.

"I can give you some seeds to get you started." Lucien slapped several packets onto the counter—tomatoes, squash, lettuce, pepper, beans, melons— and smiled warmly.

"We may need these," Alin said, buying two spades, a hoe, and a heavy rake.

In the bright clear morning, the whole family headed down the lane toward their new plot of land on the edge of town, near the spot where the hill began to rise toward the mountain beyond. The field was a badly overgrown unpromising mess.

"I don't understand," a winded Louis said perplexedly. "How will you ever get it tilled?"

Just then Lucien appeared, rolling along the narrow path from the village on a small tractor with a big plow attached to the rear. The mothers sheltered their nervous children as the tractor growled and its plow bit into the grasses and weeds, turning over rich earth.

With the land properly prepared, the Severin brothers loosened their ties. Without removing them or their suit jackets, they commenced this new phase of their lives.

They started with carrots, which hadn't been grown in Bédoués in memory. But Lucien had extolled their simplicity so why not try?

André applied his studies of when to plant various crops, the soil type and fertilizer each preferred and how to store them after harvesting. He kept meticulous records in his notebook, making a line drawing of the plot's layout and keeping charts of the plantings, including the beans he and Alin soon added to the carrots, and pea seeds André bought in Florac. In Florac's more numerous stores, André also had found and acquired a small supply of chemical fertilizers to supplement the natural fertilizers from stabled and penned animals.

It was warm and sometimes stifling in the valley, particularly since the brothers persisted in wearing their wool suit jackets and ties. André tended to take short breaks to analyze operations, but Alin soldiered on ceaselessly, overcoming obstacles with physical aggression, pouring into the job his many frustrations—including that of working in dirt, which offended his fastidious nature.

Yet Alin wished he could do this all himself. He was proud of his older brother and hated to see him "reduced" to working with his hands.

"You've met Einstein," he said. "Talked with Einstein."

"Yes," André replied. "And he's a man like any other..."

"Not like any other."

"...perhaps with a bit more imagination. But remember, Einstein produced his major advances through 'thought experiments.' He says his needs are simple: paper and pencil, and time. Well, I have plenty of time here, not to mention my notebook and pen. Why shouldn't I do some of my own best thinking while we labor together in this field?"

With the garden fully planted in neat rows, there was little to do except weed and apply more fertilizer now and again. Unfortunately, that left more time for fretting about the relentless German advance. Cherbourg, Brest, Le Mans, Dijon, and Lyons all fell.

By the twenty-first of June, Hitler declared the war in the west at an end. The next day, a Franco-German armistice was signed, with the French forced to accept all German terms: the return of Alsace-Lorraine to German sovereignty, and the occupation of the Channel and Atlantic coastlines as well as all major industrial areas.

Fortunately, most of southern France would remain unoccupied, under the jurisdiction of a French administrative center at Vichy. But the French Army and Navy were demobilized and disarmed, and France had to bear the entire cost of the occupation. Worse still, all French prisoners of war were to remain in Germany until the completion of a full peace treaty.

In London, de Gaulle formed a French National Committee and the British recognized him as head of the newly established Free French Army. Then Hitler appeared in Paris.

The sight of the Führer driven triumphantly through the nearly empty streets of the capital—visiting Napoleon's Tomb and touring the Eiffel Tower—dealt another devastating blow to French pride. A British blockade of war matériel and food to the whole of France threatened real hardships ahead—making the Severins exceptionally glad they had found and planted their plot when they had.

June turned into July. The Severins could see and admire the preliminary results of André and Alin's hard work: the first plant shoots poked through carefully graded earth. But with Pétain's government starting to incarcerate "Jews and dissidents" at a prison camp called Gurs and young Frenchmen being conscripted into German labor battalions, complacency wasn't possible.

At André's prompting, the family began thinking about leaving Bédouès for a place farther up in the mountains, away from any real town. Eventually, they feared, some unhappy person who had lost a husband or son would tell the authorities of their presence and then they might be sent away to who knew what horrible fate?

"But the mayors of Florac and Bédouès know we're here," Geneviève declared, aghast.

"I mean other authorities," André explained patiently. "I mean the police."

Still the people of Bédouès—apart from the de Montforts—treated the Severins with ever-growing kindness. Some even expressed hope that the Severins would remain at least through the summer.

As the crops began to mature, a number of farmers stopped by to offer advice and praise. Denise and Geneviève started lending a hand. Even the children helped as best they could.

"If we have to head off again," Geneviève declared, "it better not be before we enjoy the fruits of our labors."

In mid-July, Pétain was overwhelmingly elected president by the French parliament. Within a week, Vichy France banned the employment of "aliens"— nonnative-born Jews.

The Battle of Britain raged, bringing fresh fears about the fate of the Freedmans across the North Sea. Denise and Geneviève were extremely anxious about their brother Francis.

The summer rains proved gentle and reliable. The garden thrived and flourished. The Severins' vegetables grew faster, taller and more abundantly than those of other gardens planted in the vicinity year after year, always cultivated with the same methods and producing the same modest results. Some argued that the Severins' plot had lain fallow so long it was bound to do better than adjacent overworked soil, but the family was convinced André's scientific approach—particularly his chemical fertilization—was the key to their success.

Their garden became a much-discussed marvel. Its profusion stirred amazement and wonder. Many made a pilgrimage to "the land of the Belgians"—a true local curiosity.

Unfortunately, the Severins' success served as a reminder of the lack of manpower for bringing in everyone's crops. Would the young men of Bédouès ever be seen again? Many had died in the doomed attempt to defend their country. Rumor had it that the Nazis had placed many others in concentration camps. Now the Germans demanded that the few remaining young adult males work in French factories supporting German war production. Newspapers reported some young men were being taken into Germany to work in the factories there.

Fields were ripening. Orchards were heavily laden with peaches, plums, and cherries. Who would gather, sort, distribute, and store them? They would rot quickly if not picked. The Severins saw an opportunity to help and to supplement their own garden.

Alin talked with Lucien Mauriac. "If you help bring in the cherry crop," Lucien said, "you can eat any cherries while working and keep half of what you pick."

The Severin brothers and the Freedman sisters set to work immediately. The farmer who owned the trees provided each with a big apron to wear, featuring a large front pocket in which to store fruit as they retrieved it.

Climbing the gnarled trunks of the aged trees, in order to reach branches bent down under the full weight of the fruit, required temerity, agility, and tenacity. Rose and Louis, suffused with pride as they watched, marveled at their sons. But the skill, strength, and persistence of their daughters-in-law astonished them.

By mid-August, Lucien Mauriac had become very nervous. Bédouès had a problem no longtime resident could solve. But there was an outsider he could approach for help.

Early on Monday the nineteenth of August, Lucien trudged up the dusty path from his own home to the Severins' plot. André was hoeing weeds between rows of beets. Alin pulled up weeds by hand.

After preliminary pleasantries, Lucien said hoarsely, "The plums. They're ripening. And the preserves factory is closed for lack of youthful manpower. I'm afraid the fruit will rot." Politely, hopefully, anxiously Lucien asked, "Monsieur le professeur, is it possible you know or can devise some less labor-intensive way to preserve our plums?"

The mayor was sweating and just this side of panic during the long minute it took André to formulate an answer.

"I'll need space to work," André said. "There's not enough room in the attic." Lucien almost whooped for joy. Then André added, "Perhaps you could ask de Montfort. He's got plenty of rooms he doesn't use."

Now Lucien had a violent headache. He hated to ask de Montfort for anything. "Why not ask him yourself?" he suggested. "It would sound much more serious coming from a scientist." Silence hung heavily between them.

Then Lucien realized something that pleased him enormously. He grinned cagily. "Actually André, I'll do it. Let's settle this now."

Minutes later the mayor was pounding authoritatively on the château's great door.

"What is this?" de Montfort demanded of the men who dared disturb him.

Lucien felt the old timidity, but stated simply, "We have a request, or rather a demand."

The ex-governor of Djibouti was too shocked to respond. On behalf of the good people of Bédouès Lucien asked him to give André a room.

"With a supply of water and a large table," André elaborated.

As de Montfort spluttered with inarticulate rage, Lucien inquired almost sweetly, "Do I understand correctly that you have been charging the Severins rent?"

The ex-governor shifted his glower back and forth between Lucien and André as if he couldn't decide whom he loathed most or would choose to destroy first.

Lucien drove the dagger home. "Surely you know that's against regulations. And as a former government official you know how important regulations are."

De Montfort pressed his lips together so tightly they turned white.

"I hope not to need the space for too many days," André said.

Struggling, de Montfort growled, "The pantry. One week. No more!"

"Is that enough time?" the mayor asked André.

"If I can't solve the problem in a week," André replied, "I can't solve it at all."

André at once gathered plums from a tree near the château hoping to discover how to remove the waxy covering then dry the plums into prunes. It would change the local diet a bit but...

His chemistry textbook, small as it was, helped him determine the composition of the plum and the makeup of the tough skin protecting the juicy pulp inside. He spent the entire day reading and trying to remember chemical formulas affecting fruit. He sat up late into the night jotting in his notebook and performing calculations.

The next day he walked into Florac to buy caustic soda, alcohol, vinegar, salts, and an acidic brine. Retiring to the ex-governor's pantry he tried to approximate the laboratory conditions he had enjoyed in Belgium and suddenly realized how much he missed his previous life—the studies, his experiments, the conversations.

He created a series of solutions then bathed the fruit in one after another and waited for results. No matter how he mixed his chemicals and household ingredients and hoped for a softening of the outer skin that wouldn't degrade the sweet-flavored fruit, the plums held on tenaciously to their seemingly impervious skin.

Morning became afternoon. Late afternoon turned to early evening. Night wore on and on. Still no answer came.

Early Wednesday André had barely taken a sip of the coffee Nichette had thoughtfully brought him before Claude de Montfort poked his head into the pantry, grousing about how long the project was taking and demanding to know when he could have his room back.

"It's only been two days," André explained patiently. "You agreed to a week."

"*Only* a week," the ex-governor fumed.

Alone again André worked with vinegar, but it left the liberated pulp with a bitter taste. Alcohol gave a fine flavor to the plum but on its own couldn't penetrate the skin. Brine successfully dissolved the wax but the resulting fruit was more like an olive than a prune.

Late that night, André finally devised a bath with caustic soda. He tried several strengths for varying lengths of time then carefully watched and jostled the plums sitting in different pans of solution, unable to perceive any difference whatever. Sitting down and rubbing his eyes, he wondered whether and how he might succeed with his limited number of chemicals and agents.

Well past midnight, he got to his feet, ready to stop for the day, and hoping the answer would come to him unbidden as he slept. The dim light of the pantry cast intriguing shadows on the pans of plums that seemed to await—no, insist upon—the determining poke of a finger. Unable to resist one more try André gave a last push of his forefinger into each pan. Wherever he pressed the plums continued to hold firm. But in the very last pan, the skin unexpectedly gave way and the liquid of the pulp began to bleed through.

Too excited for sleep André took several plums from the pan and set them on a grill to drip and dry overnight. Had he stumbled into a possible answer? He began to feel the same excitement he had felt at the Free University of Brussels whenever an experiment worked.

Thursday morning he took the weeping plums and set them out in the bright sun. After a couple of hours, the purple fruit began to pucker and crinkle.

Impulsively he went down to the mayor's store and invited Lucien to the château the following morning.

Early Friday the mayor appeared at the villa with other leading citizens. De Montfort caught sight of their procession toward the pantry and imposed his unwelcome obtrusive presence.

André led them to his experimental plums set into a red-and-yellow dish to provide a vivid contrast with the dark purple of the fruit. He passed the dish around and each of the visitors—excepting de Montfort—took one of the dried plums, squeezed it, and then with trepidation took a bite.

Each chewed deliberately, swallowed hard and—much to André's relief—took another bite. Slowly their faces relaxed into grateful smiles.

"It's a prune!" the mayor declared joyfully. The other taste-testers nodded happily.

Lucien gave André a kiss on each cheek. The others followed suit except for de Montfort. He wanted to know if André was ready to return the pantry to its owner.

Saturday morning, at André's request, the mayor gathered a number of townspeople in the quiet idle plum factory. André demonstrated how to mix his caustic soda formula. The villagers would only need to pick the plums, place them into a vat of the winning mixture, and after the skin had dissolved spread the plums out in the sun to dry, concentrating the sweetness within.

The crop was saved!

The next day André slept late, but Alin wanted to talk. Despite the success of the plum project and a great show of thankfulness from the citizens of Bédouès, Alin couldn't bear to stay in the château a minute longer and not just because he hated de Montfort. As the summer's end approached, he was increasingly concerned that Bédouès, which was on the Atlantic Ocean side of the Massif Central, would soon face cold winds and winter snows bound to blow in from the west.

"I don't like the situation here," he complained to Denise in André's stead. "We're too exposed not only to the weather, but also to the new regional headquarters of the national police, in Mende. That's not even thirty-five kilometers north."

Denise listened and leafed through the Sunday newspaper. "Goodness. It says here all Belgian refugees have been ordered back to Belgium to reestablish the national economy."

"If that anti-Semitic mayor in Florac learns of this," Alin said gloomily, "he may send instructions for us to leave. Or he could send the police to force us out."

"I bet that awful de Montfort is showing him that article right now," Geneviève complained.

Denise sighed. "When I was down in the village yesterday, I heard the Vichy government is sending officials to all small towns to ensure compliance with new regulations."

"What new regulations?" André asked, entering the room and yawning. Alin explained and André instantly agreed, "We're too vulnerable here."

A timid knock at the attic door announced Nichette who made a quick curtsy and informed them de Montfort wanted Alin and André in the front parlor immediately.

The enormous ex-governor of Djibouti stood with his back to the brothers as they entered the front room in which they had had their first unpleasant interview. De Montfort took up most of the space and much of the oxygen.

"Well, well," he said facing them. "The RAF has bombed Berlin. That shows anything can happen—like plums turning into prunes."

The brothers exchanged a puzzled look.

Leaning forward, de Montfort announced in a commandingly large voice, "You have to leave. The French authorities require that you return to Belgium. And now, since everyone knows, I can't charge you rent anymore. I have no reason to keep you."

Afraid Alin might physically assault de Montfort, André said, "We would leave this instant if we had someplace to go. But we can't go back to Belgium. Our wives are British subjects and England is still at war with Germany."

"Where you go is not my problem. Here!" de Montfort barked, holding out a form and rattling it. "Sign!"

The Severin brothers read it together and André cried out, "But this says we're leaving at the end of the month!"

"Days," Alin seethed. "Not even a week."

"I can't sign that," André declared definitively. "But we'll get out as soon as we can. We wouldn't want to abuse your 'hospitality' one second longer than we must."

"If you don't want to sign," de Montfort said scornfully, "I'll sign for you."

The massive man sat at a small desk, scrawled "André Severin" on the contrived document, and left the room before the brothers could express their outrage and dismay.

Stunned, Alin said, "Now we know how the French ran Djibouti."

The brothers went to visit Lucien Mauriac in his shop late the next day. Before they had a chance to deliver their bad news he told them, "I've just heard on the BBC that the Luftwaffe has been bombing London for six hours straight."

Alin nodded knowingly. "Retaliation for the attack on Berlin."

"I'm just glad you're safe here with us," Lucien said.

When the Severins described their latest "interview" with de Montfort Lucien raged, "That bastard! Betraying the very nature of this place!"

The Severins explained that their mistreatment by de Montfort wasn't the only reason they had to leave. They had spent all day staring at a detailed map of the Lozère département in search of a location even more remote than Bédouès. On the far side of the Massif Central, in an area facing the Mediterranean, they had discovered the small village of Vialas. They knew nothing of it but instinctively felt drawn to it.

"We saw the bus driver and asked if he knew it," André explained.

"He was very quick and firm," Alin put in. "'It's fine. You'll fit. They'll accept you.'"

"I wouldn't know personally," Lucien said. "But I've heard it's pleasant."

The three stood awkwardly in the gathering gloom.

"Even if you go," the mayor of Bédouès warned, "you'll have the problem of being illegal Belgians. You'll have to register to live in Vialas too."

"Is it possible," André asked gingerly, "that we could receive official dispensation? Should I go up to Mende and throw myself on the mercy of the departmental governor?"

Lucien considered. "I'm told he's quite humane."

Alin asked bluntly, "What if some person of standing spoke up on our behalf?"

Lucien quickly took the hint. "I'll do better than that." Even though he would miss his friends, he would do anything in his power to help them. "I'll provide you with an official certificate of commendation attesting to the value you bring to the region."

The departmental governor at Mende proved as thoughtful and decent as Lucien had said. He was impressed by the story André told of the Severins and even more by the formal yet warm and sincere commendation the mayor of Bédouès provided praising André, "chief of work at the Free University of Brussels," and Alin, "exporter of postage stamps," for having pitched in to till a field in the "commune." And the solution of the plum problem was serious business for which André deserved no end of praise and gratitude.

"I must tell you Monsieur Severin," the departmental governor said, "these are difficult times and yours is a ticklish situation. I know my *responsibility* but I am not always in agreement with the new government of Marshal Pétain. You see I did my duty in the Great War. I fought the Germans; so I know who they are and what they are. And as long as I am the governor here, I will protect this region and its people. So..."

André looked at the governor expectantly, hopefully.

"...it is my judgment," the good man concluded, "that we need you as much as you need us. Therefore, my secretary will give you the written authorization you require. Take care of it and present it when you register in Vialas."

In shock, André returned to Bédouès the same way he had gone to Mende: by bus to Florac and then on the old red bus the rest of the way. Relieved by André's success, the Severins quickly decided that André, his family, Louis, and Rose would go to Vialas first to seek out a new place for them all to stay. Alin, Geneviève and their children would remain behind to harvest the last of the family's crops.

All too soon, it was time to pack again.

View of La Font

Looking Over the Cévennes

Chapter Seven

INTO THE CÉVENNES

August 30, 1940

Friday morning André wasn't certain how to get to Vialas or how long it might take to find a farm suitable for the duration of the family's exile. Everyone was sad to leave Alin and the others behind even temporarily. But that provided incentive for the search.

André drove carefully along the narrow road of gravel and sometimes just dirt, leveled in some places, but not all. The occasional hairpin turns twisting around the mountain ridges threatened a plunge down the steep slope. The ride provided spectacular views, but when the trailer wobbled wildly over loose stones, it was all too easy to picture it crashing into the rugged valley below.

As the Buick wound along the hilly road, the vegetation became increasingly sparse and the trees smaller. Streams chased down the mountainside, careening off of rocks, settling into clear cold pools before leaping over boulders and plummeting to the next resting place.

As André pulled off the road to study the map, the rest got out to stretch amidst the scattered chestnut trees. A warm wind blew through the valley, rustling the dangling bunches of foliage and fruit, filling their ears with whispering music while simultaneously dazzling their eyes with shadows dancing to the tune.

"The chestnut tree is the real emblem of this region," André said as they got back underway. "It's also called the 'bread tree' because the nuts can be ground for baking."

Minutes later, the Severins entered tiny Le Pont-de-Montvert, a village that had been a significant Huguenot stronghold. The only road through town curved along the Tarn, smaller and shallower here than in Millau, but spanned by an ancient arched bridge, narrow and constructed of stones now splotched and gray from lichen, rough after three centuries of weathering. The crystal clear river ran green, and then white, as it coursed around the abutments of the bridge.

André pulled the car and trailer to a stop under trees close by the bridge. Shops lined one side of the road overlooking the water. Several old men in similar black coats sat on benches across the way, berets pulled down over notably round heads.

Ida and Christel scrambled up onto the bridge to watch the water flow by beneath, while André and Denise entered one of few open shops.

All the bread was gone, but a striking middle-aged woman with a severe expression, offered encouragement. The local Cévenol dialect was stronger than in Bédouès or Florac—some words distinct from classic French—the accent hard to penetrate—but the shopkeeper gave them directions and encouraged their hopes of finding a new home.

"There are plenty of abandoned places," she said sadly, "with all the men off slaving away for the Germans—even mine."

Louis and the children drowsed lightly in the car, heads bobbing. The mountainsides were covered with heather now—purple, green, gray—gathered among rock outcroppings. The sun was high in the sky, yet despite the height of the mountains, the rays of the sun poured through the Buick's open windows bringing welcomed warmth.

As they negotiated the narrow, twisting road downhill, Denise waved her hand excitedly. "That must be Vialas," she said indicating a small village far away in the valley.

Nestled amidst the seemingly endless greenery of vast tumbling mountains, a small cluster of old stone buildings glistened gray in the late-day sun; red tile and gray slate roofs seeming to wink at the Severins, appearing and disappearing as the car made its curving way. Coming into Vialas, The Hotel Guin perched alongside the main road, its stone walls rising three stories to a severely peaked roof and anchoring into the slope of the mountain, offered simple lodging.

"Amazing," André said, pointing to the date-stone set at the highest point of the hotel's gable: 1687. "The style hasn't changed since the seventeenth century."

The hotel was surrounded by smaller stone buildings, mostly houses, several featuring shops at street level. Farther down the slope, the only structure to challenge the prominence of the hotel was the Protestant temple, with walls of heavy granite stones, large, thick, and solid. The roof, constructed of dark flat stones, featured a rounded apse and a bell-adorned steeple.

"So," André asked as the sun began to sink behind the mountain and the Severins tried to absorb the nature of Vialas, "should we try to stay here?"

They looked out across the valley, so quiet and peaceful, its small fields still green, with fruit trees growing along the terraced slopes of hillsides. No sign yet of the war.

"It seems agreeable," Denise replied, as sunset bathed the mountain with a vibrant orange.

"Father?" André inquired solicitously.

Louis looked to Rose for approval. She nodded and that was that!

Alin consulted Lucien Mauriac about a new place to stay in Bedoues. One day after the others left for Vialas Alin and his family moved—just in time to honor de Montfort's demand that they vacate his premises by month's end—using their cart to carry what little they had to their new abode.

An older house, it would be theirs exclusively and it had the additional benefit of being closer to the center of the village. Though no château, it was one of the larger houses around and belonged to the well-regarded Porfile family. Divided between inheritors, one end of the house had fallen into a ruinous state. But the Severins' side was quite livable because Maximilian Porfile was determined to keep his legacy intact.

"My brothers and sister don't care about their heritage," Maximilian told Alin and Geneviève, "but this means a great deal to me."

Monsieur Porfile never mentioned any rent.

The old stone house had a spooky feel when sunlight left the valley and wind blew around and between the walls. Katie told Philippe the rush of wind was a ghost's whisper, which frightened him, prompting Alin to secure the two rooms each night.

The place lacked indoor plumbing. Fresh water came from an old-fashioned pump. Since there was no outhouse, one either had to use a pail inside and then go out to dump it or find a private spot outside.

The children didn't like it. Geneviève was appalled.

"We'll just have to get used to it," Alin told them. But he couldn't keep his own nose from wrinkling at the thought.

During the first week of the search, André drove up and down and all around. "The shopkeeper in Le Pont-de-Montvert was right," he told his wife and parents at dinner one night. "So many places abandoned and not just in the last few months."

A peculiar yet oddly charming gentleman they kept meeting in the hotel dining room told them of the sad economic history of the region: a silkworm industry periodically decimated by a disease of the formerly abundant mulberry trees, the exhaustion of most mines, and the depletion of the population by abandonment after the Great War. A confirmed bachelor in his mid-forties, Alphonse Elzière had never recovered from the trauma of serving in the trenches during the last war. Returning from the front, he had come into a small family sum on which he had lived frugally in a one-room apartment in Alès, home to his sister and her family.

"You must meet her!" he repeatedly told André. "She's a teacher too—a high school teacher as her husband used to be—and she's starved for intellectual company!"

The return of war had brought back Monsieur Elzière's battle anxiety. Seeking a more remote situation, he had taken up residence at the Hotel Guin, near his sister's summer place at La Planche. With the proprietor's indulgence, he grew winter vegetables in a small plot out back.

Reaching into his coat pocket wordlessly one day, he presented Christel a small but perfect turnip. After that, the Severins called him *Monsieur Topinanbourg.* And "Mr. Turnip" confirmed to André that the village notary had the most detailed knowledge of the area hamlet by hamlet.

In his early sixties, the notary seemed pleased by André's clean white shirt, tasteful tie, somber suit, and agreeable manners, all quite different from those of the farmers and laborers who typically entered his modest office.

André explained his need of a serviceable farm and farmhouse. The notary nodded. "No difficulty there. The countryside has emptied rapidly. Even without fighting proper, war is pressing its punishing effect into our remote hills and villages." Then he brightened. "But you are here so things are looking up! We've already seen some refugees, though no other Belgians before you. The others are mostly Spanish fleeing Franco and a couple of Germans fleeing Hitler. What a pleasure to hear your urbane accent—so measured and precise. But have you ever farmed before?"

André fished Lucien's commendation and the mayor of Mende's letter from his jacket.

Admiringly the notary said, "We will do what we can for you and yours, Monsieur."

All went smoothly filling out forms until the question of religious affiliation arose.

"Monsieur Severin," the notary said, "we Cévenols are an understanding people. We don't have much experience with Jews. Before the war, we accommodated a few Jewish families who came here to vacation from the north of France, Germany, Belgium…"

André told about the mayor of Florac. The notary laughed uproariously.

"I'm certainly not laughing at your predicament Monsieur," the notary swiftly explained, "but rather what the mayor of Florac called you, 'Israelite refugees.' A neat evasion eh? Why don't I do the same? That way your official profile will be consistent throughout the south of France."

The notary dipped his pen ceremoniously into his inkwell. André reached out to stop him.

"Don't worry Monsieur," the notary counseled soberly. "The people of Vialas would sooner die than betray those they have taken under their protective wing."

Completing his entry the notary closed the ledger and pulled out another large book.

"Now let us see if we can't find you a useful property."

Each day on his way to and from their field, Alin stopped at the café to gather the latest on the war. The Germans were concentrating attacks on British airfields, but the British claimed to be getting the better of them, destroying two or three German aircraft for each RAF fighter lost.

Meanwhile, Vichy France implemented rationing of certain staples. Adults were restricted weekly to 135 grams of sugar, 100 grams of margarine, 200 grams of spaghetti and 50 grams of rice. That wasn't an impossibly heavy burden, but it confirmed the need for Alin and Genevieve to continue to grow and preserve as much of their own food as possible, including beets, onions, squash, carrots and barley. Struggling to wash bunches of carrots as Alin worked the pump then cutting the root vegetables into long strips she set to dry in the sun, Geneviève complained, "I still hate doing this. I wasn't made to be a gardener. I miss Brussels." She wiped a moist forearm across the sweat beading up on her forehead, leaving a long thick muddy smudge above her eyebrows.

"At least we have something to eat every day," Alin said gruffly.

"I know I should count my blessings," Geneviève continued miserably, "but I'd still rather buy these carrots than grow and pick and wash them."

"That would be fine until we run out of money and have to sell our precious diamonds."

Geneviève felt badly about provoking her husband into one of his darker humors. She was very surprised when he stepped toward her and put an arm around her waist consolingly.

"We'll get used to this," he told her, melting her heart.

But she couldn't help thinking he was expressing hope not confidence. Geneviève suddenly realized *she* had to be *his* confidence.

From that moment on she decided, no matter what she might be forced to face and endure, she would try to be as optimistic and strong as Denise. If ever she faltered, she would picture her sister and take comfort and encouragement from that beautiful inspiring image.

Entering the tiny hamlet of Soleyrols, three kilometers west of Vialas, one of a half-dozen recommended by the notary, André decided to take a break. His search had proved fruitless so far. Plenty of farms were available, but none André could convince himself would do. Most had fields that, like Lucien Mauriac's plot in Bédouès, had long gone untended; but since so much more land was involved, it was a much more considerable problem. And the houses were much too small for ten. Some didn't even have roofs, which had collapsed due to neglect and exacerbated by the weight of thick-falling snows in winter and the beating of heavy rains in other seasons.

Most farms had no springs; and water coming only from irrigation trenches presented a major challenge. André understood spring-fed water was rarely found along these rocky hillsides, but he had no desire to depend on the runoff from another property, although ancient right allowed the use of such water. His family's health was the overriding consideration.

Parking beside a small café opposite the only house on the road, André looked over the small gathering of homes of Soleyrols ranging down the valley side below, their red-tiled roofs sticking up through the trees. Breathing in the loamy smell of summer's end he could readily imagine that almost nothing had changed since these buildings were erected 200 or 300 years ago when families much like his own had come to this remote locale to escape persecution and attempt to scratch out a precarious existence on this marginal land.

Perhaps a bite to eat and a cup of coffee would restore his energy and lift his spirits. The café's proprietor might know something about the farm suggested by the notary that supposedly sat on the mountainside well above the road. The café looked inviting—a two-story building with a single front door opening directly onto the roadway, flanked by three windows, the shutters of which had been flung wide open. Smoke drifted up from the chimney in white wisps curling in the gentle breeze. André entered the larger of two rooms containing a few tables bare of any setting except for salt and pepper shakers and an ashtray. A woman stood beside the counter up front. Several older male customers hunkered over glasses of wine stopped speaking when André appeared.

"You're new here," Madame Brignand announced, introducing herself as a member of the family that owned and ran the café. In her early forties Madame was ample but firm and wore her blonde hair pulled tight, tied in a knot at the back of her head. As her arms reached out to serve the coffee André requested, her sweater pulled up enough to reveal a hint of belly. Her fingers were red and cracked from constantly washing and drying dishes and from carrying in wood to feed the small fireplace. Her teeth were straight and white. Little crow's feet poked out from the corners of her blue eyes.

Smelling the soup simmering on the stove in the back room and the round earthy bread sitting out on a cutting board with butter, cheese, and country pâté laid out beside it, André asked if he also might have some of these. Madame Brignand nodded assent and led him to a table. The clientele resumed their talk.

Then Madame brought him his big bowl of soup and asked, "What brings you here?"

Blowing across the surface of his dipped spoon to cool the soup André answered, "I'm looking for a farm known as La Font. Suggested to me by the notary in Vialas as a place where my family might live."

"Refugees?"

André acknowledged his situation. "Perhaps you can tell me about the place."

It might not have been discreet to ask directly, but he hoped Madame Brignand or one of her patrons would say more about the property than the notary had. But Madame and the others held back until André explained how he had come to be there, including a brief reference to Mr. Turnip. Then Madame Brignand underwent a remarkable transformation.

"That crazy brother of Suzanne Maurel's?" she asked excitedly, and when André confirmed that by asking in turn, "The high school teacher?" Madame began chattering on familiarly about what a wonderful person Madame Maurel was and what a shame that they saw her in Soleyrols so rarely—though that was understandable, her poor husband having gone blind.

Silently she led André by the hand to the front door and pointed across the road.

"That house is ours," she said with obvious pride, "and it's available."

André complimented her on the attractiveness and quality of the dwelling but explained it was simply too small for so many Severins and sat on a plot too tiny for farming on the scale he anticipated. At best, it would accommodate an herb garden. His family could not live on herbs.

Grasping André's real need, Madame suggested hiking up the slope behind the café. "I'll show you the way." Bringing him back through the café into the storage room she opened a small door hidden from the road and indicated a path leading uphill to and through trees. "You might find what you're looking for there. At La Font." She smiled and gave him a little push. "You can pay up when you come back to tell me what you think," she said winking. "And when you do, call me Albertine!"

The next day Denise hid her trepidation, keeping an encouraging smile on her face because André was so excited—more excited even than after solving the plum problem. He couldn't wait to take her to Soleyrols and the farm to which he hoped they'd move.

It would be good if she agreed this was "the right farm," to end André's wearying search and because Louis, Rose, and the children were restless after a week and a half at the Hotel Guin. But she was worried. André acknowledged that the property was a little rundown and he hadn't met the owner yet. What if the owner, like Claude de Montfort, proved to be a brute?

Approached from the east, Soleyrols seemed pleasant but not particularly distinguishable from other little hamlets nearby. But its tiny size and anonymity were appropriate for people who wished to blend undetectably into the landscape.

André led Denise into the crowded café. The clientele consisted mostly of older gentlemen dressed in traditional farming garb. Two young women in their late teens—nicely built light blondes, wearing matching floral-print cotton dresses draped just above the knee—skittered about responding to constant calls for "a bit of marc."

Emerging from the café's back room Albertine Brignand explained. "Marc is our locally made brandy. Goes with coffee!"

André greeted Albertine as he would an old friend and she—effusively delighted to meet Denise—expressed her hope that Madame Severin would be as enthusiastic about La Font as her monsieur. She informed them the farm's owner, Gustave Chatrey, would be up there soon. But there was no reason André and Denise couldn't hike up the hill to look around. The hillside was steep enough to make Denise grateful for her athletic youth and the enduring strength of her legs. She could just make out the property some twenty minutes away.

Soon she could see the place more clearly. Impressively large, it consisted of an exceptionally long farmhouse and four outbuildings all made of stone. The house and two small barns had roofs but the other structures had lost theirs.

It was the highest residence on the mountainside. Denise could just identify the extent of the pasturage.

As they got closer, the farmhouse looked even more massive. The stone walls stood tall and straight—solid enduring testimony to the hard thoughtful work of the farmhands and masons who had set these great weathered stones in place long, long before.

The farmhouse was built against the slope of the hill, which rose through various mountaintops to the peak of Mont Lozère, "The highest mountain in all the Cévennes," André said. Huge horseshoe arches undergirded the stone veranda that ran the length of the house. Underneath where the ground sloped up and away, the arched areas were filled with brush and other remnants of the distant time when this had been a working farm.

"Shelter," André enthused, "for chickens and rabbits, maybe even pigs."

With the pride of possession, André showed his wife the other buildings. "The big barn has two sections, one we can use for the goats and sheep, the other for hay and feed. The smaller barn will be right for winter storage of potatoes, turnips, cabbage, carrots, beans and maybe more in the loft". He pointed out a small woodshed presently empty apart from rusting hoes, rakes, and pitchforks. Beyond the woodshed lay the main gardens and the grave of the Chatrey family's older brother—the depression was never filled in after the surviving brother and sisters moved off the farm and took the body with them.

At the rear of the main house, a back door led to what had been kitchen gardens and into the pasture sloping up the mountainside. Farther beyond, a few apple trees had been planted in careless rows. Then came the chestnut trees which covered land too steep to cultivate and unsuitable for haying. Above that, the soil gave out leaving only scrub, scraggly grasses and isolated thinly wooded copses.

"There are some old fallen trees up there," André said, "with naturally hollowed-out trunks that house beehives—so we'll even have honey. If we take the place, I mean."

What pleased André most was the freshwater spring uphill, not far from the house and from which the house derived its name, short for *la fontaine,* "The Fountain." The water came clear and cold from the mountain above, running untouched down the hillside to La Font before coursing on to provide water to the café, farms and houses below.

"The only farm of all I've seen with its own source of pure water," André proclaimed.

They mounted the front steps to the stone-paved veranda of the farmhouse and entered through a simple wooden door. The walls of the house were two feet thick.

Left rough, the outside walls had weathered over the centuries to look like the surrounding mountainsides. Inside wood partitions defined the rooms, guarded against cold drafts, and exemplified the simple modest style of the place.

The four rooms were laid out railroad style. Each had one small window set high. At one end of the house was the storage room, its walls and rafters lined with hooks.

"That's where we can keep all the foodstuffs we'll need on a daily basis," André said.

Then came two bedrooms, each containing an ancient armoire—tall and severe—and a large wood-framed bed covered with a canvas mattress and filled with old straw. In the middle bedroom, an extra bed had been improvised with two chairs facing each other to support a number of boards.

"I suppose the children will have to sleep here, two to a bed," Denise said.

"Not ideal but it might suffice," André suggested,

Last and largest was the common room: kitchen, dining room, living room, and playroom all in one. The kitchen part, running along a section of the back of the house nestled into the hillside, featured a long refectory table and a sideboard that had stood in place since the 1700s. The wooden chairs had seats of canvas or straw and reeds. Most had holes in them.

"Two of us can sleep here. Again not ideal," André said, "but if we can make do…"

The source of heat was an open fireplace in the common room—a huge space lined with large stones, with a great mantel above it and a solid chimney venting into the sky. The fireplace was the only place to cook food or heat water in kettles hung on a metal rod stretched above the fire.

"We can get a woodstove too," André recommended. "Perhaps Alin can have Lucien Mauriac look into it or Alin might find one himself in Florac."

Denise lingered in the back of the kitchen, looking.

"There's no running water," André answered before she could ask. "We'll have to use chamber pots."

Not ideal. But Denise understood they couldn't have everything. She didn't even mind that there were no window curtains since privacy was not an issue without any near neighbors. Besides, she would be able to purchase material in Vialas to sew curtains of her own for some domestic warmth in the otherwise primitive setting.

"It's one of the very few farms with electricity," André said encouragingly. "At least we can have a little light at night. Maybe we can even get a radio."

After long thought, Denise said, "I think this will be all right for most of us. But I'm concerned for Louis and Rose. It's quite a trek up the hillside."

"I thought that too," André said grinning. "But here's a solution: the little house across from the café. The Brignands have agreed to let us use it rent-free as their contribution to the struggle of refugees like us. It's just two rooms, but I think my parents will be happy there. It's level with the road. It already has a woodstove for heat and cooking." He looked at Denise and said quietly, "Of all the places I've seen this is the largest and most remote. Hopefully we'll not be obvious to the Vichy authorities or the Germans."

Denise smiled and shook her head in agreement.

Looking around they were silent, each lost in their own thoughts, until someone outside called out, "Hallo!" Gustave Chatrey pushed open the door. A gnarled, grizzled older gentleman, he was no longer interested in working the slopes of La Font or gathering the plentiful chestnuts. These days, he found living in the village far more agreeable and was pleased to think someone might again make the farm productive.

"We'd like to rent your place," indicated André.

"I am a hunter of long habit," Gustave Chatrey responded, "of rabbits and pheasants and the occasional deer. I ask only for the game. And you must give me half the apples and chestnuts you gather as is the tradition. Agreed?"

André asked, "How much do you think that will be? What quantity?"

"Between twenty and twenty-five hundred kilos," Gustave allowed. "That's what we used to collect anyway."

"Is that the apples and the chestnuts?" André asked.

"Just the chestnuts."

"And is that the whole or half?"

"No, no, that's all of it." The old farmer saw André's troubled expression. "It's some work without doubt. But you'll see it's possible. I've done it."

Gustave showed them his hands rough and calloused from decades of hard work.

André gave Denise a look as if to say, *The quantity of chestnuts is fantastic, all to be picked by hand.* Denise tried to answer also with her eyes, *We must do what we must do, and you know how hard I'll work to help you.*

"Naturally," Gustave added, "the property must be cared for. But the first year at least I can help you. I'll show you the best way to pick the chestnuts and dry them."

As he described the age-old drying process, Denise foresaw the demanding labor that lay ahead. *But,* she thought, *La Font is available and viable. It can be made to meet our needs and André believes it's the best we'll find.*

Gustave repeated his willingness to help get them started, smiled, and held out his hand.

Very briefly, André turned a questioning glance on his wife. She replied with a quick nod of agreement, encouragement, and reassurance.

André took Gustave's hand and said, "We'll take it."

The old farmer grunted and gave André's hand a hard friendly squeeze.

"Good," he said warmly. "The pact is made."

Walking home after church, Lucien Mauriac tried not to think about ongoing air battles between the Luftwaffe and the RAF. The loss of so many fighter planes was almost unimaginable, but the loss of human life troubled him more deeply. Those numbers too continued to rise. To distract himself, he called to mind the astonishing discovery made by four schoolboys of wall paintings thought to be ten thousand years old at the Cave of Lascaux. Shouldn't the people of the world concentrate on preserving such cultural marvels rather than destroying everything humankind had struggled across countless millennia to create?

Passing the Porfile place, he was startled by a piercing shriek. Geneviève was chopping logs to fit inside the woodstove and the wedge holding the steel head onto the shaft came out letting the ax head fly into her leg. Blood flowed copiously as she sat on the ground in shock.

"Alin," she called weakly.

The mayor of Bédouès couldn't tell if she was aware that he was standing there. Alin came on the run from the other side of the house and the two men stooped to help her.

"You certainly didn't miss—your leg I mean," Lucien said lightly.

"I suppose you've seen cut legs before," Geneviève said flatly, without amusement.

In a quiet aside, Lucien told Alin they must stem the blood loss quickly.

"I'll take care of that," Geneviève, overhearing, announced. She pulled off the scarf tying back her hair and the mayor helped her bind her leg clumsily, trying to tighten the scarf enough to staunch the flow without cutting off all circulation.

As he and Alin helped Geneviève hobble toward the house, blood spurted from the sodden material and Geneviève fell into a swoon. Lucien supported her while Alin clasped his hands tightly around the leg. The scarf slipped to Geneviève's ankle leaving the gaping wound exposed to dirt. The cut's red flesh edges throbbed with the pulse of pumping blood vessels.

The mayor held Geneviève under the arms. Alin lifted her legs, pressing the scarf against the wound. They carried her into the kitchen area and set her down carefully on a short bench.

"It really doesn't hurt," Geneviève said, amazed and bewildered.

"She needs a doctor," Alin said.

Geneviève chuckled a low chuckle. "You don't believe in doctors."

"There is no doctor in Bédouès," Lucien said anxiously. "Or even in Florac anymore. Because of the war, they're all away, in hiding or forbidden to practice by law."

"What does the big book of homeopathy say?" Geneviève asked.

"I think she's delirious from blood loss," the mayor said softly to Alin.

"We need to wash out the wound," Alin said. Positioning Geneviève's hand to hold the scarf in place he went to the sink for soap and a pan of water. "Is there any medicine available?" he asked the mayor as he bathed the wound gently.

"I'm afraid not," Lucien replied, impressed by Geneviève's bravery.

"Then I'll have to use some wine to disinfect the leg," Alin fretted.

"I hope not good wine!" Lucien joked as Alin fetched a bottle. Geneviève still didn't smile.

After the application of wine and a fresh clean cloth, the men carried Geneviève to bed.

"Now you are truly one of us," the mayor said sympathetically. "You'll see: even without stitches or medicine your body will recover with its own natural powers. Just like ours."

"Oh that's nice," Geneviève said, beginning to drift away. "Funny. It hardly bothers me at all. And I'm glad of the excuse to get some rest."

Alin's night was long but Geneviève's was longer. Katie had a hard time too, calling her father several times for reassurance her mother would recover.

Alin was only grateful that Philippe—still too young to understand fully—slept in a blissful peace.

In morning's first light Alin examined Geneviève's bandage. White oozed around it.

Roused by increasing pain Geneviève whispered, "It's not doing so well."

Alin unwrapped the cloth. Red streaks showed above the wide, open festering wound.

Geneviève was afraid to look. Hovering by the bedroom door, Katie couldn't wait to see—until she really did. Catching the merest glimpse of the bloody cloth, Katie blenched.

"I don't feel so well," Geneviève confessed. "It hurts, it hurts, it hurts."

"Just stay still and rest," Alin counseled tenderly. "I'm going to see if anybody in the village knows anything about medicine."

"Don't worry about me," Geneviève responded weakly. "I'm not going anyplace."

If only Geneviève had said that with a hint of humor.

Alin asked Katie to stay with her brother. "Don't leave the house. Or stay out front."

"Yes Papy," Katie replied, impressed by the gravity of the situation.

"That's a good big girl. Be sure to listen for your mother. Bring her anything she wants."

"I'm just going to try to sleep," Geneviève said. "Maybe that will help."

She drifted off again without another word.

Alin did not return until the sun began casting shadows into the valley.

"Oh Papy!" Katie called as soon as he appeared. "Maman is not good. But she says she'll be happy again when you get back."

"Well I'm here," he said comfortingly, giving Katie a kiss on the cheek and Philippe a pat on the head. Then he hurried into the bedroom.

Geneviève was moaning softly and twisting uncomfortably, using her unaffected leg to try to change position and ease the pressure on the injured one. Alin had tied another clean rag around the wound but that rag had long since soaked through. The yellowish pus of infection seeped around it.

Alin felt Geneviève's feverish forehead. When she opened her half-lidded eyes more fully they were rheumy and red.

"I'm glad to see you back," she said hoarsely.

"I tried to find a doctor but Lucien was right. I did find some alcohol—cognac—better than wine for bathing the wound and getting rid of the infection."

Geneviève smiled a vague half-smile. "I don't know whether that will work the trick but at least it will smell better than the wound."

Alin unwrapped the leg again, tipped the neck of the bottle over the cut, and drizzled a little dark liquid up and down the wound. Geneviève clutched the bed as the alcohol burned into the infected area. Tears sprang from her eyes as she cried out in a tiny high-pitched whine that caused Alin to stop pouring. He blew gently on the leg hoping to ease the impact of the liquid still running into and around the exposed flesh.

After a few moments, when the pain began to subside due to the alcohol's anesthetic effect, Alin said tentatively, "I did find out about someone who might be able to help. A healer who has knowledge of these things. The villagers depend on her when other remedies fail."

Geneviève struggled to lift her torso into a half-reclining position. "When will she be here?"

"The villagers sent word to her hamlet. She could be here tomorrow."

"I'm willing to believe." Geneviève dropped back onto her pillow, gritting her teeth against a surge of searing pain. "Tell me it helps to believe!"

Pale and sweaty, Geneviève passed another bad night, keeping everyone from sleep. Before dawn Tuesday, Katie was almost desperate with fear, which was affecting Phillipe as he sobbed in sympathy. Alin told them their mother would get well soon, but he was uneasy and unconvinced himself.

They all jumped when they heard an insistent knock from outside. Alin opened the door to an old woman so dreadful looking she might have modeled her appearance on a storybook witch. Of indeterminate age, she had matted gray hair hanging down around her shoulders in uneven ringlets. The wool shawl drawn tight to her throat couldn't disguise her hunched back. When she talked the sound whistled out around crooked, cracked, black and missing teeth.

"I understand your woman has a bad cut," she said in a hoarse scratchy voice that frightened the already frightened children, "infected, maybe blood poisoning."

"You have experience with these things?" Alin said, suddenly hopeful.

Without asking permission, the old woman went into the bedroom. She walked past with such fierce determination that Alin doubted he could have stopped her had he wanted.

Turning around in the doorway, the old woman pointed to the lamp on the kitchen table, fixed her eyes on trembling Katie, and commanded, "Bring me that lantern!"

Her father nodded. Katie brought the light forward, letting the old woman see well enough to unwrap the cloth, examine Geneviève's leg and mutter, "Bad—Messy—Dried blood—Oozing white—Infection—Suppurating."

Alin took the lantern from Katie and told her and Philippe to go back to bed. But Philippe whimpered and Katie insisted she wouldn't be able to sleep anyway.

The old woman opened her shawl and drew out a small pot. Silently she put her finger into a sticky potion and lathered up the wound, spreading her "concoction" into and around the reddened ends of the flesh, humming to herself and muttering mysteriously as she worked her fingers quickly back and forth. Then she drew back admiring her work while Geneviève gritted her teeth against the pain.

The old woman asked for a new bandage. Alin got an undershirt out of a drawer, tore it into strips, and handed a length of it to her. The healer carefully rewrapped Geneviève's leg, tying a tight knot. Sitting on the edge of the bed, she clasped her hands in her lap and swayed, singing in patois. The gentle tune floated across the room. Geneviève, slightly better, settled into a deep sleep.

"Tomorrow," the old woman said leading everyone out of the room, "she'll be fine. Keep her still today. And hot broth is best for her."

The sun had pushed up above the far ridgeline. In the kitchen again, the healer didn't look so ancient or terrifying. Her skin was clear and there were surprisingly few lines on her face. Her eyes shone with the intensity of kindness. Even her hunch didn't look that bad anymore.

"What may I pay you?" Alin asked.

"No pay! No money! That would break the power. All I've done would go to waste. But if you could give me some vegetables you've grown, there would be something of yourself in them. That would enhance the power."

"How?" Katie asked, emboldened by daylight.

The elderly healer quickly put a finger to the little girl's lips. "It's God's gift," she said. "And it is not for me, you, or anyone else to wonder how or why."

Late the next morning, after having slept well and long, Geneviève called each family member by name. When they entered the bedroom, they found her smiling. Alin was anxious but afraid to lift the sheet from her leg.

"Go on," she said. "It feels so much better."

Alin carefully undid the healer's knot and unwound the bandage that came off clean. Geneviève didn't wince. The skin underneath had closed up. It wasn't even red anymore. There was no way to tell the leg had ever been injured!

"What do you think?" Geneviève asked, sounding her old self again. "Was it the cognac or the faith healer?"

Laughing joyously Alin said, "The cognac wasn't good enough to affect such a cure."

That afternoon, there was another sharp knock at the door.

"Who is it?" Alin called through the wooden panel.

"The bus driver. I have a message from your brother."

Alin filled with dread. Had the end of one nightmare led to another? Had something bad happened to one of the Severins, possibly Louis or Rose?

The driver of the old red bus stood on the threshold, smiled broadly and said, "I've just come from Vialas. André wanted me to tell you they've found a place to live—at last!"

André and Denise spent most of a week straightening, cleaning and scrubbing, trying to ready the farmhouse to move into the next Monday. By Saturday that seemed feasible and on Sunday evening they sat down to a family farewell supper at the Hotel Guin. Backed by a fervently nodding Christel, Ida begged Monsieur Navet to join them. When Alphonse Elzière accepted, he mentioned that his sister and nephew had come to town. They also were invited.

In her mid-forties, Suzanne Maurel was a smidgen shy of five feet tall. She wore a gray-and-black delicately patterned dress well below her knees, its collar tight to her neck and as high as her chin. She had a charming habit of fluffing out her respectably coiffed prematurely gray hair with small gentle hands. Suzanne laughed easily and spoke with a delightful candor that made everyone feel like old friends.

Suzanne wanted to know everything about the Severins, but she focused most of her attention on André "as a fellow teacher." Suzanne was even more surprised to learn that André had accepted the Freemason membership. André explained that the Grand Orient of Belgium was truly revolutionary within the Freemason fraternity due to its democratic and liberal orientation and because it had abolished the obligatory obeisance to a divine "Grand Architect of the Universe." As a member, André had been delighted to discover men from remarkably varied backgrounds working together toward the common good in an open spirit rich in faith. "I am particularly interested in those sects that focus on an individual's direct encounter with God."

Suzanne interjected genially, "That's very interesting, but it doesn't sound very scientific."

"The more science I know, the clearer God's reality becomes to me; for whatever explanation of physical phenomena we devise, there is always a mystery beyond it and another beyond that irreducibly. Isn't that mystery God?"

"My son André," Louis broke in proudly, "has an insatiable curiosity. He brings relentless energy and discipline to all intellectual pursuits."

"Ah," Suzanne said, "then you will adore the people of the Cévennes. You'll find they have a real love and respect for learning—far more than my students in Alès. You'll be surprised and pleased, I believe, by their reverence not only for the Bible but for all literature."

"Then I am happy to be among them," André said enthusiastically.

"And it is because of this character of freethinking, this continuing heritage of the Huguenot tradition that the people of the Cévennes resist against the loss of freedom not only of thought, but also of a true and freely organized government. As an example, my husband, Charles, started a resistance movement in Alès among the students, with my help of course and that of Françoise, our thirteen-year-old daughter who's home with him right now. We printed up and passed out leaflets declaring the dangers of collaboration and the weakness of the Vichy government. Charles saw immediately that the German defeat of France did not free the French from danger. He believes fervently that we must make an aggressive effort never to succumb to Nazi pressure. Unfortunately, engaging in these activities weakened Charles so he had to give them up. I carry on as best I can. He's been quite an influence on the children too. But for goodness sake, Max can speak for himself!" as she pointed to her son, a lanky, fresh faced, handsome young man of twenty, dark hair with hazel eyes, quick and bright.

Throughout the evening, André had taken note of Max Maurel's thoughtful attentive presence, even though the young man contributed as little to the conversation as Monsieur Elzière. Max did respond politely to direct address, however. Now, when Rose asked whether he was still in school, he sheepishly noted that he had enrolled the previous year at the University of Montpellier—his mother's alma mater, some hundred kilometers south of Vialas—to study medicine for which the university had been renowned since the twelfth century. But the war had forced him to return to Alès at the end of his first spring term.

With that, Max fell silent again. As the dinner dishes were cleared preparatory to dessert, talk turned to Vichy's decision to allow the Japanese to enter French Indochina—a perplexing move that seemed to clear the way for Japan's pursuit of territorial expansion. This sparked Max as nothing else that evening.

"Wait and see," Max said angrily. "This just proves the Axis powers of Germany and Italy are aligning themselves with Emperor Hirohito and his military government. Mark my words, the Japanese will soon be full participants in this terrible war—on the wrong side!"

André was impressed by the young man's passion and capacity for analysis. He wished he could find a way to speak with him in private where the youth might express himself more freely. After dessert, André manufactured an opportunity, offering the young man a cigarette. The two stepped out onto the hotel's balcony for a smoke and a glass of brandy.

André immediately expressed his regret that Max had been forced to abandon his studies. "My own studies were interrupted by military obligations. You must continue yours as soon as possible," he said encouragingly.

"I assure you I will," Max said fervently. "Nothing can stop me. But for now—you know not every Frenchman is willing to bow down to our new German masters or to that puppet French government." Max took a long drag on his cigarette and expelled the smoke into the air as if venting his anger. "It's funny. I didn't want to say this inside but…though I didn't know anything about my father's actions in Alès until later, it happens I joined a group of like-minded students and former students at Montpellier to write and distribute informational tracts against Pétain. Unfortunately, the school's administrators got wind of it, which is why I had to leave. Not that they threatened me—they just expressed 'disappointment'—but it made me realize it would be dangerous to stay, especially when the orders came down for young men like me to go and work in Germany. Though more dangerous naturally for my friend and fellow medical student, Fela Klinghofer—a Polish Jew. I could go home to hide but she…she had no place to go. So I took her with me. She's there now too with Françoise and father. At least we've been able to help mother and Françoise with the leafleting."

"Is that a delicate situation," André asked, drawn to and concerned for this young man, who reminded him of his very best students in Brussels, "living in the same place as your girlfriend?"

"What? Oh! Fela's not my girlfriend! I don't have a girlfriend! She's my comrade! And tomorrow we're both going into *Les Chantiers de la Jeunesse*. I may have managed to escape the call-up for Germany but…"

"Les Chantiers de la Jeunesse?"

"'Building sites for the young'—Pétain's latest brainstorm. It's supposed to get unemployed youth out of the cities and into the countryside—to thin dead trees out of the forests and hack out paths and lanes…on mornings anyway. Afternoons we're supposed to have 'educational opportunities.' *Moral* education they call it—an investigation of the ethics and legacy of France—but I think it's all about indoctrination. And they want to keep an eye on us. Keep us out of trouble. Keep us from *making* trouble. Ah well. I'll enjoy the fresh air."

By then the two men's glasses had been drained and their cigarettes had gone out. As much as André enjoyed Max's company and his stimulating perspective, he realized it would be rude to remain apart from the others any longer, especially now that he knew it was only a matter of hours before Max and his mother would be separated for some time to come.

With the evening at an end, André reflected on how remarkable the Maurels were and how much he would miss them even though they had just met. He had found some kindred souls. He was especially touched when Suzanne said good night and embraced him with tears in her eyes.

"We will see you soon," she assured him, smiling through her tears—or was she reassuring herself? "After all, now we are officially neighbors!"

"Yes," André said, happy at the prospect. "Soleyrols isn't all that far from your summer house is it? We must have you to dinner as soon as we settle in."

"And you must visit La Planche. Of course, if you ever find yourselves in Alès I know Charles and Françoise would enjoy meeting you as much as we have."

As the others drifted out of the dining room, André lingered for a final word with Max.

"I just wanted to tell you what a pleasure this has been," André told him. "I trust we will meet again before too much time has passed. And I'd love to meet your friend Fela."

"And she will look forward to meeting you," added Max. They shook hands as the evening ended.

While Louis napped in the back bedroom, Rose sat in the large front room of the house across from the café, looking out the window, waiting for the bus. The previous week, the bus driver had delivered the news of La Font to Alin. He returned with a message on a plain sheet of paper, written in the same tiny elegant penmanship Alin used to mark his ratings on the backs of collectable stamps: *We will soon start sending bags of carrots, beets and whatever else we can still harvest.*

When Alin's shipment finally arrived the last Thursday of September, it was not a disappointment. In addition to the large sacks of carrots and beets he had promised specifically, and which the bus driver was kind enough to lug out and set beside Louis and Rose's front door, there were two chickens and two rabbits in four separate cardboard boxes.

Chickens! Rabbits! Rose wondered what Alin knew about acquiring or raising them. Would André know what to do with them?

Distracted by these concerns, Rose forgot André wanted another message delivered to Alin until the bus driver was climbing back into his conveyance. Racing to reach him before he drove off she called out, "Please! When you see Alin could you tell him André hopes he'll find and buy a cast iron wood-burning stove in Bédouès or maybe Florac that he can send along with you?"

"How on earth will we get it onto the bus?" the driver asked incredulously.

"Dismantle it," Rose replied, having been prepared by her eldest. "André is certain you can manage it."

Friday was Ida's sixth birthday. Denise saved the newly arrived carrots and beets—which had taken André several difficult trips to haul up the hill—for that night's dinner. Throughout the day, Ida had the great pleasure of chasing the chickens and petting the rabbits.

The biggest treat was the small birthday cake Madame Brignand was thoughtful and kind enough to bake and bring uphill with her teenaged daughters Alice and Yvette—the young women who worked in the café. The unusually pleasant young people were always smiling if not laughing, bubbling with energy and enthusiasm, and were remarkably close in age, temperament, and thought, each repeating the other's words almost before they had all come out.

Though the cake was nowhere near as good as those remembered from Brussels, Ida was happy to have it. And having the family's first social visitors at La Font helped make her birthday seem special indeed. If only her aunt, uncle, and cousins could have been there.

Unfortunately, in addition to the cake Albertine delivered the news that Germany, Italy, and Japan had signed a mutual defense pact.

Outraged and despairing, André—who immediately recalled that Max Maurel had predicted this—declared, "This is a day that will be remembered for its treachery."

"Hush," Rose said. "Is that how you want Ida to remember her sixth birthday?"

Ida looked up perplexed. "What's 'treachery'?"

As the days and weeks went by, André became anxious for his brother's helping hands. In addition to the harvesting of apples and chestnuts that would have to begin soon, there was much work to do to winterize the farmland. They had all the old farm equipment necessary; but it was very primitive and in need of thorough mending. Yet, they would need those tools to work the difficult and stony ground.

The primitivism of the place extended to the interior of the farmhouse. The house was often cold, despite the great fire they struggled to keep ablaze in the fireplace. Though never a complainer, Denise complained that the straw-filled beds had no springs for support and the straw retained the cold. "It's fortunate we brought all our own sheets and blankets from Le Coq," mused Denise to André "It does make the archaic beds a little more accommodating."

The kitchen was filled with rustic, often ancient items: earthenware pots and big black iron cauldrons, old jam jars, glasses, and crude china that would likely make Geneviève yearn for her beloved Limoges. Denise hoped her sister would be mollified by the heavy silverware from Belgium marked on every handle with the "SF" monogram that brought the Severin and Freedman families to mind, and by the Severins' large heirloom tablecloth embroidered with an ornate letter "S."

The window curtains, which Denise had made, were a nice touch. But there was nothing to be done about the plumbing. And everyone had to be careful to dump their "business" below and away from the stream so as not to contaminate the single source of water.

The longer Alin and his family delayed the happier with La Font they would be. Certainly, they would be pleased with the wood-burning stove that Alin had purchased, and with the bus driver's help, dismantled into three pieces. When it arrived in Soleyrols, André was fortunate that the other principal in the café, Albertine's husband Louis, owned a horse-drawn cart, which he volunteered for the demanding task of getting the large heavy pieces uphill.

Once the pieces had been maneuvered into the kitchen, André succeeded in reassembling the stove himself. The great iron top was an enormous help in cooking and the water compartment on one side was large enough for three jerry cans of water. This most welcome additional source of warmth made heating up water to fill the tub—at least once a week for washing clothes and cleansing bodies—much more feasible and efficient.

Alin had chosen well. The stove grew hot swiftly; its fire starting quickly with dried sticks from the bush of broom or heather that even the children could help gather.

Without doubt, maintaining a sufficient supply of firewood for the fireplace and woodstove would be a big ongoing necessary project. Already into October, Soleyrols was dauntingly cold. The Severins could only imagine how much more bitter the weather would be when the long winter set in.

Shortly after moving into La Font and during the first of the strong rainstorms that swept across the mountains from the west, the Severins heard a tick tick tick from leaks in the roof. Once again the Brignands—the Severins' lifesavers in so many ways—stepped in, recommending an "old carpenter" for the repairs. He was able to come up and do the job almost right away. Despite his sixty years, he proved adept at negotiating the old roof's perilous slope.

"Good thing I'm here now," he said laconically, looking up at the sky and nodding agreement with himself. "Weather's going to change soon. Snow's on the way."

Still no sign of the Bédouès contingent. Instead a huge sack filled with forty-five kilograms of barley arrived—and onions too, lots and lots of onions. Alin also sent along a crate with another dozen chickens and a note explaining that he thought it more important to have more chickens rather than extra rabbits since the pair of rabbits he had sent were male and female; with luck, they would fulfill the old expression and multiply.

On her family's last day in Bédouès, Geneviève was packing. In the last several weeks, the friends the Severins had made became exceptionally generous, selling them food and other goods they could ill afford to do without themselves, sometimes offering desirable items as presents. The pair of breeding rabbits the Severins had been given was particularly valuable and the owners had refused payment—an astonishing sacrifice in such hard times.

More recently, becoming aware of Alin and Geneviève's impending departure, a number of neighbors had come to say good-bye—including Nichette, the maid from the de Montforts' château who had been the first local to befriend them. One acquaintance offered to sell them a couple of goats at an impossibly low price to which Alin had agreed without a moment's hesitation. What a happy surprise discovering one of the goats was pregnant!

Initially Alin and Geneviève had intended to stay through the end of the month. But when they learned that the Germans had ordered all Jews in occupied France to register with the authorities, they felt they should move before things got worse in unoccupied Vichy, France.

Late in the day, Camille Mousand, a favorite neighbor who had lived in Bédouès all her life, stopped by. She wore a work apron over a blue dress faded by endlessly repeated washings and bore a farewell gift: a huge slab of pig fat with a little bit of bacon attached.

"Thanks so much," Geneviève said, glad she had been brought up well enough to make offering a thanks reflexive, because she was thinking, *What on earth am I going to do with this?*

Despite their brief acquaintance, Camille knew Geneviève fairly well. "You say 'thank you' but I don't think you know the value that fat will have for you."

"Of course I do. And I'm very grateful on behalf of my family. Besides I love bacon!"

"Further proof you're no true Jew," Camille said with a hearty laugh. Then she grew serious, wished Geneviève the best always, kissed her on both cheeks, and walked away. Geneviève could read her sadness in the slump of her retreating shoulders.

"Isn't her husband a poacher?" Alin asked, returning from the mayor's garden plot for the last time.

"I guess that's why they always have meat that isn't on the ration list," Geneviève replied. "But why would they give us all this fat? For a couple so tight with its money..."

"We have been well treated here," Alin acknowledged somewhat grudgingly.

The next afternoon, Alin and Geneviève loaded their belongings and their children onto the old red bus. Handing everything in, Geneviève couldn't help musing. *It's so dirty and smelly; and it's getting to seem normal to me.*

At the last moment, Lucien Mauriac came to hug Geneviève and shake Alin's hand.

"Bédouès will never be the same without you," he said. "It feels as if you belong here now. You will certainly not be forgotten."

"We'll be back," Alin said bluffly though he had no idea whether or not that was so.

"I look forward to it," Lucien called out, waving as the bus pulled away noisomely.

Only when her nostrils filled with the scent of fatback did Geneviève begin to realize how meaningful the time in Bédouès had been. They all had discovered so much there: their internal resources and their ability to cope with true adversity.

As the kilometers passed by, Geneviève found herself crying.

The bus driver had told André when to expect the Bédouès contingent. As the bus rumbled slowly toward Soleyrols, André could hardly conceal his excitement. Louis and Rose joined him in front of their house. Denise ran down the path from La Font with Ida and Christel.

The lumbering conveyance chugged to a stop in front of the café. Ten adults and children became a joyful blur of hugs and kisses. Then the children led a scramble uphill to the great farmhouse. Toward the rear, André marveled that Alin had taken to dressing like the local laborers. He himself had given up ties but still wore a wool jacket and white shirt every day.

Soleyrols was on the southeast face of the mountains, but it was higher than Bédouès. Harsh wintry winds—as the old carpenter had warned—were already beginning to bite. Denise and the children had made La Font as cheery and welcoming as possible, but even with the woodstove and fireplace stoked and blazing, the farmhouse remained cold.

Ida and Christel acted as tour guides for Katie and Philippe. Geneviève expressed appreciation of the place and all her sister had done, but André knew she was disappointed. Alin had a clearheaded practical response; he wanted André to show him the rest of the grounds.

The sun's setting brought a bitter tang to the still, chilled air. André hurried Alin through outbuildings, fields, and stands of trees. With a now-practiced eye, Alin assessed the property positively, praising his brother for finding and choosing a farm well-suited to their purposes, including keeping them hidden from prying eyes.

The brothers talked briefly of work to be done and improvements to make. Alin was anxious to see about piping water into the kitchen to reduce the time spent out-of-doors in the soon-to-be freezing temperatures.

For dinner, Denise served a stew made from the barley, carrots, and onions Alin had sent from Bédouès, and the first chicken André had slain, which Denise, with advice from Albertine, had plucked and cut apart. Beets from Bédouès served as the one side dish. André poured wine acquired in Vialas and topped off the meal with fine coffee brewed from grounds from the café.

It took longer than dinner for the family to discuss everything that had happened since the end of August. The tale of Geneviève's ax accident and the miracle of her healing made André laugh loudly about this "evidence" of the efficacy of homeopathy. He too was stunned when Geneviève lifted her skirt to show no trace of the wound.

The lack of indoor plumbing was something the newcomers had gotten used to at the Porfile place, but they did object to the smell caused by the goats kept in one of the spaces under the house and the chickens and rabbits in another. The animals were right below the bedrooms and the floorboards were made out of old dry wood full of cracks.

"At least the animals' body heat helps with the cold," Denise suggested.

"It would be easier to put up with the smell," Geneviève retorted, "if it came with *enough* heat. Perhaps if those rabbits hop to it..."

That night all slept soundly and long. They awoke to the season's first snow.

The four cousins couldn't wait to go out and play. But André and Alin got out first, afraid the early snow would dash their hopes of installing a water tap.

Rounding the corner of the café, the brothers were startled to see their father outside his house chopping wood in the light but persistent snowfall. Despite the cold, Louis had removed his coat and laid it carefully aside. Still he perspired.

Alarmed, André cried out, "Father! Be careful! You're not used to such physical labor!"

"But it helps me keep warm."

"We can do all the chopping you need," Alin insisted, gently but firmly taking the ax out of his father's hands. "There are safer ways to stay warm."

The brothers finished up for their father then hurried to the café, crowded and abuzz with lively chatter about Hitler meeting with Spain's Generalissimo Francisco Franco and his plans to meet with Pétain.

The brothers explained to Louis Brignand what they had in mind.

"Baptiste," Louis called, introducing a compact balding man with scarred grimy hands.

"Good thing you got to me when you did," Baptiste told the Severins cheerfully. "By tonight the snow will freeze hard. Then it will be too late."

The brothers and Baptiste went into Vialas and bought the last piping available: lead. The question of lead poisoning was controversial. André allowed himself to be swayed reluctantly.

"Galvanized iron or stainless steel would be better but there's none to be had," Baptiste complained. "Copper would be good too but it was always a luxury up in these mountains and it was all used up in the French defense effort."

Snow fell throughout the afternoon. Baptiste seemed impervious to it. There was just enough pipe to reach from the spring through the rough hole he laboriously carved into La Font's thick back wall and then to the spigot which splashed water into the newly installed basin.

The basin was shallow and the water flowing into it was icy cold. They worried about what would happen in a hard freeze but Baptiste assured them the water would always be there.

In the middle of the night Geneviève was awakened by a moaning sound right beneath her bedroom.

"Alin. Alin!" she whispered shaking him, hoping not to wake anyone else.

"What? What is it?" Alin grumbled groggily.

The eerie keening unnerved Geneviève, but Alin said, "Must be that pregnant goat. Want me to have a look?"

"No you sleep," Geneviève said slipping into her farm clothes.

She lit a lantern and carefully made her way down the stone steps to the lower level. Alin's offer to go had been sweet, but what did he know about pregnancy and birth? Not that Geneviève had experience with gravid animals. She just hoped there was some similarity between the two- and four-legged kind.

Inside the arched space, she immediately realized the goat was in trouble—wheezing, moaning, and writhing in the dirt. The goat was well past her prime and probably shouldn't have gotten pregnant.

The creature looked up at Geneviève with such pitiable pleading in her huge liquid eyes that Geneviève sat beside her despite the unpleasant smell. She stroked the beast's brow and softly told her to try to stay calm though she felt foolish talking to a goat.

As the night wore on, Geneviève felt hypnotized by the steady stroking and the goat's stertorous breaths and periodic whines. Then the goat gave a start and a terrible cry and started licking feverishly at her nether region. Peering through the very dim light Geneviève saw the head of the kid had appeared. She was about to participate in an animal's birth!

The goat's desperate struggle panicked them both. Didn't beasts of burden simply and easily drop their newborns in the field? Not now. All progress ceased.

Acting on instinct, Geneviève tenderly took hold of the kid's head and began to pull gently but steadily. The process was agonizingly slow but at last one shoulder came through and then the other. Soon the slick sticky body was lying before her. It didn't move at all.

Inexperienced though she was Geneviève understood the kid had been born dead. But the mother goat didn't. Instinctively the old goat licked and licked in a frantic futile effort to bring the stillborn back to life. It was painful to watch the poor thing keep at it. Then it just stopped.

The miserable creature put her mournful head on Geneviève's shoulder and moaned a very different moan. Were those tears falling from the heartsick goat's eyes? Geneviève couldn't tell because she herself was weeping inconsolably.

The old goat recovered quickly and began producing milk. Denise contrived to relieve the goat's swollen udders by a process of trial and error. Soon she was an old hand at the twice-daily milking, delighted to be able to supply the children with this excellent source of nutrition. At first, the children complained about the flavor—so different from cow's milk. Before long, they acquired a taste for it.

That was important because having ration coupons did not guarantee the apportioned foodstuffs would be available when Denise and Geneviève made the six-kilometer roundtrip between La Font and Vialas. Some days the greengrocer and butcher had good items on display, but often there was nothing to buy with or without coupons.

Shopkeepers sometimes held back what they could for favored customers. That included the Severins because André was highly regarded as a professor. But when there was simply little or nothing edible at hand, the family was grateful for the lactating goat!

On the last Tuesday of October, Denise made the trek to Vialas alone. The day was frosty but Denise was bundled up and the exertion helped keep her warm, as she was enjoying her rare solitude. She tried to make her mind blank—better to take in the lovely pristine landscape and the marvelous bracing air—but she couldn't stop thinking about what she might find in Vialas.

For basics were all she hoped. She certainly didn't expect much meat. Even the farmers the Severins met at the café, who always showed them the greatest kindness, could only afford to sell them some lamb occasionally—and even less frequently rabbit since everyone wanted to hold on to a breeding pair till spring.

Meals had acquired a sameness that aggravated everyone—Louis in particular. The Severins had no choice but to partake of the traditional local breakfast: *bajana,* a soup consisting primarily of dried chestnuts from which the husks had been laboriously peeled by hand. The chestnuts would then be left to soak overnight, after which they would be cooked for the better part of three hours along with some goat's milk, onion, and maybe garlic.

It took the Severins, especially the children, quite a while to get used to the flavor and texture. Fresh bajana was reasonably agreeable, and with a little wine added, as per village custom, even more so—sour though, even a pig might refuse to touch it.

Eggs were a special treat for which the Severins were grateful to their chickens. Big round loaves of dark heavy country bread could sometimes be purchased in Vialas. Like the bajana, this bread took getting used to, but it was very good with the soup and for mopping a plate clean.

Dinner, the day's largest meal, was taken in early afternoon. Although Denise did the little she could to produce variety, dinner, like breakfast, almost always consisted of soup—usually barley soup, for now and for as long as the large sack of grain Alin had sent from Bédouès lasted. The soup was supplemented with a bit of rabbit when they could actually get some, or sometimes fatback of which they had a fair supply thanks to Camille Mousand and her poacher husband.

"I finally understand the value of Camille's gift," Geneviève said. "It certainly makes it a little easier to withstand the chill we must put up with even inside."

Supper tended to be comprised of leftover soup and some added-in goat cheese. It wasn't always appetizing, but even Louis managed to be cheerful about it since at supper he felt free to indulge his penchant for wine. Rose could hardly chastise him for this indulgence given the circumstances, but she was a little surprised that wine was so readily available.

"I think the Germans made a conscious decision to leave the winemaking industry alone," André said. "Maybe they hope the French will drink themselves into further acquiescence."

"The German Army drinks a lot of wine too," Alin put in. "They may be patriotic but they can't deny French wine is far superior to the swill they produce in Germany."

When Denise arrived, the butcher shop was closed "for lack of product." But the greengrocer's was open, and though the shelves were mostly bare, the shopkeeper reached under the counter for some secreted supplies.

"This is very bad about Laval," he said weighing out white flour.

"Excuse me?"

"If you ask me the former prime minister invented Vichy. I blame him for this hideous armistice. And now, that idiot Pétain has named him foreign minister. I bet Laval is working hard right now to cede even more power to the Nazis. The politicians disgust me! But you'll see. The Americans will save us just as they did the last time."

"I wouldn't count on that," Denise told him. "My husband likes many of the Americans he's met individually, but he says they're a terribly isolationist people."

"I believe that. But now they're drafting young men even though they're not under attack. Surely that's not just for self-defense."

Denise doled francs from her small purse one by one. The greengrocer amiably double-checked her count and thanked her.

When she turned to go he called, "Just a moment, Madame Severin!" He ducked behind the counter and came up with a handful of sweets. "For the little ones," he said warmly, giving her a friendly little wink.

Walking home with her tiny but precious bundle of purchases, Denise marveled at the greengrocer's unexpected generous gesture. Surely he had legitimately been thinking of the children, but it also seemed as if he had been trying to communicate something more: that the people of Vialas as well as those of Soleyrols knew all about the Severins and intended to treat and protect them as they would their own.

These Cévenols might not have much, Denise cheered and encouraged herself, *but they will never let us go hungry.*

The big black Buick and its trailer had been stashed temporarily in the big barn, but the brothers believed they needed a better hiding place. Anyone who saw it would know they weren't ordinary farmers.

"Not that anyone would ever mistake us for locals," Alin laughed, pointing to the berets he and André had taken to sporting, "even if we wear these."

André insisted, "We still shouldn't make it any easier for anyone to unmask us."

"Not that they couldn't just unmask us by checking the notary's records," Alin sighed.

They found Albertine alone at the café washing and drying dishes.

"Do you know of any spare space available in a barn around here?" André asked.

"For your car and trailer?"

André and Alin looked so startled that Madame Brignand couldn't help laughing.

"You should know by now," she said cheerfully, "there are no secrets in these mountains." She polished a glass and set it on the shelf behind the counter. "Louis and I have already discussed it. We have a barn off the road you're welcome to use."

Later that day, the brothers drove the Buick and trailer down into the barn and closed the door behind them to work to conceal their vehicles.

"It feels strange to give up the car," Alin said wistfully.

"Now we'll really be like the rest of the inhabitants here."

"No André. No matter what, we'll never be like the inhabitants here."

They used a jack to raise the car's tires and then placed blocks under each axle. They disconnected the battery; poured the fluid into a glass jug they carefully sealed and hid the battery and jug in the loft under some hay. When they spotted a piece of old canvas lying about, they drew it up and over the car.

"It's not perfect," André said glumly.

"No," Alin agreed, "but unless someone also finds the battery and the battery fluid it's not going anywhere. What about the trailer?"

"If anyone sees it let's hope they assume it is in storage because there was no car to attach it to."

Early Wednesday morning on the sixth of November, Genevieve dressed Katie and Ida neatly in clothes more like those of the other children in Soleyrols than her more familiar Brussels attire. Today she had an appointment with the local schoolmaster about enrolling Katie and Ida in the one-room schoolhouse.

Hastening downhill and around the café through another dusting of snow blowing wispily around them, Genevieve and the girls spotted Louis across the road leaning over the woodpile, but not chopping. He seemed to rest his full weight on his ax handle and to sway slightly side to side.

Apprehensive, Geneviève raced across the road dragging Katie by the hand.

"What's the matter Father?" she cried. Louis always looked pale, but something about his pallor now and the grimace on his face seemed terribly, irremediably wrong.

"Uh, uh," Louis grunted as he slumped down onto the woodpile. His eyes pinwheeled then settled briefly on his granddaughter. "Katie," he sighed, smiling fleetingly as he slipped from the wood to the earth, falling flat.

As Katie cried, "Bonpapa! Bonpapa!" Geneviève ran to the café shouting for help. Albertine grasped the situation immediately, picked up the public phone bolted to the outside wall and cranked it to call the one doctor she knew still practicing in Vialas, a young man who had somehow escaped notice during the Army call-up. He agreed to come immediately.

Hearing the commotion, Rose opened her front door and ran to her fallen husband. Albertine sent her second daughter up to La Font to bring the rest of the Severins quickly.

Geneviève hurried over to Rose who held her husband's hand, worried his face, and pleaded with him to speak to her. His eyes glazed over and then he lost consciousness.

Several regulars from the café scampered across the road, lifted Louis' limp form, and carried him to the bed that almost filled the back room of the little house. André, Alin, and Denise arrived on the run just as the doctor drove up.

The doctor strode rapidly past the small crowd that had gathered outside the house in which the stricken man remained unresponsive. Rose, who had regained her composure, sat by her husband's side clutching his hand as the doctor conducted a short examination.

With a serious expression and a curt nod, the doctor signaled to Louis' sons and daughters-in-law that he would like a word with them in the front room.

"I'm sorry," the young doctor said without preliminaries, mostly addressing André as the eldest son. "Your father is in bad shape. There's not much I can do."

Denise covered her mouth as a wrenching cry escaped her. Geneviève suspected the doctor felt true sympathy, but found his manner dismayingly abrupt.

"This is a very seriously sick man," the doctor continued, shaking his head. "He's had a stroke. I could perhaps do a little to help him, but it would hardly be worthwhile. No matter what, he will remain severely paralyzed for however little life remains."

No one made a sound. It was as if they were all afraid to breathe, for who knew which of them might inadvertently take Louis' last mouthful of air?

"It's up to you," the young man concluded, a neutral professional. "In my considered opinion it would be far better for all concerned to let nature take its course."

"In which case," André said somberly, "he will die."

"It won't take long," the doctor said. "He should pass peacefully."

The young doctor took their silence as agreement and put on his hat to take his leave. André stepped over to shake his hand firmly, and with that decisive handclasp, said for them all that needed to be said.

The siblings set up a vigil in the little living room, each taking a turn to sit with Rose by Louis' side. Albertine brought over coffee and pastries—"To keep up your strength," she said—but no one felt like eating. Neither André nor Alin took even a sip of coffee.

Louis remained unconscious for two hours. The room seemed to grow smaller with every passing moment. Then he was dead.

Tears welled up in Rose's eyes and flowed soundlessly down her cheeks as she cradled her dead husband's head. Geneviève reached out to touch her late father-in-law too—to brush his white hair back from his forehead—but recoiled as if shocked when she realized how quickly his body was cooling.

André, Alin, and Denise were drawn into the dark room as if bidden. The brothers watched intently and Denise gently laid her hands upon her mother-in-law's shoulders as Rose stroked Louis' goatee and moustache, settling each whisker into its proper place.

After some time, Geneviève delicately disengaged Rose's hands from the body that had been her husband for forty years, and embraced her with touching solicitude. Stillness filled the air. Rose sank to the floor and wept.

This is a most melancholy mission, Pastor Robert Burnand thought the following morning bicycling up the road from Vialas. Leaning his bicycle against the café's outer wall, he walked over to the little house and rapped tentatively at the door. André introduced himself and thanked the pastor for coming.

"I am heartily sorry for your loss," the pastor said feelingly. "I'm only glad that Madame Brignand thought to call me and that you agreed she should. Our young doctor had already told me the sad news."

"Of course you will want to meet my mother," André said escorting the pastor through a small gathering of mourners.

The son led the way into the little shuttered room. The pastor lowered his eyes, moved his lips in prayer, and went directly to Rose, who sat alone on the edge of the bed.

Rose got up and took the pastor's hand. He felt certain he would never forget the warmth of her touch, or the penetrating look of understanding and appreciation in her eyes.

"I know that Louis would feel comfortable in your hands," she said kindly.

Pastor Burnand felt humbled by her graciousness and generosity. "We take strength from the long tradition of the Huguenots."

"It's terrible," Louis Brignand said, as if he would much prefer to spit than speak. "That good man lies dead and Vichy France orders all Jewish businesses sold or expropriated for 'Aryanization!'"

"It makes me so ashamed of being French," Albertine exclaimed, mourning her country as much as the deceased.

"We must do something," Monsieur Brignand grumbled. "We must! Both to uphold our honor and to do what is right."

Despite the cold, and because he simply could not think of any other place to conduct a tactful conversation, Pastor Burnand gestured for the Severin brothers to join him outside. Though this was not his intention, he found that the three of them naturally gathered around the woodpile—site he understood of Louis Severin's last stand.

Sensitive to the fact that the Severins were not Protestant, the pastor began by expressing his regret that it wasn't possible to see to the interment as quickly as required by Jewish tradition.

"We just aren't equipped to provide such service on the very next day," he explained.

"I'm sure Father would understand," André said immediately, as if it was incumbent upon him to relieve the pastor of his discomfort rather than the other way round. "Although he was brought up as a Jew he was not a practitioner or a believer. But he was a wonderful man and I'm certain he would be honored to find his final resting place among the people who have proved so warm and welcoming and sympathetic to our plight."

"No matter our backgrounds and beliefs," Pastor Burnand assured the brothers feelingly, "we are the same in God's eyes. God understands us in whatever language we use to speak to Him, even if we choose not to speak to Him at all. None of this matters to God. Our prayers, formal or informal, go through different channels but all reach the same source."

"And so our history as Jews," Alin asked quizzically, "doesn't trouble you?"

"Never," Pastor Burnand affirmed, "and especially not at a moment such as this."

The undertaker arrived at the little house early Friday morning, leading a horse and cart carrying a plain primitive coffin. Introducing himself to André, he expressed his regrets and apologized.

"It's not much," he said referring to the simple pine box, "but it's the best we can do in times like these."

"I deeply appreciate your efforts and your concern," André said kindly. "This simplicity is exactly as it should be."

The man that had been Louis Severin was dressed in his best suit. The undertaker took special care as he single-handedly lowered the body into the casket. Then he noticed that the rest of the family, including the four grandchildren, were wearing the straightforward garb of the region's farmers. That surprised him. He had anticipated a display of big-city finery from these Belgian refugees. But it soon became clear from the little he overheard and the gestures he could construe, that this apparel was purposeful. The Severins had arrayed themselves to fit in with the local population as a sign of honor and respect.

The procession began and proceeded slowly the few kilometers to Vialas. At the beginning, the funeral cortège was quite modest: the widow, her two sons and their wives, the grandchildren, the Brignands, and Lucien Mauriac from Bédouès. Every time the undertaker turned around though, he saw more and more people following. Soon almost every resident of Soleyrols had turned out to accompany Louis Severin to his rest.

In Vialas, the Protestant temple was filled with residents of the town and nearby hamlets. Even the staff from the Hotel Guin and the shopkeepers of the village were in attendance.

The warm greetings from a striking number of local inhabitants showed that many were familiar with the Severins, but quite plainly, a larger number were not. For them, the Severins served as a symbol providing the Cévenols a rare opportunity to show what they were truly about. To these people, whether Louis Severin had or hadn't been Jewish wasn't important. What mattered was that they were all too well aware of the daily increasing persecution of the Jews, those who harbored Jews, and anyone else who had fled from the German occupation of the Low Countries and northern France. This funeral service, short as it was—and as kindly as the pastor spoke of the deceased, his family and their friends—offered an unusual chance for a strong show of defiance of the Vichy government and of the German conquerors of their beloved country.

Then the unadorned casket was carried to the cemetery that was perched alongside a farm lane and shaped into terraces sloping toward the valley below. They all entered through the old cast iron gates, which long ago had been set into the stone boundary wall, then proceeded down several levels of steps to an open grave. After a few further words from Pastor Burnand, the coffin was lowered into the ground. André led the mourners in shoveling dirt onto it.

The Severins exchanged a few words with each of the many considerate well-wishers. Slowly the residents of Vialas drifted away.

Then the new head of the Severin family went out of his way to thank Pastor Burnand warmly and to say, "We are so grateful to be here. We draw courage and confidence from the faith and independence of the residents of the Lozère. In fact, I hope you will allow me to pay a proper visit to your temple soon. You see I am engaged in a quest of faith of my own and would gladly learn from your teachings."

"You will be most welcome," the pastor replied with equal warmth. Then he lowered his voice. "At the proper time," he said gazing at André as if to deliver his message through his eyes as much as his veiled words, "we must talk of other matters too—so that we make sure no other Severins are lost to us."

As André considered the meaning of this mysterious speech, he returned to his family for the slow melancholy walk back to La Font. He noticed that the undertaker was still standing alone with his horse and cart beside the grave. The grave had already been filled in.

It was all so sudden, André thought.

Then it was all over.

Chapter Eight

SURVIVAL

November 10, 1940

The sudden death of Louis Severin was an irretrievable loss and an ominous sign. Until then, the family's members had all been riddled with fear about their fate, but each had felt certain that someday they would return to Brussels. Now death had given hope the lie. And the little ones had been forced to confront life's saddest truth. Never before had it come so close.

Yet, life went on implacably. The adults struggled for sheer survival and the six-year-olds had a new distraction: their education in the one-room schoolhouse in Soleyrols where the single teacher taught twenty lower-school students who would go on to high school in Vialas.

Each weekday Ida and Katie managed the trek—fifteen minutes in the morning mostly downhill and twenty-five minutes back up later in the day—though the journey grew trickier with steadily increasing cold and deepening snow. Remarkably, the girls inserted themselves easily into a roomful of strangers who knew each other well and spoke mostly in the Cévenol dialect.

Christel and Philippe—much too young to accompany their sisters—stayed home and played with each other, the farm animals, and their grandmother.

Coping with sorrow was especially difficult as the feeling of isolation multiplied with each day's fresh blanketing of snow. The Severins' new friends and neighbors were remarkably kind and attentive the first week after the funeral, but this was a hard time of year for everyone in the Cévennes. The family quickly found itself left to its own devices.

To alleviate the sense of solitude—and to share their sad news—Denise and Geneviève began writing to almost everyone in the address books they had brought from Belgium.

First, they wrote to Anna, Rose's sister in Brussels. Then they attempted to contact other relatives in Belgium, the Netherlands, and Great Britain as well as those who had escaped to other countries before the Severins entered France.

Focusing on practical matters, André wrote to an agricultural products company in Switzerland. After reading deeply in the great green textbook, he had decided to grow soybeans—a novelty in the area—and hoped the neutral Swiss would send viable seed.

As days went by, the Severins awaited any response with growing impatience. They understood international mail in wartime could be slow, but the wait was difficult. They not only longed to hear from loved ones, but also wanted proof their letters were getting through.

Impatient for any communication, Alin pulled his brother aside one afternoon. "Do you think we can purchase a radio so we can get news that isn't days or weeks old? We need information—on the war, on the Vichy government—to stand a chance of keeping ourselves safe."

After sunset, André made his way downhill to the café.

"A radio?" Albertine spluttered after acceding to André's half-whispered appeal to step into the back room. "You really are new here. Radios are scarce in the Cévennes and no one has one in Soleyrols. Getting one that works may be impossible. But having access to news could help us all. You have electricity and La Font is high enough on the mountainside to get good reception."

"And we speak English," André informed her. "News broadcasts on the BBC are often the most accurate and reliable."

Albertine agreed. "And here's a joke for you: one Frenchman says to another, 'It's terrible. At nine-twenty a Jew killed a German soldier, cut him open and ate his heart.' 'Impossible,' the other replied. 'First, a German has no heart. Second, a Jew eats no pork. And third, at nine-twenty everyone's listening to the BBC!'"

André promised that were a radio obtained he would never reveal its source.

"I'll see what we can do," Albertine said, making André wonder who "we" might be.

The prickly outer husks of the maturing chestnuts started to open. It was time to harvest.

"This is worse than picking cherries in Bédouès," Geneviève complained as she, Denise, Alin, and André struggled through a thick stand of trees, bending repeatedly with clumsily gloved hands to retrieve and sack the precious objects. "Why is reaching down so much harder than reaching up? And these spiny outer shells! Why not wait for the soft nuts to fall out?"

"We'd lose too much to the birds and wild animals," André explained patiently.

"Move along," Alin growled, hand pressed to the small of his back in pain. "Each day's shorter than the last. You want to gather chestnuts in the dark?"

The next day the weather was dreadful, but they busily gathered again. A cold wind whipped across the mountain, spiraling around the trees and causing wisps of snow—which had settled onto stones and rocks and compressed dead leaves against the frozen earth—to lift and drift before settling down again. The chestnut gatherers drew scarves up over their ears but still the cold seeped in around their necks. When they took short breaks, they jammed their gloved hands tightly into their wool coats seeking warmth in the depths of the lining.

Thankfully, the landscape was beautiful. The grays and browns of the fields and the oak and chestnut copses heralded the onset of wintertime repose. If only they could finish this.

Suddenly Gustave Chatrey appeared with two women and another man, all elderly.

"I said I'd get you started," Gustave called cheerfully. "And I've brought friends."

The experienced hands placed themselves and the four Severins in a row several feet apart, facing uphill. They began their demonstration by tying canvas sacks around each one's waist, leaving the sacks to drag behind as they filled up.

"Here," Gustave called. "Everyone take a wooden rake."

These curious implements—surprisingly short, with four tines each—were specially adapted to the task.

"As we walk up the hill," the other man—the women's brother—explained, "we rake the chestnuts into little piles."

"For the ones still inside their spiny hulls," one of the sisters suggested, "just take the side of the rake and hammer them open."

The old woman leaned down to demonstrate. She was quick and proficient—and so obviously practiced that Geneviève doubted she herself would ever do half so well.

"Simple," the other sister said encouragingly.

Slowly all began walking up the hillside, manipulating their rakes. Though the four old-timers were perpetually stooped, their steps were far livelier than the decades-younger Severins'.

Geneviève wasn't as strong as the others were and fell farther behind minute by minute. She found it easier though still painful to remain bent over rather than to stand back up and then bend down again. Exhaustion began to overwhelm her, but the work needed to be done and she felt ashamed watching four old peasants keep at it with steady unflagging energy.

Work gloves couldn't keep painful blisters from developing on their fingers. At the farmhouse for the midday meal, Geneviève wrapped a clean cloth around a rapidly reddening wound.

"That's bad," one of the old sisters said. "Infected."

"Here," the other spinster said, taking Geneviève's hand tenderly and applying a home remedy. "Put a half a lemon on that sore overnight and the pus will dry right up. Be sure to care for it like this every day and you'll see how soon the infection will go away."

"Homeopathy," Alin said nodding significantly at André.

They devoted the afternoon to a lesson in drying to preserve the bulk of the chestnuts through winter. Chestnuts would be the primary staple until the first vegetables ripened in the spring.

Each worker loaded and carried a basket to the drying shed about halfway down the hill. A special two-story structure built of stone apart from the wooden rafters inside, the shed was designed to hold the chestnuts high in a small attic.

The brother and his sisters shoveled chestnuts from baskets into the attic while Gustave started a smoldering fire below. Then all climbed the built-in ladder to the small trap door through which the chestnuts had been heaved. There they spread the chestnuts evenly and not too deeply on wood boards positioned to leave small cracks in between allowing the heat from the smoky fire below to rise and reach the target.

Back downstairs, Gustave explained, "We use huge logs for this fire. First, get a good blaze going then smother it with old hulls to control the burn and create smoke. You must keep the fire going no matter what, with new logs added and smothered with more dry husks, to ensure constant heat, even when rain comes lashing through the mountains. That's why even the roof is made of stone: stone gains and retains heat despite winter's chill."

"Remember," the old brother cautioned, "turn the chestnuts again and again. You don't want them to burn, but you do want them absolutely dry or they'll rot."

"When one batch is done," a sister said, "replace them with fresh chestnuts. That way the entire crop gets its time in the attic."

"It takes a month to do a good load," the other sister added. "So drying goes on through much of the winter."

Geneviève felt faint. So much work for preservation. And before any nuts could be eaten plain, made into soup, or baked into bread, they would need to be boiled more than two hours.

Between this realization and the pain from her throbbing hand, Geneviève wanted to weep. Yet she knew she mustn't. Like the old peasants, she had to soldier on.

The last Friday of November, a Brignand daughter appeared in the field the Severins were gleaning and spoke to André. When she left, he told the others, "They've found us a radio."

After the sun had set and the moon had begun to creep above the mountains, the Severin brothers hiked down to the café and entered by the back door.

"Here it is," Albertine said proudly, shutting the door behind them. "A good one I think."

"Where did it come from?" André asked admiring the marvel in her hands.

"Over the mountains," Albertine answered. "The bus driver brought it from Florac."

So, André thought, *the bus driver is one of "us."*

Alin examined the radio—an old model from an unfamiliar French manufacturer.

"It will pick up the broadcasts you want," Albertine insisted unruffled. "That much we were assured. And one more thing," she said as Alin discreetly paid her from the Severins' dwindling supply of francs. "When the postman comes, give him whatever news you have. He's reliable and will share the news on his rounds—only with those we trust of course." Back at the door she cautioned, "Always turn the dial away from the BBC frequency when you finish. Anyone could stop by and that would be a foolish way to betray yourselves."

In the family room, they connected it to the single electric cord that ran through the house. Astoundingly their position on the mountain allowed them to pick up British stations without static. They were immediately rewarded with an address by General de Gaulle urging his countrymen to take heart: Free French forces now numbered thirty-five thousand trained troops and one thousand airmen. He promised operations would begin soon. Soon the true French would once again rule all of France.

Katie and Ida were still awake and listening.

"Now girls," Alin warned the excited children, although he doubted they understood what they heard, "don't repeat this or anything else you hear on our radio, especially not at school. Don't even mention our radio. And don't touch that dial ever!"

Over the next several nights, the Severins heard the Germans jam portions of BBC broadcasts. Aware that many listeners were foreigners, the British announced the news first in English and then in French. The Germans almost always jammed both. Within half an hour, the same program would be broadcast unimpeded in Flemish by Belgian exiles in London.

Alin grinned. "I guess the Germans know nothing about Belgians. They don't realize how many of us speak Flemish as well as French."

"Still," André said, "the jamming is frustrating."

After Sunday supper on the first of December, the adult Severins gathered in the family room to listen to a live report about the blitz from U.S. correspondent Edward R. Murrow.

"I can't stand it," Alin bristled.

"War is so terrible," Denise agreed, "and sad."

"I mean these Americans," Alin scoffed. "Everyone else is careful about what they reveal, but the Americans don't realize they're giving away important clues about strategic Allied positions."

The next morning, the postman appeared at La Font far earlier than usual and not to deliver letters, but rather to gather the news. Thanks to the radio, La Font was now the first stop on his rounds.

Alin told him about the latest bombings in Britain and the postman startled him by saying, "I hope your brother-in-law is all right—so brave, flying with the RAF."

Alin eyed him suspiciously. The family had made no secret of Francis Freedman's activities but hadn't spoken freely of them either.

"There's no privacy here so far as correspondence is concerned," the postman said amiably. "The Vichy government checks every letter, censoring what it doesn't like. But there are others who open the mail too"—here he lowered his voice and his eyes—"on *our* side. Pro-Nazi messages sent to Vichy and Germany don't reach their destinations intact either."

So, the rumors Alin had heard in Bédouès were true: there was some kind of Resistance—a growing underground. Now it was mostly a conduit for information, but it would surely become increasingly active as German abuses and atrocities inevitably mounted. The Brignands, the bus driver, and the postman were all obviously part of this underground.

The Germans understood and continued to jam the BBC. Accurate uncensored information was the yeast that would grow the Resistance. And the Fascists had reason to fear a homegrown opposition for they knew the Vichy government had been weak from its inception.

Someday, Alin thought, *with or without André, I will join this Resistance.*

On St. Nicholas Day Eve, Denise and Geneviève did their best to recreate the feel of Brussels. They even helped the children put little wooden shoes with their names on them onto the floor by the fireplace. It was hard not to think of Louis at a time like this.

Denise managed to make speculaas, the special Belgian Christmas cookie, though she didn't have the wooden molds for the shapes the children liked best. At least they tasted like home.

By then, André had attended services at the Protestant temple in Vialas several times and at Ida's request had taken her with him. Having tired of her children's books, Ida read the Bible. She enjoyed the stories and she liked Pastor Burnand's sermons, as did André. André explained about his search for God and Ida decided she would look for God too.

Then she asked if she could participate in the Christmas pageant at the temple. With Denise's permission, André agreed. Excited, Ida told her sister and cousins, and they wanted to be part of the pageant too.

Getting Alin to let his children go to the temple took some doing. Denise was able to convince Geneviève that it would be good for all the children to be better integrated into the community. And André made two points that proved telling to Alin: first, participation would help conceal their background; and second, since André would take the children to and from the temple for services and rehearsals, Alin would have some time to himself.

"Without the children underfoot and in my hair you mean?"

Naturally, he gave his consent.

After the first batch of chestnuts had been thoroughly dried, the Severins began spending evening hours with specially adapted little knives to peel the outer husks and scrape the dark brown skin from the rock-hard meat—a difficult, tedious, slightly disfiguring labor: one's hands took on a chestnut-colored stain. Working at the chestnuts long and hard, they desperately needed distraction, which mostly came from the radio, though the news could be distressing, heartbreaking and—due to the jamming and resultant static—headache-inducing.

There were the usual reports of back-and-forth bombings (the British bombed Düsseldorf, the Germans bombed Sheffield; the RAF bombed Naples, Mannheim and Berlin, the Luftwaffe bombed Liverpool, Manchester and London) and there were ongoing stories from North Africa and the Mediterranean. America seemed irreconcilably divided, with the public against getting involved in the war, even as President Roosevelt initiated actions supportive of Britain's struggle against Nazi tyranny.

In a very different way, France was more seriously divided. Six months earlier, Marshal Pétain had appointed pro-Nazi Pierre Laval foreign minister and then had sacked and imprisoned him only to free him days later thanks to the German ambassador's intervention. Many pre-war Socialist and Radical-Socialist leaders had been indicted for "war guilt," though they had been among the precious few to stand up for France in the face of the Fascists.

"It amazes me," Denise stated ruefully one night over a great bowl of shelled chestnuts, "that such heroic figures would be persecuted. Isn't it the state's responsibility to foster and maintain the integrity of the individual?"

"I'm afraid," André countered with an equal measure of rue, "Pétain would say it's the individual's responsibility to sacrifice himself for the cohesiveness of the state."

"That policy works wonders," Alin said sardonically.

"All the more reason for us to enjoy the freedom we have within the walls of La Font," André said, "for as long as it might last."

Startled, Denise pleaded, "Don't say that. I'm just beginning to feel settled in."

"Every day the world is less certain and more dangerous," André replied levelly. "How can we guess what the French will do next? When they laid down their arms, they surrendered their souls."

"Pétain tries to maintain national unity and French pride," Alin added, "but with half a country at his disposal, subject to German authority, how long will that last?"

"All I want to do is cry," Geneviève declared.

"Now is the time to look to our own souls," André counseled, "to stay true to ourselves and all that we cherish of our human dignity."

"I don't know about these 'souls,'" Alin grumped.

"Think of it ethically then," André insisted, "or politically. It's too easy to forget oneself; to take comfort in becoming part of the great amorphous mass of the thoughtless, the spineless, the soulless, as I would say. To go along with the wrong instead of standing up for what's right. To become nothing because so many are nothing and being nothing takes less effort than becoming something worthwhile. Of course, we all must die eventually, but to die for nothing—*as* nothing—is too cruel to contemplate. To lose one's way and remain forever lost. To participate in the dissolution of society and the degradation of all human worth."

"That's pretty talk," Alin complained, "but what nobility do you perceive in our running and hiding? What is this 'something worthwhile' we're doing besides saving our skins?"

Without hesitation André replied, "Maintaining sanity in our world however small or circumscribed it may be." André took out his large white handkerchief to wipe his brow and polish his glasses reflexively. "It may be a 'Thousand Year Reich' as Hitler has proclaimed. He may win the war, but not the hearts and minds of the people. Not totally. Not forever. People like us, and the descendants of the Huguenots who shelter us, keep the promise of humankind alive."

"Please!" Geneviève cried. "If we can't talk about something else I swear I'd rather do this tiresome work in silence!"

"Maybe one of us can read as the others peel," Denise suggested, dropping her scraper and reaching for a book on the mantelpiece.

"I'll do it," Geneviève declared, snatching Robert Louis Stevenson's *Travels with a Donkey in the Cévennes* from Denise's hand and beginning to read. "'The journey which this little book is to describe was very agreeable and fortunate for me...'"

Night after night Geneviève read while the others scraped, amused by Stevenson's misadventures with his willful pack-donkey Modestine. They also took pleasure in the familiar settings Stevenson described—walks through locales the Severins had experienced recently.

"'A little after,'" Geneviève read, "'the stream that I was following fell into the Tarn at Pont de Montvert of bloody memory.'"

"That's where we entered the Cévennes," Denise recalled.

Geneviève continued, "'One of the first things I encountered in Pont de Montvert was, if I remember rightly, the Protestant temple—'" She interrupted her reading. "It's uncanny."

Stevenson's book didn't serve as mere travelogue and reminder. It proved practical when Geneviève read about chestnut trees, "'The slope was strewn with lopped branches, and here and there a great package of leaves was propped against a trunk; for even the leaves are serviceable, and the peasants use them in winter by way of fodder for their animals.'"

"I hadn't thought of that," André allowed.

"Helpful as the old farmers have been," Alin remarked, "no one mentioned it either."

Later Geneviève read, "'...that the chestnut gardens are infested with rats.' Ugh!" she grunted. "You won't catch me going back into those anytime soon!"

"We'll set traps," Alin said dismissively. "We'll take care of it."

"But let's have the children play elsewhere till we do," Denise suggested.

That Stevenson confirmed some of their impressions of the vicinity and its inhabitants, suggested neither had changed in the previous sixty years and so might be assumed unlikely to change anytime soon: "'I had not only come among new natural features, but moved into the territory of a different race. These people...questioned and answered me with a degree of intelligence, which excelled all that I had met...'"

Much of the rest was congenial to André especially because it dealt with the spiritual dimensions of the Cévennes. André felt encouraged by a number of passages, one of which spoke to him as no other. He even took the book to bed one night and sat up late to memorize Stevenson's words in order to have them with him as he went about his labors:

> Outdoor rustic people have not many ideas, but such as they have are hardy plants, and thrive flourishingly in persecution. One who has grown a long while in the sweat of laborious noons, and under the stars at night, a frequenter of hills and forests, an old honest countryman, has, in the end, a sense of communion with the powers of the universe, and amicable relations towards his God...he knows the Lord. His religion does not repose upon a choice of logic; it is the poetry of the man's experience, the

philosophy of the history of his life. God, like a great power, like a great shining sun, has appeared to this simple fellow in the course of years, and become the ground and essence of his least reflections; and you may change creeds and dogmas by authority, or proclaim a new religion with the sound of trumpets, if you will; but here is a man who has his own thoughts, and will stubbornly adhere to them in good and evil.

No one could have been more surprised or less delighted than Alin Severin was to find himself in the Protestant temple in Vialas Christmas morning. But he could not have avoided it; his children and nieces were appearing in the pageant. The little ones' excitement might have been contagious even to him if the whole business hadn't seemed such a foolish waste of time.

Rose had begged off because of the cold blustery weather. The rest had bundled up for the tramp to the French Reformed Church, which wasn't as bad as it could have been, for the day was crisp, the sun was out, and even Alin had to admit it was dramatically beautiful on the road with snowcapped mountains majestically surrounding them, crystalline in sparkling sunlight.

The church was packed with worshipers excited for the lengthy celebration of Christ's birth to begin. They greeted the Severins warmly. André plainly fit in.

Alin defiantly didn't. Sitting with his wife beside their brother and sister, he felt uncomfortable, not only physically because of the hard bench, but also mentally because he didn't share the faith by which—in Alin's not-humble opinion—everyone else had been brainwashed.

The children disappeared into the back to prepare for the "show." After a long time, Pastor Burnand began preaching a long sermon. Others seemed enraptured by it, but Alin was mind-numbingly bored and not a little angered. Worse still, when the sermon was finally finished, the parson invited others up for an extended series of readings from the Bible, mostly from the New Testament, which Alin had managed previously to avoid.

His back stiff and his legs asleep by the time the children finally filed out to perform, Alin still felt a thrill of excitement since the Severin progeny looked incontrovertibly adorable, even to his curmudgeonly self. But he quickly concluded that he had only perked up because the intolerably dull and utterly preposterous readings had ended.

Preposterous also was his word for the traditional Christmas pageant unfolding before his disbelieving unbeliever's eyes. But Katie and Ida acquitted themselves admirably as members of the chorus and little Philippe appeared every now and again too. Christel had a memorable nonspeaking role as one of three girls at play in a field—presumably one of the fields of the Lord. An evil person came along and for no apparent reason killed them by beheading them, of all hideous things, represented by each girl pulling a blanket over her head.

Then St. Nicholas happened along and miraculously brought them back to life—that is the little girls threw off the blankets again.

The only real miracle to Alin was that he kept from laughing out loud. He actually enjoyed the extravaganza's climax: a choral rendition of a Protestant hymn taken from Handel's oratorio "Judas Maccabeus": "Thine is the Glory." The children sang, and though the sentiment rang hollow, Alin could appreciate the music.

Then midday dinner was served. The parson had somehow found enough rolls baked from scarce white flour to give one to each child to take home as a Christmas gift.

During the dinner interlude, Alin and Geneviève slipped away. A few grocers were keeping hours that day so last-minute items could be picked up for a Christmas "feast." As they passed one open store, the shopkeeper waved them in.

"I'm glad to see you," she exclaimed, picking up and proudly displaying a box of figs. "I've been saving these for you. The local folks won't eat them— they'd rather keep their money. But I know you Severins have more cultivated tastes and will appreciate these."

The shopkeeper placed the box atop the counter expectantly. Geneviève gave her husband a look of request and demand. Alin smiled indulgently.

"This will be our Christmas treat," he agreed, placing his payment into the little dish on the counter. "Sweeter even than a roll."

Back at church, the Severins said good-bye and swathed themselves. Snow fell and the wind, into which the road home faced, picked up, whipping freezing white powder into their lowered faces and making remaining upright steadily more difficult.

"It's good that mother decided to remain Jewish today," André shouted to Alin only inches away.

"I wish I hadn't pretended to be a Christian," Geneviève shouted back, voice muffled by the scarf in which she had buried her mouth.

"It was a nice service though," André insisted.

"Lovely," Denise called out supporting him.

To Alin, it was the box of figs that made all the effort and suffering worthwhile.

Despite the pleasing spiritual interlude, André was distressed by the way 1940 ended and 1941 began. There was simply too much work to find the time he wished to devote to his interior life. And listening to the radio gave little cause for optimism let alone joy.

Though encouraging noises kept coming out of Washington, D.C.—
President Roosevelt declared that the United States "must be the great arsenal
of the democracies"—words were not yet matched by meaningful deeds. And
there were other words that had to be considered, such as Hitler's New Year's
message to the German armed forces in which he promised "the greatest victory
in our history" on the Western Front.

News from the Eastern Front was disturbing too, and puzzling. Despite
the 1939 signing of both a nonaggression pact and an economic agreement
between the Soviet Union and Germany, André had understood as far back as
the Spanish Civil War that there was no love lost between the Nazis and the
Communists. He had hoped the Russians would enter the war on the Allied
side, possibly sooner than the Americans, but now the Soviets and Germans had
signed a new series of pacts, recognizing their respective "spheres of influence"
and affirming previous trade agreements. Was it conceivable the Russians would
sit out the war for a modest economic advantage? Surely it was as obvious in
the Kremlin as in Soleyrols, that Germany unchecked was a mortal threat to
all sovereign nations.

Nothing in Indochina made sense either. How could France protect
its territories in Laos and Cambodia from incursions by Thailand when the
Japanese supported Thai rights to the disputed lands? Surely, Vichy France
would not be allowed to stand up to Germany's ally!

Now that the RAF was bombing occupying forces from Brittany to
Bordeaux to Cologne, André was grateful yet again that the Severins had
sequestered themselves in a remote strategically insignificant locale. But what
was he doing with a chestnut in his hand? He didn't think himself superior to
the mundane demands of existence, but couldn't help wondering if there wasn't
something more important for him to do than peel husks from dried nuts.

After Stevenson's *Travels*—a quick and pleasing read as promised—
Geneviève read *Chronique des Pasquier,* a beguiling book she had already begun,
but was happy to begin again. The story of a poor family's struggles in Paris
could hardly have been more different from the Severins'—especially that of
the Freedman sisters who had grown up economically privileged. But that was
a large part of the book's appeal: Duhamel's ravishingly detailed contemplative
narrative drew these Belgian refugees into worlds and lives so unlike theirs it
helped them forget present troubles—even the damage to their fingers—for
hours at a time. And that this volume consisted of five complete novels was a
blessing, since so many chestnuts remained to be shelled.

Recalcitrant nuts didn't go to waste since the goats and rabbits were willing
to eat them even with their peels on. The rabbits fattened with noteworthy
speed on this unusual diet.

Alin closely tracked and recorded the details of the care, feeding, and growth of all the animals and chickens because charting the barnyard creatures' behavior and life cycles impeccably could profit the family. For example, the chickens also turned out to be quite willing to eat cast-off chestnuts, but Alin was able to prove such ingestion reduced egg production and in some cases stopped it altogether. Then again, when Alin's records indicated a particular chicken was no longer laying eggs anyway, the Severins could begin a regimen of deliberate chestnut feeding to quickly fatten that chicken for the table.

Before eating chickens though, they had learned to kill and grill pigeons they discovered pecking at chestnuts in the loft of the barn. Alin kept careful records of them too. The pigeons attracted hawks and their documented depredations against the chickens and rabbits helped speed the Severins' determination to get the pick of tasty pigeon treats.

Toward the end of the first week of February, André trembled with delight, believing he had discovered how to stop the German jamming of radio signals.

"The key you see," he told the others that night, "is oscillation. By rapidly shifting the broadcast frequency back and forth ever so slightly the jamming signal can be evaded and the broadcast can still get through since a radio's tuning mechanism isn't all that precise."

"You mean we'll constantly have to twiddle the dial?" Denise asked perplexedly.

"Not if the oscillations are fast enough. Anyway, it's worth a try. It can't sound any worse than it already does."

André was so taken with this that idea he addressed a letter to "The BBC."

"The only problem is where to mail it from," he said. "I've signed it 'PHOTON' to maintain anonymity but I don't want to take any chances even with the postman. I don't want to get him into any trouble either."

"Why not go to Alès and mail it from there?" Alin suggested.

The next day André returned from his mission to Alès in an unusually foul humor.

"I got the letter off easily enough," he hastened to explain. "But I'm outraged by the black market I found. The world is at war, the true French are under siege, everyone is suffering, and there are black-hearted selfish people profiting from misery."

"You're not just right but righteous," Geneviève sniffed. "We should feel fortunate you let us accept cow's milk for our children even though we don't have proper ration coupons."

The cow's milk was another great gift to the Severins arranged by the Brignands. When the old goat stopped giving milk, jeopardizing the children's health, Albertine convinced an elderly farmer and his wife who lived down the road and owned a milk-giving cow to happily share "with the little ones."

"That's altogether different," André insisted. "No one *profits* by it—the farmer and his wife give the milk for free. That's as it should be. These good people demonstrate we're all in this together, as we must be if any of us is to survive."

"Careful, André," Alin said acidly. "With thoughts like that, next thing you know you'll be taking up arms against the enemy."

"Never."

"That's enough." Denise interposed herself between the two brothers. "André, something came for you while you were away."

She thrust an envelope into his hands and watched his eyes open wide.

"So mail really can get through from outside the country," he exclaimed, quickly tearing open the envelope.

"If we would only hear from our relatives," Geneviève said wistfully.

André peered into the envelope and laughed joyfully. The others watched in astonishment as he poured twenty-four little seeds into his hand.

"Soybeans. From Switzerland." He declared. "Amazing! Wonderful!"

Over the next few days, letters finally started arriving from family in Canada, Portugal, and Switzerland. Each of these exiled relatives had been relieved to receive evidence of the Severins' successful escape and wanted to know what they might do or send to help them. They also provided good news about members of the family elsewhere. Ominously there was no information about those who had stayed behind in Belgium.

The greatest joy was definitive word of the fate of Jack Freedman. He had bided his time in Biarritz as suspected but, spurred to action by the German drive down the Atlantic coast, had caught the last ship out the previous June. Now he was safe with other Freedmans in England.

The Severins asked the postman why he thought mail was so slow getting to unoccupied France. He suggested censorship was more prevalent and intrusive as the Vichy government grew increasingly nervous about dissension and conspiratorial communications. Regarding contact with friends and family in Belgium, he believed the Germans were restricting exchanges between occupied and unoccupied territories and that the Severins ran a risk by writing to Belgium at all.

When André confirmed that, some of those they wrote to in their homeland were Jews the postman said, "I don't recommend trying that again—

not directly. If known Jews write to you from Belgium Vichy postal authorities might be alerted by the Nazis, compromising your security and the security of those associated with you."

"We're already registered as Jews," Alin burst forth. "How much worse could it be?"

"It's one thing to be Jews who keep to themselves," the postman explained. "It's something else entirely if someone imagines you fomenting rebellion with coreligionists in another country. I recommend that the next time you attempt to reach anyone in Belgium you send those letters to relatives elsewhere—in Portugal or Switzerland—and ask that they forward them. That would insulate you and paradoxically might get you a quicker response."

The calendar promised spring but, as March trudged by, precious little gave hope that the long-dreamt-of softening weather would arrive by the twenty-first—Philippe's second birthday. And how else could they make that a special occasion?

Philippe could hardly take a single spoonful of bajana anymore and who could blame him? The Severins had eaten so much of it they could identify the trees the chestnuts came from by the slight difference in look and sweetness. They often ate chestnuts several times a day—as soup, in puddings, mixed with carrots or roasted in the great fireplace. The barley from Bédouès had begun to run low and the fatback was rapidly diminishing so they could rarely leaven their diet of the despised nuts.

But based on Alin's reading, charting, and planning there was reason to hope some of the rabbits born at the end of February would be ready to provide a fresh taste sensation soon.

"Shall we have rabbit for Philippe's birthday dinner?" Alin asked Geneviève, surprising, pleasing, and relieving her.

Immediately after lunch, Alin went out to ready the chosen rabbit for roasting. The least squeamish Severin did his bloody work behind the barn so no one else had to see.

Grabbing the pudgy creature by its ears and using steady pressure from his boot on its hind legs he held the rabbit on its back on top of the great chopping block then drew a six-inch knife across its throat letting the blood drain out onto the ground; it was a quick business.

He sliced the knife down the underside of the dead rabbit's soft still-warm body priding himself on his skill at skinning. To use almost the whole animal he only cut off the tail and the bottoms of the feet making it easy to pull the skin down and even to bare the head so it too was available for the pot. Methodically scraping the carcass down to the meat Alin saved the abundance of fat for André to make into soap—now a scarce commodity.

It was not a pretty job, but the results were delectable. Fortunately, Alin's newly prattling son had not yet connected the "rabbit" they would eat with the "rabbits" he helped feed and loved to pet.

A few days later, the brothers began working the terraced garden plots to prepare for planting. Even if a tractor had been available, gas was hard to come by and the hill to La Font was too steep. What they really needed was one of those sturdy Brabant draught horses from Belgium.

But they persisted by hand and got the job done. Then they prevailed upon a neighbor to part with some pig manure that they mixed with hay to make high-quality fertilizer. Disking it into the poor soil was a laborious nose-holding chore that got worse as the days grew warmer.

They planted Swiss chard, green and yellow beans, tomatoes, beets, lettuce, and even some corn purchased in Vialas. They cut up potato seed stock and implanted each eye in a small mound of soil. They drilled their two-dozen soybeans into the ground.

The change in the weather also changed the family's social life. Everyone in the little hamlets thereabouts could finally get out after the long hard months as virtual shut-ins. Many strolled up to La Font to make sure the Severins had survived the winter.

The farmers were intrigued by the brothers' agricultural "experiments." None of them had ever considered planting soybeans. The corn rows were also a curiosity because only a little corn was ever planted in the Cévennes and then the green stalks were fed to the cows since the ears never matured.

Each day after Philippe turned two, Christel grew more excited because her birthday came next. She couldn't wait to be three. Knowing this milestone was approaching made her feel bigger than ever—so big she wanted to go to school with Ida and Katie more eagerly than before. She begged and pleaded until one morning her mother told the two older girls to take Christel with them. They were embarrassed to be saddled with a child too young to attend school, but Denise would not be denied.

Christel was excited, but the schoolmaster Patrick Molines was not. Given the great disparity in the ages of the students he already had, his hands were full. He didn't wish to be mean to Christel, but told her to sit on the bench on one side of the classroom and stay quiet.

This was miserably hard for Christel who was used to running around freely and speaking whenever she wished. Determined to prove she was ready for school she tried hard and did well. But Monsieur Molines never smiled at her or talked to her once.

When Christel needed to relieve herself, she was afraid that if she said anything Monsieur Molines that wouldn't let her come back. So she kept her mouth closed and had an accident. She was wet everywhere. The teacher just made her sit there.

"Monsieur Molines says she can go to school," Katie explained later at La Font, "but she'll still have to sit on the bench and he's not going to teach her anything."

"It's not fair," Ida said trying to comfort her little sister who was weeping with abandon. "She's so young and Monsieur Molines only wants to work with the older kids. He's not even interested in me and Katie!"

"You must understand," Denise said stroking Christel's hair. "His honor and a promotion depend on his students passing tests and obtaining their certificates."

Christel wailed more so Geneviève suggested, "I could teach Christel since I spend less time working outside than you, Denise. I'd be delighted to help her learn to read and write."

Ida and Katie jumped up and down chanting, "Good for Christel!"

"And good for us," Katie concluded. "Without her it won't take so long to climb back up the hill!"

By early May, the Severins still hadn't heard directly from Jack Freedman, which worried Geneviève to distraction. She and Denise had taken turns writing to him in England but they had no way of knowing whether any of their letters got through. And they knew that André's anonymous letter about evading jamming had reached the BBC—because they had responded in one of their broadcasts!

"We acknowledge the letter from PHOTON," was the cryptic response. The Severins never knew whether or not André's advice was taken seriously. The radio signals from Britain remained as obstructed as before.

Shortly after mentioning PHOTON, the BBC aired instructions for those in Nazi-controlled lands who wished to write to England. "Don't use exact postage," the announcer recommended. "Either add too much or affix too little."

When the postman arrived, he explained that exact postage implied to French postal authorities the writer's British sympathies since he knew the precise cost of such communications. Inexact postage suggested greater ignorance and therefore lesser danger.

"You'd be surprised at the different tricks people employ now," he elaborated. "For example I know of other Belgians who send letters to London via Léopoldville in the Belgian Congo. It sounds crazy, but it can be easier to send a letter through Africa than across the English Channel. And if you put your postage stamp on upside-down, it might not mean a thing to the Nazis, but this tells local postal workers the writer is against the Germans. They make sure the letter gets through."

The Severins obtained a new goat that Ida and Katie named "Louise" after the grand Avenue Louise in Brussels. Louise needed milking every day—a job Geneviève took on even though it was lots of hard work for limited results.

The goats' odor added to the challenge. All the animals in the great space beneath the house smelled but the goat stench was so noxious Geneviève insisted they be moved to the barn where she would sit on a little stool with a bucket between her legs and gently stroke the milk out of the udder—an activity which gave her mind time to wander.

A sound in the rafters distracted Geneviève. Looking up she suddenly saw a gigantic disgusting rat clinging to the underside of a wooden beam, carefully making its way backwards to just above her head.

Geneviève screamed and jumped up involuntarily, accidentally spilling the bucket of milk and frightening poor Louise as she ran out shrieking.

"I'm not going back in there ever!" she shouted to Denise who had rushed to her screeching sister's aid.

Geneviève told her about the rat. Denise put her arm around her quivering sister.

"Poor darling!" Denise said soothingly. "That rat was probably as scared as you."

"Then it was plenty scared!"

Denise gently rubbed Geneviève's back and spoke calmingly. Slowly Geneviève settled down.

"I'll tell you this," Geneviève laughed. "Louise better get used to being milked outside!"

May 18 was Katie's seventh birthday. André left La Font for a walk after lunch and came back hours later with a surprise for everyone—most enchantingly for Katie, who loved animals and spent most of her free time looking after the chickens and rabbits—most disturbingly for Alin, who thought his brother had gone mad with a whole flock of sheep complete with a sheepdog.

Everyone ran to see. Petting the sheep, the children declared themselves smitten.

"They're cuter and softer and cuddlier than the goats," Katie cheered.

"And they smell a little better too," Ida added, "though still not good."

Their love for the dog was instant.

"Sheep," Alin spat, "are so stupid. They don't even know to come in from the cold when it gets dark. André, forget about lamb! Let's stick to chicken, rabbits, and goats. They're as stupid as sheep, but a lot less trouble. Tell me you don't expect that sheepdog to do all the work!"

André explained that the old man who had sold him the sheep and sheepdog had assured him that all he ever had to do was send Touté into the fields and the sheep came trotting right back.

"Touté?" Alin barked.

"The dog," André said. "Touté."

"So it's a pet," Alin grumbled. "The children will get more out of 'Touté than we will."

"The only problem is he doesn't seem to understand my commands."

Happily petting the dog stretched out at her feet Katie said, "Maybe he only speaks patois. I wonder what 'Touté means in patois?"

Alin groused, "Now we've got to learn the local dialect to speak to a dog."

"Well we don't want Touté to realize we're not from around here," André said amiably. "In fact if we don't learn Cévenol, anyone coming here will realize we're not natives."

"Please Papy, may we keep Touté?" Katie begged her father. "We'll do all the looking after him, I promise! Please? For my birthday?"

"Well," Alin agreed though the concession pained him, "it is your birthday."

"I don't know about you," André said with a funny little grin, "but I really like lamb."

"So do I," Alin admitted. "If they fatten up before next winter they'll make good food for us—or someone else if we decide to sell any. But if we have to keep them over the winter, stuffing them up with chestnuts, they'll just be old mutton. I hate mutton."

Alin shook his head with disgust. But if it made the birthday girl happy...

Occasionally André would take a break from backbreaking labor and walk uphill to a shaded spot to rest and think. Usually the sheep were cropping grass nearby. As soon as André sat with his back braced against a tree Touté would lie down and place his head in his lap.

The dog was far more attentive to the sheep than Alin had feared. But no one could communicate with him verbally even though Touté was an enormously affectionate and clever mutt. Every weekday morning he accompanied Ida and Katie to school and then ran home to tend to the sheep. Just before four o'clock each afternoon, he somehow knew to race back to the one-room schoolhouse in time to trot home beside his pair of scholars. Incomprehensibly Touté never failed or showed up so much as a minute late.

André liked these little breaks for the chance to meditate cooled by fresh breezes. Frequently, he pulled out his faithful notebook to review notes or make new ones. Recently he had taken to jotting down the Cévenol patois. These private moments were perfect for practicing his vocabulary and accent without fear of mockery—from his brother who doubted men their age could acquire new languages and from the children who picked up the dialect easily.

Sometimes though—as on June 2, 1941—André couldn't keep focused because of disturbing news. In this instance, Vichy had published more anti-Semitic legislation, banning Jews from public office and placing all Jews under "administrative arrest." A census of Jews was also to be taken, many suspected as a prelude to deportation.

All knew the Severins' status as "Israelites." Many commented on the recently established *Commissariat General aux Questions Juives* designed to assist the Germans with "Aryanization" of Jewish businesses in the occupied zone. Some decried this further despicable evidence of Vichy collaboration but others insisted it was an effort by Pétain's government to make sure matters got no worse.

Soleyrols was sufficiently removed from the immediate reach of the Vichy government and it wasn't likely anything would happen to the Severins anytime soon. Still it had been a difficult couple of weeks for all anti-Vichy French and especially for Jewish residents of France, occupied and unoccupied alike. In mid-May, more than three thousand Jews had been arrested in Paris and Pétain had announced the replacement of the Franco-German armistice with a whole new set of economic-collaboration agreements—agreements so pleasing to the Germans that they agreed to release and repatriate one hundred thousand French prisoners of war.

Roosevelt had condemned this collaboration and had informed Vichy France it must choose between Germany and the United States. Vichy's reaction had been to pass more laws restricting the movement and activities of Jews within France. The Nazi Göring had ordered that no Jew be allowed to emigrate from any occupied territory "in view of the imminent final solution." André had no clear idea what this new vile phrase, "final solution," meant, but it was likely massively murderous. Then a Vichy military court sentenced in absentia, to hard labor or death, fifty-six noncommissioned officers and privates allied with de Gaulle. Orders were issued to confiscate all property in unoccupied France belonging to Free French fighters.

André shook his head. Revolving dreadful thoughts in his mind could do no good, so he decided to concentrate on the Cévenol words in his notebook. How hard it was to twist his Brussels' French into the patois of the mountains, to emulate its gentle singing!

Suddenly Touté raised his head sharply and his ears stood up straight. André tried to pronounce several more local words. Touté began to whimper and whine.

Had André stumbled upon words sufficiently familiar that the mutt could understand them despite André's mangling? What if Touté could be made still more useful with the sheep, helping them file out into the proper field mornings and back down to the barn late afternoons before snuggling up with the children at night?

For the first time it struck André that in coming to Soleyrols, he had inadvertently ended up where he truly belonged. Or perhaps God had arranged it.

Alin enjoyed breaking up rock-hard ground, chopping down and lugging away dead trees—all farm labors. But he was troubled about doing nothing to help bring down the Nazis and their collaborators. Sure he listened to the radio and passed on news that could be valuable to the Resistance. But how much effective resistance was there when the Vichy government was able to announce mid-month the arrest and internment in concentration camps of twelve thousand Jews purportedly engaged in a "Jewish plot" to hamper Franco-German relations?

Those actions reminded Alin of nothing so much as the Phony War. And phoniness struck him as a major factor in the mid-June denial by Tass, the official Soviet news agency, of widespread rumors of the massing of German troops along the Russian border.

Those rumors proved true. The world-at-large proclaimed astonishment and shock as the Nazis launched an attack on the Soviet Union that made prior Blitzkriegs look like warm-ups—just what Alin expected of Hitler.

And what did the Americans do? Offer to send "assistance." Churchill announced a similar intention: "Any state that fights Nazism will have our aid."

Undeterred by these threats of "aid," Finland, Hungary, and Albania declared war on Russia. Less bold Vichy France merely broke off diplomatic relations.

By the end of June, the Germans had the Russians on the run. Believing Hitler had finally overreached, Alin actually felt elated. By attacking Mother Russia, Hitler like Napoleon before him had signed a death warrant for his dream of world domination.

Others panicked; but feeling celebratory, Alin purchased a pig. If André could buy sheep and a sheepdog without discussion, surely Alin need feel no compunction about pursuing his porcine predilection! Besides they could unquestionably use a pig. The previous winter they had all learned the value of a little fatback or a bit of bacon in making bajana more substantial and palatable. And thanks to the lush results of their plantings, they were now learning the value of pig manure-based fertilizer.

When Alin brought the porker home and placed it in the third space beneath the archway of La Font's open-air basement, Geneviève complained about the stench. The warmth of the pig rising along with the smell was equally unwelcome at that time of year.

"It's so offensive," Geneviève sniffed.

"The smell or the heat?" Denise wondered.

"They'll always be together," André reminded them.

"Just think how glad you'll be for extra heat," Alin shouted, "when cold weather comes!"

Realizing how disappointed Alin was by their response, Denise quickly agreed. "I guess we'll get used to the smell just like that of the rabbits, chickens, and goats."

"Speak for yourself," Geneviève pouted. "I'll never get used to the stink of goats."

"How about this?" Alin said angrily. "Whenever the pig stench bothers you think 'ham,' 'bacon,' 'sausage,' 'pork chops.' Then the smell won't be so bad, will it?"

Alin focused his outrage by naming the pig "Adolph." Adolph turned out to be a dirty pig, only adding to fastidious Alin's revulsion for the animal.

At first, Alin only let Adolph gorge on water to enlarge his stomach and increase his capacity for food. Then Adolph's diet was leftover chestnuts and kitchen scraps. He gained weight rapidly, but became fussy about the grub so Alin tried a mix of grain and chaff boiled into paste-like flour. This gruel pleased Adolph for a while, but then it turned away from it in disgust. Soon he would only eat bits of greens from the bounty of the garden.

Alin hadn't anticipated the need to keep a pig interested in eating. At least the creature kept putting on pounds. To judge by the look of him, Adolph would be fattened up for the slaughter by the time cold weather arrived.

The Severins were slowly becoming self-sufficient like the region's long-established residents. Every day they felt less need to go to Vialas. As they produced more of what they had formerly bought, they found their ration coupons lasted longer. They did so well they even felt free to sell off the last of the previous season's chestnuts.

Agricultural disappointments were few. The potato yield only increased fourfold above seed stock. Even though the textbook suggested growth by a factor of ten to twelve, that still meant lots of potatoes. And as if to compensate for that "failure" they pulled a great many more carrots out of the ground than expected. The Cévenol summer had passed its peak but these root vegetables continued their exceptional productivity.

The corn proved a triumph as did the soybeans. In fact the twenty-four soybean seeds produced a crop sufficient to help feed the family and their livestock and to save a great many more seeds to plant the next spring—if necessary.

The need to stay in Soleyrols was a distressing but increasingly likely prospect. Pétain broadcast a speech asserting that Hitler had attacked Stalin's Russia "in defense of civilization" and that he had taken measures to suppress opposition political parties in the unoccupied zone, to create a stronger police force and—most frighteningly—to establish special courts.

Denise felt encouraged by a joint declaration by Roosevelt and Churchill. The "Atlantic Charter" described their vision of a free peaceful democratic world to be constructed after the destruction of Nazi tyranny. She believed these leaders would never have enunciated such a vision if they did not intend and anticipate its realization.

The Severins were well housed, well fed, comparatively safe, and—most important—together, which need not have been true. Much had gone badly for the Jews in France since late August, when the Germans opened a major concentration camp in the northern Parisian suburb of Drancy. The holding facility was a transit point for Jews who would later be sent—well no one knew where, assuming they weren't executed—a real possibility since German authorities threatened to shoot Drancy detainees should attacks on German troops and interests continue.

Continue they did. In a matter of days, Pierre Laval and a prominent pro-German newspaper editor were shot and wounded near Versailles by a young man acting independently. Always seeking to impress its German masters, the Vichy government ordered the immediate roundup of many opponents, generally branded Communists.

Distinctions were drawn between French and non-French Jews in France. The non-French were better off because only French police rounded them up. French Jews were rounded up by the Gestapo since the brutes didn't trust the French police to arrest their fellow countrymen, which did not make the Severins especially comfortable. They would have to be increasingly careful in their travels and associations as the Germans and their henchmen became more entrenched.

The sheep behaved well until chestnut season. Then they revealed a taste for falling nuts.

"They like them more than we do," Denise suggested while penning the sheep for the night.

"That's not saying much," Geneviève said sullenly.

"Who cares whether we like chestnuts?" Alin demanded. "The sheep eat what we need. Do you really think they're worth the effort?"

"Their behavior is certainly exasperating," Denise conceded.

"Isn't it interesting though," André asked archly, "that the lambs always follow Alin?"

Denise giggled.

"They're still stupid," Alin said miserably.

He left to expend his anger slopping pigs. Over the summer, the family had acquired two more. Besides "Adolph," they now had "Herman" and "Emmy," named after the Görings.

With those names, Alin thought, *slaughtering them will be a pleasure.*

Early on the morning of October 24, Alin went out alone to look at trees. He and André had already scavenged the dead and fallen for the hard winter ahead. Now they would have to chop down a few live ones, sanctioned neither by custom nor by tradition. Therefore, he did his best to select those that didn't produce anything valuable enough to rival the family's need for heat. He had to wander farther and farther afield for such trees, which meant hauling as well as chopping. And they would have to fulfill Rose's needs as well as their own.

Returning to the house for breakfast, Alin ran into the postman and told him about the evacuation of Moscow. The postman reported the latest rumor: de Gaulle had met the previous day with leaders of the French Resistance asking them to spare the innocent and bide their time.

As the postman started back downhill, Alin was glad to see Emmanuel and Sebastian coming up, two Spanish Communists, who had come to France as refugees from their civil war and somewhat later had visited La Font to satisfy their curiosity about the Severins. Now they returned every few weeks out of friendship, and to see the children—as they yearned for their own.

Swarthy gentlemen with black hair and deep-set eyes lined at the corners, Emmanuel and Sebastian looked older than their twenty and twenty-two years respectively. Born into farming families they had worked their native land until joining the Republican Army to fight Franco.

"We were lucky to get away," Emmanuel, the taller leaner one—his body hardened first from digging in the baked soil of his family's farm and then from several years of fighting—had explained to the Severins with whom he and Sebastian had immediately felt comfortable. "Once Franco's Army started winning, they hunted for us hard and knew just where to look."

"The climb through the mountains was difficult," Sebastian had added explaining how they had come into the Cévennes. Shorter than Emmanuel, but more heavily muscled, his chest was deep, his shoulders were broad, and the black hair on his chest curled up above his shirt. That and being cross-eyed helped to create a special bond with Ida. "Leaving our families behind was unbearably sad, but at least we think our women and children are safe. I don't know about my father though, but I can hope. Not Emmanuel. His father was killed in our last battle—right before his eyes."

Emmanuel had sighed heavily. "That was enough for me."

"So now our women work the fields while we work in the mines."

"The work is hard but it's better than evading Franco's police."

"Crazy," Sebastian had said. "Now we have to hide from Pétain's police."

The Severins knew little else about the Spaniards except that they lived in a hamlet farther down the valley and labored in the barium mine. Also they were knowledgeable in agricultural matters and happily lent Alin and André a hand in exchange for a little food. Farm work gratified them. Each time they set to it, their tough protective exteriors softened.

In addition, they glowed spending time with the Severin children, taking special delight in tossing the youngsters high into the air and carefully catching them when they came down. The children loved it too.

Today, the two were glad to help chop firewood and lug it from far up the hill to outside the kitchen. Working, they spoke with regret and disgust of rumors they had heard concerning a volunteer Spanish brigade joining the German fight against the Russians.

"We would fight on the other side," Sebastian asserted, "if it all didn't seem so futile."

At the end of the day, Alin was anxious to think up a new way to show his appreciation, which wasn't as easy as when the gardens were producing. Then he had an inspiration.

He had long wondered what to do about the old goat that had lost her kid in childbirth. The goat was of no use anymore except as meat, and Geneviève would never allow her kin to eat the poor thing. Yet feeding the goat was a drain on their domestic economy. Perhaps Emmanuel and Sebastian would be interested.

The Spaniards declared goat a favorite meal among the miners. But they wouldn't simply accept the animal. Though Alin didn't want their money, he finally agreed to take a few francs—far fewer than even a thin goat was worth.

Chapter Nine

CRISTIAN

October 26, 1941

S peaking with André had been on Denise's mind all day, in part because the twenty-sixth of October was her brother Francis's twenty-third birthday—such a baby really, yet flying in fighter planes. But she could never find the right opportunity. Before she knew it, supper was done, the dishes were washed and put away, and there her husband and she were, snuggling in bed, trying to warm each other against the mid-autumn chill.

Denise whispered excitedly, "I think we're going to have another little one!"

In the dark awaiting her husband's reaction—shock? Displeasure? Delight?—she filled with trepidation. Listening to his steady breathing she sensed André's eyes open wide and felt him shift position, propping himself upright on the thin mattress recently restuffed with cornstalks. When he leaned over and gave her a long tender kiss she flushed with warmth—released to enjoy fully carrying another of André's children.

"That's wonderful," monsieur le professeur Severin whispered at last, the palpable thrill in his voice making up for the slight delay. "When will it happen?"

"Hard to say," Denise responded gaily now. "Maybe late May. I'm so happy. It may not be convenient, but what joy!"

"I love you," André burst out, more loudly than seemed wise.

"Careful." Denise giggled. "Let's not upset Alin with a display of affection!"

"I dread his reaction." André sighed. "I suppose I should tell him myself?"

"And I'd like to tell Geneviève."

André embraced his wife again, resting his hand gently on her belly. "Why do I think you got the easier assignment?"

The following morning while Denise announced the news to her sister in the kitchen André told his brother as they stepped outside to release the sheep into the fields.

"What a stupid thing to do!" Alin shouted. "How could you let that happen?"

Instantly angered André realized it had been absurd to expect Alin to react like anyone else and simply offer congratulations.

"Geneviève and I would never be so reckless," Alin groused.

André grinned. The more he thought about the pregnancy the more pleased he was.

"There's a war going on!" Alin exploded. "It's a struggle to survive even without an extra burden."

"I think we'll be fine," André replied peaceably though he was becoming aggravated by Alin's inability to be happy for him and Denise. "And may I remind you," he said stiffly, "that you and Geneviève knew it was a troubled world with more trouble to come when you got pregnant with Philippe in '38? Yet you chose further life. And Denise and I choose life now."

"We've just gotten Philippe out of diapers," Alin groaned. "To go through that again..."

In the kitchen, Denise and Geneviève smiled broadly.

"I think it's wonderful," Geneviève said to Alin. "Don't you?"

Alin reflexively shook his head no. "What if we're forced into hiding?" he demanded. "A squalling infant will give us all away."

"We'll take care of it, Alin. We'll manage."

"What about a doctor?" Alin breathed, uncontrollably vexed. "The doctor from Vialas who tried to help Father isn't around anymore."

"We'll manage," Geneviève said soothingly, rubbing her husband's back.

"It's all such a bother," he complained.

"The doctor is an issue," André allowed. "But I think Max Maurel could help."

"Max!" Denise clapped her hands. "So warm and so intelligent."

"Do you think he'll be available?" Geneviève asked.

"We can't be certain he'll be free from Les Chantiers de la Jeunesse," André replied. "But we can hope."

"How will that help if he's living in Alès?" Alin asked dubiously.

"He might agree to stay at La Planche," André countered, "once he knows."

"A young man with no experience," Alin went on, "who never finished his studies."

"He's a fine fellow," André said firmly. "I'm sure he already knows enough."

"What fun to have an infant around again," Geneviève cheered.

"Given the midwifery skills Geneviève demonstrated with the old goat maybe Denise *would* be better off in the hands of an untutored boy," Alin scoffed storming out of the farmhouse.

"He doesn't mean it," André told his wife and sister-in-law.

"Of course he does," Geneviève said knowingly. "But don't you worry." Sweetly she gave her big sister a little hug. "Everything will be all right—even Alin. He's just afraid." Then she excused herself to go to him.

"That went well," André told his wife sardonically.

"It all will be fine." Overwhelmed with exhaustion, Denise slumped in her seat.

"Shall I go tell Mother?" André asked gingerly. "I think she should hear it from one of us."

"No," Denise replied rising slowly and slipping her hand through her husband's arm. "Let's go together. I want to see Rose's face when she learns of this new life."

Early November brought the solemn first anniversary of Louis Severin's passing. A week later André and Denise turned forty and thirty-two but the family was in no mood to celebrate.

The weather had turned cold enough to prevent meat from spoiling so they decided Adolph should be slaughtered. Almost all the villagers of Soleyrols showed up to assist since hog butchering was traditionally a communal activity—a big job requiring an experienced hand at the helm and much additional help to assure the fullest use of every bit of the animal, including the head and feet which would be turned into souse.

All the messy work involved such as cleaning the intestines disgusted sophisticated Geneviève. But the previous winter's experience of fatback had developed her visceral sense of the value of viscera. And with the stuck pig's carefully saved blood she, Denise, and Rose could make *boudin*—blood sausage—in the Belgian style Louis would have appreciated.

And then there were the chestnuts to collect. It went slightly more swiftly this year since their hands and fingers were experienced. But it was still painful and painfully tedious.

The Severins' St. Nicholas Day Eve celebration was spare and quiet again but enjoyable. Two days later though they had quite a shock when they learned of the Japanese attack on Pearl Harbor and the loss of three thousand American lives.

Yet, some good came out of this latest atrocity. It finally forced the United States to declare war on the Axis powers.

Soon after, the BBC brought news that was more dreadful: German mechanized forces had destroyed much of the Soviet Army and the Germans had overrun almost all of European Russia. Fortunately, harsh winter weather, as so often before, had come to the aid of the Russian people. For the moment, the Nazi drive on Moscow was stopped in its tracks.

On a different scale, winter made life difficult for the Severins too, as before. They only went outside when necessary for the briefest time possible.

When a huge snowstorm blew in on Christmas day, the children were prevented from attending the pageant at the Protestant temple in Vialas, which they had spent months looking forward to and preparing for.

The Severins also felt lucky to have special foods to share. In addition to the wealth of their larder, including the wonders of "Adolph," there were dried fruits and of all things, sardines that Uncle Paul Herz had sent from Portugal.

Another luxury was coffee. Real coffee beans had become nearly impossible to obtain, but André had devised a system for making them last by combining them with ground soybeans. As long as one added a dash of imagination, it was somewhat flavorful.

Perhaps the greatest gift to arrive at this time was a response, at long last, from Anna Severin. The letter from Brussels was circumspect to say the least. Aware that all mail was read by the authorities, Anna had felt terribly constrained. At least the Severins in Soleyrols could gather that the family in Belgium was managing to survive.

In late January, there was an unexpected knock on the door. Marc Donadille, the pastor from Saint-Frézal-de-Ventalon, had learned of the Severins from Sebastian and Emmanuel and had decided to pay a call as part of his ministry and to express his concern for the exiles' welfare.

Primarily he was concerned that the Severins were living relatively openly, under their own names.

Alin snarled, "And what are we to do about that? We're registered under our own names here and elsewhere."

"There's always the possibility..." Pastor Donadille trailed off briefly before completing his thought. "Certain sympathetic officials in interesting situations—in towns where the churches that held birth records have burned down...Let me look into it."

As soon as the pastor was gone Alin said, "So he's part of the Resistance?"

"I suppose," André agreed. "Everyone knows the Protestant pastors of this region are associated with the Resistance. But no one speaks that truth out loud."

In the depths of February, a significant lessening in the quantity of milk produced by the family's goats worried Geneviève. There was no obvious cause. But a careful examination of the goats' udders revealed the smallest of puncture wounds in every teat.

"Snake," Albertine Brignand declared nonchalantly. "Not uncommon here."

Geneviève shuddered, as frightened of snakes as of rats.

Albertine laughed. "Time to call the faith healer!"

In another time and place Geneviève would have dismissed this as superstitious nonsense. But after her experience in Bédouès...

Albertine placed a call and that very day the aged and mysterious figure of the faith healer of Soleyrols appeared at La Font.

"Snake, yes," the old woman confirmed examining the goats. "There's never any infection but we still must drive the snake away!"

All Geneviève could ever say was that the faith healer "used her powers." The next morning when Geneviève went into the barn, there beside the goats was a dead snake.

The flow of milk returned to normal. The problem never arose again.

On the tenth of April, Pastor Donadille returned with several members of the Resistance and a bit of equipment. The mayor of Saint-Michel-de-Dèze had agreed to sign new false identity cards for the Severins, but since the small village was some thirty-seven kilometers distant, the terrain somewhat treacherous still at that time of year, and Denise seven months pregnant, a roundtrip had been deemed impractical. So the Resistance had come to the Severins and they proceeded to photograph them, take their fingerprints, and obtain their signatures on the official documents in question. "Severin" became "Milard" and the visitors went away.

The Severins fretted through the weekend: what if their photos, fingerprints, and fake signatures somehow went astray, subjecting them to investigation? But their fears were allayed early on Tuesday the fourteenth, when Donadille returned with the properly executed identity cards, duly stamped, attested by the mayor, and dated 13 *Avril* 1942.

In late April, with the snows gone from even the farthest reaches of the Lozère, André resumed regular attendance of Sunday services at the Protestant temple in Vialas. Pleased to see him again Pastor Burnand greeted the news of Denise's pregnancy as a sign of divine favor.

The pastor was excited to introduce André to another occasional visitor: Irene Bastide, who lived in Le Salson, an even more isolated hamlet than Soleyrols. André and she shared a common interest: Irene was one of the few Quakers in all of the Cévennes.

Irene was thrilled by André's fascination with her faith. "There's always room for one more," she said, going on to describe their infrequent gatherings: the *veillée* as she called it—an evening gathering around a fire. She invited André to attend the next one though she couldn't say where or when since the meetings were held in varying locations.

André wondered aloud whether he couldn't offer La Font for that gathering. The suggestion pleased Irene and they picked a date. André hoped to convince Alin to leave during the session, for even if Alin kept his mouth shut, his skepticism could permeate and poison the atmosphere.

The evening in early May more than fulfilled André's hopes and expectations. Sitting in a circle of thoughtful caring, Friends silently communing with each other and their God, brought peace and hopefulness into his soul such as he had only dreamed possible. Denise and Geneviève, though sitting in their rooms, were impressed with the way La Font felt throughout the veillée. Even the children were wordlessly responsive to the atmosphere created by meditating Quakers.

Afterward Irene thanked the Severins profusely and offered her very best wishes to Denise, whom she would keep in her prayers. Then Irene caressed little Christel's face and told her she hoped they would have a chance to spend some time together someday.

The baby seemed certain to arrive in late May but the Severins had still not made arrangements. Max had agreed to help if available, but that couldn't be counted on.

"You should go to aunts Léonore and Régine in Aubenas, Denise," Alin insisted after dinner one evening. "Surely you'd be welcomed by your aunts."

Geneviève agreed. "It would be a mistake for us to try to deliver the baby up here without a doctor," she said gently, looking at her sister with large sad eyes. "We both know how hard labor is and how dangerous confinement can be. If there are any complications…"

"But I don't want to leave the farm, you, André, or the children!" Denise responded stubbornly.

"Sweetheart," André said softly but firmly, "it will be much safer for you and the baby in Aubenas. The aunts will see to you and we know they have a doctor who cares for Beatrice."

Denise focused a look of trepidation on André. Geneviève knew the baby was kicking.

"It's settled then," André announced with quiet authority. "I'll go down to the café in the morning and make the call."

The bus was cramped for the very pregnant Denise but the train from Génolhac to Aubenas was more comfortable. Though terribly excited, the girls were well behaved. Their first view of Aubenas was an impressive thirteenth century castle, the tallest structure on the highest point in the center of town, surrounded by narrow crooked streets. Silk pennants flew before resort hotels crowded onto little open squares, perched above the town walls, and overlooking the river below.

Aunts Régine and Léonore and Cousin Pierre waited for them at the station and proved as gracious and accommodating as could have been wished in their pleasantly appointed apartment.

Pierre was busy that summer drawing and studying for his baccalauréat exam. But with his older brother away—presumably a prisoner of war in German hands—Pierre was the man of the house, a role he fulfilled admirably despite his relative youth.

Grandmother Beatrice was on her deathbed so she couldn't terrorize the children as she had at weekly teas in Brussels by crooking her cane's handle around one of their ankles or knees to pull them to her. When Denise asked why no one had told her how ill her grandmother was, Aunt Léonore bit her lower lip and said, "We were afraid you wouldn't come."

Léonore led Denise into the dimly lit back room. Ida and Christel followed timidly. The elderly woman—once so strong, stern and determined—rested almost motionlessly in a large tall bed, her beautiful white hair spread out on the pillow.

"Ah Denise, Ida," she said softly. "Is little Christel with you?"

Still at the door, Christel strode forward boldly as if no longer afraid of the family's ill tempered matriarch. Going straight to the bed she rose up on tiptoes, presented herself and called loudly and distinctly, "Great Grandmother are you going to die like Tante Fanny?"

Aunt Fanny? Toward the end of the Severins' life in Brussels the death of Jack Freedman's sister may have been mentioned in Christel's presence, but no one would have guessed the words would hold any meaning for her, that she would remember them from such a tender age, or that she would bring them up in such a circumstance.

"It's all right," Aunt Régine said later, making Denise feel better about the embarrassing incident. "Mother's well aware of her condition and Christel has always been a favorite."

Then Denise presented Régine the monogrammed tablecloth brought out of Belgium and said, "A small token of appreciation for taking us in at a time of need."

"It's lovely," Régine said clutching it to her chest and crying softly.

Oddly, being a Jew or the descendant of Jews could be beneficial as well as dangerous. The Nazis had only banned Jews from practicing medicine in occupied France so the Vichy government didn't even acknowledge the few Jewish doctors who hadn't yet fled the unoccupied zone, such as the one caring for Beatrice Herz. The doctor, a member of the small Hebraic community that had lived and thrived in Aubenas for generations, attended to Denise too.

He recommended "little walks in the park" as a daily regimen and assured her his clinic wasn't far. "It won't be a long ride when the moment arrives," he told her. "And if you have problems getting a taxicab, phone and I will come get you."

Late Friday the twenty-ninth of May, Beatrice Herz passed away quietly. The Severins' great tablecloth served as the dead woman's shroud.

Denise went into labor the next morning—Life and death so close together! Aunt Léonore took Denise to the clinic. Pierre looked after Christel and Ida. Aunt Régine arranged the funeral.

The phone call to the Brignand café—late Saturday, May the thirtieth, brought André news of the birth of Cristian Louis Severin and the death of Beatrice Herz. Since he couldn't ascertain that a train would be running from Génolhac to Aubenas on Sunday he borrowed a bicycle from Louis Brignand. Louis worried that eighty kilometers over very rough terrain would be too much for André, but André laughed, remembering his bike ride from Brussels to Le Coq—a longer trip in much worse circumstances. And André was much stronger now.

After a grueling ride with many steep hills and hairpin turns, André went straight to the clinic where he was asked to sign his son's birth certificate in a great leather-bound book. Reading his son's name for the first time André flushed with pride and then suffered a brief spasm of panic: had he and Denise chosen rightly to assume that it would be safe to use the name Severin instead of Milard, which now appeared on their identity cards? But Aubenas and Vialas were in different départements and there was more than enough distance between them to make communication between officials of the two towns unlikely if not impossible. There had been no need for Denise to declare any residence other than Brussels.

Then André noticed with surprise and relief that no religious affiliation had been listed. Reassured that his newborn's safety had not been compromised André signed the birth register with the deepest feeling and a fine calligraphic flourish.

In Denise's private room, healthy gurgling sleepy-eyed Cristian rested his full head of shimmering dark hair on his mother's chest. André held and kissed Denise's hand. The doctor stopped in to ask if they wanted him or the rabbi to perform the circumcision.

André and Denise agreed circumcision made medical sense. André couldn't explain why he wanted the rabbi to handle it but Denise didn't object.

"Samuel Freedman would insist," she said mischievously.

When Ida and Christel saw their baby brother for the first time later that day Ida said, "I love him. But will he always look like a frog?"

Next day André rode back to La Font and Denise brought Cristian back to the aunts' apartment where they stayed in what had been her grandmother's room.

Within a week the Jews of occupied France were ordered to wear yellow armbands with the Star of David whenever they appeared in public.

"Will they make us wear a star too?" Léonore asked nervously.

Régine considered then slowly answered, "If the Germans want the star worn in the north of France it won't be long before Pétain makes it the law in the south as well. I'm sure it betokens worse to come." She turned her eyes on Pierre. "You must be more careful than ever. I don't want you and your friends hanging around in public places anymore. Avoid downtown. Stay away from theaters."

Each time an aunt ran an errand she returned with news of increased gendarme presence.

"We almost never hear from the family in Belgium," Léonore said dolefully one evening, "but now mail from friends in Paris has stopped. I don't want to think what that means."

Both aunts believed Aubenas had become too dangerous for Denise and the children.

Denise agreed sorrowfully. "We'll leave soon."

On June 22 the government enunciated a new policy: *relève*—"relief." One French prisoner of war would be released for every three skilled French workers who went to Germany.

"Three for one," Léonore said disgustedly. "How does that help France?"

Secretly, Aunt Régine prayed that one of the ones released would be her other stepson.

In early July, the BBC relayed a London *Daily Telegraph* report that more than one million European Jews had already been killed by the Nazis. Almost simultaneously a letter arrived from André couched in terms, that read by Vichy authorities would suggest nothing out of the ordinary but nevertheless conveyed to Denise that he had learned definitively (from one of the pastors? the mailman? Max Maurel?), that after a person went to "camp" (Drancy) they were sent on "vacation" (out of the country) "permanently" (no interpretation necessary). He also wrote, "Touté is not the only dog about to round up some sheep," and by "sheep" Denise understood he meant foreign Jews in Vichy France.

Denise told the tantes they should come with her to La Font since Soleyrols was safer than Aubenas. But the aunts still believed their age and sex would protect them.

"Pierre though," Aunt Régine said tearfully, "should go with you."

But Pierre insisted on staying with his friends. They had agreed to share their fate.

"They're not all Jews," his stepmother said fearfully. "And you're the only foreigner."

"So that brings you up to date," Denise concluded. She was glad to be back, but worried about her aunts and Pierre—until they appeared at La Font in mid-July to check up on Denise, Cristian, and the rest of the family. Distressingly, Aunts Régine and Léonore had drifted into lethargic despair. Pierre had become rebellious as never before, spending more and more time out with his friends.

They found no relief at La Font.

"We've been listening to the radio," Alin told the visitors soon after they arrived. "During the night, police rounded up all the foreign Jews registered with the authorities in Paris and shipped them off to Drancy, even those who had lived in France for years and years."

A few days later, the guests had gone back to Aubenas and the reports were confirmed: almost thirteen thousand Parisian Jews had been arrested and interned during one long night. Then the newspaper said that on the fourth of August, nearly a thousand Belgian Jews had been deported to Auschwitz.

But the worst news for the Severins arrived mid-month by telephone. Pierre had been taken away. He had gone out with friends, stopped into a pharmacy on the main street to pick up medicine for Léonore. After making the purchase, Pierre and his friends had spotted police herding men into a van at the end of the block and Pierre had led his friends into a movie theater to hide. The movie stopped almost instantly, the lights came on, and policemen blocked all exits. The gendarmes told the women to leave and told the men to show their identity cards. Then they ordered the men to drop their pants. Any circumcised man was declared a Jew and taken away—including Pierre.

The Severins were inconsolable and terribly afraid.

"We should try to leave," André told Alin. "There's still an American embassy in Vichy. We could try to get permission to immigrate to the United States."

Alin was stunned. "You really think that would work?"

"Probably not. But it's worth a try."

From the Protestant temple in Vialas, André knew a teacher named Leo Rousson. Having seen him talking privately with the pastor, André was convinced he was part of the Resistance. Via nods and winks, the postman had suggested Leo sometimes went to Vichy on "business." So André went to Vialas to ask Pastor Burnand whether Leo could be trusted to go on a mission for the family.

The pastor was impressed by André's choice and arranged for Leo to meet him at the Brignands' café. There André handed Leo a dozen of Jack Freedman's diamonds—part as payment, the rest to convince the Americans that the Severins were solvent.

One week later André and Leo Rousson met again at the Brignands' café. But Leo's effort had failed. Approaching the American embassy in Vichy he had spotted a *collaborateur* from Vialas so he walked around the block and went to lunch in a café. Each time he returned, the collaborator was there. Leo hadn't dared enter the embassy.

Expressing his regret and sorrow he returned all of the Severin diamonds. "Never before have I had so much value in my pocket. And never again, I know."

On the beautiful sunlit first Monday of September 1942, Pastor Robert Burnand walked the winding road between Vialas and Soleyrols, a newspaper tucked under his arm, his dark clouds of thought a confused and sorrowful contrast with the clarity of the sky. He had spent the previous afternoon at a conclave of Protestant pastors of the Cévennes gathered in the hamlet of Mialet to discuss what to do about the "final solution." Recently, the Grand Rabbi of France had sent a letter to Cardinal Pierre-Marie Gerlier, Archbishop of Lyon, informing him that Jews weren't sent from France to Germany to work. They were sent to be exterminated.

The pastors knew they had to do everything in their power to save their local refugees.

André apologized to Pastor Burnand for himself and Alin being so sweaty and dirt-smeared. They had just come from working the upper field, slicing through row after row of hay with great wide swings of their scythes. The hay would be left to dry in the sun for two days then turned, gathered into piles and brought down to the barn for storage.

"I never knew how many muscles I had," André stated uncomplainingly.

Skipping past pleasantries the pastor unfolded his newspaper and handed it to André, who adjusted his glasses and set his beret more evenly on his head before starting to read.

"Another new law has been passed," Pastor Burnand said not waiting for André to finish, "allowing the Vichy government to conscript specialists and send them to Germany. All French men are required to register."

"We've already heard about this," Alin groused.

The pastor shook his head. "I suppose you also have heard about the roundups."

"Yes," André said gravely, adding hoarsely, "I can't believe I had Cristian circumcised."

"You need to know," the pastor said softly, "that many of our young men are leaving their homes and going into the mountains."

"Yes, like…"

Alin made a quick gesture cutting André off. Best not to name names. But the Severins knew from the young man's sister that Max Maurel had left Alès for a mountain redoubt.

"You know these young men?" Alin asked.

"Some of them have come to me," Robert Burnand replied evenly, "seeking advice. Should they obey the law and sign up with the gendarmes? I suggest that they consider their actions carefully."

"That's very noncommittal of you."

"I choose my words carefully," Pastor Burnand allowed, "but my message gets across." Averting his eyes, he continued quietly, "I believe the danger to you is growing. The gendarmes know you are here and it appears that government agents in Vichy will soon attempt to rid themselves of all refugees, particularly Jews—practicing and non-practicing alike."

"What should we do?" André asked huskily.

"Prepare to go into hiding at a moment's notice—to join the others in the mountains."

"And you can help us find them?" Alin inquired.

"I believe we can help, yes," the pastor said. "Preparations are being made."

"We?" André quizzed.

"Obviously I am not alone."

"Is our family in danger?" Alin asked. "Are 'preparations' being made for them too?"

"We think they will be safe for the time being," Pastor Burnand answered somberly. "The Germans are not interested in women and children, yet."

"I knew we should never have registered," Alin angrily told his brother.

"What choice did we have?" André muttered, resigned yet despairing.

"They would find you soon enough either way," the pastor said pacifically. "Remember there are many who support Pétain—maybe even in Soleyrols—who will do anything to preserve the present peace of France. Who knows who would come to your aid at their own peril and who would turn you in to the authorities as though that were a patriotic act?"

André turned the newspaper over in his hands. The pastor gently relieved him of it.

"Best not leave evidence of your interests lying about," he said, secreting the paper in his clothes. "For now act as if everything's normal—until someone comes, as someone surely will."

The brothers focused on their hay. Though they spoke of their concerns and fears rarely, they thought of them constantly, their minds freed by the monotony of the movement of their scythes.

Alin couldn't stop thinking about a BBC report he'd heard: *Vichy's Jewish victims, children deported to Germany.* André mulled over the Vichy government's latest distressing moves: firing the military governor of Lyon for refusing to participate in the arrest of local Jewish citizens and ordering the arrest of all Catholic priests caught sheltering Jews.

"Did you hear?" a familiar voice called startling both André and Alin out of their reveries as they worked the lower field. It was the postman, climbing up to La Font on his daily rounds. "New regulations have been posted at the mayor's office in Vialas. All male foreign refugees are to report to French authorities to volunteer for an additional work force in Germany. The gendarmes are making a wide sweep looking for potential 'volunteers' everywhere."

"So the last roundup wasn't enough," André said neutrally, resting on the handle of his scythe. "Have the local police started looking?"

"Not that I know of," the postman replied. "They don't like the Germans. But eventually they won't have a choice. They'll even come up here." He encompassed the surrounding mountains with a wave of his hand. Then he pulled a worn stained envelope out of his old leather pouch, smiled, and handed it to André. "From the Belgian Congo, originally mailed from England."

The letter from Jack Freedman provided the relief Denise and Geneviève had longed for. But André and Alin had other news from the postman that was no comfort at all.

"The roundup," André said mournfully, "in which Pierre was picked up was not an isolated incident."

Alin railed, "It was coordinated not just in Aubenas, but everywhere— Nîmes, Marseille, Mende, Lyon—all over southern France."

"So the danger gets closer and closer," Geneviève breathed.

That night, the danger seemed closer still. The family was surprised and terrified when Cristian unexpectedly began singing tunefully—unmistakably— the distinctive opening notes of the BBC news fanfare.

André and Alin went into Vialas the next day to purchase canvas bags to pack against the need for a sudden departure.

Then they heard from Aunt Paulette in Switzerland about an underground movement to smuggle imperiled children out of France into the safety of her neutral host country. If the Severins could find their way across the Rhône to Chamonix-Mont Blanc—a journey fraught with dangers including discovery throughout its four hundred kilometer length—Paulette would send a guide to lead the children to the other side.

How to respond? The Severins wanted to preserve their children from harm but couldn't bear the thought of separation. And Cristian was simply too young to leave his mother's care.

The agonizing decision was taken from their hands. Pastor Marc Donadille paid a special visit to say that after several groups of children had made their way into Switzerland the Germans and the Vichy French had found their route and shut it down. Some children had been caught and sent to German prison camps.

In the dusky gloom of late afternoon on the Sunday marking mid-October, Max Maurel hurried up the path to La Font hoping not to be detected by unfriendly eyes. He was relieved and gratified by the warmth of his reception. They just were finishing supper, but insisted he sit and eat. He was more than glad because he and his compatriots in their hidden camps found food and other necessities in perpetually short supply.

The Severins spoke of their failed attempts to leave the country.

Max asked, "So what will you do?"

"Watch," André answered. "Wait."

"Keep an eye out for interlopers and the police," Alin added angrily.

Trying to steer back to what she hoped would be a happier subject, Denise asked Max about his family.

"We worry about father," he answered dispiritedly. "Mother misses Françoise."

"How is Fela?" Geneviève inquired. "She's rather special to you isn't she?"

"Certainly she's very nice," Denise suggested leadingly.

"You really do like her?" André asked.

"Maybe even love?" Alin added teasingly.

Max blushed charmingly. "Love," he said tentatively. "I don't know. I like her and I miss her more and more. She's different. Special." There was a catch in his voice. He looked around.

"One day the Germans had rounded all the Jews in the Klinghofers' hometown in Poland into the town square. A German officer grabbed a crying baby by its feet and flung it against a wall, smashing its head and killing it instantly in front of its mother and everyone else. Without a moment's hesitation, Fela's father, the town's doctor, took his wife by the hand and kissed her. 'Good-bye,' he said softly, and then walked over to the murderer and spat in his face. The soldier pulled out his pistol and shot Dr. Klinghofer dead.

"When the Germans sent everyone home Fela's mother had to drag Fela's brother away. As a lesson, the Germans left Dr. Klinghofer's body where it had fallen. The townspeople were afraid to move it, but Fela's brother slipped out after dark, gathered his dead father into his arms, carried him home, kissed the cold body, hugged his mother tight, and fled into the night."

"Horrible," Denise said miserably.

"It can't last," Geneviève said with the coldness of fury. "It can't go on forever."

André still had a few cigarettes left from his month's ration so the three men went out onto the terrance and smoked quietly, enjoying the crisp air and bright stars.

"I'd like to get Fela up here," Max said softly. "She'd be safer at La Planche."

"I'm sure your mother wouldn't object," André said, "and Françoise would be delighted."

Max smiled broadly. "But Fela has a mind of her own. I'll have to go to Alès to try to talk her into it when the time is right. But not with winter coming on."

"And where might you spend the winter?" Alin asked. "We don't even know where you stay now."

Max tensed and then relaxed knowing he could trust these people with his life.

"You know of the Resistance," he said fervently. "It has begun to spread from the towns to the countryside. Some stay in private homes even more secluded than yours. Others stay in the woods and forests in cabins and camps, many built by the young men themselves when they were in Les Chantiers. And I...for now I stay in a camp a little way from here. I won't say precisely where to protect you as much as us."

"Very wise," André agreed. "But what is it like for you?"

Max laughed. "I'm the camp doctor! I try to make sure no one gets sick. So far so good—only fungus of the feet and the occasional cough—inevitable for newcomers to mountain living." Instinctively Max lowered his voice. "We've begun to coordinate with the Gaullists. The Resistance has moved well beyond leafleting. There's going to be shooting sooner or later so I guess we'll find out how much doctoring I learned at school."

This was serious business, but the three men chuckled softly. Max marveled at the persistence of natural human feelings and reactions in an increasingly inhuman, unnatural time. He felt so warmly toward the Severins, he finally said what he had really come to say.

"You two may find yourselves in a Resistance camp soon enough." Max extinguished his cigarette. "I know you've thought about leaving. Today I tell you it's going to be necessary. I can't say when. But we'll know. Be prepared and don't worry."

"I do worry!" Alin exploded. "If André and I must leave, what about the family?"

"We'll look after them too," Max assured him. "We know what we have to do and we're determined to do it."

After a long silence, André said, "I wonder what it's like to be in one of those camps."

"Hard," Max replied forthrightly. "Tense. There's a good deal of grumbling and arguing. We suffer from short supplies and short tempers. And we all have such different views. You can't imagine the fights that break out between the socialists and the Communists."

"That's terrible," André declared. "They need to overcome their differences, to unite against the common enemy." An even longer silence followed. André pondered deeply before asking, "Is it possible I could help? I hold no truck with either philosophy: the socialists seem naïve to me and the Communists are dangerous. But that doesn't matter. Perhaps, I, as a neutral party, can talk sense to them. Do these groups have leaders? Could you conceivably get them to come to La Font? Away from the camp, perhaps I could try to broker a peace."

"Possibly," Max answered noncommittally. Then he said he must go.

André asked if Max wouldn't consider spending the night.

"Isn't traveling in the dark dangerous?" Alin demanded.

"Less than in the light," Max replied laughing again. "I've got to get back to the camp anyway—in case some socialist coughs on a Communist!"

Several nights later, Max brought the socialist and Communist chiefs of his Resistance camp to La Font. André masterfully managed these tough argumentative men, patiently convincing them—over not a little food and wine, tobacco, and soybean-enhanced coffee—to "bury the hatchet" at least until their mutual oppressors had been overcome and their own future and that of France as a proud independent nation had been secured.

Alin came away from the meeting impressed by the willingness of these hard-bitten determined figures to fight, and was half-convinced he should join them.

On November the eighth, André and Alin listened to the daily broadcast of the BBC in French. They heard the cryptic phrase "The fish are in the river" just as the jamming started. It was repeated in Flemish. The brothers interpreted it as confirming the start of an Allied invasion of North Africa.

On the eleventh, Hitler ordered the occupation of the rest of France. Then the mailman reported that Germans had arrived in Alès and now directly controlled the French police.

"Also," he said darkly, "the Gestapo is in Mende."

Late in November 1942, a tall overweight man trudged up the path to La Font black bag in hand. He wore a dark coat and despite the seasonal chill, loosened the black tie that bound the neck of his white shirt already soaked with sweat. His generous jowls jounced up and down on his otherwise spare face. He felt old, gray, winded, and disgusted as he mounted the last steps onto the terrace.

"I'm the doctor," he said when André and Alin came out. "Sent to check on your health."

"By whom?" Alin demanded.

"By order of the prefect from Mende. I need to report back to the police."

"Why do they want to know about our health?" Alin snapped.

"To make sure the air of the Cévennes agrees with you," the doctor replied dryly. Then he added more seriously and heavily, "To see if you're healthy and capable of work."

He set down his black case and brought out his stethoscope. After a quick examination, he declared the brothers healthy.

"Do you agree?" he asked

Alin barked, "You're the doctor. You tell us!"

"I am," the doctor replied miserably, "and you are, which is what I was sent here for, so now I'll leave." He prepared to go then turned back and told André, "By the by, the governor of Mende asked especially that I give you his regards. He hoped I would find you well. I will tell him I did."

When the doctor was gone, André said, "This is only the beginning. I'm certain the governor of Mende was sending us a message. If authorities that far away are thinking about us here in Soleyrols we're not safe at all."

In the depths of December, the Severins could muster no enthusiasm even when the BBC broadcast encouraging news. Nor did they have the Christmas pageant in Vialas to look forward to, because by then, they were afraid to be seen anywhere and not only for their own sakes. The laudable involvement of Protestant pastors in Resistance activities made the presence of any refugees in their temples, let alone a family as numerous as the Severins, a potential compromise of their security and their much-needed anti-Fascist activities.

New Year's 1943 brought no brightness either. Soon enough, the puppet Vichy government instituted an additional police force to work in "cooperation" with the Gestapo. The Milice, as they were called, were more active, aggressive, and authoritarian than the regular gendarmes. Directed by the German authorities in Mende, the Milice were instructed to apply more pressure to any Jewish refugees and other foreigners in the Lozère who had somehow eluded previous less-concerted efforts to extract them.

Consisting of carefully selected thugs, the Milice were only too happy to rid France of outsiders, especially Jews. But the Milice didn't discriminate. Anyone who objected to Fascist ideology and policies, or worse, actively opposed them, was subject to the roundups or *rafles* for which the Milice evinced brutal enthusiasm.

In turn, this placed enormous strain on those coalescing in the secluded mountain villages and hamlets of the Cévennes. As more and more men like Max Maurel joined the Resistance, it became difficult to find places they could stay. And since the youths who found their way to the few isolated camps brought very little beyond energy and determination, all food and clothing had to be supplied, stretching to the utmost the limited resources of local trades people and farmers—including the Severins, who clandestinely provided whatever they could.

Rumor had it that the resisters had begun to train rigorously in arms and guerrilla warfare. Meantime, another four thousand Jews were rounded up in Marseille.

When school resumed after the holiday break, Katie and Ida seemed uncharacteristically reluctant to resume their studies. Denise was greatly puzzled, but both she and Geneviève agreed it was important that the children go if only to get out of the house for a few hours every day.

Before the week was out, both girls separately complained about irritation "down there." Upon examination, Denise was shocked to discover redness. When she looked up into her daughter's face for an explanation, she saw a torrent of tears.

Ida confessed first and Katie confirmed the abuse. During recess periods in December, the older boys had taken them out into the woods to show them "what the animals do." And they were doing it again.

The household spent a miserable sleepless night. The next morning both Denise and Geneviève escorted their daughters to school to confront Monsieur Molines. Appropriately appalled, he swore the culprits would be punished and the heinous practice stopped. But that didn't mollify Denise. The more understanding, compassion, embarrassment, and regret Patrick Molines expressed, the more Denise bore down on him.

It wasn't until Denise and Geneviève had walked halfway home that the bitter winter cold worked its way into Denise's clothes and cooled her down enough for her to understand what had happened. The rape of Ida and Katie was an inexcusable offense, but by berating poor Patrick Molines viciously, Denise wasn't just pouring out righteous indignation. She was releasing all the pent-up sealed-off emotion and trauma inflicted on herself, her family, and the world-at-large by the hideous never-ending war.

Chapter Ten

INTO THE NIGHT

February 22, 1943

In mid-February, the French agreed to deliver another ten thousand foreign Jews to the Germans from the so-called unoccupied zone. Another rafle began; André and Alin were not surprised. They were relieved when late one night toward the end of the month, they found Pastor Donadille—with his sallow cheeks, graying temples and thin nose almost hooked over his upper lip, and wearing his habitual ill-fitting suit of black—hammering heavily at their kitchen door.

"Thank God," André said softly. "We thought you'd never come."

The wives joined and hugged their husbands.

"*Mesdames,*" the pastor breathed, reflexively offering a quick courtesy.

Two packed duffel bags rested next to the door. Heavy coats and berets hung on the backs of kitchen chairs.

"Listen," the pastor told the men, "we have just learned your names have been entered onto the list. Early tomorrow morning the police will come to take you away."

"Damned Milice," Alin growled.

"No, the gendarmes I think," Pastor Donadille said.

"Thank you for coming Pastor," Denise said feelingly. "We were hoping not to be forgotten."

The pastor looked perplexed so André explained, "We knew it would come to this. We just didn't know when."

Alin declared angrily, "But it was clear what would follow after Vichy recruited thirty thousand toughs into their mini-SS."

"And even clearer earlier this month," André added, "when the government established *Le Service du Travail Obligatoire.* Once they were forced to call up whole age-groups of native-born citizens for obligatory work in Germany, how long could it be before they finally came for us?"

"How did you learn about tomorrow?" André asked the reverend.

"Let me just say 'friends,'" Marc Donadille offered reluctantly. "I would prefer not to be so mysterious, but it's better this way. You understand: too much knowledge is dangerous. One must guard against such information falling into the wrong hands."

"Bastards," Alin snorted. "Traitors."

Pastor Donadille shook his head. "It's a sad day when the French throw in with the Germans. Have we learned nothing from so many wars, so much bloodshed, and so many lives lost?"

"What happens now?" Denise asked, trembling.

Rounding on the brothers again the pastor explained, "I will escort you to others. They will take you to safety some little distance from here—but hurry. We have no more time to lose."

"What about our family?" André begged. "Will they be safe too?"

"The Resistance will see to them," the pastor replied. "Don't you have reason to believe? Because of someone else you know?" He looked deeply, knowingly, into André's eyes.

"Perhaps," André said vaguely.

"Then let us begin our journey."

Denise clasped her husband. "It's cruel and unjust," she said sorrowfully. Then she released him.

"Just one more minute," André said to the pastor. He reached into his pocket, pulled out a small velvet pouch, and handed it to Denise. "The diamonds," he told her. "You know where to go and who will help if you need to sell them."

Alin went to the mantel above the fireplace and returned with a thick leather notebook he gave to Geneviève. "Here are our livestock records and the plan for the garden that has worked so well. If you're still here when spring comes, just follow this schedule of plantings."

Geneviève listlessly turned the pages. "So meticulous," she said, her voice husky with unshed tears. "February twenty-first. You made your last entry today."

"Ready?" Pastor Donadille asked prodding gently.

"Just let me kiss the girls," André pleaded.

"Don't wake them," Denise counseled. "We'll give your love to them and Rose."

"Come quickly," the pastor urged, looking at the clock showing close to midnight. In an instant, they were gone as Marc Donadille led André and Alin out the door into thick snow. The night was still and cold. The sky was filled with a multitude of stars, but only a thin sliver of moon.

"Can you see well enough?" the pastor whispered to the brothers.

"Just," André responded for both.

"Best make do," the pastor insisted. "Who knows who might be up even at this hour?"

Lapsing into silence, they picked up speed going downhill.

"Be careful not to dislodge any rocks," the pastor cautioned. "Make no unnecessary noise."

They reached the darkened café at the base of the hill, turned west, and went on. After leaving the main road, André's wasn't certain where they were. But the night was intensely beautiful. He could just discern the peaks of the nearby mountains standing out against the sharp night sky. Little villages and small clusters of houses half-hidden in the darkness loomed, sheltered by trees nestled along the mountainsides.

No lights could be seen. Only the occasional bark of a dog disturbed the tranquility.

"You're sure of the way?" Alin asked the pastor anxiously. "This path is safe?"

"I'm not going to lie to you Monsieur," Pastor Donadille said gravely. "Men have died of the cold in these mountains, falling and freezing in the snow. So watch your step."

They tramped uphill and down around bend after bend. Despite Pastor Donadille's familiarity with the terrain, his ability to find his way surely on a lightless night was remarkable.

As the three approached yet another road, the pastor stopped short and softly whistled a strange distinctive series of notes like the call of an exceptionally musical bird. All listened intently. Another low whistle sounded the same notes as the pastor's.

He led them forward again slowly. André could just make out a shadow breaking away from some deeper dark, shifting direction and growing larger as it neared.

"Donadille?" the shadow called softly.

The pastor motioned the shadow forward. It assumed the silhouette of a man.

"Christophe Brett," Donadille intoned, "I leave these brothers in your capable hands."

"I will do all I can for them," Christophe promised. "You take care."

The pastor shook hands all around then drew away into the night.

"Come," the new guide said, motioning, and leading the brothers across the road.

"Where are we going?" Alin asked once the new guide had gotten them onto a wooded path.

Christophe Brett made no reply, so André said quietly, "I'm sure we'll be there soon."

"How far must we travel?" Alin persisted. "I don't like being kept in the dark."

Not catching the joke, Christophe said somberly, "Those who will hide you live about three kilometers from Soleyrols. But it's down then up so it takes longer than it should."

They walked on quickly, but slowed when the way fell into the deep shadow of trees. They could hear water streaming down the mountainside into the broad valley they traversed, helping to direct Christophe. Far, far away another mountain could barely be discerned.

Then they came to an old mill perched on the side of a dam long since breached. The spillway was empty now and water the dam could no longer contain rushed by, some feet below.

The brothers followed Christophe across the mill's threshold. What once had been a door had crumbled against the stonewall inside, years or even decades before.

"What now?" Alin demanded.

"We wait," Christophe answered serenely. "Someone will come for you soon."

Only a few of the roof beams were still intact. The small building itself was solid stone. Some fallen timber gave the men a place to sit. Christophe took off his knapsack and tossed it into a corner. André and Alin set down their duffel bags.

"It's safer to talk here than outside," Christophe told the brothers.

As their eyes became more attuned to the dark, they could tell he was young, fresh out of the lycée and roughly the same middling height and build as the Severins. With a fair complexion, his angular face was dominated by a prominent whisker-free chin.

André asked, "Why would you risk your life to help strangers like us?"

"I am Cévenol," Christophe responded in a voice rich with sympathy. "My family lives here. My ancestors are buried here. We have always been a strong people who value independence of thought, conscience, and action, and who cherish freedom—not just from ignorance and harassment, but from laws that protect the few and degrade the many." Christophe spoke more and more quickly, his voice rising in pitch but not volume. "Now the Germans have come and our cowardly French authorities and police have sold out our heritage, pride, and very name. But I am not one of them and neither are most of us in the Lozère. So I resist, working with others of like mind. I know how to write and I'm good with figures; when I dress like a shopkeeper, I can blend in; and I have legs strong enough for the longest walks, so I serve as a courier for the pastors and the growing Resistance. But it is dangerous. Too many cooperate with the Germans hoping to get into their good graces. One needs to be careful."

"More careful than that," a deep voice sounded unexpectedly from the doorway, startling Christophe and the Severins. Then the large shadowed man chuckled warmly and Christophe relaxed visibly. Something about this fellow seemed eerily familiar, but the Severins couldn't place him. "Remember my young friend," the big man continued, "for now *they* have the upper hand so *we* must be stealthy and cagey—do all we can but hold our tongues and wait patiently."

"For what?" Christophe asked.

"Opportunities. Organization. Direction. Right now, we're too fragmented, too weak to take action. We're lucky we can do as much as we already do: protect people."

"Like us?" André said.

"Like you," the other agreed. "By the by, I'm Émile Brignand." He laughed his deep warm laugh. "Don't look so surprised. My brother and I look alike but not as alike as you two!" Émile squatted down beside them. "I'm here to take you the rest of the way. But don't thank me. I'm glad to help, but I'm more glad to do something against the Germans." He stood again. "We should go before it gets too light."

Striding to the door, he glanced about then motioned all to follow. At the threshold, the brothers looked at Christophe, and tapped their berets as they would have tipped their hats in Brussels. Then they followed Émile one way as Christophe went the other.

They leapt rocks to cross the stream. Émile led them through a grove of chestnut trees interspersed with oak, poplar, and ash, which formed a leafy canopy over sparse underbrush.

Climbing upward on paths lined with ancient stone walls, they finally came to an opening on a level plain. Sky lightening with the approach of dawn they saw the gray shapes of stone houses crowded close together along a path wide enough for an ox cart.

"Here," Émile whispered gently lifting the door latch of one of the larger houses, next to a barn. The three slipped inside almost silently.

"There," Émile said. "We're home."

Standing awkwardly, Alin muttered, "Thanks."

André quickly added, "We will never be able to express our appreciation adequately."

Émile waved off their words in embarrassment.

"I don't want to light a lamp yet," he told them gruffly, covering his emotion. "Someone might see and it wouldn't do for anyone to suspect I've changed my routine."

Émile hovered over the broad deep fireplace of the house he shared with his mother. The fire had been banked to smolder overnight but Émile wielded a poker, disturbing ashes and exposing a soft red glow. He fed in a few small sticks and as tongues of flame licked them, added some larger chunks of wood. Shortly, warmth crept out taking the edge off the profound cold.

Outside a dog began barking. Then the rooster started in waking the hens and some fifteen residents of a settlement too small to call itself a village.

The sun began rising behind the mountains casting long shadows onto the clustered houses of the farmers of this difficult and much-loved land. How beautiful it was: the trees close together on the sheltering hillside, the gently sloping fields, and the careful stonework of the old masons who had deployed their skills as no contemporary could match. Émile wondered whether the Severins would cherish the way those men had worked the rock into homes that would last for generations—how though driven by hard necessity they had been proud enough to take the time to create lovely arches over doors and passageways. Would these city-bred brothers even notice the painstaking care taken in carving the moldings around windows and doors?

Smoke rose through the tall chimney to the open sky. Even in this remote habitation, people felt compelled to shut their doors at night against the threat of the hated German interlopers and their French lackeys. Still, Émile believed this place was secure for the moment.

In this hamlet, everyone knew everyone else as their parents and grandparents had and on and on. Émile believed each of them felt the same troubled way about the latest in the region's long line of oppressors. Nevertheless, the history and hard experiences of the Cévenols had bred a preternatural caution into him. He knew nothing could be taken for granted.

Having dozed uneasily for a few short hours on a wooden bench and three rush-seated chairs pushed together, Émile's guests blinked, rubbed their eyes, and looked confused.

"It's okay," Émile called out. "Coffee's on its way."

"Where are we?" André asked sleepily.

"Le Massufret," Émile replied reaching past pots, crocks, and trivets hooked over the fireplace to the coffeepot held above the flames by a crane. "Too small to find on a map—with luck, too small to find at all." He poured the brew into tin cups that grew hot instantly, but the handles were cool enough to hold. "It's not much," he admitted, offering the cups to the brothers, "and not real, but better than nothing."

André shook himself, stretched, and stood up to take his cup. Alin remained motionless.

"I can't stop thinking about our family," the younger brother said anxiously.

"We can't control the situation." André sounded stiffly professorial. "Their safety, like ours, now rests in the hands of others."

Émile held out the second cup again. Alin accepted it wordlessly.

"I'll be just a minute," Émile said flatly, stepping over to the front door to give the brothers a minute to themselves and to take a precautionary look outside.

He pulled the solid wooden door to and immediately was revived by the fresh mountain air after his own sleepless night. Le Massufret appeared peaceful. He didn't see a single soul until the door to the next house opened and Pasqual Platon emerged.

"Morning," Pasqual called cheerfully, heading straight Émile's way.

"'Day," Émile offered—his standard reply.

Pasqual was small, but strongly built. His shirt and brown sweater with holes at the elbows were a too-tight fit. Like Émile, Pasqual wore the blue cotton pants common to the region—comfortable, easy to wash, and not very costly.

"So?" Pasqual asked.

"Yes," Émile responded.

"Where?"

"In there."

Émile returned to the dark interior. Pasqual followed in his wake and welcomed the Severins, smiling enthusiastically, taking each one's hand in turn, and giving it a short hard shake.

"Friend?" André asked Émile, puzzled and slightly unnerved.

"Brother-in-law."

"Good," Alin said relaxing his tensed shoulders. "Family."

"So you know about us too," André said to Pasqual.

"We all do in Le Massufret," Pasqual explained. "Which I assure you is okay. You can trust us. As for the other little villages hereabouts—well most are like us. Some are a little strange and may have funny ideas." He began muttering in a Cévenol accent so thick the Severins couldn't understand much, but could make out "Fascists" and "bastards."

"You must be hungry," Émile told the brothers, changing the subject.

"I'm too nervous to be hungry," Alin complained.

"It's fine to be nervous or hungry but not at the same time, eh?" Pasqual joked.

"You still have to eat," Émile insisted, glaring at his brother-in-law.

Going over to the cupboard, he brought out a round loaf of crusty bread blackened by baking in the beehive oven at the back of the fireplace. Then the bedroom door flew open.

"You're making an awful noise for men who are supposed to be secretive."

The rotund, wizened woman—white hair tied loosely into a bun at the back of her loose-fleshed neck—shuffled forth with a broad smile of welcome.

"Mother," Émile said. "Did we wake you?"

"I've been up for hours," she said. "You know I never sleep much anymore."

Émile presented Lucille Brignand, who said with satisfaction, "So these are the famous Severin brothers." Wearing a faded blue dress and a lighter blue checked apron securely fastened around her ample waist, she was pale and wrinkled; but her fine brown eyes were clear and bright. "So what do you think of my boy?" she asked reaching a hand to tousle Émile's thinning black hair. "I keep telling him to do something about this mop. It's ridiculous no?—growing out like a great big bush at the sides and the back. No wonder he's never found a woman." She gave a little laugh to show she didn't mean it. "But I love the blue of his eyes, don't you?—even if those brows are too bushy. He has good color too—ruddy from long hours in the sun and from the wind that always blows down into this valley. Here," she said taking the loaf out of her son's hands, which seemed too large for the rest of him and were spoiled by dirty uneven fingernails "All of you sit," Lucille commanded, motioning to the single large table. "You can stay too," she told sheepish-looking Pasqual. Then she shot him a sharp look. "Unless you have something better to do."

"I'd better get back to my wife," he said meekly.

"My daughter you mean."

"I'm sure she's got breakfast ready now," Pasqual said, backing out the door.

Émile's mother cut the bread into large slices then fetched a crock of butter from the small room off the kitchen and returned to spread a small amount onto each slice. She also brought back a jar of blackberry preserves with which she was more generous. Not bothering with plates, she just handed out the slices.

Émile tore off a piece and dipped into his coffee. Lucille stoked the fire muttering, "You'd think a grown man would know how to get more warmth into this place."

After some minutes, André asked quietly, "Now what do we do?"

Émile shrugged. "Stay here for a bit. Then we'll take you someplace safer."

"Believe it," Lucille said, patting Émile's head. "Such a good boy."

"I just can't get to sleep." Denise returned to the kitchen, drawing a blanket around her shoulders.

Geneviève, staring blankly, gathered her shawl about her. The stove was already cold though embers glowed softly under ash in one corner of the firebox.

"I can't sleep either," she said.

The sisters sat silently, side by side, listening to the gentle rhythmic breathing of their children in another room. One of the older girls uttered the softest cry. Then all was quiet again.

"I'm so afraid," Geneviève finally admitted.

"We need to make plans," Denise said. "The police will come for us sooner or later."

"How are we to manage in the meantime—on our own?"

"Don't worry so," Denise counseled herself as much as her sister, "we will do what we must."

"But what do we tell the children and when?"

"We'll figure it out in the morning," Denise said suddenly weary of talking. "Let's get some sleep," she suggested yawning. "We're going to need it."

"I'll sleep later," Geneviève replied in a thin voice. "Not yet."

She got up and went out onto the terrace. The night's stillness was broken by the call of an owl hunting. The pigs and sheep bedded down below rustled about. The goats in the little barn sounded restless too, but that was just their way.

Geneviève knew the gendarmes were bound to walk up the path soon. She listened for footsteps or muffled voices floating on the breeze. Staring out into the dark, she could barely perceive frost on the rocks of the path poking black above the thin mantel of snow and glistening in the starlight.

Exhausted, she went back into the kitchen and cradled her head on the refectory table.

Feeling the warmth of the sun on her back, Geneviève opened her eyes. There was Denise surrounded by children, holding Cristian in her arms.

"I'm hungry Didi," Katie said using her nickname for Aunt Denise.

"Me too Maman," Ida echoed.

"Shortly," Denise promised. "First, I need to tell you something." Katie and Ida perched on stools. Christel and Philippe clung to her skirts. "Your fathers have gone away," she said in a clear comforting voice. "They didn't want to. They had to."

Katie's eyes began to water.

"But why, Maman?" Ida demanded sounding close to tears herself.

"To be safe. Now you must get ready for school," Denise said heating up the bajana.

"But where did they go?" Katie asked. "Somewhere nearby?"

"Spain," Denise answered spontaneously—to protect the children from the truth (*I don't know!*) and to keep them from accidentally saying anything revealing to anyone. "Where our friends Sebastian and Emmanuel come from."

"Then we will see them again?" Ida asked almost prayerfully. "Soon?"

"Oh certainly you'll see them again," Geneviève assured them all. Fully awake now she joined Denise at the stove and ladled thick chestnut soup out of the black pot.

"But when?" Katie squealed. "When?"

Geneviève carried the soup to the table and sliced coarse brown bread and a little cheese.

"Maman," Christel asked, "is there an apple? I'd like an apple."

"No dear," her mother replied. "They're all gone. You know that."

"Is the war coming here?" Ida asked calmly.

Geneviève and Denise exchanged a look.

"We hope not," Denise replied steadily, hoping the children could neither see nor feel her sadness. "Come," she said, forcing a smile onto her face. "It won't do to be late for school."

Geneviève dropped Christel, Philippe and Cristian off to play with Rose then walked Katie and Ida to school. Denise sat on the terrace shielding her still-tired eyes against the early morning sunrays, slanting across the distant mountains. Overnight frost turned slowly to dew.

Fear of the gendarmes kept her wide-eyed and alert. Since they wouldn't find André and Alin, would they arrest the mothers instead? Or worse, want the children? She paced the veranda then saw what she expected: two French policemen in their distinctive blue uniforms and caps walking slowly up the path. In a sense she was relieved. At least she would soon know what would happen.

"Good morning," the younger of the two men called lightly in a surprisingly kindly tone.

Looking down, Denise judged him to be about fifty—too old to have been drafted in the war's earlier days and now safe from other duties since the Germans needed police to help keep order locally. The second man was older. He trudged up to the terrace with a slight limp, likely from service in the Great War. After that horror ended, ranks of the gendarmes had been filled by returning veterans.

The policemen touched their caps politely with their forefingers as they reached the landing. The man who had already spoken said, "Madame, I am Officer Pellet and this is my superior Brigadier Salager. Sorry to disturb you, but may we see Messieurs André and Alin?"

"They're not here," Denise replied surprised by the offhand manner she simulated.

"Excuse me Madame Severin," Brigadier Salager said politely, "but where are they and when will they return? We have been ordered to ask them to come with us."

"Why?"

"I don't ask why Madame," the brigadier replied. "I get my orders and follow them."

"I don't know where they are or when we'll see them again," Denise replied truthfully.

"We don't doubt you Madame," Pellet said, "but may we look inside? We must make a report no matter what. So we must see with our own eyes."

Salager added, "Almost all the men searched for in the Lozère are not home. But it's not our problem if your men have gone. And the authorities are not interested in women or children...today."

The officers went through La Font rapidly then returned to the veranda.

"Just as you say," Officer Pellet affirmed. "They're not here."

"If and when you do see your men," Brigadier Salager admonished, "tell them they must report to the police in Vialas immediately without fail."

The gendarmes walked down the path more rapidly than they had come up. When they rounded the bend and disappeared among the trees, Denise breathed a sigh of relief.

The Resistance got it right, she thought. *We can trust what they say.*

The first few days underground passed slowly for the Severin brothers. They ate. They caught up on lost sleep. They fretted about their loved ones and the future. They talked with Émile, his mother, and his brother-in-law until there was nothing left to say.

"It's no good! I'm worried about our family!" Alin exploded one morning.

"But we'll know in good time," Émile said, perplexed by this unprovoked outburst.

"What? What will you know?"

"When they might be in danger."

"How?"

"How did we know about you?" Turning abruptly Émile snarled, "I'm going out," and stormed off.

Émile's departure exacerbated Alin's agitation. Émile could step out whenever he liked, but the Severins were trapped in the house because of a barium mine across the ravine, from which they could be seen. They knew something of the mine because of Sebastian and Emmanuel.

"Some of the miners come every day from Vialas, La Planche, even Génolhac," Émile had told them. "They don't concern us. But many live in small houses close by. Mostly they support the Resistance, but about some, we're not sure. I think that at least one is a collaborateur, so we have to be very careful, especially at this time of year. With the leaves off the trees, everyone and everything is plainly visible."

"I miss the fresh air and sunlight," André confessed to Alin after Émile had gone out. "Of course we had those days in Brussels too, but never experienced them in such abundance as here in the Lozère."

Alin grunted, sitting in the corner by the fire, trying to stay warm. "I just don't see how Geneviève and Denise can keep up with all the work at La Font while taking care of five little ones. It's not as if Mother can help much at her age, apart from minding the children—when they're on their best behavior."

"At least the chestnuts are dry and peeled. And there are plenty of root vegetables and jellies, jams and canned goods. And they still have Emmy to butcher."

Alin tensed up again. "But turning the soil and starting the spring plantings..."

"Why worry now? Who knows where we'll be when the ground melts?"

Alin got up and paced. "Everyone thinks selling stamps is a tedious business, but I can't remember ever being this bored," he complained. "Anything would be better than just sitting."

"We could be 'just sitting' in a camp like Drancy," André reminded him. "Here at least we're among friends, friends we've never met before who are taking a terrible risk by hiding us." He lowered his voice, hoping not to be overheard by Lucille in the kitchen. "The Brignands don't have much, yet they feed us three meals a day without complaint or compensation. All we have to do is withstand a little monotony."

Émile came back for lunch. Alin assaulted him verbally when he stepped through the door.

"What are we going to do?" Alin demanded. "I'll go mad if I stay inside much longer."

"We have some ideas." Émile rubbed his big hands together. He was as fed up as Alin with the present situation and just as anxious for a change.

They ate their meager meal of coarse bread and watery soup in silence. Then Émile pushed back from the table and jammed his blue beret onto his head, completely covering his large round bald spot but leaving tufts of hair as a fringe around the rim of the cap.

"You stay inside another day or so," he said. "I'll be back."

Émile opened the door, looked about cautiously, shut the paneled door behind him, set the latch securely, and left quickly.

"Now what do we do?" Alin whined.

"Wait," André said tonelessly. "Just...wait."

Hours later, Émile returned in better humor and announced, "It's settled. Up and over the ridge, past the road that runs along the crest line of the mountains, and down into the next valley, there's a couple by the name of Guin..."

"Guin?" André interrupted. "Like the Hotel Guin in Vialas?"

"Related," Émile replied smiling. "But these Guins live in the little village of Le Tronc—well not really a village anymore because the five homes are empty except for the Guins. All the fields and barns are theirs now since everyone else either died or moved away—including their son who was taken into the Army. Sadly, like so many, they don't even know where he is. So they're on our side and they'll be happy to have you. Plus if you're willing to help out on the farm you'll be able to work outside again and the Guins will be grateful."

"When do we leave?" Alin asked hoping it would be immediately.

André turned his most serious gaze on Émile. "You believe it's safe for us?"

"As safe as we can make it," Émile answered compassionately. "As long as the Germans occupy France, there's danger everywhere. But I'm convinced you'll be safer there than here, maybe safer than ourselves."

Again Alin asked, "When do we leave?"

"Tomorrow night should be good. The partial moon will provide enough light to see by, but not so much that we'll be spotted easily, especially if we keep to the shadows as we'll have to when we get close to the mine. They have some dogs down there—not fearsome, but they do like to bark, and we don't want them announcing us."

"Will you come right back?" his mother asked from the kitchen entrance, the tremor in her voice betraying worry.

"I'll have to stay over," Émile replied, "but only for one night. Le Tronc is too far for me to get home before daylight breaks. You wouldn't want me to be discovered would you?"

As Émile looked out, a chill crept down the mountainsides, swirling silently among the trees, backing and filling around the buildings, pressing the last of the day's warmth deep inside the interiors of the outbuildings of Le Massufret. The stars were shining, crisp in their mottled patterns across the sky, some brighter than others, all pulsing faintly, irregularly. A sliver of moon had just appeared above the deeply dark horizon.

Shutting his front door, Émile felt the cold push against the closed shutters of his house. He knocked lightly on the door to the back room where André and Alin had spent nights sleeping on thin narrow beds.

"Time," Émile called feeling an odd mix of anticipation and regret.

The door cracked open. André stood fastening his coat. Behind him, Alin finished lacing up his boots. Each brother picked up a canvas duffel bag and slipped its large corded handle loosely over a shoulder. Neither spoke as Émile led them into the kitchen.

"Here," Lucille said handing out packets containing bread, a large piece of hard cheese, several slices of cold ham, and a small cake. "You take care. All of you."

Émile opened the front door again, glanced out, and led the Severins into the night.

They walked quickly along the side of the house then ducked into the small passageway between the Brignand barn and the village wall that held the slope of the earth in place. Frost was just beginning to form on the outlying rocks.

At the end of the barn, Émile hesitated then started again, giving the Severins a slight encouraging wave from a hand held close to his waist. They moved rapidly across the open area in front of the last abandoned house of Le Massufret before slipping into the shadows of the path leading down into the valley. Émile slowed down for stones that were not set firmly in the path. Though he could negotiate them safely, even in the dark, the brothers Severin could not.

Despite the slower pace, the frozen gravel tended to slip out from under the brothers' feet. Following Émile's lead, they felt for the sides of the surrounding walls at regular intervals, maintaining their balance as the trail wound down one way and then another in the steeper places, gradually straightening as the slope leveled out.

Coming to a mountain stream, Émile listened to the soft noise of branching rivulets and the plunging of water starting its long journey to the Rhône River and thence the Mediterranean. Then he led them carefully across a narrow footbridge that offered no support railing. As all three climbed up and away from the streambed, they reached the dirt road to the barium mine. The outlines of the workers' houses set into the hillside looming above and to the right appeared in the dim light.

All was quiet, the mine's machinery having been shut down as sunlight faded and the exhausted miners having gone to bed soon after. Suddenly a dog barked. It growled and barked again, louder this time. The door to its house opened and a man stood framed in the doorway by the light of the lantern he held above his head as he peered out into the dark.

Émile and the brothers crouched down instinctively and stayed motionless, hardly daring to breathe as the dog gave one more short sharp bark and came close, its excited panting and the scrabble of its paws on the cartway stones audible as it neared. Émile picked up a large rock but just then, the dog's master gave a whistle and a call stopping the dog in its tracks. The miner gave another stronger call and the dog hesitated, caught between its determination to seek out the strangers and its desire to obey.

At last, the dog turned around and slowly trotted back to its doorway, scrambled up the wooden steps, and ran back through the open door. Then the door shut and darkness enveloped the cartway again.

The Severins released their long-held breath.

"I don't like other people's dogs," Émile whispered heatedly. "No telling what they'll do." He carefully put down the rock and stood up stiffly. "Let's go," he commanded, "before that dog needs to come out again."

They ran to the left, sheltering behind small trees and wagons, and then moved faster still, the rut of the road having been smoothed by the passage of carts down the sloping hillside. Émile took a path that turned off the road and led up the mountainside. The travelers scrabbled up the embankment, passing through grasses and brittle brown broom bushes. Before long, the path was surrounded by trees. Émile kept going until shadows hid them and the road they had left behind and below was fully obscured.

"We're safe now," he whispered breathlessly, "at least from the miners." His chest heaved as he gulped and gasped for air, bracing himself against a tree.

André took his bag off and set it down, breathing as deeply as Émile. Only Alin appeared to have taken the effort in stride.

Several minutes later, Émile forced himself to say, "We'd better be going." Without complaint, André shouldered his burden again and all started back up the path, which grew steeper and steeper, zigzagging back and forth as they staggered toward the ridge. Trees gave way to broom bushes again and short clumps of heather, dotted occasionally by stunted trees, permanently bent away from the wind.

At the crest, it was easier to see. The moon, three-quarters high in the sky, caused the silhouettes the men cast alongside the path to stand out more clearly. As they came close to the highest point, Émile whispered, "Let's rest here."

He picked out a large rock outcropping on which they all sat gratefully. They opened Lucille's packets and ate hungrily.

Émile left the Severins to scout out the Route des Crêtes, carved more than two thousand years before by the Romans during their conquest of the Gauls. The thinly layered gravel road ran from mountaintop to mountaintop overlooking the valleys below. The headlights of any approaching vehicle would be visible from far away, but Émile knew to be cautious. Before the war, he had gone wherever he liked altogether unafraid. Now he had to guard against assumptions and overconfidence.

No lights were on in the buildings, far below where a few families lived. Even small birds and hawks had abandoned this high ridge for the night.

Émile returned to the brothers and reassured them. In single file, they climbed to the high road and walked rapidly several hundred yards.

"We'll go down here," Émile announced, gesturing toward a cartway that diverged from the route along the crest.

They walked through flickering starlight filtered through trees that grew wherever the mountainside provided shelter. The farther down the mountain they went, the trees grew to a more normal height and less bent from the wind. Still short by lowland standards, these oaks were large for the mountains of the Cévennes, their thick trunks indicating great age.

A small stream worked its way down the mountain seeking the valley floor. As the moon reached its apogee, Émile saw a cluster of buildings in the cup of the tilted valley.

Le Tronc was far more remote than Le Massufret. Surrounded by bushes, with grassy slopes and rocky outcroppings instead of trees, Émile felt sure the Severins would be less subject to exposure there. As far as he knew, département officials in Mende weren't aware it existed let alone that Léon and Yvonne Guin still managed to scratch a modest living out of the hard unforgiving ground. Perhaps the mayor of Saint Frézal-de-Ventalon knew about them, but he never interfered. How could he? Léon Guin held no truck with governmental obstruction or dictates. He lived as he chose.

Moving through the last turnings of the cartway and along the walkways that divided the buildings of Le Tronc one from another, Émile rounded the last corner and felt relieved seeing geraniums flowering in pots ranged alongside a doorway. The plaster on the house's front façade was still in place after three centuries. The wooden door's lion-headed knocker was strangely ornate for this obscure place.

Émile rapped with his knuckles since the big brass knocker would sound throughout the valley. It made no sense to announce their arrival at an unseemly hour to anyone but the Guins.

A voice called from the other side, "Yes?"

"I'm here with the brothers," Émile said as loudly as he dared.

The door's bolt drew back and a very thin face peered out. Light from a lantern set on a table inside cast a pale yellow glow onto the new arrivals.

After examining the three faces closely, Léon Guin stepped back. The men entered without further invitation and Léon quickly shut the door, slid the bolt into place, walked back to the kerosene lantern, and adjusted the wick to burn more brightly.

"You made good time," Léon said crustily. "We weren't expecting you for hours." Solemnly, he put out his hand to offer strong handshakes all around. "Welcome," he said as if taking in two refugees in the middle of the night was just ordinary hospitality.

Léon was a spare rustic gentleman, thin and angular, of medium height, with wisps of white hair floating above ruby cheeks and a prominent nose bent at the tip as if the Romans had left behind a reminder of their former dominance. An impish smile broke across his face.

"Come Mother," he called cheerfully to his wife. "I don't think they'll bite."

Yvonne Guin emerged from the next room, a greatcoat wrapped around her nightgown. Her bare feet made her appear even shorter than her five feet. She too was thin. Her soft sparse graying hair was tied back in a tight bun leaving only a few straggling strands to dance across her forehead. She offered her welcome with unmistakable warmth that contrasted powerfully with her husband's inscrutability.

"Good to have you," Yvonne said holding out her hands for her new guests to take in turn. "Come sit. You've had a long walk."

Léon shot Émile a look of deep concern. "Any problems?"

"No. Though a dog by the mine gave us a start with its barking."

At Yvonne's cheerful insistence, each man pulled a chair up to the large well-lit table, which was used, as was the custom in the region, for everything from preserving fruits and vegetables to butchering sides of meat to kneading dough to sewing.

"These are the Guins," Émile said properly introducing the parties he had brought together. He hadn't thought to do so sooner since everyone knew everyone else in the area, making introductions unnecessary. "And these are the Severin brothers. One is André and the other is Alin. Even after spending five days together I still can't tell them apart."

That was Émile's way of letting Alin know all had been forgiven.

André identified himself and Yvonne, turning, said, "Then you must be Alin. And you must all be hungry."

She brought several pieces of three-day-old bread out of the cupboard. From the small pantry at the back of the house—below ground level since like La Font the house had been built into the slope of the land—she retrieved butter and raspberry preserves.

"Émile," she asked invitingly, "you'll stay?"

"Just for a bit of rest," he sighed. "I was going to wait a day to go back but there's no danger in me walking around mid-afternoon. Only at an hour such as this could my appearance arouse suspicions."

Late winter lay about La Font with the cold, sometimes snowy, broken by occasional warmer, days in which clouds from the west broke open to reveal bright blue skies. Every now and then, a gentle softness breezed in from the Mediterranean forcing the bitter Atlantic air north. But even when new-fallen snow melted quickly, the ground remained frozen. Would this winter never end?

Denise and Geneviève swiftly settled into constant work and worry. They took comfort in Albertine's assurance that the greater part of the local gendarmerie was friendly, sympathetic, and resistant to distant authorities. But official orders working their way from Mende to the post in Le Pont-de-

Montvert and then on to Vialas, came directly from the Gestapo, making them impossible to ignore. Thanks to secretaries sympathetic to the Resistance, most times the police knew before the orders were sent out and did their best to help the intended victims.

Unfortunately, the treacherous, devious, merciless Milice thugs acted on behalf of the Gestapo independently of the police. So the postman kept Geneviève and Denise abreast of the Milice's latest movements by hinting and winking, and starting sentences he never finished.

They also got the idea from him that the Resistance was daily becoming larger, better organized, and more reliable. Old-timers at the café agreed, insisting the enemy weakened as the resisters—newly dubbed "Maquisards"— grew stronger and more numerous.

Overwhelmed by their tasks and fearful of their fate, the Freedman sisters still did their part to fight the Fascists by listening to the BBC each night after the children had settled down to sleep. Denise faithfully remembered what she could—say the fighting in Tunisia with von Arnim's Panzer attack on British positions at Majâz-al-Bâb or Montgomery's assault on Rommel's position along the Mareth Line—and then passed it along to the postman as André and Alin had done.

Denise and Geneviève were now barely distinguishable from the other hardworking women of the Cévennes, who also suffered from the enforced absence of their men. Denise was particularly struck by what Geneviève had become capable of doing and putting up with.

"I don't mind the smell of the animals anymore," Geneviève told Denise one day in early March, "not even the goats, maybe because now we all smell pretty much the same."

But neither could get used to not hearing from their husbands.

"I should be stoic and bite my tongue," Geneviève complained, "but you're my sister and I have to tell someone: I'm constantly worried about Alin, and André too of course."

"The postman says they're safe."

"Too vague," Geneviève keened. "If only he could tell us where they are."

Before Geneviève could upset her too much, Denise said, "What we don't know we can't reveal."

"Madame Denise!" the postman called out hurriedly. "Madame Geneviève!"

As he reached the veranda stairs, Ida came around the farmhouse followed by the other children.

"'Madame' is in the field," Ida called out gaily, skipping and running. Excited and bright-eyed she asked the postman, "Anything for us?"

"Let me check," he said playfully feeling around in his leather pouch. "Oh dear. Sorry. But as long as I'm here may I please speak with your mothers? Run and get them for me won't you? Quickly now, my darlings. I've still got a long way to go."

Ida and Katie ran off to the upper field and the postman strolled over to sit on the stone wall by the barn, glad for a moment to rest. Christel and Philippe followed and Christel asked, "What do you want to say to Maman?"

The amused postman chucked her under the chin. "Nothing that would interest you two. Grown-up news, maybe. Or just thoughts. Yes that's it. Just thinking."

"We think too," Philippe asserted.

"And what do you think about?" the postman asked.

"About when the rabbits are going to have little bunnies again. Also about our chickens and why they don't lay as many eggs as they used to."

"We're the ones who feed them," Christel added proudly.

"But Ida is the one who writes it all down in the book my father used to keep."

Philippe scuffed his wooden shoes on the grass alongside the gravel path. He had outgrown his last pair of leather shoes and since leather was hard to come by, had switched to wooden clogs, common footwear throughout the Lozère.

"I'm glad you think," the postman told him. "Not enough people think—not for themselves at any rate. As they should—and must." He leaned down, bringing his face close to Philippe's to make an impression. "Never stop thinking for yourself." He slowly straightened up and looked down at Christel who peered up at him intently. "You too little girl."

Then he spotted Ida and Katie racing back down from the field that stretched above the house and its collection of outbuildings. Their mothers followed.

"Mesdames," the postman called politely, standing. When they were within range of his speaking voice, he said, "Perhaps we could talk for a moment? Away from the children."

"Children," Denise called, suddenly apprehensive. "Back to your chores."

As the young ones left reluctantly, the postman quickly said, "The Germans are preparing the Milice for another sweep of refugees. This time they'll also search for women."

"Why?" Geneviève gasped.

The postman looked over his shoulder. As high on the ridge of the mountain as they were, they could see a great distance and therefore be seen.

"The Resistance has begun to take action. The other day they raided the offices of Le Service du Travail Obligatoire and burned draft cards and destroyed furniture and equipment. Also a train was blown up."

"Oh my!" Denise cried.

"When will they come?" Geneviève demanded.

"Soon I think."

The women nodded. Then Geneviève begged, "Any word of our husbands?"

"Sorry. But today you may be in greater danger than they are. Now I must go," he said dolefully. "I'm afraid you're not the only refugees I need to warn."

"Now what?" Geneviève asked, numb.

"We need to start packing."

"What about the animals?"

"Others will surely want them," Denise stated flatly. "But we'd better make arrangements. Who knows how long we have?"

Denise marched up to the house and straight to the girls' room. Geneviève hurried after.

"We'll start with the children's clothes," Denise said opening cupboards and sifting through small mounds of clothes on the shelves. "Pack them into the little sacks we came with. Sweaters and coats. We'll only have room for a few summer items." She laughed ruefully. "It's good we left something behind each step of the way. We have hardly anything left, which means it will take little effort to figure out how to deal with it all."

"What about the silver and whatever we can't carry?" Geneviève asked. "We can't just leave it on the veranda or we certainly won't ever see it again."

"Into the big metal trunks," Denise replied. "Someone will hold them for us."

They packed sacks rapidly, leaving out what each child needed to wear for a few days.

"What do we tell them?" Geneviève asked.

"Nothing until we have to."

The children raced into the house chattering excitedly.

"Two chickens got loose!" Philippe shouted.

"But it's okay," Ida hastened to explain. "We got them back again."

"But it was hard," Christel said proudly.

"We led them into the pen with corn kernels!" Katie crowed.

Later Denise added dried broom bush branches to the fire and stirred the soup in the big kettle on the quickly heating stovetop. Geneviève laid out the big table with the silver service. She turned the large serving spoon in her hand, examining its details as if hypnotized.

"What are you doing?" Denise asked gently.

"Just thinking we should enjoy some of our finer things one last time before packing them away. It's funny how inanimate objects tied us so completely to life before the war."

After supper the Freedman sisters put their children into their rooms and shut the doors. Then they went into the nearest barn to retrieve the old metal military trunks from Great War days.

Back in the farmhouse, Denise gathered the clothes they would have to leave behind. Geneviève began covering the kitchen table with everything else they would pack away.

Starting to fill the trunks, Geneviève said, "If these things aren't here when we get back..."

Denise cut her off. "They're just things. They're not important."

"They're important to me."

"What's important is that we survive," Denise said pointedly. "Not this stuff."

Suddenly, Geneviève broke down.

"I'm through making decisions!" she cried. "I'm tired of trying to figure out everything and of taking everyone else into consideration. All I want is to be safe. To live a quiet simple life in a little house where I can enjoy what I have instead of packing it up. Without having to worry that the next person to cross our threshold might take us away." She collapsed into the big chair with its heavy wooden arms, put her head into her hands, and began to weep. "I can't live with never-ending fear. We don't even know where we'll be tomorrow."

Denise knelt before her, clasped her knees, and looked up at her steadily. "It's going to be all right," she said with conviction. "As long as we have friends in this region—and as long as we keep up our courage and strength—we'll be fine, I promise."

Geneviève wiped her eyes and managed to give her sister a little smile. Then they started packing again, together.

Soon the trunks were filled. The sisters stuffed an extra layer of sweaters on top of each to keep the silk, linen and silver in place. They carried the trunks into the shed behind the kitchen. Returning, they sat down across from one another at the kitchen table, near the stove. The wind blew forcefully outside penetrating and swirling about the interior, chilling every inch.

"I was hoping to have a little party for Philippe's fourth birthday," Geneviève said more resigned than sad. "At that age it's such a special day."

"We can still have a party," Denise insisted.

"What if we have to leave first? His birthday's not quite a week away."

"We'll hold the party early, marking the end of a phase for us all."

"Then we'd better start planning," Geneviève said firmly. "Best not waste another day."

Katie and Ida were terrifically excited Thursday morning. Monsieur Molines had promised to take the class outside to teach how animals survive winter. That afternoon was Philippe's premature birthday party.

At breakfast, Philippe insisted he already knew how animals survive winter. Katie taunted him into saying, "We put them in the barn and feed them." Then he stuck out his tongue at her—when his mother wasn't looking.

All the children were surprised as Geneviève shaved bits of leftover ham into each bowl of bajana. Stranger still, she doled out unusually large portions of the long grainy bread and then gave them extra cheese.

"Maman," Katie asked suspiciously, "why are you being so generous?"

"Because it's cold outside," Geneviève answered icily. "Eat well so your bodies stay strong." Putting slices of ham next to the bread and cheese she added, "Let's just say it's a special day," and walked away.

A few moments later, Ida went to the bedroom the two sisters now shared to ask her mother a question. Drawing near she overheard Tante Geneviève explain to Denise about giving the children the ham they'd been saving. "Well we may not be here Sunday and we can't take it with us."

"Let's be sure to eat well at supper tonight too," Denise said, "just in case."

Tante Geneviève sank down onto the bed, sniffled and said, "Maybe going through this will make us more like Alin and André."

Denise asked, "You think it's okay for Ida and Katie to go to school today?"

"If they don't someone might become suspicious."

"I'd better pick them up right when school lets out," Denise said, "just in case."

Ida wondered, *Are we going to Spain?* and *In case of what?* But before she could learn any more the bedroom door opened and she hurried back to the kitchen completely forgetting what she wanted to ask.

Patrick Molines sat in front of his class considering how much his work and the schoolhouse itself meant to him. Katie and Ida entered in a rush, took off their coats, and quickly settled on the bench closest to the great round stove.

The schoolmaster rose to add several branches of dried broom bush to the gentle fire that warmed only the center of the room. Ordinarily, he did that habitually, absentmindedly. Now he was intent on noticing everything, even the way the branches crackled as they settled over the glowing coals and burst into flame.

"Attention please, children," the teacher called. When they closed their varied reading-level books he said, "I'm sorry but we won't be going out today." A chorus of disappointment sounded. "I know you were looking forward to visiting the barn down in the village. Maybe we'll do that tomorrow. Today I want to focus on the mountains, streams, trees, and vegetation all around us. I want you to know how they were formed and shaped, how to find your way around them, even how to stay alive in their midst if you ever get lost."

That was foolish, he immediately thought. *I mustn't frighten them. But time is of the essence. Perhaps if they're a little afraid, they'll pay attention.*

Time was of the essence as much for Patrick as anyone. He knew that an intensive roundup was about to begin, since he had been warned by those members of the Resistance who trusted him that he too was in danger. Just thirty-eight years old, he had only been spared in the Vichy government's rafles because as an educator he had been exempt from the march of forced labor. But soon, like so many before him, he would have to leave the village he loved, disappear into the mountains and join the Resistance.

Until then, he was determined to give his charges practical knowledge of their surroundings: the paths through the woods, the secret places known only to locals. He wanted to point out springs it was safe to drink from, tasty and wholesome berries, edible mushrooms and those which must not be touched. Reading, writing and arithmetic were important, but not as important as knowing how to survive.

Patrick kept recess short to use every available minute for instruction. Besides, he wasn't sure it was safe to let the children play in the yard for extended periods anymore. What if the Milice came to snatch away one or more of them? Swift as these little ones might be, he doubted they could outrun full-grown vicious men. Not that Patrick could protect his students if the Milice came in to get them.

Instruction wound down as the fire in the stove burned away to ashes and the children put on their coats to keep out the chill. Patrick called for early dismissal. Most of the youngsters scattered quickly, happy to get home to their chores and to enjoy the warmth of their homes before the late-winter darkness fell. But Ida and Katie Severin requested and received permission to wait for Ida's mother to walk them home.

When Denise knocked and entered, Patrick rose from behind his desk to greet her.

"May I stand by your stove for a moment?" Denise asked moving closer to it.

"I'm afraid there's not much heat left," the schoolmaster apologized.

"Any will help."

Patrick stepped up beside her. "May I talk to you?" he asked softly, somberly. "Alone?"

"Ida? Katie?" Denise immediately called. "Through the hedge, at the next cottage where the smoke is coming from the chimney—doesn't one of your classmates live there? Maybe you can go play with her for a few minutes."

"But we don't want to be late for the party!" Katie objected.

"You won't be. I promise."

After Ida tugged at Katie's sleeve and led her away, Denise explained to the schoolmaster, "My nephew turns four on Sunday. We're going to celebrate a little early."

Patrick gave Denise a look of intense worry. "So you know?"

"Know what?"

Patrick waited, hoping Denise would guide him through this minefield. Since she said no more he took the lead.

"It's becoming more dangerous here for you and your family. I have received reliable information that the Germans now insist all refugees be taken away, even women and children."

"Where did you hear this?"

"Let's just say my source is trustworthy. There really is reason for concern. It's quite likely they'll also come for me."

"When?"

"Soon. Very soon I'm afraid."

After an unsettling silence Denise took Patrick's hand. "Thank you," she said warmly.

Yvette Brignand didn't think it fair to be left alone at the café while her mother and sister went to La Font to celebrate Philippe's upcoming birthday. Especially when the café was so quiet.

Standing outside talking with a friend, Yvette was surprised by the noise of a motorcycle: the pastor from Le Pont-de-Montvert coming around the bend. She was even more surprised when he stopped right beside her.

"Good afternoon," the pastor said evenly. "Are your parents inside?"

"Sorry. Mother and Alice are up at La Font. Father's helping a neighbor fix his cart."

"May I talk with you privately?"

Yvette assumed an air of formal reserve, waving good-bye to her friend and leading the minister into the otherwise empty café. Had the time come for her father to flee?

"I need your help," the pastor said as soon as they were alone, taking an envelope from his coat and handing it to her. "Hide this and bring it up to the Severin mothers quickly."

Before Yvette could make a sound the minister walked back out, hopped onto his motorcycle, and roared away. Shutting the door behind him, she shuttered the windows and hurried into the back room. Though alone, she felt her face redden as she slipped the message into her bosom.

They'll never think to look there, she told herself, feeling important and afraid.

She put on her coat, opened the back door a crack, looked around cautiously, and stepped out. But when she set foot on the path to La Font she spotted something moving on the road and crouched down until she realized it was her uncle Émile in his cart full of hay drawn by his old horse Coquette.

"Oncle Émile!" she cried leaping up and running to greet him.

Breathlessly she told him of her mission and the big man said "Hmn" to himself. "I bet the same information that sent the minister here sent Pastor Donadille to me." Looking thoughtful, he told Yvette to go swiftly. "I'll be right there with Coquette. But don't say anything to anyone else, understand?"

"Wasn't I right to tell you?" she quailed.

"Yes. But hurry."

Yvette walked as quickly as she could without running, which might attract too much attention, having realized the Germans might leave her unmolested but the Milice were another matter.

Oh my God, she thought, a knot forming and tightening in her stomach. *They're French. No Frenchman would ever hesitate to reach into my bra.*

Yvette's mind raced as she came around the last bend of the path. She had to deliver her message confidentially in the midst of a party.

Philippe called excitedly, "Your mother said you couldn't come!"

"Gracious, child," Albertine cried out to Yvette. "Who's minding the café?"

"Where are the mothers?" Yvette whispered heatedly into her own mother's ear.

Imitating her daughter's strange behavior Albertine whispered back, "In the kitchen."

Yvette hurriedly entered through the door by the woodshed. Geneviève was readying a small birthday cake. Denise was emptying a large sack. Yvette recognized Françoise Maurel, a contemporary she knew only from brief summertime visits.

"Yvette," Geneviève called pleasantly. "We're so glad you could make it."

"Please," Yvette said haltingly, turning away, reaching into her blouse, blushing and handing the slip of paper to Geneviève. "It's from a pastor."

Geneviève read the message rapidly, her face falling. Then she handed Denise the slip as if it had burst into flames and singed her fingers.

"It's happened," Denise said flatly, pulling strands of hair back from her forehead.

Puzzled, Yvette doubted anyone would enlighten her.

"Let's just finish up the party as if nothing has happened," Geneviève suggested.

"I'll stay after," Françoise said, "to help."

"That's not necessary dear," Denise said gallantly. "And it's not worth the risk to you."

Albertine stormed in and pulled Yvette to one side brusquely. "All right. What's going on? Why is Émile here with his old horse and cart? Philippe keeps saying, 'A hay ride! Hurray!'"

Geneviève intervened, explaining the situation briefly. Albertine's expression and tone changed instantly.

"Yvette," she said commandingly. "Run and telephone the operator in Florac. Tell her, 'Send the white jacket of summer for Yvette immediately.'"

Yvette felt more confused than ever.

"Repeat it back to me," her mother insisted and she did. "Good. Now go. Then get back into the café as if nothing has happened."

Geneviève gave Yvette a kiss and said, "Thank you. You're a good brave girl."

As Yvette raced away, Françoise asked if "white jacket for summer" was a secret code.

"Yes," Albertine acknowledged. "To trigger calls to everyone involved in the Severins' escape."

There was no hayride. With the few guests gone, Émile stood alone, wind gusting around trees and blowing straight into his face. Touté stood on the veranda barking at the unfamiliar horse lazily browsing on a patch of grass.

"Good Touté," Denise said as she and her sister came out of the farmhouse. She patted the dog's head and scratched behind his ears. Then the sisters walked slowly down the stone steps, their faithful dog at their heels. "The children are settled down to supper now, so we can talk," Denise told Émile.

"I'm sorry we must meet under these conditions," Émile acknowledged. "But I helped your husbands as I will now help you."

Geneviève flushed. "Are they staying with you? Please tell us they're all right."

"They're fine. But no, they're not staying with me anymore. Come. There is much to do if we're to take care of you too—and very little time." He placed one foot on the corner of the lowest step. Suddenly self-conscious he realized how scuffed and scratched his boots must appear to women like these. But the boots were practical: firm, dry, warm. "Have you thought about your animals? They're quite valuable especially in times like these. I can see that they go to those in need."

"Just as we hoped," Denise agreed. "If possible though, we would like them to go to those who have helped us most generously, especially here in Soleyrols."

"I will do it carefully," Émile promised, "so no suspicions arise. A sheep here, a goat there, a rabbit someplace else."

"I suppose we can let the cats loose," Geneviève said. "They'll be all right."

"But not the dog," Émile muttered as Touté went in and out between his legs, wagging his tail. Émile caught the dog's eyes and Touté stretched out at his feet, tongue darting in and out, ears standing straight up. "Even if we give him away he'll follow you. Smart dog. Knows how to find sheep; he'll find you too."

"What can we do?" Denise gasped.

"Can't take chances," Émile insisted dolefully, "with your lives at stake."

The sisters clutched each other's hands.

"I'll take care of him." Émile glanced around and saw a heavy pitchfork standing in the manure pile by the lower level of the big barn. "Not good," he mumbled, "but necessary."

Denise shook her head tearfully. Geneviève set her jaw, grim but determined.

"Please don't pay attention," Émile said regretfully. "Don't even look." He took hold of Touté's collar. The dog looked up at Denise and Geneviève then rose to his feet trustingly beside the mountain man. "You have a rope?"

The sisters exchanged a terrible glance. Geneviève stepped into the space beneath the house and quickly returned with a short stout line. The women stood stock still as Émile led the dog down to the side of the barn, tied him to the latch of the door, and drew the line up tight. Inside, sheep and goats rustled about nervously, baaing and neighing at the scent of Touté, expecting to be let out of their pens again.

Stupid animals, Émile thought. *Better to take care of them than clever Touté.*

Long schooled in hard necessity, Émile did not hesitate. He pulled the pitchfork out of the pile of manure and swung it around with both enormous force and deadly aim, crashing it down mercilessly and paradoxically mercifully upon Touté's head. The dog, having completely transferred his trust for his masters to this stranger, was too surprised by the blow to dart aside or make a sound before being stunned to his knees.

Émile brought the pitchfork up and then down again quickly. Touté let out a whimper as a huge crack sounded, his right eye bulged, and he collapsed onto his side, his tongue hanging out of his slack jaws, blood bubbling and foaming at the corner of his mouth. Swinging the pitchfork one more time Émile made sure the poor dog was dead. Lifeless Touté's head rested against the edge of the manure pile.

Émile took up the pitchfork once more and manipulating it expertly and scooped enough manure from the pile to form a deep hole. Then he forked the dead animal into it and covered him with dung, mounding up the manure until the pile resumed its natural appearance.

He stabbed the pitchfork into place and turned back to the farmhouse. Denise and Geneviève looked as stricken as he expected, but he was surprised to see two little children on the veranda. They had watched the whole scene.

"I'm sorry little ones," Émile called out knowing his words were useless.

Crying, Christel and Philippe raced to their mothers.

Denise reflexively embraced her sobbing daughter. "You were supposed to stay inside!"

"Why Mommy?" Christel wailed. "Why did that mean man kill Touté?"

The trunks were to be transported to the loft in Louis and Albertine's barn underneath the load of hay already in Émile's cart. Outside, Coquette neighed, growing as impatient as her master. Inside, Geneviève and Denise hurried to finish up.

"You think we'll be intercepted?" Geneviève asked her sister.

"No," Denise answered anxiously. "I have faith in Émile and Louis."

"I hope Emmanuel and Sebastian get here in time to help cover our tracks."

Émile entered the farmhouse. "I'll carry the trunks out."

"We can help," Geneviève insisted.

"No," Émile said definitively. "If anybody saw me letting women lift a heavy load they'd know something's up."

Denise watched Émile labor alone, folding and unfolding her hands inside the apron about her waist. Every minute, it grew colder; but Denise wasn't warming her hands. She just didn't know what else to do with them.

Émile loaded the trunks onto the bed of his cart then spread the hay over them, piling it up on top until it looked as it had when he arrived.

"All right then," he said climbing onto the hard wood plank behind Coquette. "Louis will be back just after midnight so be ready. And let's hope for a bit of moon. You don't want to use a lantern to find the way because that could draw attention."

Émile lifted Coquette's reins and gave them a snap. Only when Geneviève heard the squeaking of cart wheels rounding on their un-greased axles and the scraping of metal rims bouncing over the stony cartway to Soleyrols, did she comprehend the moment they had so long dreaded had finally arrived.

Supper was simple, but there was tension in La Font even among the children. Taking a break from final preparations Denise and Geneviève sat at the table. Rose was kind enough to bring out the last of the soup of chestnuts, garlic, onions, potatoes, and carrots. Breaking off chunks of bread to dunk, everyone ate quickly. There was even some cheese to help fill their stomachs for tonight there was no need to stint. Whatever remained would go to others or to waste.

"Now children," Denise said when they were done, rousing herself from melancholy, "we need to do a few more things to get ready."

"But why do we have to go Maman?" Katie cried out.

"You know all that," Geneviève snapped.

Ida said, "At school we hear the Germans don't like Jews."

"Even some French people don't like Jews," Katie added.

"Who told you that?" Geneviève asked sharply. "And what has it got to do with you?"

"One of the older boys," Ida answered softly, "whose father owns a leather shop."

"He said some families hiding in these mountains have Jewish relatives, but aren't Jews themselves," Katie explained.

"Maman?" Ida asked quietly. "Were we ever Jews?"

Rose let out a sob and left the table. Never having seen their grandmother cry before except when their grandfather died, the children were confused and upset.

"The Germans and their supporters don't care one way or the other," Denise answered carefully. "If they believe you, your parents, or your grandparents used to be Jews then you are Jews to them. Forever. And every refugee is suspect no matter his or her family history. That is why your fathers went away and that is why we must go too."

"Are they safe?" Katie asked nervously. "We never hear from them."

"They're with others who also are in danger," Denise said comfortingly. "But because they're all together the danger is less."

"Does that mean we'll be safe too?" Until then, Christel had been quiet, staring down into her empty soup bowl. Now too upset to hold her tongue she watched her mother with wide-open eyes, their hazel tint darkening with fear.

"Yes. We will be safe," Geneviève answered simply and surely.

"Will we go to Spain too?" Ida asked imploringly.

Realizing the children could no longer be protected from the truth, Denise somewhat sheepishly said, "Your fathers never went to Spain. That was just a little untruth we told so you wouldn't accidentally say the wrong thing to the wrong person at the wrong time."

"Why tell us now?"

"It doesn't matter now," Geneviève cut in, "now that we're also going into hiding."

"So we will see them?" Ida persisted.

"Yes," Denise said, "I believe we will. Just not right away."

"Let's get started," Geneviève insisted. "We still have work to do."

"We've already packed most of what you will need into sacks," Denise told the children. "There's room for each of you to choose one little thing to bring for yourselves. But remember each of us has to leave some precious things behind."

Philippe took the little stuffed rabbit, without which he couldn't sleep. Christel selected her special doll. Katie took her small pocketbook with a mirror and her ever-present comb inside. Ida chose a book she'd read so often the pages were falling out.

"Won't you be bringing anything precious?" Ida asked the mothers sweetly.

Geneviève handed Denise a small velvet pouch: the diamonds.

The children surrounded their grandmother who sat slumped in the big armchair, watching them all silently.

"Are you coming with us tonight *Bonnemama?*" Katie asked.

"Yes Bonnemama," Ida echoed. "Please come!"

"Not tonight," Rose replied with a heavyhearted smile as she caressed each of her grandchildren's chins and cheeks in turn. "I'm just a little too tired my darlings. So I'm going to stay on for a bit."

Denise was saddened by the prospect of parting from the woman who had meant so much to her for so long. She was pleased though that she and Geneviève had made arrangements for Rose's safekeeping well in advance of this night. In a matter of moments, Rose would descend the path to the little house across the road where she would pack her few things yet again. Shortly after that, the Resistance would help her to the old mill house at La Planche. Eventually she would join Suzanne Maurel in Alès and be introduced around as Suzanne's aunt.

"We all need to get a little rest before it's time to go," Denise told the children, "so I want you to give your Bonnemama a kiss and a great big hug."

With each successive hug, Bonnemama's embrace of her grandchildren became a little tighter and lasted noticeably longer.

The children trooped off to bed, their sacks at the ready for the knock at the door. Denise checked on Cristian, already asleep, surrounded by the last of the hanging garlic and other foodstuffs. Then she bid the rest of the children good night.

"Tante Didi," Philippe asked bashfully, "do we really have to wear our wooden shoes?"

"Are you embarrassed by them?" Denise replied surprised. "Don't be. Back home in the low countries wooden shoes were once considered an improvement on leather."

"Why?"

"For one thing they don't sink so easily into the mud!"

All the girls were lying down except for Ida. She sat up writing carefully in the family's black notebook in which she had kept track of egg production.

Looking over the eight-year-old's shoulder, Denise watched her meticulously make her last entry: March 18, 1943.

Chapter Eleven

Underground

March 19, 1943

Shortly after midnight, Louis Brignand rapped softly but insistently at the Severins' back door. The bolt slid back and the door cracked open. In the thin glow of wood coals burning their last in the stove, Louis saw that Denise already wore her coat.

"I have seen no one," he told her.

"Good," she said thankfully, but then added fearfully, "Does that mean no one saw you?"

"Let's hope not. Are all the shutters closed?"

"Yes. Securely."

"Then it's okay to turn on a light since the kitchen window faces away from the valley."

The single bulb came on and Geneviève appeared. After a brief exchange of greetings Louis said, "We must hurry."

Geneviève and Denise went to get the children. Ida and Katie started talking together. Christel gave a muffled cry.

"Quickly now," Denise urged.

Entering the kitchen carrying their little sacks, Ida and Katie wore wool coats, scarves and hats.

"We're ready," Katie told Louis proudly. "Philippe and Christel need to get dressed."

As Katie finished speaking, Philippe came in rubbing sleep from his eyes.

"Where's your sack?" his older sister demanded. "You need it!"

Philippe ran back to his room. Denise returned, pushing Christel ahead of her. The little one's eyes were red from lack of sleep.

"I've got to get Cristian," Denise said placing Christel between her sister and cousin.

Louis began to fret, but a minute later, all the Severins were lined up at the kitchen door holding sacks or small valises. Denise also held Cristian, so bundled up Louis couldn't see his face.

"Let me take your case," Louis offered Denise, relieving her of her bag before she could protest. "You just take care of that little one." Turning and smiling at the four other children he said, "And remember: no noise. We don't want to disturb anyone else's sleep."

With Philippe on his shoulders, Louis took the lead followed by Christel, Denise carrying Cristian, with Ida, Katie, and finally Geneviève bringing up the rear. As soon as they set foot outside the door—the little ones with the thrill of anticipation, the mothers with misgiving—they heard a rumbling that echoed across the valley.

"What's that?" Denise gasped clutching her baby more tightly.

"It's them," Geneviève intoned coldly. "They're coming."

"A truck I think," Louis said. "And motorcycles. Headed up the road toward Soleyrols. Come. Now."

Louis put Philippe down and Philippe slipped on a rock. The sharp kick of his sabot pierced the night, louder in everyone's ears and more heart-stoppingly unnerving even than the growing growling motorized sounds of vehicles coming closer.

"Sh!" Christel hissed.

"Good girl," Louis said quietly, "but be sure to take your own advice." Louis addressed all the Severins without raising his voice. "We'll wait until we're sure those vehicles have gone on toward the pass at Saint-Maurice-de-Ventalon." Trying to quiet his breathing and his racing heart, he listened to the truck gear down and the engines work harder until the noise finally faded. "Quickly," he said showing the way. "Watch out. The stones are covered with frost."

The whole journey, he knew, was a dicey proposition. He was thankful though that the landscape was bare of snow. At least they would leave no tracks.

Rounding the corner by the café, Louis was relieved to see that the light no longer glowed in the little house across the way. Rose Severin must have left too and, therefore, had a chance of being safe—this night anyway.

The road was empty; but it seemed to Louis that they had walked along utterly exposed for a dangerously long time before coming to the turnoff. Again, he heard the motors, this time from somewhere above—which confused and concerned him.

"Maman?" Christel whispered. "I'm afraid. I don't like this."

"Monsieur Brignand knows what he's doing," Ida whispered back.

But Louis could appreciate Christel's apprehension. He worried too, imagining members of the Gestapo or Milice hidden in every dark group of trees lining their route.

For the moment though, all was still. They soon entered onto the path that Louis hoped would carry them more safely toward the rocky slope below and thence to the ruins of the old mill where Émile had met André and Alin during their escape one month before.

Hard to believe how little time had passed. It seemed so long ago.

Nearing their first destination, Louis noticed that the sporadic sound of motors had grown louder and clearly came from the road on the ridge above. Apparently, the vehicles had ground to a halt with their engines idling.

Male voices wafting on the chill night air, spoke guttural German mixed with sibilant French. A motorcycle alternately gunned and sputtered. Then a loud, exasperated, threatening voice reverberated through the dark. Motors revved and vehicles roared toward Vialas.

Louis and the Severins moved on, but soon Louis whispered, "Wait. I'll be right back."

Slipping around a turn in the path, he cautiously approached the old mill and stepped across the sill. Dim skylight filtered in and Louis tensed involuntarily as a human form emerged from the shadows whispering, "Louis?"

"Yes," Louis answered, relaxing in recognition of his contact's voice. "Anything?"

"Nothing."

"Then I'll go get them."

One by one, the refugees emerged from the shadows. Denise visibly startled as the figure standing in the old mill's doorway came forward.

"Madame," he said in formal greeting.

"Max! What are you doing here?"

"I've come to guide you on your way..."

"But..."

"...while Louis gets back to his house."

"...where are we going?"

"To Georgette Guibal's, in Villaret. There you and your three little ones will stay while Madame Geneviève and her two go on."

"What do you mean? You can't split us up!"

"There's no choice," Max said consolingly. "No one in the region has enough room to accommodate seven of you."

"But where will they go?"

"It's better not to say."

"And when will we see each other again?"

Max looked to Louis who had no answer either.

"Times are so uncertain," Max explained, "there's no way to say. But you must believe it will happen. We all are intent on making it so, on reuniting all the divided families—yours as well as our own—as soon as possible."

"I should go now," Louis said.

Denise shifted Cristian in her arms and with enormous dignity told their guide, "You have done us a great service. Thank you."

"It's nothing," Louis replied shrugging his shoulders.

"Good luck," Max said offering Louis his hand.

"And to you." Louis turned back to Denise. "And good luck to you and your children."

He put out his hand. Denise took it, leaned forward, and gave him a kiss on each cheek. Geneviève did the same.

Louis turned to the three girls and one boy standing woefully next to one another.

"It won't be long now," he said, knowing they must be cold, tired, hungry, frightened, and miserable. He patted each on the head then turned and walked away.

After a short rest in the old mill, the party proceeded. Ida and Christel held hands and strode along behind Max. The path grew steeper. Here and there, the travelers had to inch around large rocks jutting out from the hillside. The sound of rushing water grew louder with each step until they came to the narrow log bridge without a handrail to protect them. At least the wood, unlike the stones on the path was free of frost.

They made their way across at a cautious pace, clasping each other's hands, arms, and elbows. Suddenly, Max heard someone cry out behind him. Instantly turning back, he reached out to grab Cristian, just as he slipped from Denise's arms tumbling towards the creek. While lifting the infant and securing him against his chest with one arm, Max reached for Denise with his other to help her steady herself.

Despite the sudden jolt, little Cristian let out only the smallest of cries. Then he rested quietly in the cradle of Max's strong right arm.

Before long they reached Le Massufret. Several hundred yards farther along a straight path that angled upward, they made their way into the gathering of the half dozen houses of Villaret. Passing a large barn that served Max as a landmark in the dark, they abruptly entered a narrow passageway between the cartside wall and the barn's adjoining house, readily identified by the finished stone archway over its entrance. The door of the house faced the side of the barn, hiding it from the houses farther up the hill.

Edouard Ours stood quietly by the head of his horse and his two-wheeled cart awaiting the small fleeing group. At this decisive moment, the Severins clung to one another, rooted as firmly as the Lozère's oldest trees.

"Please," Edouard finally said. "We must go on before all our efforts go to waste."

Gently, Max and Edouard separated the family. Max lifted two little sacks onto the hay in the cart then heaved Philippe into place in one swift motion. Katie tried to climb in on her own, but it took so long that Edouard felt compelled to lend her a hand.

Geneviève let out a long sigh, climbed up on the tongue of the cart and settled down on the bare wood plank. Denise couldn't even bring herself to ask again where her sister, niece, and nephew were going. She knew it was useless.

As the cart headed off, Ida and Christel ran after it crying and reaching for one last grasp of hand. Katie and Philippe leaned over as far they could but when the cart got going faster than Ida and Christel, they stopped and waved until the cart was swallowed by the dark.

Georgette Guibal urged Max and the Severins to hurry into the only large room of her small house. Georgette's adolescent daughter Simone hung back shyly near the fireplace that radiated welcome heat from the far wall.

Ida and Christel dropped their little sacks onto the floor. Christel grabbed and held her sister's hand, though she sensed immediately that the Guibal household offered refuge—the first true safety she'd felt that long night.

Exhausted and emotionally wrung-out, Denise sat down on the bench along the near wall and looked carefully around this sheltering structure. The room's stone walls were plastered white. The fireplace offered a bold contrast of gray granite stones set in a wide arch. On an iron crane in the middle of the fireplace's deep cavity, a pot hung over hot coals of soft firewood glowing deep orange.

"You must be tired," Georgette said in a kindly way to the children. "Come take off those coats. I have some soup for you."

She bustled to the fireplace and spun the crane on its pintles to bring the bubbling pot within easy reach of her large pewter dipper. Then she reached for several bowls set out on the great wooden table not far behind, and began ladling the steaming mixture into them.

Without taking off her coat Christel ran to the table, pulled a chair up to it, and began to eat before her mother, sister, or Max could take their places.

"Ugh!" Christel said just as suddenly, making a terrible face, putting down her spoon and looking to her mother as if for protection.

Max took a taste of the thin soup made of nothing but garlic, onions and a little bit of cut-up carrot floating in the broth. He really couldn't blame the poor thing for her reaction. But her mother could.

"Don't you dare say another word," Denise hissed under her breath, giving her younger daughter a menacing look and then glancing over at Georgette to make sure she hadn't noticed this embarrassing behavior. Fortunately, Georgette was busy stoking the fire. "Eat," Denise quietly commanded Christel and then said sweetly to Georgette, "It's so cold out tonight. Thank you for this thoughtfulness."

Georgette kindly took Cristian from Denise. The others sat silently, staring apprehensively at the soup. Finally, they moved hesitantly to swallow one shallow spoonful after another. Max found the distasteful soup went down more easily with the chunk of rough country bread Simone served each of them.

While others ate their soup, Christel put her spoon back into the bowl and idly stirred until she realized her mother was watching out of the corner of her eye. Jolted into action Christel once again scooped up the smallest conceivable quantity of soup and raised it ever so slowly toward her mouth. After her mother shot her yet another stern glance. Christel shut her eyes, brought the broth up to her lips, and with a terrible effort, swallowed. Then she opened her misting eyes and looked over at her mother pleadingly.

"I can't eat any more maman," she said pitifully, letting her head sag.

Denise took Christel's hand, held it, and pulled her head against her own shoulder. "It's okay," she said softly.

"Here, Simone," Georgette said motioning to her daughter for assistance. "You help the little ones out of those cold coats." Then she told Denise, "We have a room overhead I think will work for you." She turned to Max. "And you need to stay here tonight too. It's too dark and dangerous for you to hike about these mountains one minute more."

Max nodded, too tired to protest.

"You're most kind to take us in," Denise said gratefully to Georgette, retrieving her youngest. "I don't know where we would have gone or what we would have done if you hadn't."

"Someone else would have helped you," Georgette said graciously. "Max has been such an aid and comfort to so many in the little hamlets and villages hereabouts, almost anyone would have answered his call." She bowed her head. "It's always good to have a man around, especially when it's been so long since one's seen one's husband."

"My father's been away a long time," Simone said simply and sadly.

Max glanced surreptitiously at the Severins to gauge the effect of these words on those who suffered similarly though not yet for such great duration. He was glad they made no comment and asked no questions, because he knew how painful it was for the Guibals to discuss the absence of the man of the house, who had joined the Resistance when he—like so many—became aware of the danger of being rounded-up.

Simone guided the little ones up narrow steps to a small room with a window facing the other houses of Villaret, which could clearly be seen through the intervening limbs of trees still bare of leaves. Beyond the hamlet and the stream below, the barium mine also was visible.

"You have to be careful," Georgette warned Denise downstairs. "No light in that room, and don't let anybody go in front of the windows—ever. It's most important that no one suspect anyone else is here besides Simone and me." She pulled her shawl more tightly around her shoulders since the room had grown cold after the fire died away. Georgette lowered her voice as if someone might draw near and overhear. "The children can go out to play only at night and if we all are very careful and keep a close watch for strangers. Even then, they must play only inside the barn."

Max smiled in silent agreement. He knew Georgette would look out for her guests as if they were family—which was important to him since that was how he himself felt about the Severins.

Albertine loved her customers. As the frosty sun reached above the iced-over rocks of the mountains on the far side of Vialas, slowly wearing away the rime and exposing the grasses, there they were as always—in the café at the same early hour.

The small place was nearly full. Despite the depredations of war, a dozen men above the age of seventy sat at the few tables and talked quietly. They slurped unselfconsciously from tiny cups of what passed for coffee a mix of coffee beans, roasted chestnuts and a smaller quantity of the Brignands' "secret ingredient"—blackened soybeans. It was a trick Albertine had learned from André Severin who had supplied the unusual legume from the fields of La Font.

Sweetened only by a few precious granules of rationed sugar, the coffee was ersatz. Fortunately, for these old-timers the marc was still real.

The men were real too—*real* men—but the Germans and the French authorities who served the Germans, neither understood nor appreciated their value. To the Gestapo, these men were too old to work—worthless but harmless. Yet the foolish Fascists could not have been more wrong. These old men were more robust than most men half their age were, their bodies having been strengthened by long years of strenuous farming, which they continued to this day. And despite their indulgence in marc, their minds were clear. They were cunning, alert, and thoroughly aware of everything going on around them and—insofar as possible given their remote location—in the outside world too.

Word of the latest events had reached them as it always did. No one could explain how news passed from one to another, for no one was ever seen or heard talking about the Resistance, the Maquisards, or the present movements of the police and the Milice. Yet all the old men knew what they needed to know, which was why they listened so attentively that morning.

From afar, they heard the coughing motor of a small van winding around the curves the road cut into the side of the mountain. The sound got louder and then softer, muted by the shoulder of the mountainside, and then it gradually got louder again until the van they all expected rolled slowly into view, stopping in front of the café.

Two men climbed out and entered wearing the blue uniform of French gendarmes. Everyone eyed them warily, measuring their every move. But Albertine remained unperturbed.

"Good morning," the older of the two said immediately.

"Good morning," Madame Brignand replied, ready to begin an elaborate charade. She recognized the policemen as Officer Pellet and Brigadier Salager. She knew from Pastor Donadille that they were the ones who had warned of the danger to the Severin men and they had probably sent word about the women too. But she would pretend she knew nothing of them. It was important not to give the game away so the game could continue.

"Coffee?" she asked Pellet.

"If you please."

"I'm afraid it's not very good," she said drawing it. "There's a war on you know."

No one laughed or cracked a smile. A couple of old-timers rose without a word and shuffled to the back leaving a table open for the police. But none of the regulars were about to leave. The appearance of these gendarmes was a momentous event in Soleyrols. Everyone wanted to see what would happen.

The gendarmes took the seats politely vacated for them. Albertine brought over small white cups of coffee. Brigadier Salager took the first sip.

"Very good," he said without irony or flattery. "Better than the stuff in my own house, which we only drink Sundays, because as bad as it is, that's all we can afford."

Officer Pellet sipped his coffee too, but instead of commenting on it he asked Albertine, "Can you please tell us if and how we might drive our van up to the farm known as La Font?"

Albertine's customers glanced at each other knowingly, but the policemen's eyes remained focused on her.

"Turn off the road just up here," she said pointing, "then take the first gravel track off to the right. I wouldn't recommend it though, especially at this hour when it's slick from melted frost."

"I suppose we must risk it," Pellet told Salager, finishing his coffee with a smack of his lips. "Duty is duty."

"The bill please," the brigadier requested slipping into patois—thereby tipping his hand to the regulars. "A cold morning," he said as Albertine handed him *l'addition* on a little tray. "But no snow, which is good. Our van's tires are too smooth to hold a snowy road."

The officer placed a few coins into the tray, but neither he nor the brigadier made any effort to go.

"We have orders to bring in the Severin family," the brigadier said heavily and softly enough to simulate confidentiality. No one else talked or missed a single word.

"Do you know them?" the officer asked.

"Everyone knows everyone else in Soleyrols Monsieur," Albertine allowed.

"Are they up there?"

"Perhaps."

"Maybe we could have a little glass of brandy?" Pellet asked his superior. "To protect us against the cold."

The brigadier nodded.

"Right away," Albertine said smiling.

She brought the gendarmes their marc. All eyes were trained on them as they lifted and slowly drained their glasses in one fluid motion. Salager shook his head a little as the warm sharp spice of the local brandy coursed down his throat. Then he licked his lips as if to capture the smallest drop that might have attempted escape, and finished by smoothing down his well-trimmed handlebar moustache with his fingertips. Meanwhile, the younger officer put a little more money into the tray to cover this extra fortification.

"Now we must be off," the brigadier announced easily as he stood, straightened his belt, and pulled his greatcoat tightly about him. "Madame," he said to Albertine, bowing formally.

When the officer and the brigadier stepped back outside the inhabitants of the café listened attentively as the van stuttered back to life and shuddered off. When it had achieved a safe distance the café came alive with chatter and laughter.

"What was that all about?"

"They certainly took their time."

"I think they know more than they let on."

"Madame Brignand what do you think?"

Albertine said nothing, but she couldn't keep a sweet pleased smile from pulling up the corners of her mouth. She hummed quietly to herself as she washed out the grounds that had settled and dried hard in the bottoms of otherwise empty coffee cups.

The old men lingered, anxious to learn what would happen next. But as the minutes ticked by, habit reasserted itself and the hardworking men of Soleyrols gradually left the café to resume the familiar routines that filled their every working day.

Forty-five minutes later, Albertine heard the van roll back down the road. The brigadier opened the café door and she stepped over to him since he seemed reluctant to cross the threshold.

"Madame there were only a couple of Spaniards there and we weren't sent for them." The brigadier sounded relieved, but Albertine knew he would never admit it. "I still need to make a report." He pulled a small notepad and a special pencil out of his coat. "Do you know where the Severins are?"

Albertine shrugged her shoulders. That was all the answer she was willing to give and it was all the answer the brigadier needed or expected.

"Well then," he said making note of it, "another family has disappeared." He sighed so ostentatiously that Albertine felt certain it was intended for show—in case some other official came by to inquire into the tenor of the brigadier's investigation.

Salager gave Albertine a little salute and turned to go. As the van shifted into gear again Albertine looked out the window and watched it putter off. She could have sworn the brigadier allowed her to see the hint of a grin.

The following morning the café was as busy as ever with the same old men in their accustomed seats. But this morning, the conversation was much livelier than usual.

"I hear the Severin women's RAF fighter pilot brother came in the middle of the night and flew them away."

"I heard a racket that disturbed my sleep some nights back."

"I bet he put the plane down in the valley to pick up their husbands too."

"Those Brits are very clever."

"Surely they're all safely in London now."

Albertine listened with enormous satisfaction. She knew better than to believe what she heard—and she knew that her customers knew better too. They were very, very clever—more clever than they suggested the British must be—because they had a tremendous talent for generating and spreading useful rumors. Far better that the authorities in Mende believe the Severins were living in England than to suspect them of hiding out in the nearby mountains—like Roux the Bandit.

Denise awoke unknowable hours later still terribly tired, but unable to get back to sleep. She dressed again, threw on her coat, and slipped back down the stairs.

"Sleep well?" Georgette asked much too energetically.

"I suppose. I hardly remember lying down."

"You had a long day and there's another ahead as always."

Georgette brought out coarse mountain bread, a little butter, a pot of honey, and a cup of coffee for her guest. She spoke of awaking early despite going to bed so late—because the work of the farm had to go on. Simone also had gotten up early for school.

Brushing aside ash to start up the morning fire, the mistress of the house chattered about bleating goats and chickens that spent their days scratching around the outbuildings for grubs and bugs and the remnants of dry brown grasses revealed beneath the recently melted snow.

"What happens next?" Denise asked in a subdued tone. "Do we stay here? Do we go?"

"You stay here for now," Georgette said in a sympathetic hush, "till someone tells us otherwise or you can't stand me and Simone one minute more."

"I'm sure that won't happen." Still not eating, Denise walked to the fire to stop herself from shivering. "So my sister and I won't be able to get back together?"

"Not immediately, no."

Denise took her hands out of her coat pockets and extended her cold fingers toward the fire. "Will our husbands know we have left La Font for Villaret?"

"I'm sure they'll be told something." Georgette stepped over to Denise and put her arms around her. "It will all be all right. You'll see."

"I just keep thinking how fortunate Albertine is to have her husband with her."

"And our other brother's still around too," Georgette said, lighting up. "Émile."

"Brother? Isn't your last name 'Guibal'?"

"Married name, yes. But I was born a Brignand."

Just then, Ida inched down the steps trailed by Christel. Both rubbed their eyes.

"Maman," Christel said proudly and sheepishly at once. "I have to go pee-pee."

"Here," Georgette said reaching into a small side room and bringing out a glazed clay object. "Use the chamber pot."

Ida looked scandalized, Christel simply horrified.

"But Maman," Christel complained, "can't we go outside?"

"Not unless Georgette says so," Denise replied. "You know we have to be much more careful now than ever before."

Reluctantly yet bravely, Ida and Christel trooped into the side room to take their turns using the new facilities. Meanwhile Denise went to get Cristian as Georgette started warming the bajana, adding a few new ingredients to the pot that was always available in the fireplace.

Ida returned from the side room first. "Can we go out to play?"

Denise looked to Georgette who shook her head "no," reminding Denise of the warning she had issued the previous night.

"But Maman," Christel also whined, "we went potty like good girls!"

Denise looked at her daughters helplessly. She had run out of ways to explain.

Georgette swung the great iron cooking pot out on its crane and gave the soup a stir. With infinite patience and concern, she explained again about going outside only at night and never being seen at the windows. Then she served out the soup.

That evening, after the children were once more in bed, the sun quickly set across the range of mountaintops to the west and the deep gray shadows of night surrounded the ancient stone buildings of Villaret. Georgette led Denise out of the house at last; and in the pale light of stars shining through a haze of clouds, Denise could just make out the little passageways between the several houses and the many small barns and outbuildings. The two women stood quietly, hidden in the lee formed between the corner of the house and the adjoining barn, listening to the Guibals' livestock bedded down beneath their two-story stone house, just as the Severins' animals had been at the much-larger La Font. Creatures of the night crept out of their daylight hiding places, scurrying here and there in search of life—another's for their own. This led Denise to dark thoughts of human hunters.

"It's all right though," Georgette said as if she had read Denise's mind. "They can't see us from the mines when it's dark like this. Besides," she added with a confidence born of long years in the hamlet, "I can hear anyone coming from across the way. We're safe here for the moment."

Denise stood silently in the dark corner, sheltered from the wind, but keeping her coat buttoned up against the cold.

"I'll go back in now," Georgette said thoughtfully, appreciating the delicacy of the moment. "You stay out as long as you like."

Denise stared up into the dark searching for the invisible moon. She tried to count her blessings. Though it was terribly sad she wouldn't be able to be with Philippe when he turned four, she was glad at least some of the family had a chance to celebrate his birthday together.

Le Tronc is hard, Alin reflected, forking manure out of the lower level of the barn that he and his brother lived in—less comfortable and more monotonous than La Font. But he preferred sleeping in a barn and working outdoors to confinement in a prison camp.

The stone barn would have been too cold if not for the built-in fireplace that, due to the stone, could be used without fear of conflagration if one made sure every last wisp of hay was far enough away to prevent stray sparks and cinders from igniting it. With the fire bright and the Guins' limited livestock gathered in the nearest stall, the smallish barn was fairly warm.

There were a couple of chairs and a rough table, but no beds. The brothers slept on piles of hay they regularly re-formed into usable shapes, which weren't as comfortable as La Font's already uncomfortable beds, but were better than the hard barn floor or the unheated ground outside.

The Guins were almost the only people Alin and André saw. Food was in very short supply and basic—simple and none too tasty, despite Madame Guin's best efforts.

As for the brothers' work—gathering firewood, feeding sheep and goats, shoveling manure—Alin preferred it to doing nothing or moping about the Brignand house in Le Massufret. In the cold air of early spring, he like André and Léon wore heavy wool pants, a white cotton shirt grown faintly brown from dust and dirt that refused to come out despite repeated washings, and a wool suit coat, its three tightly sewn buttons buttoned in hopes of preserving as much body heat as possible. Not that forking mounds of manure over a stone wall didn't make Alin sweat.

"Amazing," Alin muttered to André laboring beside him, "how so few creatures can produce so much stuff. We've been pitching it for days."

"I don't think Léon has ever cleaned out this barn," André said.

Surveying the dark mass of animal defecation, Alin shook his head. "Now I know why he wanted helping hands."

"I don't have much," was Léon's favorite phrase. "Just my animals and my land. At least the authorities are far away—though they're never far enough away." Whenever he spoke of "the authorities," Léon coughed and spat derisively. But, he always followed this display of disgust by growling pleasurably, with a twinkle in his eye, "Of course I have Yvonne."

Very much her husband's opposite, Madame Guin was always smiling, helpful, and supportive. She could ameliorate Léon's nastiest moods and she sent him out to the brothers every few hours with warming mugs of some mixture of beans, tea, and goat's milk she contrived in her kitchen.

"Here," Léon said each time, thrusting steaming mugs into the brothers' hands. "This will help. Though it's not like Brussels, eh?"

Alin had been drinking ersatz concoctions so long he had almost forgotten the taste of real dark-roast coffee. Every now and again, he could trick himself into believing charred beans of undistinguished mixed pedigree supplied a hint of civilized satisfaction.

In late March, three weeks after Émile Brignand had dropped off the Severin brothers at Le Tronc, Alin took a brief break from his dung-removal efforts. Wiping away the sweat beneath his beret, he looked out over the valley stretching far away below to the slope of the mountains rising up on all sides. From here, he could see a great distance, making it difficult for anyone to approach unnoticed during the day. So when he saw Pastor Donadille bicycling down the path to the Guins' isolated farm, he and André raced to the Guins' door to greet him.

"Marc Donadille, what brings you here?" Léon demanded, stepping out of his house.

Panting the pastor said, "I want to let the brothers know about their families."

"Are they okay?" Alin and André asked anxiously over the pastor's gasping.

"Yes, yes," Pastor Donadille answered weakly, "but they had to leave La Font."

"When?" Alin felt his heart thump against his rib cage and pound in his ears.

"Last week. The police were coming for them as they had come for you."

"Where are they now?" André asked.

"Madame Denise and your three aren't far. They're staying with the Guibals—a good woman and her daughter—in Villaret, a hamlet rather like this. Off the main road."

"The Milice don't like to get off the main roads," Léon spat, "and the Gestapo like it even less. We make it dangerous for those cowards."

"Where is my family?" Alin demanded. "Why aren't they all together?"

The pastor put his hand over his heart as if to apologize.

"No room at the inn," Léon chortled.

"Or in Villaret," the pastor explained. "Seven Severins in one tiny hamlet would have made for too much activity and visibility."

"So where are they?" Alin insisted.

"Two places," Donadille revealed regretfully. "Madame Geneviève and your daughter are in the next valley over, in L'Herm, also with a nice family, that of Pierre Guin."

"Your brother?" André asked Léon.

"Cousin," the old farmer answered.

"And my son?" Alin asked, almost apoplectic.

"Philippe is just a little farther away with the family of Edouard Ours in Le Lauzas, part of Le Collet-de-Dèze, south of Saint-Frézal-de-Ventalon. They have many children. I'm sure he's safe and happy there."

"Away from his mother?"

"Just one of the precautions the Resistance judged it wise to take," the pastor said carefully.

Alin continued to stare at Pastor Donadille. Slowly his look softened. "Forgive me," he apologized. "I'm worried, concerned, upset. But it has nothing to do with you or any of the good people doing all they can to help us."

"We all understand," Donadille said, putting out a hand, which Alin took in his.

Talk turned to the question of security throughout the Cévennes.

"The Maquisards are strong around here," Léon said. Then he smiled broadly. "Of course, the strength of the Resistance is mostly due to the Communists."

Alin was surprised by this. He had had the impression that factions within the Resistance locally were much less significant than before André had staged his intervention at La Font.

"Léon only says such things because he himself is a Communist," Pastor Donadille told the brothers good-naturedly.

"Naturally I'm a Communist," Léon declared. "Only the Communists have a real feel for the people. The government never cared about us even before that idiot Pétain took over. And neither do the socialists or the conservatives."

"Léon's a good man," the pastor said grinning, "but he holds to his own opinions."

"Still a Communist!"

Donadille winked at the Severins conspiratorially. "And like all Communists, he doesn't hold much stock with religious people like me. You don't think much of us Protestants, do you Léon? Neither your forebears nor your contemporaries."

Léon stamped the ground and gave a firm negative shake of his head. "Ah you're all right Donadille," he conceded. "You're a good man too—not so much for the religious part, but because of your Resistance work."

"You wouldn't have the one without the other," the pastor insisted.

"If you say so. But I still don't believe all that religious gobbledy-gook— not to be insulting to you two," Léon said to André and Alin. "You can be Jews or not. I don't care one way or the other."

"I feel about religion as you do," Alin quickly told Léon, "but I'm no Communist."

"My religious views are ever-changing," André explained, "but they're much closer to those of Pastor Donadille than to those of my ancestors."

The weather, having become pleasant by mid-May, prompted Georgette to bid her household farewell and set off for Vialas. The sun was lovely and warm, the air fresh and filled with the exhilarating scents of spring. Georgette felt wonderful, as if the Severins were no problem, just welcome company. If at times Georgette had felt a little down...well maybe she just needed to get out more.

Light hearted and optimistic, Georgette did not immediately notice the souring mood of the town. But on either side of Vialas's market street, she spotted pairs of Milice thugs dressed in crude but obvious imitations of Gestapo uniforms, interrogating ordinary people doing nothing more than a little Saturday shopping.

Georgette's impulse was to turn and run but she realized instantly she had to go on, because any sudden movement would single her out for the investigation presently underway. Even deviating from her path might attract unwanted attention, though that path was about to lead her right by an older woman attempting to appease two questioning goons.

The terrified woman wailed, "I heard the men were flown away by the Royal Air Force!"

The Milice spat. Georgette was horrified by the way the brutes treated this old woman, but her words were worse: she was talking about the Severins. The Milice were pursuing them!

All the villagers of Vialas knew something about the Belgians in their midst, but what each knew remained an open question. No one was likely aware of where the Severins were just then, but if anyone chose to cooperate or accidentally let slip that they might be hiding nearby...

Despite the enormous peril, Georgette lingered by a vegetable stand hoping to learn enough to determine how immediate the threat was to the Severins—and to herself and Simone.

"*Messieurs,* we have not seen these brothers for months and months."

"What about their families?" the Milice demanded unrelentingly. "The women and the children—they fled La Font too. Where are they?"

"Truly Messieurs, I do not know. I have never had anything to do with any refugees let alone these. Please, you must believe me."

One of the Milice monsters spat again at this miserable woman's feet. But the other said she could go, which she did—skittering away, terror in her eyes, strain distorting her face.

Georgette put down the greens she had pretended to look at and, as casually as she could, turned and followed the "witness," simulating a leisurely pace even though she could not have been more anxious to get away from the Milice. Soon she overtook a pair of women engaged in heated discussion.

"Good for them," one said. "I hope they never find them."

Georgette was grateful for this support of the Severins and by extension herself. She knew she had to be even more resolute than before and felt encouraged by these women, because it was brave of them to speak in public. In the little gatherings of houses on the mountainsides one could speak freely, but *here...*

Georgette's worrying intensified. Everyone knew the butcher was a collaborator. Were there others? Maybe someone would talk. With the Milice stopping people randomly on the streets...

Warmer weather will make it easier for the Milice to track down refugees, Georgette thought striding home rapidly, *even in remote places like Villaret.*

She knew she would have to tell Denise everything. What else could she do? But she certainly wouldn't say a word until the children went to sleep.

Then an idea struck her with the force of revelation: *Tomorrow, I'm going to the church!*

When Georgette returned to Villaret from the services in Saint-Frézal-de-Ventalon late the next afternoon, she sat Denise down in the great room to say, "Marc Donadille will be visiting his parishioners this week. His regular ministry." She laughed. "Of course we all understand his 'regular ministry' now: helping to save everyone he can from the Nazis and their sympathizers."

"So...?"

"So we wait. The pastor will be here—today, maybe tomorrow, certainly this week. With a plan." A light film of perspiration covered Georgette's flushed face and long gray wisps of her hair came loose, falling in front of her ears and sticking to the moisture on her cheeks and lips. "We need to be ready to act quickly when he says the time is right."

Dazed, if not stricken, Denise said, "I shouldn't be surprised. At least this time will be easier since we stored almost everything in Soleyrols."

"Sh!" Georgette warned. "Don't tell any more than I need to know."

"Sorry," Denise said softly, chastened. But after two months of intimacy it seemed only natural to tell Georgette everything.

"It's all right. It's just the war. It does things to all of us. Before the war, we all knew everything about everyone else. And after the war we'll know everything again. But now, we can't. We mustn't." Georgette sat beside Denise at the table and held her hands. "Nothing should be this way. We'll miss you when you go."

But they didn't go, though their canvas bags and suitcase were packed and waiting by the door. Night after night, the week dragged on. Still Pastor Donadille did not appear.

When the quick, solid knock finally came during supper Saturday night Denise jumped.

"Who is it Maman?" Ida asked excitedly. "Is it him?"

"We won't know until we open the door," Denise said trying to sound calm.

Simone leapt up to get it. Soon she brought in the pastor who shook himself to ease the strain on his back caused by the little pack he carried.

"Mesdames," the pastor said formally, "you are well, I trust?"

"Now that you have come, yes," Denise replied, marveling how despite the war and all they had already gone through together, propriety was still appreciated and sustained.

"Pastor," Georgette offered politely, "will you have some soup and a little bread with us? There isn't much left tonight, but you're welcome to what we have."

"No need." The pastor patted his belly gently and laughed lightly. "I ate well at midday." Then he resumed his formal manner. "Madame Denise, I have come to lead you and your children across the ridge to Le Salson. To Ernestine Roux and her daughter Irene Bastide."

"Irene?" Ida squealed delightedly.

Pastor Donadille smiled. "She looks forward to seeing you again too. Did you know Irene and her mother are cousins of the Guins, with whom the brothers Severin stay?"

"Is Le Salson far?" Denise asked, almost as excited now as Ida, but anxious about whether she and her children had the strength to make the journey.

"Not so far, no. But more isolated and much safer than here." The pastor turned back to Georgette. "Other sources have confirmed what you told me last week: the Milice seem energized. They are going out into many villages now, asking more and more questions. I doubt they even know Villaret exists, but we dare not take chances."

"So they go now?" Georgette asked apprehensively.

"As soon as Madame is ready."

Denise looked at Georgette, who was on the verge of tears, and patted her hand. "It's best for us all that we go quickly."

Pastor Donadille gazed at the two women steadily. "You are both very brave. None of us could have gotten this far if you weren't."

"Thank you, Monsieur," Georgette said bowing slightly to him and wiping her eyes with the backs of her hands.

"Come children," Denise said gathering the girls, picking up her son and moving toward the front door. "Tell me Pastor Donadille, will we be closer to André and Alin? Do you think we'll be able to see them?"

"Perhaps." The pastor followed the Severins to the door then turned back to Georgette who followed him. "When did you last see your husband? I neglected to ask last Sunday."

"Three months," Georgette said in the hushed voice she assumed on the rare occasion the painful subject came up. "My man left home around the time the Severin men left La Font." Again, Georgette seemed about to cry, but instead she snorted with anger and derision despite the pastor's presence. "The bastards. The filthy rotten creatures, who do the dirty work for the Bosch and turn their countrymen in to the Gestapo to save their own useless skins."

Georgette balled the hem of her apron and worked it nervously back and forth. "But don't worry about me Pastor. I'll survive. I have Simone and I know my husband is out there with the others. Of course, I pray for him constantly. Every day." A single tear ran alongside her nose. She wiped it and sniffled. "But what am I thinking? You'll want to take a little something with you! Simone will you help me?"

The pastor stood waiting. Denise helped her children into their heavy outerwear since it could still be chilly at night.

The Guibals returned with several small packages.

"This isn't much," Georgette said. "Just the remains of that big round loaf of bread we had for dinner and several pieces of our hard goat's cheese."

"That smelly stuff?" Christel complained.

"Christel!" Denise chastised. Her daughters were wonderful, but they still needed to be reminded occasionally to mind their manners.

"That's all right," Georgette laughed. "It *is* smelly. And the smellier the better I say!" She winked at Christel. Christel squirmed. "You'll also find slices from that joint of smoked ham hanging in back of the root cellar."

"Look Maman," Ida said pointing to Cristian, who sat on the floor with his back to the doorway—all but swallowed by his coat—his little head nodding as his eyelids fluttered uncontrollably. "He's almost asleep. But don't worry. I'll carry him."

"I'll help," Marc Donadille said sweetly, grinning appreciatively at Ida.

"Let me try first," Denise said lifting her son gently to her shoulder. "Amazing...it is only eight days till his first birthday and he's still so light."

The Severins and Guibals made their good-byes. Ida clung tearfully to Simone. Simone also seemed moved.

"Must we go Maman?" Ida asked. "I really like it here."

"But I don't like having to bend down all the time not to be seen at the window," Christel countered. "Where we're going will we still have to stay away from the windows?"

"I don't think you will little one," the pastor said pleasantly, crouching down beside Christel to reassure her. "The place where you're going is far, far away, where no one else can see. I think you'll be able to stand up as much as you like, even in front of the windows!"

"Well that's better," Christel said somewhat petulantly.

Georgette leaned to give Ida a hug and a kiss on each cheek. Then she picked up Christel and held her for a long moment before giving her a little kiss on each cheek.

"You take care," Georgette said, smiling though looking forlorn. "And be good girls like you have been here. I'll think of you often."

"But we will see you again won't we?" Ida asked becoming emotional. "Simone, will I see you?"

"Of course," Simone said in a hoarse whisper.

"When?"

"Soon. Very soon." Simone turned away as she said, "I hope."

Denise and Georgette made one final quick display of affection.

"Thank you so much," Denise said, hoping to convey the intensity of her gratitude as much with her eyes as her words. "I can't begin to say..."

"I know," Georgette said feelingly, squeezing her hand. "I know."

Simone stepped forward and with a little curtsey, offered Denise a kiss on each cheek. Then Marc Donadille opened the door and without another word, stepped out into the night.

The dark was softened by the glow of a half moon and the sparkling of a million stars. The Severins followed the pastor down the path. Suddenly alert, Cristian began babbling to himself and waggling his head, delighted by the change of routine and mysteries of the night.

Denise concentrated on the narrow gravel paths and the even narrower tracks in the woods. Despite the cool night air, the brisk walk heated them until they regretted their heavy coats, but still easier to wear than to hold them. Every once in a while, Donadille—carrying the suitcase—slowed just enough to let the lagging girls catch up.

After they'd been walking about half an hour the pastor told Denise, "It will take us another two and a half hours to get to Le Salson. Can your daughters handle it?"

"They'll have to," Denise said simply, negotiating around several large rocks.

"Listen," the pastor said holding up his hand and stopping them all in their tracks.

From far away Denise could hear all the noises of the night: insects, birds, nocturnal animals creeping about.

"Noise is good," Pastor Donadille said cheerfully. "If anyone was out and about prowling, all God's creatures would sense danger and quiet down. So their noise is a comfort."

They continued their dogged way uphill so long that Denise hoped they'd made good progress.

At the crest of the mountain, the pastor peered and pointed below. "That way," he said. "Le Tronc."

Le Tronc. Denise's heartbeat strengthened. *André. Alin.*

But as she knew he must, the pastor led them in another direction. He found a path that ran down the mountain into the same great valley that contained Le Tronc, but would usher them toward a different place: the little collection of homes Denise could just make out in the distance.

"Le Salson," Donadille said pointing again. "You see that flickering light?" He gesticulated more excitedly. "It must be the lantern Irene said she'd leave shining through the window of the main room of her little farmhouse. I admit I'm relieved. I trust my wonderful fellow Resistance workers, but when making arrangements we have to work with a word here and a lifted eyebrow there. So each time, it's good to see how effective their efforts can be. They said Irene and her mother would wait up for us. Thank God they did."

At an hour when she was usually long and fast asleep, Irene Bastide was a bundle of nerves though not because she feared discovery. The local gendarmes rarely set foot in Le Salson, and the Milice and Gestapo had never been seen there. Her nerves also were not caused by the close proximity of the other three families living in her tiny hamlet—each of those families had at least one man in the Resistance. Rather her concern was that her husband was not in the Resistance. A French soldier, he had been captured by the Germans in the first days of the lost war and imprisoned in northern France. Three years had passed, yet Irene had no idea where her man was or even if he was still alive. The last letter she received from him had arrived more than a year before and she had worried every day since. A young, recent bride when her husband went off to fight, she had been worn thin, or thinner, given how large she was to begin with. Now she appeared prematurely aged due to her relentless emotional pain and anxiety.

Her accustomed apprehension was tinged tonight with as much excitement and hope as fear. The thought of those children—those two darling little girls and now a baby boy—thrilled her. They would be her special charge. She would care for them with unending delight.

Her mother Ernestine, widowed by the Great War as so many were, would gain renewed interest in life too. Irene suspected Ernestine would especially appreciate the company of another adult—especially one as worldly and sophisticated as Denise Severin.

But the children...oh! For Irene Bastide, to have a hand in raising and comforting young ones in a house she had once hoped to fill with children of her own...

When the knock came, Irene jumped. Within seconds, she was fumbling with the bolt.

"Come in," she sang out gaily.

There was Denise—so much more slender, with a bundle of joy in her arms. There was Pastor Donadille, carrying a suitcase and with a pack on his back. There were Ida and Christel holding small sacks. Once Irene set eyes on the two girls, they were all she could see.

"The Severins," the pastor announced.

"Of course," Irene replied hoping the big grin on her face didn't make her look like a simpleton. "Welcome to our humble home. I had hoped to see you again in different circumstances, but Mother and I hope you'll be comfortable here."

"This is Ernestine Roux," Pastor Donadille said waving his hand toward the older woman coming out of the back room.

Weary though she was, Denise accepted Irene's and Ernestine's warm embraces. Ida and Christel were exhausted; they swayed back and forth on feet they could barely keep on the floor.

Irene bent down to them and said, "You must be so tired after your long hike—but you also should be proud you made it. It's late though. Let's get you to bed."

Embracing both girls with her warm ample arms, she alternately led and pushed them ahead, helping them mount the stairs to the small room at the back of the house. Days before she had made up the bed with clean stiff sheets and a down quilt that covered the entire expanse.

"Here is your room," Irene told them proudly, certain they would appreciate it in the morning. "Just put your things in that chest over there. And here's the chamber pot for the middle of the night or any other time you just don't want to go out. Tomorrow I'll show you the outdoor place to go."

Christel's tired eyes opened wide. "You mean we really will be able to go outside?"

"Here in Le Salson," Irene assured them both, "you can go out whenever you like."

She chuckled, which made the folds of her stomach, slackened by worry, bounce up and down. Then she gave Ida and Christel another big hug, kissed each on the cheek and prepared to leave them to adjust to the new room in private, recommending that Christel sleep crossways at the foot of the bed, leaving room for Denise and Ida.

"Where will Cristian sleep?" Ida asked yawning.

"Here!" Irene cheerfully pulled out one of the drawers in a chest, already arrayed with a blanket and small pillow.

Downstairs Denise had plopped into one of the chairs in the front room, the center of farmhouse activity.

"May I hold him for you?" Irene asked returning and removing Cristian from his mother's arms before the too-tired woman could think to resist.

Ecstatic, Irene clasped the infant close and made soft cooing noises to him. She had practiced these sounds in anticipation of this moment.

Seated beside Denise, Donadille smiled at Irene. "It's good of you to take them in."

"Ah, but we wanted to," Irene returned reddening. "Ever since I saw Ida and Christel at our Quaker group's veillée, I wanted to be part of their lives. Now I will love this little one too and take care of their precious mother. Besides, my mother and I are grateful for a chance to do our part for the cause." She asked the pastor solicitously, "You'll stay the night won't you?"

"Oh no," Pastor Donadille replied. "You don't have room."

"Unfortunately, there's just the settee over there for you to sleep on. But even that's got to be better than hiking more tonight."

The pastor nodded. "In that case yes. And thank you."

Without ceremony, the minister crossed the room, took off his shoes, stretched out on the thin cushion covering the long wooden settee and immediately fell asleep.

"Come," Ernestine Roux said rising and leaning over their other guest. "You look exhau*th*ted. Le*th*' get you to bed too. Irene?" Her daughter understood her mother's lisp from her missing teeth.

Assisting Denise to the stairs, Irene tried not to feel embarrassed by her mother's slight lisp. After all, it wasn't the older woman's fault she had lost most of her teeth. In earlier times, Le Salson had been a thriving village. But over a long period, almost every family had moved away in search of easier livings to be made in the towns and cities of the lower, flatter country to the south. The local dentist—primitive as he and his practice were—had long since decamped, leaving Ernestine Roux's strong rectangular face to cave in at the lips. What a sight she was, her strange face topped by what remained of her long gray hair piled up in an unflattering bun.

Irene continued on as Denise happily, sleepily, made her way up the narrow staircase.

Waiting at the top, Irene pointed and said, "In here. Little Cristian is all settled in, still asleep and dreaming."

"I'll gladly follow him," Denise said, too done in to bother with further niceties.

Heading back downstairs to help settle her mother in for the night, Irene couldn't keep from smiling or from feeling warmed by satisfaction. She had put Cristian down without waking him up: a very good sign.

Chapter Twelve

DISAPPEARING SHEEP

APRIL 25, 1943

Every day there seemed to be more work—preparing the fields for planting then broadcasting or drilling seeds into the soil. The Guins and Severins worked from dawn to dusk.

Desperate to break the monotony, Alin asked Léon, "What is there to hunt here?"

"Wild boar Monsieur." Léon winked and sneered—his version of a smile. "You want meat to eat? Wild boar is good—not like a well-fed pet pig but..."

Monsieur Guin supplied Alin with a rusty old single-action carbine. Alin hardly had more than an hour or two to use it any given week and he never had much success. But the very act of hunting enlivened his otherwise tedious existence.

Sunday was no day of rest on the Guins' farm. It was a day of hard work like any other. But on the first Sunday of June, work stopped for a visit by Max Maurel, and if for any particular reason it wasn't immediately apparent.

The most noticeable thing about him—besides his bright shining eyes, big eyebrows, ready smile, and fine white teeth—was his bulging biceps. Max had always had strong legs from hiking, mountain climbing, and skiing but his life in the Resistance had made him powerful overall. And his speech was considerably more expansive than before.

He told the Guins and Severins about Le Crespin, the nearby camp of the Resistance. It also was close to the *Route des Crêtes*, the Route on the Crest of the lower mountains. It was a location from which the Maquis could keep an easy watch on the Milice and Gestapo who frequently used the road.

"How does the Resistance know so much about the movement and activities of the enemy?" Alin asked.

"Some of those the Milice believe are their sympathizers, are really for us," Max said. "They bring us information at great danger to themselves, for if they're ever discovered not to be true collaborators, they'll be arrested and sent to Germany or put on show trial and quickly executed. There's another risk for them too: those who have infiltrated the Milice on our behalf may be mistaken for actual collaborators after the Germans are defeated. Then our people who have suffered at the hands of the Fascists and their friends may seek retribution. It could be hard to protect these true patriots from those more anxious to exact vengeance than to await the facts."

"You're confident of victory," André remarked.

"I know we will win. Then reprisals will begin. It has happened in this region many times before. Of course, those of us in the know will do all we can to prevent miscarriages of justice."

Max stared into his mug of pseudo-tea. When he looked up again, Léon and Yvonne were nodding knowingly.

Standing to stretch his legs Max intimated that he had a few matters to discuss with the Severins. The Guins discreetly suggested they themselves had much to attend to, but insisted that Max and the brothers feel free to stroll about.

Striding out into the fields, André asked Max about his family. Hesitantly Max said, "My father died in March." The brothers were stunned. Max explained, "I didn't know until I visited Alès a few weeks ago for the first time since the beginning of the year."

"Didn't your mother let you know?" Alin demanded. "Didn't Fela?"

"They wouldn't know where to write him," André said. "I'm sure Max protects them by concealing his whereabouts."

"And have you heard about what happened in Nîmes?" Max asked. "In late April, two twenty-year-old Resistance members were stopped and arrested coming out of their house. The French government in service to the Nazis ordered and carried out their executions in the old Roman arena. By guillotine."

"Barbarians," Alin wailed.

"Nîmes is only an hour south of Alès," André remarked.

"Right after that," Max added, "there was a noticeable surge in the number of young men fleeing into Resistance camps. They said these public beheadings scared them more than anything before." Max stared at his feet for several long moments then said, "There's a reason for my visit today besides friendship. As you might have guessed."

"What is it?" André asked anxiously.

"The leaders you hosted at La Font think you both could be useful to our cause."

"Doing what?" Alin demanded.

"Many things," Max said evenly, "that will be necessary."

"Involving guns?" André asked apprehensively.

"Not necessarily."

"When?" Alin asked impatiently.

"Soon, is as much as I can say. You need to be prepared at a moment's notice."

"We've been in that position before." Alin spoke with irony, seethed with anger.

André resettled his glasses on his nose and stared into the middle distance. "Alin and I have talked of it before," he said contemplatively, "long certain the time would come."

"I'll understand if you say no," Max allowed, "given your devotion to pacifism."

"'To everything there is a season,'" André said slowly, dreamily. "No, we won't say no. Ever since we were forced to flee La Font there has been no question that given the chance, we would help those who have helped us." Gazing meaningfully into Max's lustrous eyes he concluded, "You may depend on us. We're ready whenever you say."

Three days later Max came strolling down the path to Le Tronc again. Awash in sweat in the narrow garden of a terrace formed by a great stone wall that several generations of Cévenols had taken several centuries to build, André and Alin momentarily stopped planting potatoes.

"That man has a purpose," Léon insisted, holding his ground and continuing to work.

The brothers returned to their labor until their friend reached them. His striking dark eyes flashed brightly from his sun-browned face. A sly smiled appeared as he asked, "Are you ready to help?"

"What do you want us to do?" Alin asked bluntly.

"Leave Le Tronc for a time," Max said simply, mysteriously. "We have... certain plans."

"Which we're not to ask about?"

"Oh you can ask," Max replied still smiling, "but I can't tell you."

"Let's go," André said giving his brother a sharp look. Then he turned to Léon. "We hate leaving you in the lurch."

"You think I can't plant potatoes without you?" Léon groused. "I've managed on my own almost longer than you've been alive."

"We'll be back soon," André said soothingly. "Won't we, Max? To help with the turnips?"

"I should think so," Max answered.

"Just go," Léon said sharply.

André didn't take that personally. Even Alin understood that years of war had taken a toll on Léon, making him progressively more short-tempered than he was to begin with.

"You won't need much." Max glanced at André mischievously. "We hardly ever change clothes. Not exactly like a well-dressed professor."

"Teaching is one thing," André retorted. "Surviving is another." He gestured to his laundry-free work clothes. "And it has nothing to do with clean clothing."

"We would rather dress in rags and live to tell the tale," Alin snapped, "than be victims of murderous oppressors."

Max peered up the path toward the crest of the mountain. "I don't think the Milice are out today. We've had no information suggesting otherwise." Then he said, "Get your things. No more than you can carry easily. For hours."

In the barn he'd called home for three months, André wondered how much less comfortable a Resistance camp would be.

When André and Alin got back from the barn, Max and Léon were engaged in heated debate.

"The Resistance is made up of more than just Communists," Max insisted, exasperated. "There are Socialists and Republicans and for a long time more and more unaffiliated Frenchmen have come into the camps. Politics may have been a problem once, but no one cares about that anymore. You don't have to be a Communist to fight to get your country back."

"But the Communists were first," Léon asserted coolly, "and they're still the strongest in standing up for the people. The others only came when they saw the problems we Communists *foresaw*."

Max struggled to match Léon's infuriatingly even tone. "I have been with the anti-Vichy forces from the first. I have been in the mountains with Les Chantiers de la Jeunesse. Now I'm in the mountains with the Maquis, and I can assure you very few Frenchmen look to Russia and its Communist government to save them. We look to ourselves. Together we fight for a free France."

It was a fine speech and a strong argument, but it had no effect on Léon, who remained unshakable in his beliefs. He was not about to waste any more breath arguing.

"Get on with you," he said dismissively, bending to continue seeding the ground.

Max led the brothers up the path, stopping frequently to survey the valley slopes and the ridgeline ahead. "You never know who's going to come down that road," he cautioned pointing toward the Route des Crêtes.

He stopped abruptly. After confirming his location he worked himself into a thick stand of oak trees, their thin brittle branches bent heavily beneath fresh green leaves.

"Crouch down here," he called to André and Alin, who had followed him into the stand.

The brothers quickly did. Hidden from the road, all three listened intently. There it was again: the sound of an engine.

A small truck came up the road from the south laboring mightily at that altitude. The driver created a grinding noise shifting down to first gear then back up again when the road leveled out enough. Peering through leaves and branches the men could make out first the color and then the make: a Citroën.

"It's okay," Max told the brothers, breathing more easily. "That's our ride."

He stepped out onto the road almost jauntily and waved. The truck slowed to a stop as the grim-faced driver, who wore a beret and smoked a Galois, rolled down his window. The driver puffed away and studied the scene carefully as André and Alin edged cautiously toward Max. Then the driver motioned them into the back, as he flicked off a long ash from his cigarette.

Max and company wordlessly, hurriedly, climbed in and shut the door behind them. The back of the truck was full of logs and bags of chestnuts, which they moved to make space. Max piled some of the bags between them and the rear door.

"If we're stopped," he explained, "we'll just pull the chestnuts over us for cover. Of course, if they start to pull things apart they'll find us anyway."

"What's that burning smell?" Alin asked worriedly.

"This truck is fitted out with a gasogene?" André speculated.

"Right," Max confirmed.

Alin looked puzzled so André explained, "An older technology that gas rationing and shortages have brought back I suppose. It requires modifications in standard vehicles—a gas generator, a gas reservoir, changes to the carburetor and extra plumbing and filtering to get the gas into the engine. After that you have options for fuel: coal, charcoal, wood."

"That's why we're stuck with all this lumber," Alin grumped.

Max nodded. "These days, gasoline is reserved exclusively for Germans and Vichy functionaries. We resisters must make do. And yes, the smell is dreadful."

For a while they said nothing, breathing only as deeply as they dared. Max shifted awkwardly and spoke through a little window opening onto the driver's compartment.

"All right?"

"All right," the driver replied. "And on time."

"Germans?"

"Haven't seen any and hope not to."

Max turned back to the Severins. "It's safe for you to know now: we're heading to one of the main camps in the Cévennes, past Le Pont-de-Montvert and hidden away ."

"And then what?" André asked as lightly and genially as he could. Some of the smaller logs kept pushing up against him in all the wrong places. Each time he moved slightly to get away from an offending branch, another chunk slipped and pressed against him.

"It takes a lot of food to feed everyone," Max said, "and with more men coming to us, we're setting up additional locations. We need more to eat than ever.

"The farmers in the next valley have had an annual spring roundup for centuries, driving their sheep across to Le Pont-de-Montvert and greener pastures. This year we have learned the Germans intend to make sure all the sheep end up feeding German soldiers instead of the French people. So it's our job to divert the sheep—and for that we need help. We chose you for your sheep herding experience."

"Too bad we don't have Touté," André said wistfully, "the family's real sheepherder."

"When will this take place?" Alin asked.

"It starts the day after tomorrow," Max replied, "when the farmers collect the sheep and newborn lambs and begin driving them over the fields toward town."

"And what is our job exactly?" Alin persisted.

"That I can't tell you," Max admitted. "The Chief gives us our assignments and he hasn't told anyone specifics yet. It's smart that he keeps them to himself."

The next two hours passed mostly in silence. Each man was profoundly engaged with his own thoughts and the struggle to get comfortable and breathe.

Finally, Max felt the truck rumble over the ancient arched stone bridge that crossed the headwaters of the Tarn and gave the town its name. Soon, the driver slowed to a prearranged stop by a small alley to pick up a compatriot. Then he quickly started off again.

The truck wound up along the hills surrounding Le Pont-de-Montvert, crossing little streams and passing occasional gatherings of homes until it entered an ancient village close by the mountain pass leading into another valley. Skirting the fountain in the town square that pulsed water beneath a metal cross commemorating all the wars fought and sacrifices made since the village had been established, it turned into a side street, which devolved into an old farm path—nothing but rocks, ruts, gravel, and dirt.

The driver brought the truck to a halt and the recently added passenger hopped out to open the huge door of the largest barn at the Resistance camp. Then the driver pulled the truck in and turned off the engine.

It wasn't easy, but Max, André, and Alin disengaged themselves from logs and sacks, opened the rear door, and climbed out stiffly. The driver was busy removing burning charcoal from the gasogene—a far longer process than shutting off the engine.

Some twenty men were scattered in the dim light of the barn's interior. There were no animals or other indications that this was part of a working farm. It wasn't. There was a great deal of work going on in the camp, but none of it had anything to do with farming.

There was a mix of languages—French, Spanish, Polish, even German, for the Maquisards included refugees from Nazi Germany. One man approached the apprehensive Severins eagerly.

"Welcome," he said grasping the brothers' hands. "We're happy to see Max got you here all right. Now you go over there. That fellow will find you a place." The greeter pointed toward a lean man who stood up abruptly and said, "Follow me."

A beefy hand clapped Max's shoulder. His grizzled middle-aged Chief said, "Welcome back. Tomorrow then." and "You're sure they can be trusted?"

"Anyone forced to flee Belgium and hide in this rugged terrain can have no love for the Germans. I know the Severins well. Good people."

"And what did you say they do normally?"

"One's a professor. The other's a stamp dealer."

The Chief broke into a broad gap-toothed grin. "I don't think we've ever had either of those before." The smile fled. "But they know about sheep?"

"They kept sheep on their farm in Soleyrols, and there are sheep where they're staying now too."

His thoughts already turning elsewhere the Chief said, "They're going to learn a lot more about animals before we're done with them."

The taciturn, lanky gentleman led André and Alin to their quarters for the night in one of a handful of wooden shacks of simple frame construction built by Les Chantiers de la Jeunesse. Something in the nature of this man's silence discouraged questions.

The brothers were shown to a tiny room with improvised beds of straw on the floor. They settled down wearily.

The next morning, they were surprised to have slept long and well despite their stiffness and assorted aches. Tired though they were, they still woke with the first light of dawn seeping through the cracks in the roughhewn wood walls.

Max came in almost immediately. "We all wake up early too," he said, "especially in the barn and particularly before an operation when everyone's nerves are on edge. Not that we're not hopeful."

The day was gray but dry and crisp. The brothers mustered quickly and joined the other Maquisards gathered around the Chief in the dim light of the large barn.

"Tomorrow," the Chief announced standing on a bale of hay, "our local farmers start driving five hundred sheep toward Le Pont-de-Montvert. We're going to make sure none reaches the intended destination. You all have been assigned, mostly in pairs, to farms and farmers we know support the Resistance.

After we 'divert' the sheep—some of which belong to collaborators—they will be hidden by our supporters."

The Severins were impressed that the Maquisards knew which farmers were with or against them, who they could trust or must fear, who could be asked to help with this operation, and who should be left in the dark.

The Chief broke into a great grin. "The Germans have already paid for these sheep. So we'll finally have reason to be grateful to the Nazis—for buying us French lamb and mutton."

The resisters laughed appreciatively, whistled and clapped. But one asked, "When we get our sheep into one of these local barns, then what?"

"The farmers will immediately slaughter one or two so have some meat for yourselves. Then bring back as much as you can carry. But don't be too obvious about it eh? Oh and several camps are working on this operation so others will have new provisions too. After that the farmers have agreed to keep the sheep as long as necessary, mixed in with their own flocks."

The Chief stepped down from the hay bale and put on his hat and coat. The greatcoat was worn not for warmth at that time of year but to conceal the pistol in his belt.

He assigned the teams and gave individual instructions. The men drifted out. André and Alin accompanied Max, relieved to be working with someone they knew.

Some Maquisards walked north, crossing open fields on well-worn farm paths. Others rode bicycles. A handful left in one of two ancient trucks. Several more drove off in one of very few cars. It was remarkable that the Resistance had that many vehicles—all converted to gasogene.

Max and the Severins made their way on foot with Max as guide. First they followed some others on a small path north. Then they veered alone to the west.

They walked most of the day making the Severins glad they had grown stronger and hardier by working outdoors for three years.

"See that farm?" Max said now and again, pointing as they trudged through little hamlets. "The farmer and his neighbors will take all the sheep we bring them."

Just past sunset but before complete dark, they entered the small village in which they would spend the night. Smoke rose from chimneys in several houses. Occasionally a light could be spied shining from a window onto the only lane, which bisected the small community: five houses on one side, outlying farm buildings on the other.

Max approached the largest house and rapped on its door with the great black metal knocker that proclaimed the owner's financial success. The traditional bolt shot back and yet another Cévenol farmer stood in his open doorway peering at the new arrivals skeptically.

"Sheep?" Max asked: the password.

"Sheep," the farmer replied standing aside to let them in. An older man— tallish, rangy, firm-muscled, with calloused hands and slightly bent from long working the earth—he offered no name and neither did Max: part of the Chief's security plan?

"Come eat," the farmer encouraged. "You're hungry and we've been waiting for you."

The room was bright with several electric lights, another sign of the farmer's above-average productivity. His wife—short, slender, quiet, with modest clothes and a gentle careworn face—brought out country bread and butter, and beef left over from previous meals. Not bajana!

Everyone ate rapidly. Alin hesitated to taste the wheel of homemade cheese because it was fearsomely encrusted with mold and dirt. But the farmer and his wife dug into it heedlessly, appreciatively, so he decided to run the risk and was rewarded with a remarkably smooth tangy flavorful sensation. When he remarked upon the unusual savor the farmer laughed, doubting Alin had ever eaten cheese made from sheep's milk before. Even if he had, this wheel would still taste different because of the distinctive grasses the sheep grazed in the high pastures during the warmer months.

The farmer and his wife aged the cheese in their own root cellar. The apples and pears, which had lasted the winter and which all ate for dessert had picked up some of the flavor from sitting alongside the cheese as it set and softened over many months.

With dinner done, the farmer pulled his chair closer to Max. "Well?"

"We start out early," Max said including the Severins with a gesture. "We'll get into position, watch the sheep come together, and move along as one until close to dark. Then our teams will move in and separate out the animals a few at a time for the receiving farms—most in the high country here, but several closer to Le Pont-de-Montvert where the Germans will be waiting with trucks to move the sheep to the city. They'll have a long wait."

"That's a lot of sheep to hide isn't it?" the farmer asked with hard-won skepticism.

"Sure, but there are two or three dozen farms involved. If we disburse the sheep carefully—say you normally have fifteen sheep and now you'll have thirty—you think anyone's watching your flock that closely?"

"I wouldn't know. But the Germans have made us declare the size of our property and the numbers of our livestock. And another thing, I have enough feed for my flock, but I doubt I can sustain twice as many. And I'm one of the more prosperous farmers around."

"Remember we need food. Some sheep will be slaughtered now and the rest as needed. Besides, spring is here. Your pastures are mostly green again. They'll support the extra sheep."

"We'll have to watch closely, run everything carefully," the farmer demurred. "There could be trouble ahead. But to help you help us—it's worth the risk." He stood up, pulled on a coat, said, "Come," and walked to the front door, lighting and lifting a lantern before stepping outside. He led Max, André, and Alin to his barn where the goats and sheep were bedded down for the night. Two cows chewed their cud standing next to a team of workhorses.

"We can add the sheep in here," the farmer said. "Nobody will know." He held the lantern high so the glow shone not only on the pens separated by little fences and wooden walls, but also on the four men. Then leading them back out of the barn he tilted his head in the direction of several other barns in the hamlet and said, "The others will do the same." When they reached the house again he told them, "You can sleep in the back room. It was the boys' before they went off to the Army."

"And?" Max asked gently, concerned.

The farmer sighed heavily. "We haven't had word in over a year. That's one reason we'll help in any way we can."

The morning was still when Max and the Severins awoke in the crowded back room. A little frost glistened on the fields. Fresh breezes blew softly from the west.

The air in the room was electric. This was the Severins' first Resistance action and though Max was an old hand, each new chance to strike a blow against the Nazis excited him.

"There's a certain risk," Max whispered to keep the farmer and his wife from overhearing his concern, "mostly from a collaborator who might give us away. It's worst when they don't have a name or other specifics. Then the enemy gathers a whole village and shoots some men at random as an example. It's an effective technique of intimidation and repression but each such act ends up serving as a recruitment tool for the Maquisard. So the countryside becomes even less safe for the Germans and still more dangerous for their traitorous French accomplices."

These sobering thoughts accompanied the three friends to the dining table where the farmer's wife had laid out a full breakfast. André was nervous, but Max encouraged him and Alin to eat heartily because there was a strong possibility they would have no opportunity to eat again until they returned to the farm much, much later.

In exceptionally high spirits the farmer said, "I want you to take my sheepdog Blackie. He'll know how to separate out the sheep and he can find his way home even in the dark."

The would-be rustlers began their long hike over the pass into the next valley with Blackie gamboling by their side. Wherever they went the path was clear, for though it was frequently used by local farmers to guide their flocks from pasture to pasture, no one was using it today.

The sun shone clear above the horizon. Only a few wispy clouds laced the sky. Rounding the hillside, Max pointed into the distance where white shapes moved and merged into a large symmetrical object only to break apart again farther along, strung out in a line.

"That's where we're going," Max said enthusiastically, picking up the pace.

Approaching their destination, Blackie grew more excited. Other sheepdogs worked the flock, which kept getting larger as more and more sheep joined from other paths.

By noon, the trio reached the little valley rendezvous. With the bearing and allure of a natural leader the Chief stood out in the crowd. André and Alin already recognized many of the men gathered around the Chief, some sitting on rock outcroppings, most standing. They stayed a step or two behind Max who approached the Chief to let him know they had arrived.

"All the sheep are here too," the Chief said. "These farmers all are with us. The ones paid to deliver their sheep to the Germans are back in their own homes protected by the Milice—today. Tomorrow—who knows?" He raised his voice to be heard by the two dozen men ranged around him. "The drive will go on most of the afternoon. But when you see the trail or path that leads to your assigned farm pick off as many animals as you think can be hidden where you spent last night. If there are any sheep left, I'll take them on to the final village. It's a little close to Le Pont-de-Montvert, but it will do." He paused to look at each man closely. "None of these animals have been tagged or marked. If you notice distinguishing characteristics, be sure the farmer slaughters those sheep first."

The Severin brothers trailed along behind Max all afternoon, Blackie obediently at their heels. The size of the flock diminished until Max finally said, "We'll take ours here."

The Severins took a deep breath and walked slowly toward the flock from the rear.

"Eh Blackie," André called softly. Then using the singsong mountain patois he had practiced with Touté he gave the dog instructions and, he hoped, confidence. He was relieved to be rewarded by the dog's practiced response. It was important not to spook the flock.

Blackie worked back and forth carefully, herding the sheep, heading them onto the right path, not letting any rejoin the larger flock. In a gratifyingly short time, Max and the Severins managed to move their small flock over the hill on the way to their new home.

As the sun began to set, the handful of local farmers stood talking quietly, waiting. When Max, the Severins, and the sheep appeared, Blackie, at his owner's direction, brought the flock to a halt in the center of the road.

"You take these three," the farmer told one of his neighbors. "They look like yours." He did the same with the other sheep and farmers. In the end, fifteen nervous "diverted" sheep were left. "Okay Blackie. To the barn."

In minutes, everything was back to normal. No one entering the village would have guessed that a few more sheep had been mixed in with each farmer's flock.

In the morning, Max and the Severins began hiking back to the camp, avoiding all roads associated with Le Pont-de-Montvert. Great care was taken to cross only where adequate cover shielded them from unwanted view and even then only when all was quiet.

"Today or tomorrow at the latest, the Germans will miss their sheep," Max said. "I'd love to hear how the collaborators explain it."

Late in the day, they climbed the last hill to the camp. Smoke swirled into the sky from two chimneys on the grounds. Though it was quickly lost in the gloom of dusk Max thought he should talk to the Chief about it since it was imperative that the Maquisard conceal their hideaway.

In the large barn, everyone had a story to tell or a comment to make.

"I had to act as the bellwether. They would only follow me."

"Dumb animals. Stupid sheep."

"But good eating."

"No matter how old, mutton makes better eating than turnips three times a day."

The banter died away as the men laid themselves down and dozed off.

"We'll stay a week or so," Max whispered to André and Alin, leading them back to their quarters. "It'll be safer staying together in an armed camp. Once the Milice tell the Germans five hundred sheep have disappeared, the Gestapo will go everywhere to hunt them down."

"To hunt *us* down," Alin corrected him.

"So," André asked wiping off his glasses briskly, "are we now one with you?"

"You are now Maquisard," Max grinned, grasping each by the shoulder. "Welcome!"

André settled his glasses back. "So there's more for us to do?"

"Eventually. Meantime, I'll get you back to Le Tronc as soon as it's safe to leave."

Max and the Severins sat around pondering the future. André expressed a heartbreaking sense of helplessness about Denise and their three children.

"We're in your hands," he said, over and over. "Yours and our fellow Maquisards."

Alin acknowledged similar thoughts and feelings about Geneviève, Katie, and Philippe. Both fretted about their mother and their relatives in Aubenas and Belgium.

Then word came that the Germans were furious over their sheep loss, demanding of their French partners how a flock so large could simply vanish.

In the large barn, an old farmer who had helped the Maquisard, smiled toothlessly as he related what he had witnessed in the village square. "They were running all over frantically, insisting that the mayor find their sheep. But the mayor and the townspeople said nothing. They just went back to their homes. It was wonderful. The Gestapo officer grew red in the face and turned his outrage on the Milice captain next to him, yelling in German. The captain didn't understand but still was terrified."

A week later Max tracked down the Severins. "The Chief says if you want to return to Le Tronc he'll have the truck take you. The driver needs to go on his regular run anyway."

Alin peered at Max doubtfully. "Regular run?"

"Potatoes and carrots go down to the village. Wood and chestnuts come back."

"I'm sure the Guins could use us," André said tentatively.

Alin nodded. He and André had bonded with the men of the camp, but it would be good to get back to Le Tronc.

Léon got the brothers planting turnips, beets, and beans right away. After they had put in several hours of backbreaking work he suggested to André the time had come to see his family and pointed southward across the valley.

"When it gets dark tonight you can walk over if you're up to it. It shouldn't take more than an hour or two. The path is uneven so it might be best to climb up to the ridge and then go down the other path. That way you'll be out in the open a shorter time—if anyone's watching."

"When will I be able to see my family?" Alin demanded.

"Not yet. But that time too will come."

"I'm afraid to see Denise," André confessed. "I smell bad and I haven't shaved."

"Don't worry," Léon said dismissively. "We'll get you all cleaned up for the misses. Besides, after so much time you could stink like a pig as long as she can see your face."

As the sun began to set, André cleaned up and shaved as best he could. His whiskers mostly came off but his cheeks were still stippled by uneven stubble. Overjoyed to remove the shirt he had worn for almost two weeks he put on the best of the last two remaining from Brussels, which though wrinkled were not stained with dried sweat. He also shook out and donned his finest coat. Unfortunately, he thought it best to keep on his rough trousers—a pair manufactured for the rigors of outdoor existence. They might survive a mountain hike.

"I'm off," he told Alin who sat watching. Should he offer a word of consolation? No. *Better to leave Alin to his own devices,* he thought shutting the barn door behind him.

The moon was out, not shining down fiercely enough to reveal André, but providing enough light for him to find his way. Still, as he reached the high road at the crest of the mountain and sought the trail that led to Le Salson he tripped on a root projecting from the side of the road and fell hard, scraping his hand against gravel as he slapped and grasped to keep from falling the long way down. Then working his way to his knees and then to his feet he rubbed his hands together, pressed his sore hand against his pants and hurried on.

Léon had told him the Bastide house was the fourth building after the path widened. As he approached an outbuilding between two other structures he grew confused. Finally he came to a house that might have been the fourth and at least it looked lived in.

In the moonlight, shining more brightly in the open, the house's stoop struck André as clean and welcoming. An ancient pot filled with dried branches and the first wildflowers of the season rested on a great stone set beside the door. It looked like Denise's handiwork.

No light escaped through the small cracks between and around the latched shutters. André firmed his resolve and knocked gently, then again with greater force. He pressed his ear to the door and heard grumbling and a shuffling toward the door.

"What is it?" a strange voice called fearfully. "Who's there?"

"André Severin."

He heard the strange voice again, another and then one he knew.

"André?"

"Yes!"

The bolt slid back and Denise stepped through the doorway into his arms. André squeezed and held her tight, pressing his lips to hers in a long lingering kiss. Then he held her at arm's length. How wonderful to see and feel her!

"Oh my dear," Denise breathed. "Come in."

She guided him into the large front room, where he greeted Irene Bastide warmly and was introduced to Ernestine Roux. With tears in their eyes these women quickly, kindly, made themselves scarce so that André and Denise could sit on the couch talking privately, holding each other's hands tightly.

Denise spoke with great pride of their children: how well they were developing and how extraordinarily helpful, thoughtful, and brave they were being. Then she asked excitedly, "Should I wake them for you?"

"I'd hate to disturb their sleep."

"But they'd be so thrilled to see you!"

"All the more reason not to. It's better for now that they not know I've been here or that I'm staying relatively nearby. Secrecy is important for us all—and quite a few others."

"I understand. But I hope it won't always be this way." André sank into himself. He hadn't thought through how hard this would be. "The children are always asking where you are," Denise said. "I tell them you're all right, nothing more." She squeezed his hand more tightly. "But come quietly and look at them. We won't use a light—just the lantern which we'll leave outside the door."

Upstairs their daughters slept in the big bed as if to protect one another. In the drawer where Cristian dreamed, the boy's sweet face was turned to one side atop his pillow. André hardly recognized his littlest one. Dark hair now covered his son's head entirely. André could hardly believe how large he had grown even though he was still small enough to fit in a drawer. It almost was as hard for André to stand there without kissing and caressing Cristian as to realize he would soon have to leave.

In the meantime, the Bastides had slipped into the great room to add a bit of wood to the evening's fire. It gave the room a lovely warmth and provided a dancing, guttering light to illuminate and animate their faces.

"I can't stay much longer," André said regretfully, returning with Denise. Then he looked deeply and lovingly at his spouse again before addressing the older women. "I'm just happy to see my wife and children doing so well thanks to your consideration and care."

"We could do no less," Ernestine said feelingly.

"And your children are so wonderful," Irene enthused. "Especially little Cristian. He's such a darling and so proud to be walking!"

"I've missed so much," André said sorrowfully.

"We're most fortunate to be here," Denise affirmed. "Irene and Ernestine really look out for us. And I feel we're well-hidden."

"I hope so," André said concerned. Then he pulled Denise close again. "Now I have to go," he said softly.

"I know," Denise replied equally softly. "But you can come again?"

"Next week perhaps. It depends. We might be busier then."

Denise accompanied André to the door. Standing out on the stoop again he pulled her to him and kissed her passionately.

Breaking away, he gazed into Denise's beautiful eyes. A faint smile played across his face. Then he disappeared into the dark.

Chapter Thirteen

BETRAYAL

September 25, 1943

The successful harvest was pretty much at an end. Now it was time to prepare the Guins' fields for the first hard freeze and to begin gathering chestnuts. And for the first time in months, Max Maurel showed up. The Resistance had need of the Severins again.

"What do you want us to do this time?" Alin asked sarcastically. "Steal pigs?"

"Alin," André admonished. Then he told Max, "If you think we can help we're ready."

"Isn't there anything you can tell us about it?" Alin burst out.

Max looked uncomfortable. "We think we have an information leak." Alin eyed him, warily, dissatisfied. "Look," Max continued sounding defensive and pettish himself, "I don't know everything and I don't want to know everything. It's enough for me that the Chief asked for you specifically."

"How long this time?" Léon demanded.

"A day or two. Maybe three."

As much as Léon supported the Resistance, he was annoyed. But all he said was, "We'll be here if and when you come back. We're always here." And all he thought was, *Chestnuts!*

Heading back toward the mountain, Max and his friends had some catching up to do.

"I'm sorry I haven't been to see you in so long," Max said. "I do keep an eye on you."

"What do you mean?" Alin demanded. "Spying?"

Max laughed. "In a way. The camp at Le Crespin is so close to Le Tronc, some days when I walk out from under the trees, I can actually see you working in the fields."

"Well doesn't that make me feel safe—to know anyone can see us almost anytime from almost anywhere!"

"It's nowhere near as bad as that," Max insisted. "If it were, we would have moved you long ago."

Asked about the last few months, André said that hard but invigorating labor had been leavened by making his way to Le Salson frequently. Unfortunately, Alin still hadn't been able to visit his family.

"But that time will come I'm sure," Max hastened to say.

Arriving at the camp of the Maquisard, the puzzled Severins expected to see the schoolmaster from Soleyrols. Instead, a stranger with a wary expression came in. André thought he looked familiar, perhaps from the temple in Vialas. The young man seemed to recognize him too.

"Pierre, schoolmaster from Vialas," the Chief said, "this is Max, André, and Alin. Tell them what you discovered."

Now André understood: Pierre Jabot—a handsome dark-haired man, not yet thirty, with the strong build of the region's laborers—taught the upper school.

"First if I may," the young man said tremulously, "I'd like to acknowledge monsieur le professeur Severin whose presence honors this humble schoolteacher."

"No last names!" the Chief burst out. Then he did a double take. "You know him?"

"Everyone in Vialas knows about André Sev…Sorry. His excellent reputation precedes him."

"Let's hope it doesn't precede him too far," the Chief joked. Everyone chuckled politely. "Please Monsieur Pierre. Go on."

Flushing the teacher said, "Yesterday morning in class I noticed one of my older students—Thomas Vignie, the seventeen-year-old son of Maurice Vignie, a petty merchant in the village—drawing a map. This immediately struck me as unusual—Thomas has never been much for drawing—so I went to his desk and bent closer to see. He tried to cover it but I'd already seen enough. He was constructing a reliable guide to this camp and its layout."

As if jolted by electricity Max burst out, "But how did *you* know about this camp?"

"That's irrelevant," the Chief said cutting him off.

"Don't worry about me," Pierre told Max. "A farmer who provides food for the camp is a close relative. More to the point: how did Thomas know about it and why would he draw it? Troubled, I let class out early and came to tell the Chief."

"The teacher's just lucky the lookout liked his face," a lieutenant joked.

"Very disturbing," André said, not finding this a joking matter.

Alin said, "I still don't see what this has to do with us."

"I understand you put your children into the school in Soleyrols," the Chief said.

"Before they were forced into hiding," Alin complained bitterly.

"I don't care how long ago!" the Chief exploded, his patience with Alin wearing thin. "Some of the children there may have older brothers, sisters or cousins who might have said something indicating an interest in the Resistance."

"Neither of our daughters mentioned it," André said regretfully.

"Then here is what we must do," the Chief said, forcefully crunching his words through clenched teeth. "We need to stake out the roads leading from Vialas to Génolhac and Alès. I need to know if that map goes anywhere!"

"If so," André asked delicately, "what then?"

"Then Max and the others I'm sending with you will know what to do."

Max nodded, grimly determined.

The implication of a potentially violent outcome hung heavily in the air. André wondered, *Is this where Max's medical skill comes in?*

"Look," the Chief said, "this kid or his father may be a collaborator, unless it's both of them." He leveled his steady gaze on each man in turn. "This is serious business with potentially serious consequences. We have no choice but to get to the bottom of it." He settled his blazing eyes on Max. "You're in charge. In addition to Monsieur Jabot and the Severins, I'm sending two more of our hands with you. You're to leave immediately. Our best guess is that one or another of these Vignies will head for the closest Gestapo station, in Génolhac, if he hasn't gone already." He began writing out a note. "Let's not waste another second. Here." He handed the finished note to Max. "For your own protection. If you're stopped and questioned by the enemy it won't do any good—in fact it might play against you. So be prepared to destroy it quickly. But if you're approached by a member of another Resistance brigade it could save your lives."

Max folded the slip of paper carefully and secreted it inside his clothes.

"You'll want to take a pistol," the Chief told Max. "Go to the supply section. Your other two already have rifles." Then he asked the Severins, "Do you have any arms of your own?"

"No," André said, anguished but trying not to show it.

"Then you'll get rifles too," the Chief said turning to other business. "The others can show you all you need to know." He stared at them hard as if trying to hypnotize them. "This isn't a game. If you need to use force, you must do so without hesitation. Understood?"

"Understood," Max said assuming his command and answering for all.

As they left the room, Max quietly asked André if he would be all right.

"I'll carry a rifle," André answered gravely, "but I won't use it except in self-defense."

Two armed Maquis—Albert Lazare and Guy Chauvert—joined their procession to the supply barn. The resister in charge gave Max a pistol and handed each Severin a rifle. Pierre Jabot remained unarmed. He only needed to identify the Vignies.

"Ever use one of these?" the supply master asked the Severins.

André stayed silent. Alin examined the firearm admiringly and said, "The only rifles I've ever fired were a lot older."

"Well it's easy—maybe a little too easy," the supply master said demonstrating. "Put the cartridge here, press the rifle butt against your shoulder—tight or the kickback might break your collarbone. Sight your target along this line and when you're ready squeeze the trigger slowly." He lowered his weapon and grinned at the brothers. "Good hunting," he called gaily.

My God, André thought. *This Maquisard thinks killing a man is as easy as shooting wild boar!*

Stuffing bread, meat and cheese into their pockets for what might be a long stakeout, the men followed Max, who set a fast pace down the cart way. Heading over the pass into the next valley, he kept his six-man squad off the road by descending toward Vialas on a parallel path well worn by previous Resistance activity.

The sun approached the western horizon and shadows lengthened as the men neared their destination in silence. When they occasionally heard voices coming toward them from the woods Max signaled them to crouch down behind bushes or trees.

"Around the next bend," he finally whispered, "is a good place to wait and rest. Up in the woods, we'll still be able to see the road. There are places to hide quickly if we must."

After four hours of walking, all were relieved to sit on a fallen tree. With shoulders chafed by rifle straps, the Severins were pleased to lay the weapons across their knees.

Max left his subordinates and carefully picked his way down toward the road. An engine rumbled and brakes squealed as the old red bus struggled along its route between Vialas and Alès. Later a small truck could be heard going the other way. Its headlights shined spottily through the leaves until it too disappeared.

Then Max returned to lead the men to a spot closer to the road. By peering through branches and around the large trunks of old-growth trees, all could obtain a clear view.

"Stay where you can see," Max told Pierre. "Can you recognize the father too?"

"If there's enough light," Pierre replied. "He's visited the school many times. I remember him particularly because he always asks annoying pointless questions. Frankly, I don't like him even without this terrible business. Inflexible and demanding. He's got a reputation for insisting shoppers in his store have exactly the right ration coupons to buy anything. None of the other merchants in Vialas are that strict. Even if you have the proper coupons he may not have what you're looking for unless you're willing to pay more." Pierre shrugged his shoulders. "I've always thought his son nice enough. He wants to be an engineer, but he's under his father's thumb."

"Just tell us if you see either of them," Max said.

One old farmer walked by grumbling to himself, but no one else appeared as dusk gathered and deepened. Then a bicycle came along, its headlight beaming a faint glow ahead. Pierre signaled frantically. Max leapt into action.

Waving the bicyclist to slow, Max only made the rider pedal faster, trying to maneuver around the human obstruction. But the others waited a few meters on.

The bicyclist skidded to a stop, positioned to take off if allowed or to make a break.

"What's this?" the rider asked sounding simultaneously aggressive and defensive.

As the schoolmaster nodded Max asked the detainee, "Are you Maurice Vignie?"

The stunned suspect glared at the half dozen men surrounding him. "Yes and I'm in a hurry, so if you'll excuse me..." No one did. Panicking, Maurice shouted, "I need to go!"

"I'm sure you do," Max said coldly, "but first we need to ask where you're going."

"None of your business!" Maurice squealed. Then he growled, "To Génolhac. To visit a friend—Anything wrong with that?"

"At this time of day?" Max motioned to Albert and Guy. "Search him."

The two Maquisards grabbed each of the man's arms. Maurice tried to shake free but was roughly pulled off his bicycle. Then he spotted and recognized Pierre.

"Ah, Monsieur Jabot," he called bowing scornfully as deeply as his captors' grip allowed. "Isn't it a little late for teaching lessons?"

Maurice squirmed as Max turned his jacket pockets inside out, patted the lining and emptied his pants pockets. But Max found only a wallet with a few franc notes and a shopping list—unless flour, salt, sugar, fruits and vegetables constituted a code.

"Satisfied?" Maurice demanded smugly.

Max had Alin pick up the bicycle so he could feel around the frame. "Loose fittings? No. Solid." He ran his hands along the handlebars, twisted off the rubber grips at either end, pulled a flashlight from his back pocket and shined it into the exposed hollow space of the tubular handle. Next, he unscrewed and explored the little headlamp revealing only a small battery in the lamp housing.

Maurice had stopped struggling but Max wasn't finished yet. He felt around the seat and shined his flashlight under it. He felt his way along the rear strut. When he reached the rear reflector he wrenched it loose. Maurice stiffened.

Max patiently worked the reflector, finally pulling it free. Inside the cavity he found and pulled out a square of paper which he unfolded and read carefully. "Twelve names," he announced somberly, "including mine. I know the rest too. Most are still living in Vialas and Soleyrols, but several are men who have already joined us at the camp. Albert," he said to one of the men holding Maurice, "you're on it."

"*Merde!*" Albert Lazare cursed. Without warning, he slapped Maurice and spat in his face. "You bastard!"

Coldly Max showed the paper to Maurice. "What is this?"

Maurice's chest sank and his knees sagged. He said weakly, "I don't know. It's from my son. He's the one who wanted me to take it."

"Take it where?"

"To a friend. Like I said." His eyes spun wildly in his head as he looked at the small menacing group. "It's not my fault! It was all Thomas's doing, not mine!"

Pierre Jabot swallowed hard and wrapped his arms around his belly. *I can't believe I've been teaching his son. Could I have done anything to prevent this?*

André moved to within inches and examined the captive's face with scientific detachment. "So this is the enemy. He looks so normal and talks with the same accent. He's no different from anyone else in the Cévennes—except that he's a traitor."

Maurice Vignie shook. "I didn't know what that note contained—honest! I didn't even know it was there! Please don't hurt me! I won't do anything like this ever again I swear! I'm for France too! I hate the Germans just like you do! The Nazis, the Gestapo...they're the ones who have done this to us all! Spare me and I'll do anything you say!" He sank to his knees. Albert and Guy let his arms drop. He clasped his hands together in the classic beggar's attitude. "Please!" he moaned, drawing out the vowel sound miserably.

After what seemed an eternity, Max turned to his men. "You all know I trained to be a doctor, to save lives. And when this war is over, I intend to complete my studies and heal as many as I can." Suddenly he pulled out his pistol, crouched and pressed the deadly weapon to Maurice Vignie's left temple. "But I have not yet taken the Hippocratic oath. This is war and this man would betray his country—and us—to the Germans."

Maurice could no longer move or even squeak let alone continue to petition for mercy.

Albert placed a hand on Max's shoulder. "We should take him and his bicycle down to the bottom of the ravine and leave them both to rot."

Max nodded. Albert and Guy grabbed Maurice under his arms and dragged him away.

"No no! Don't do it! For the love of God!" the condemned man pleaded.

Max followed, then called back to Alin, André, and Pierre to come too.

Pierre obeyed immediately yet unsteadily. The Severins held back long enough to exchange a sharp look, both wondering, *Does Max really have what it takes to kill in cold blood?*

André slowly followed the others into the ravine and Alin followed, wheeling the bicycle by his side. They both stopped halfway down the slope out of sight of the road. From there they watched the dark forms of the Maquisards drag shadowy Maurice Vignie into a small depression filled with close-growing broom bushes at the edge of a water course. There they forced him to his knees.

Albert said to Max, "Let me have your pistol. You shouldn't have to do this."

Taking it, he set the muzzle against the base of Maurice's skull, pulled back the hammer and gritted his teeth.

"N-o-o-o-o..." Maurice Vignie keened.

Albert pulled the trigger. With a flash and a roar the bullet exploded into the skull. Maurice Vignie's head snapped back as his body flopped into the ravine.

The slight light from the rising moon revealed a half dozen stupefied expressions. Albert and Guy managed to scuff brush and twigs onto the inert body. Then they climbed up to Alin, removed the bicycle from his clutched hands, and rolled it down, twisting it to rest against the body.

Max led his squad slowly back up to the road. "Pierre?" he called. "Can you show us to the Vignie house?"

"Must we?" the schoolmaster asked, even as he began guiding the group.

"The names of twelve good men are on that list," Max said grimly. "If it were to get into the hands of the Gestapo they would be twelve dead men— including me and Albert."

Approaching Vialas, the group left the road to skirt the more populated areas. After some minutes, they came out from under cover again near Soleyrols. The still-rising moon provided a bit more light. Stars shone brightly through the crisp clear atmosphere.

They slipped off the road again just before reaching the first houses and began working their way along garden paths. A dog barked repeatedly and growled as the Maquis passed. Then it grew quiet again.

The schoolmaster held up his hand, stopping the little band awkwardly. "There," he whispered excitedly. "That's the house."

The house's shutters were closed tight for the night. A light was on over the front door. Max had André, Alin, and Pierre wait while he, Albert, and Guy crept closer.

The front door opened. A young man came out with a lantern and entered the outhouse, hanging his lantern on a hook beside the door.

The trio of Maquisards made their way in a crouch alongside the short path to the outhouse, careful to stay in the shadows of the house. They heard noises from within as Max slowly reached up to cut off the lantern light.

"Merde," a voice groaned inside.

The outhouse door banged open. A hand grabbed for the extinguished lantern. Max seized it and pulled. Albert and Guy rose to snatch each of their victim's arms. Faster than Thomas Vignie could cry out, Max stuffed a handkerchief into his mouth and clamped it tight.

Thomas struggled manfully, but was quickly subdued. His captors dragged him up the garden path and down a little trail. André, Alin, and Pierre followed quickly to a listlessly meandering stream.

Max shined his flashlight onto Thomas's face and then onto the list of Resistance names.

"Did you have anything to do with this?" Max demanded.

The youngster's eyes popped wide in terror as he vigorously shook his head no.

"Your father said you did. Is this or isn't this your handwriting?"

The unfortunate young man's eyes bobbled wildly. Max gestured Pierre to come forward. Seeing his teacher, Thomas slumped.

"Well?" Max demanded of Pierre, showing him the list.

The teacher looked closely at the slip of paper and with obvious reluctance acknowledged, "Yes that's his handwriting. Distinctive."

Thomas struggled more forcefully, his eyes on fire, and focused murderously on Pierre. The gag kept his shouts muffled deep within his throat.

"You have one chance to survive this," Max informed the young man. "Agree to work with us rather than against us."

"Don't be a fool," Pierre pleaded with his charge. "You have so much to live for."

Suddenly a female voice called out from the house. "Thomas? Thomas?"

Turning toward the worried voice, Thomas stopped struggling.

"His mother," Pierre confirmed.

"You're running out of time," Max told the prisoner.

Thomas's eyes glistened with tears but he made no gesture of renunciation.

His mother called his name again more loudly.

At another nod from Max the Maquisards dragged Thomas farther down the stream. Then Max led them along pathways that emerged from a thicket onto a small spit of land declining steeply toward a ditch.

Guy Chauvert pulled out Max's pistol, stepped to within inches of Thomas Vignie and asked softly, "Now will you see reason?"

Again, Thomas shook his head "no."

Max hissed into his ear, "You want to end up dead like your father?" The young man curled up into a tightly wrapped ball of flesh. André felt sick to his soul. "Get him up on his knees," Max ordered.

Albert and Guy forced Thomas into a squat at the edge of the ditch. Albert took the pistol and with his mouth firmly set, looked to Max who held up his hand.

Thomas hung his head limply.

"You know what you've done," Max said bitingly.

Albert placed the pistol against the back of Thomas's head. Just like his father.

"Work with us," Pierre begged his student. "You know in your heart we're right."

After a long motionless silence, Max nodded and Albert pulled the trigger. The sound of the shot was muzzled by flesh. Thomas's head jerked forward and bounced back. The dead body made a soft plop as it smacked into a slimy patch of alluvial mud.

"Someone will find them both," Max said huskily, recovering the revolver from Albert and slipping it into his belt. "They'll know what all this means."

André wasn't the only one struggling not to become sick. *Damn this war!* he thought helplessly as they crossed the small stream and moved through the woods to avoid the little gathering of homes. He didn't like swearing even to himself, but if ever there was a moment in his life…

Damn!

They slept fitfully in the hayloft, leaning against a wall or braced by a pile of musty hay, berets pulled over their ears. But that little cover couldn't block out the voice of a troubled conscience.

Max was especially distressed and remorseful. He had done what he had to and for the sake of his men, had managed with great effort to maintain a façade of certainty and strength. But left to his own devices in the dark, how could he quiet his agitated mind? Would he keep this from Fela or should he? Someday he knew he would have to tell her everything. But not until he had sorted through his feelings and forgiven himself.

A muted light began to suffuse the barn. The little frost that had formed on the straw overnight melted quickly in the warmth of the rising autumn sun. A few of Max's men began to stir. André and Alin sat side by side, picking wisps of straw out of their clothes and hair.

Max gathered his soul-sick self and said, "Better return to Le Tronc this morning. Now." The brothers looked at him blankly, too worn to process a thought. "We've all got a better chance if we separate. Once those bodies are discovered…" Max turned to Pierre Jabot. "The same goes for you. Go down to your own place. Tomorrow go back to school. The children expect you and it will raise too many questions if you don't show up as usual. Just don't talk about this to anyone. That goes without saying."

Pierre's face was drawn, bone-white. There were heavy dark circles under eyes that contained a faraway look. His unresponsiveness caused Max to call his name sharply. "Pierre!"

Shaking his head slowly, Pierre muttered, "How can I ever go back to school, look into those young hopeful faces—faces like Thomas's? But if I don't go back, what will I do when I run into them? They'll talk when his body is found. They'll look at me and wonder, *Did you know? Did you have a part in this?* And they'll guess the truth, no matter how I try to hide it." He buried his face in his hands.

"It won't be anything like that," Max said gently. "Unless you let it happen."

A sorrowful silence weighed heavily on them all. But Albert and Guy slept on undisturbed.

When Pierre finally looked back up, André said softly, "Last night always will be with us. But what you—what we—must constantly bear in mind, even when we're old men called at last to account for our actions, is that killing those two men saved at least a dozen others and who knows how many more. And consider too, all the good this dozen brave souls will yet do for a free France. Did we have a choice? No. Would it even be possible for us to go on with our lives in good conscience had we acted otherwise? Again I say no." André took off his glasses and wiped the dirt from them with his great blue handkerchief, now a worn-out hole-riddled rag. "I saw the results of killing during the Great War. People, who like us, had killed up close and were never able to forgive themselves, going through life as automatons. Others who had done the same, put their terrible experiences into a broader perspective: they did not like themselves for taking others' lives, but saw what they had fought against come to an end, and acknowledged the small but vital role they had played in bringing the horror and suffering to a rightful conclusion. Then they began to live again. They tried to do more—to contribute more—to make up for the lives circumstance forced them to snuff out. And they went on working to make a bigger difference to create a good that simply could never have come to be if not for the dreadful actions fate had forced upon them." André put a hand on Pierre's shoulder. "Now you must make a decision: to dwell eternally on the terrible fact of what we did last night and allow it to paralyze you or to rejoin the struggle to make a better future for you, your students, and all those on which you can continue to have a powerful positive impact. Nothing could be harder and no one can help you. But we can encourage and stand beside you." André released Pierre as if to leave him the room he needed to decide. "Either way you must go home now and resume your routine so you don't give us away. Besides, those children need you. They need to hear and learn of the good and the right, of values and belief, of the importance of faith, about men—real men and true freedom, of thoughtful unfettered inquiry, and of the necessity to dream and to explore and to work toward a future far better than man has ever known. For as bad as the present may be, it's the same as every bad time in history, such as the torture and killing of the Huguenots—it can't last—not forever. And only you, *monsieur l'instructeur* Jabot, can give your students the knowledge, the hope, and the courage required to build that better future of which we all dream."

Alin added, "Thomas Vignie made a terrible mistake. He paid with his life because life is serious business. But now the serious business of life must go on. And it's up to you to keep the rest of your students from making the same mistake."

André clasped Max's hand and said, "Alin and I will go to Le Tronc as you so wisely suggest. But we shall be ready to help again. Please call on us whenever necessary."

Alin shouldered his rifle. "Agreed."

Pierre Jabot struggled to his feet and said gravely, "I'm going home now too. And first thing tomorrow I will go back to school. After all, I can't leave the children sitting there waiting for me. I'm their teacher." He smiled wanly. "But like André and Alin, I say get word to me when you need me again. I'll do my part. You can count on that."

Now Max knew what he too must do. Shaking off the last of the long night's chill he left for the camp's command center to discover what the Chief had in store for him next.

Léon and Yvonne were laboriously gathering chestnuts when André and Alin returned.

"Back so soon?" Léon asked as if their comings and goings and the rifles on their shoulders were as common as chestnuts. "Success?"

Neither brother answered.

"You look tired," Yvonne told them kindly, as she continued her labors uncomplainingly. "Why not go to the barn and get some rest? We can talk later if you like."

Before they could move, Léon said, "Fine-looking weapons. Know how to use them?"

"No!' André answered abruptly—vehemently—and sounding terribly upset.

"Well I'll show you," Léon said with uncharacteristic gentleness. "No sense having them if you can't use them properly. May I?" He gingerly removed the rifle from André's yielding hands. "Hmn. Better than my rusty old thing."

"It's just for self-defense," André said abashed.

"Not mine," Alin countered. "I'm ready to use mine for its intended purpose."

"Either way," Léon continued, "you'll need to learn the proper care and cleaning and the internal mechanism in case it jams. This doesn't look too hard to figure out."

"Léon," Yvonne counseled. "Let them rest."

"Oh all right," Léon grumped. "Come back later. I'll show you how it's done."

André startled awake in late afternoon, daylight already fading. His brother continued to sleep.

As he moved his feet from straw pallet to hard floor, the cold stunned André more fully awake than the nightmare that had jolted him into unwelcome consciousness. Rubbing his eyes, he looked around blearily. There were the rifles in one corner, standing on their stocks. André flashed back to the previous night—the crack of pistol shots—the blood.

He had hoped a decent sleep would bury these memories; but they haunted his dreams and came back now with the intensity of the present. Against his will, he found himself remorsefully reviewing and reliving the killings. Even when he tried to conjure his beloved wife and children, a spectral vision of Maurice and Thomas Vignie, first alive and then very dead, appeared before his eyes and could not be wiped away.

Pacing uncontrollably, André couldn't stand it anymore. He strode to Alin and shook him by the shoulder. Before Alin forced his eyes open André said, "I have to go to Le Salson to see Denise, if not to rid my mind of what happened yesterday then at least to gain some distance."

Alin sat up massaging his scalp and pounding temples. "Yes, well," he mumbled, "I want to see Geneviève too. But not yet, I guess. Damn it! I need to be with her and I will!"

André put on his shoes and coat and pulled his dark blue beret to one side because he thought it looked jauntier that way—though "jaunty" was the last way he expected to feel anytime soon.

André hiked briskly, purposefully, up the path, protected by the encroaching night. A wearying hour and a half later he approached the house he now knew. Mercifully, the light was still on.

When the door flew open and André moved to step inside Denise came right out, closed the door behind her and, before André could question her, wrapped herself in his arms and placed her lips on his in a kiss that lasted a long wonderful time. At its end, they clung closely to one another.

After a great silence and a profound sigh, Denise murmured, "I've missed you so."

"And I've missed you more than I can say."

André kissed her again trying to imply a great deal. Another long moment passed before Denise gently released herself from his embrace, took him lovingly by the hand, and led him to the nearby stone wall.

He lifted her up onto it then sprung up beside her. The dark stones were cool, slowly losing the last of the sun's heat. Side by side husband and wife luxuriated in each other's presence and the sense of peace supplied by the early-autumn night in the Cévennes.

Much as André wished to unburden himself, he couldn't utter a word about the Vignies' execution. Even as waves of guilt disturbed his mind and spirit, it seemed wiser to suffer in silence than to draw poor Denise into his moral morass.

Fortunately, she chattered away lightly, brightly. "Ida and Christel get along so splendidly now, perhaps because Cristian demands so much of me that Christel has learned to turn to Ida as her chief comforter and protector—a role Ida has taken on with amazing grace and facility. They play make-believe endlessly—in the house, in the enclosed courtyard, even behind the wall of the terrace that runs alongside the garden. They're sad that all the sugar is gone and we need our honey to make bread and to sweeten our tea. But their imaginations have grown so vivid that they easily substitute fantasy sugar for the real thing. Christel even planted a small row of wild seeds she claims are special sugar seeds, which will grow up to be candy trees. Ida plays along, helping to water and weed. Oh, and Cristian has begun to talk! Only a few words and only one at a time, but he's only sixteen months old. That's fairly remarkable, especially for a male child."

"I bet his first word was 'maman,'" André said grinning with pride in both his wife and son. How he wished he would soon have a chance to hear Cristian's prattle.

"Yes it was," Denise laughed. André thought he saw her blush in the little light provided by the moon and stars. "But listen to me going on and on about trivial homely things when I know you have far greater matters on your mind."

Charmed and delighted by the activities of his son and daughters as never before, André was glad to be distracted, however briefly, from the terrible tale he held within himself. Feelingly he said, "How much the war has changed me. It's true that I missed the first steps and words of both our girls without giving it a thought, but now...Now I care very much about every aspect of our children's lives. Every day it becomes clearer; it's life itself that matters most in this world." Then he thought, but did not say, *Especially after yesterday.*

"I love you so much," Denise said spontaneously. It was as if she had read André's freighted mind and couldn't wait to mouth what he most needed to hear.

Stretching herself to lean up against him, Denise rested her head in the hollow of his shoulder. She may have spoken of love this way only rarely, but André never expressed his deepest emotions so simply or directly. He wished to now, but found he could not. Thankfully he knew his wife understood and had no need for him to give utterance to what he felt for her.

Long before he wished to, André felt compelled to say, "I have to go."

"I know." Though melancholy, Denise had long since learned and accepted that this was the way things had to be for now. There was no point in objecting.

André dislodged himself from the stone wall and helped his wife down. They kissed again and André hugged her passionately. Almost suffocating.

Full of longing and regret, André released Denise and walked back up the path. At the bend of the road he stopped and turned, unsure whether his wife watched from the Bastide house or could see him if she did. He waved, hoping she would at least sense and appreciate the gesture, just as he trusted she had sensed and appreciated all he could not say.

He had hoped this visit would lighten his emotional load, but the farther he got from his family, the heavier his heart felt.

In the bright sunlight of Monday morning, Denise felt exhilarated as her children played in the Bastides' courtyard. Still glowing with the memory of André's unexpected visit, she imagined she could feel the imprint of his touch, his clasp, his kiss. But she also was painfully aware that something troubled her husband, something far beyond the now-habitual worries.

Then a sound froze her heart and propelled her to move protectively toward her offspring. A man's voice was so unusual that Denise couldn't help but be alarmed. She warned her daughters to play quietly and they obeyed since both were old enough to understand their presence needed to be kept secret. Little Cristian was too young, but his sisters hushed him as necessary. Ida especially had a gentle way with him.

Feeling foolish, Denise suddenly remembered what day it was and realized the male voice belonged to the postman paying his weekly visit. He wasn't the mailman she knew from La Font, but Irene and Ernestine had vouched for his trustworthiness.

Curious since the conversation sounded livelier than usual, Denise tiptoed back into the house and toward the front door that stood partially ajar. Listening from behind it, she heard the letter carrier say, "Sometimes there's a letter inside, sometimes it's a rope."

"A rope?" Irene asked.

"So they get the message and hang themselves," Ernestine lisped.

"They send them through the mail?" Irene continued incredulously.

"Sometimes," the mailman allowed. "Sometimes it's hung in a tree or over the front door."

"Good," Ernestine spat. "Those traitors deserve what they get. Some tell the authorities where young men have hidden themselves. Those young men who believe they have something better to do with their lives than sacrifice themselves for the benefit of Nazi dogs."

Irene said, "I still don't understand where they get those little wooden coffins."

Now Denise understood. Since early summer, rumors had circulated about collaborators receiving miniature coffins. No one knew precisely where they originated but their message was clear: *We know you inform on resisters. We know you traffic in black market goods.*

"Carpenters make them," Ernestine shot back. "Carpenters that the true French can trust."

"Have you heard the latest?" the mailman asked excitedly. "About the Vignies?"

"What?" Ernestine demanded. "Who?"

Denise wracked her memory but—nothing.

"Maurice Vignie, a shopkeeper from Vialas, and his teenage son. Both shot dead."

After an extended silence Irene said, "Terrible. Think of the poor wife and mother."

Ernestine said sharply, "Ask yourself what they did to deserve it."

"No one deserves such a thing." Irene sounded heartsick.

"The village is full of Milice," the mailman said, "asking whether anyone has heard or seen anything suspicious."

"You think the Resistance killed him?" Irene asked in a hoarse anxious whisper.

"Has to be," her mother clucked triumphantly. "The Maquis."

Denise's heart throbbed. When the postman left, and the Bastides stepped back inside. Denise stood stock-still in the hallway.

"It's okay now," Ernestine said gently, a look of concern creasing her brow. "You really don't need to be afraid of the mailman anymore. He's harmless, though he does talk too much."

But Denise wasn't afraid of the letter carrier. She was afraid of what her husband might have had to do with the Vignies and what it was doing to him.

Chapter Fourteen

THE MAQUIS

September 27, 1943

Despite intense concentrated labor, a strange air of peace prevailed at Le Tronc in the weeks following the Vignie killings. Max paid a quick visit to tell the Guins and Severins the camp at Le Crespin had been abandoned, its location having been disclosed to the Gestapo after all. The Maquisard had established a new camp at Les Bouzedes and if the Guins had any more food to share or the Severins ever needed to go there…Nothing was said of the Vignies nor were the brothers asked to participate in another mission.

It wasn't until October that the postman brought word of the final liquidation of the Warsaw ghetto in June, after a months-long uprising by incarcerated Jews that had shown Poland and the world that even the most wretched and abused could display the greatest courage and dignity and engaged in daring acts of defiance. The Severins and Guins also learned of that summer's Allied victories in Africa, the subsequent invasion of Sicily, and the overthrow and arrest of Mussolini—all very encouraging, but insufficiently close to home.

André continued his weekly visits to Le Salson, always a source of comfort and renewal. And a message finally arrived from Pastor Donadille freeing Alin to visit L'Herm.

That very evening Alin shouldered his rifle and went off to see his wife and daughter for the first time in seven long months. Pierre Guin had secreted them the second floor of an old schoolhouse where they were reasonably comfortable, but had to be extremely careful during school days not to show themselves or make any noise. It was a struggle for Geneviève and Katie only to speak in low whispers, always duck beneath the windows, and carefully avoid stepping on floorboards they knew might squeak.

Traveling in daylight was risky, so Geneviève could only see her son infrequently at night. Though they never spoke, it was helpful yet never enough to gaze upon her sleeping Philippe.

Despite his isolation Philippe Severin was better off living with the large Ours family than his own. Everyone was told that Philippe was a cousin whose mother was from French-run Algeria. This made Philippe the only Severin not in hiding at all times. He was free to interact with the village children, to run and jump in the fresh air and to play without restraint.

Alin wished he could see the boy too and decided to stay in L'Herm for a few days. Léon would curse him but he and Geneviève had so much lost time to make up.

André was startled to find himself with evenings alone. Glad of the opportunity to think and write, he also was surprised and delighted to discover among the Guins' small stock of prized possessions, *Roux the Bandit,* the first substantial modern literary work in Cévenol that Suzanne Maurel had strongly recommended three years earlier. Sometimes André had trouble deciphering the patois, but Yvonne always was happy to help.

Despite Suzanne's suggestion, André did not view himself and Chamson's Roux as having much in common, but he could certainly appreciate their shared much-derided devotion to pacifism. This Roux—modeled perhaps on a member of Ernestine's late husband's family—suffered far greater privations than André Severin, making André most grateful for the warmth of his little fire and the comparative comfort of his bed of fresh straw. And he found reassuring resonance in a passage about Roux's criminal avoidance of military conscription during the Great War: "If Roux had wished to hide on a farm, the gendarmes would have known nothing about it, for nobody would have come to betray him..."

But reading this book in the wake of the Vignie assassinations, increased André's confusion about his deeply held beliefs of the sacred nature of life and the foolish notion that killing of any sort can serve a greater good and lead to better times. These beliefs contrasted strongly with the obvious need to do something in the face of overt evil.

Over dinner one night, the Guins told him how disgusted they were by the Great War and how horrified they had been throughout the thirties watching the present war coming. So many of the French had sworn they would never be drawn into yet another pointless death-dealing war. But none had done anything to prevent it.

Back in the barn, André was fascinated to discover a counterexample to Roux in Chamson's novel—the pastor of Anduze: "He did not want to fight, either, because of conscientious reasons. But he went just the same, like the others, in order not to put himself in the wrong...without taking a gun." André could not help but ponder deeply this model of thoughtfulness, bravery, fortitude, and sacrifice. Could he too be bold and determined enough to put himself in harm's way in order to serve without picking up a weapon?

Yet he also couldn't help thinking of the way Einstein had put aside his longstanding pacifism in the face of the despicable. André began to feel a strong desire to stand his ground and defend his adopted country, almost convinced that though the philosophy of the Quakers' *Peace Testimony* was assuredly worthy of the devotion of his life, there were still horrors, there was still evil, and that even the moral peace-loving man must feel compelled and right to fight.

What a conundrum. If Max Maurel and all the other resistants jeopardize their lives to shelter and defend André and his family, how could André fail to join them? Yet he remained convinced that any form of military action was wrong. Simultaneously, he knew that when bloodshed inevitably got closer still, he would have to find a way to contribute to the Maquisards more meaningfully. Not to take substantive action might well mean allowing himself and those he cared about most to be subjugated and possibly destroyed. On the other hand, wasn't there an internal contradiction between joining the fight to gain the freedom necessary to worship, as driven by a spiritual insight, and a spiritual insight that led one to reject war?

The resolution of André's conflict was taken out of his hands once Alin finally returned. Two Milice showed up at Le Tronc and went to the farmhouse searching for Léon. Terrified, Yvonne let slip that her husband was out in the far fields working the sheep.

Laboring at Léon's side, André and Alin looked up and spotted the distinctive uniforms. Fearful for their lives they knew better than to bolt, for to run away would declare their status as renegades from the government. Instinctively they felt it was better to assert their innocence by stolidly laboring on as would any hard-bitten Cévenol farmer—like Léon.

Their instincts saved them. The Milice hadn't come to capture them but rather to demand of Léon how much land he had and how much wheat that land could produce, so that they would know how much would be available to feed the German Army after the harvest. Though Léon underestimated by a substantial margin, his false answers satisfied the urban thugs. Profoundly ignorant of agriculture they went away happy.

But now that the Milice had found their way to Le Tronc, André and Alin knew the time had come to leave and join the Resistance for the war's duration. They would miss the Guins but they knew it could mean their lives if they didn't move still more deeply underground.

The lookout recognized the Severins from Le Crespin and with a quick salute, let them pass. A little larger than Le Crespin, Les Bouzedes had its own layout and landscape, but the buildings were similar and the faces mostly familiar.

The brothers made their way unremarked until Max raced over. "I wondered how long it would be before you came here!" he cried, embracing them and planting kisses on their cheeks.

The Severins explained what had brought them—Alin with bitterness, André with resignation.

"That's bad," Max acknowledged with a long low whistle, leading the brothers to a big barn and sitting beside them on a sack of potatoes. "But I'm not surprised. We've had more and more reports of the Milice and the Gestapo going farther and farther afield to fulfill Germans needs. And now we have a new chief."

"New chief?" Alin had barely gotten used to the old one.

"Roger. A man of much experience. You'll feel comfortable in his hands." Max leaned back and pointed at the brothers' rifles. "Have you practiced?"

"With Léon's help," André replied tentatively. "But I'm still intimidated."

Alin snorted. "That's because shooting can kill."

André shot Alin a fierce look.

"Let me take you to meet the new chief," Max enthused.

After a few minutes' wait, the three were ushered into the new command post. Half-hidden by the large table that served as his desk, tall, thin Roger Boudon was about thirty-five years of age. His angular face showed signs of strain and his two-day growth of brown beard made him look worn. Two strong lines creased his brow and the beginnings of small crow's feet were visible at the corners of his piercing eyes. As he rose to shake the Severins' hands, they could see the pistol he wore in the thick leather belt strapped around his narrow waist.

After Max's rapid-fire detailing of the Severins' background and previous involvement with the Resistance, the chief welcomed them warmly to Les Bouzedes. Then he excused himself and asked Max to show them to their new quarters: a cramped room in one of the outbuildings.

This will do, André told himself, setting his little sack down on one of the two slender cots, *though it makes the Guins' barn seem like a mansion.*

Roger Boudon had brought a new level of organization and discipline to these Maquisards. The camp's inhabitants were divided into three teams charged with different responsibilities: the maintenance team gathered firewood and potable water, cleared and cleaned, and cooked; the security team manned guard posts and ran perimeter patrols; the military instruction team dealt with guerrilla tactics, group combat, and the study of arms and explosives. Working with Max, the instruction team also saw to first aid and safety procedures.

There had been a remarkable increase in the number of weapons available. A recent raid on a nearby gendarmerie had yielded a startling array: American Remington, French Hotchkiss, German Mauser, assorted English rifles, Sten guns, and hand grenades.

Food supplies remained problematic, although local peasants, farmers, and the townspeople of Vialas provided as much as they could. Whatever food the Maquisard obtained was prepared amidst the chestnut trees, decreasing the chance of smoke from cooking fires being noticed by German spy planes.

Everyone knew to go into hiding under the chestnut trees when a plane passed overhead. The broad branches and big leaves provided excellent cover.

André and Alin quickly learned the daily routine.

07:00 a.m.: Reveille (without a bugle!) and toilette.

07:30 a.m.: Breakfast (which far too often consisted of the dreaded bajana).

08:00 a.m.: Free time.

09:00 a.m.: Physical training.

10:00 a.m.: Military instruction.

11:00 a.m.: Work and patrols around the camp.

01:00 p.m.: Lunch (bajana again, this time with a little meat added in).

01:30 p.m.: Siesta.

03:00 p.m.: Sports (sometimes soccer; sometimes *la pétanque*—a version of *boules* or *bocce*).

04:00 p.m.: Work and patrols.

07:00 p.m.: Dinner (bajana yet again, with noodles or potatoes, a little bread and perhaps some locally grown greens).

07:30 p.m.: Free time (which many used to play *belote,* a card game).

09:30 p.m.: Lights out (or, for those so assigned, overnight guard duty).

Despite built-in rest periods it was a demanding schedule. The brothers were surprised by the intensity of the training and labor. One night after a particularly long day of backbreaking work, André told Max, "I had no idea my body had so many muscles. Now they all speak to me with a heavy accent."

André took great satisfaction in becoming part of the camp. He participated in all its activities with a will, even learning how to take his rifle apart, clean it, and put it back together again.

More startling still, he was willing to take orders—unlike in the Belgian Army—because he believed in the cause.

Before long, the Severins were sufficiently well-trained and trusted to go on perimeter patrols, swiftly learning to scout for German and Milice dispositions. It was always nerve-racking though, particularly when the Maquisard received advance warning of their would-be tormentors' movements.

Because they were older than most of their compatriots, whose average age wasn't much above twenty, the chief tapped André and Alin to help train the latest volunteers. He even had newcomers bunk with the brothers, forcing the Severins into separate sleeping quarters.

The Severins' distinct personalities and aptitudes rapidly became evident. Alin's greater physicality and handiness were put to good use in repairing the great barn and outbuildings. André, due to his experience with and ability to judge young people, was occasionally asked by Roger to sit in as he attempted to determine if a new recruit was truly against the Germans or entering Les Bouzedes as a spy.

The need for caution was great. Everyone knew the Milice kept attempting to infiltrate the ranks of the Resistance. When spies were found out, they were summarily executed—just as the Vignies had been.

André was pleased to do his part in these sessions. But killings were something he prayed never to see again.

On the next morning, the lookout watched warily, alert to any danger. Two figures hiked up the cartway: would-be Maquis or enemy spies? The lookout was the first line of defense and guessed these two came fresh from the lycée. Both had unruly uncut hair and the wispy beginnings of soft light beards. Both were wiry and gave the impression of being used to the outdoors. They didn't carry rifles, but the lookout thought it wise to let them see his.

"Hello," he called down. "Where might you be coming from?"

"From Nîmes," one new arrival said voice quavering.

The anxiety was a good sign, but the lookout had to follow standard procedures. "What brought you into this region?"

"They want to send us to Germany," the second called loudly.

"And you don't come back from Germany," his companion elaborated.

"We're scared," the other continued. "Another friend signed up with the gendarmes as he was supposed to and the next week they took him from his home. He hasn't been seen or heard from since." The young man swallowed hard. "I'm only nineteen. I won't wait to be taken."

"I'd rather fight," his companion insisted.

The lookout suppressed a smile. He knew how they felt and how naïve they were about what was in store for them. He had been just such a raw recruit a year earlier.

"How did you know to come here?" he demanded, as he slowly climbed down from his semi-concealed position. How old he must appear—weathered and lined by long hours spent in the sun. Not quite twenty-five, he felt far older than the few years' difference in age should make.

"We started walking and ran into someone who told us to come here."

"Are you carrying any weapons?" the lookout asked.

"No," one allowed. Both looked sheepish. "But we'll fight barehanded if we have to."

The lookout grinned despite himself then quickly made his face blank. "I must check you," he said and patted them down. Their submission increased his confidence in them. Certain they were unarmed he told them, "Head up this cartway to the big house. If anyone asks tell them the lookout sent you to see Roger. Convince him of your good intentions and you're in."

The two young fellows smiled broadly, stood up straighter, and mumbled thanks in the manner of abashed youth.

"Don't thank me," the lookout said sardonically. "Thank the Germans. And thank our glorious leader Pétain."

Good God, Alin groaned inwardly, sitting on his cot when one of Roger's lieutenants ushered a new youth into his presence. *Why do they keep bringing them to me?*

"Keep him out of trouble," the lieutenant said, "until we can find him a permanent place."

"When will that be?" Alin growled. He hated playing nursemaid.

"Soon we hope," the lieutenant said chuckling as he strode away.

For a minute Alin was morose. But the new recruit trembled, bewildered and fearful, so Alin took pity on him. "What's your name?" he asked as pleasantly as he could.

"Jean-Philippe—"

"Uh-uh-uh!" Alin cut him off with a cautioning wag of his forefinger. "First names only please. It's not wise to let anyone know too much about you—not even your roommates."

"Just Jean-Philippe then."

"Good." Alin examined the youth closely. There wasn't much to him. "And what did you do? Before I mean."

"I was a student. But I've always done farmwork too on my folks' small place. In the off-seasons I apprenticed myself in woodworking, building cabinets and chairs." The young man suddenly collapsed onto his cot. "Oh God," he cried, his lower lip trembling. "I hope my Pa is okay. I tried to get him to join the Resistance too, but he just kept saying, 'Everyone needs to eat. I must stay and do my part.' Do you think the Milice will take him?"

"Not a farmer. Not yet."

"He's not in good health."

"Then they'll never want him."

Jean-Philippe wiped at his nose. "So what exactly is it we do?"

"Many things. Senseless things." Jean-Philippe looked so downcast Alin backtracked. "I mean things that may seem senseless, but they all have a purpose. Our job is to obey the chief's orders, even those we don't understand. You think you can do that?"

"I guess." The young man lowered his face into his hands.

Alin stood up uncertain what to do or say next. "We're all in this together," he tried. "We just do the best we can." Moving toward the door he said, "I've got some business to attend to. But don't worry. You'll find out all you need to know soon enough."

The young man stared at the floor. Alin stepped out and shut the door softly.

During his siesta on Thursday, November 6, André lay on his cot staring at the ceiling, feeling a little down as he always did on the anniversary of his father's death. This was the third year of such dispiriting remembrance and the pain never seemed to diminish as purportedly it would. Instead, as time went by, André missed Louis more and more.

One week hence Denise would turn thirty-four, and the day after that André would reach his forty-second birthday. He hated not being with his family, especially on such occasions. But he was inexpressibly glad that, Louis aside, they were all still alive.

By late November, the chief was bogged down in the paperwork required to coordinate all the new recruits. He hated paper-pushing, but one did what one must.

His office was now fitted out with two more tables and additional benches and chairs. As he worked, his various lieutenants, assistants, and subordinates kept coming in and going out, occasionally laying yet another piece of paper on top of Roger's increasingly messy mass of notes, memos, messages, and maps.

"Chief? André to see you," one aide announced.

"Send him in."

Sensing rather than observing André's arrival, Roger raised one finger to acknowledge him but went right on working. Finally finished, he stood up to offer André his hand.

"We have a problem that requires immediate attention," the chief told him. Then he turned to the others in his jam-packed office. "Please excuse us for a few minutes." Everyone else left and Roger told André, "I've got information that the Vichy government has placed spies in our area. We've got our eyes on two newcomers who seem to fit the bill but we're not absolutely certain. I'd like you to go out to investigate. The rest of the Maquisards I've assigned were all raised in these mountains, so they know their way around, but whether or not these two fellows really are spies...I need you to query them and see what you think."

"You mean before we do anything to them."

"Find out who they are, where they came from, who sent them—if anyone did—and what they know. After we bring them in—if that's what you recommend—well we're certainly not going to be able to send them on their merry way." Roger fixed his gaze steadily on André. "Are you up to it?"

André looked back at Roger just as directly. "I'm here to do whatever you tell me."

"Thank you," the chief said gravely. "There's just one other thing." Roger broke into a broad grin. "Remember to wear your glasses. They make you look like an intelligence officer. Someone not to be trifled with."

It was André's turn to smile. "No problem. I have to wear my glasses to see anything."

They laughed together, but within seconds Roger said, "There will be four others in your squad. Jacques is the designated leader. He already knows the role I want you to play."

"I don't know him," André said warily.

"He comes and goes frequently. But I trust him and you should too. Don't let his manner put you off. He can be a little gruff."

André grinned again. "That's all right. I've had plenty of experience with *that* kind of character."

The paths were dry. The air was brisk. With no wind, they didn't feel the cold. With little idle chatter and a steady pace, the small squad arrived in the hamlet sooner than expected. There was the typical handful of dwellings with smoke curling up from the chimneys of three. No one thought it would be difficult or time-consuming to find their quarry.

Coming down a far path, a solitary farmer returned from one of his small fields. As Jacques advanced alone to ask if he knew the men they were looking for, the farmer slowed and looked about confused and distressed. But Jacques swiftly put him at his ease and the laconic fellow nodded meaningfully toward the hamlet's smallest house.

Jacques waved to André and the others to join him. The farmer, dismayed, put down his walking stick to show he wouldn't put up a fight. He knew now that this was about the war, but supported neither the Resistance nor the Vichy authorities. He just wanted to be left alone.

"Can I go?" he asked nervously.

Jacques nodded. The farmer scurried off.

"The men we're after moved in just last week," Jacques told André as the resisters followed him to the door in question. "The other fellow says they're farmers, but I don't think he believes it—or cares."

Jacques banged on the door and without waiting for a response walked into the house followed closely by André. The others stood guard outside.

"Who are you?" a man about André's age asked as Jacques barreled past. Tall and thin, the man was obviously, understandably, annoyed and discomfited by this intrusion. His hands were rough as a farmer's, which stood in his favor, but his speech was not of the region. He cursed in Cévenol, but even to André his accent sounded off—definitely from somewhere beyond the Lozère though possibly from within the Massif Central. Certainly from the south of France.

The second suspect entered from the back. He too was middle-aged but heftier than his companion. His soft round stomach hung heavily over his belt. Maybe he'd done hard work in his life long ago. Impossible to picture him laboring in the fields today.

"New to the region?" André asked neutrally as Jacques looked on menacingly.

The fatter "farmer" answered "Yes," but sounded suspiciously tentative.

"Well, welcome," André said.

Jacques smirked.

"Thank you," the thinner man replied in a reserved tone.

"What brought you here?" André asked genially.

"The war."

That response seemed surprisingly quick, even glib, as if well-rehearsed.

"It's hard always having to search for food, even when you have the right ration coupons," the fatter one said. "It seemed easier to find a place and grow our own."

His ample girth gave his answer the lie. *He's never worried about food in his life,* André thought. Bearing down he inquired, "How long do you plan to stay?"

"Say, what is this?" the thinner man demanded irritably, sticking out his jaw defiantly. "You come in without so much as a 'How do you do' and don't tell us who you are. What gives you the right to interrogate us?"

"What do you plan to grow?" André persisted calmly.

If anyone addressed me that way, Jacques thought, impressed, *I'd sock him in the jaw.*

"What a foolish question," the fat one said. "We'll grow whatever's grown here."

"So you'll plant chestnuts," André said cagily. "When?"

"In the spring of course," the thinner one answered.

Now André knew they were lying. Imagine planting a tree in the spring and hoping to harvest from it that fall!

"What about wheat?"

"You can't grow that here," the same man answered speedily. "It's too high and rocky."

"Oh?" André said caustically. "Then why does the government demand to know the size of everyone's wheat fields?"

"You can go now," the thinner man told his uninvited guests, opening the door.

"After you," Jacques said agreeably, gesturing to the armed men just past the threshold.

"You can't make us go," the fat man wailed. "We live here!"

"Get your coats on," Jacques said, "unless you'd rather be cold."

The two "farmers" looked at one another uncertainly. Jacques settled the matter by opening his coat and showing his revolver.

"Wait a minute," the fat one said to Jacques, disappearing into the back room.

"Follow him quickly," Jacques urged.

André raced to the door.

The fat man reappeared saying flatly, "I'm ready now."

André stood aside. The burly man hesitated then went back to the front room.

As Jacques delivered the suspects to the three other Maquisards, André slipped into the back room. Swiftly sizing it up, he tugged aside a curtain uncovering a small paneled door set in the rear wall. Though he pulled at a knot in the wood panel beside it the door remained shut. Then he pushed at the other side and the door swung open.

André looked in then put in his hands and felt around. He pulled something forward.

Jacques appeared in the doorway in time to catch a glimpse of glinting metal: a small radio receiver and, damningly, a transmitter.

"That seals it," Jacques said. "Unless radio signals stimulate crop growth."

Jacques brought out the radio equipment. Flanked by Maquisards the thin one opened his eyes wide, boring into his fat friend with hatred and rage.

The resistants started walking the suspects up the path. Jacques stayed in the rear, but no one followed them. The farmer Jacques had spoken to first must have told the other residents something was up. Perhaps they didn't care—or realized there was nothing to gain by interfering.

"Where are you taking us?" the thin captive complained. "You have no right."

A young Maquisard pushed the butt of his rifle into the spy's ribs as if to say, *This is all the right I need.*

There was a good deal of grunting and groaning from the duo as they were hurried along. Then they began to stumble now and again, slowing the little procession.

Finally the fat man stopped. "My legs are giving out." With no more warning, he struggled toward a big flat rock at the side of the path and collapsed onto it.

Though angered by the delay, Jacques realized it had been a long day for his men too. "Okay," he called out regretfully. "Everyone rest."

The Maquisards unslung their rifles and sat on the ground. Jacques remained standing, but unbuttoned his coat to keep his pistol handy.

"Hey you," the slender spy said pointing at Jacques. "This your operation?" Jacques nodded. "Then why all the mystery? You can tell us now. We're out of the village."

"We can't go much farther," the portly one said cocking his head at a quizzical angle. "You want to carry us? Heh?"

The thinner man spotted André standing apart. "And what do you do? I can tell by your glasses you don't belong here."

Before more taunting occurred Jacques ordered, "Let's not waste any more time."

"You heard the man," the young Maquisard gleefully told the fat spy, prodding him again with his rifle butt. "On your feet. Move." Then he jabbed his boot into the other one's shoe.

The spies rose reluctantly, suddenly fearful of violence. Jacques just wanted to get on with it. He hoped to get back to camp before sunset because in the dark his charges would have to be bound, slowing progress and further endangering his men.

"Keep moving," he barked.

For the remainder of the forced march, Jacques kept pushing the pace though the suspects flagged and their breathing came harder. But what difference did that make?

Time for them to meet their fate.

The light began to fade as the thin captive caught sight of Les Bouzedes. In a way he was as glad to be there as his captors. He too could use water and a rest. And he would soon know whether his worst fears were justified. Either way, he would be glad when this was over.

But then the man in charge held up his hand bringing them all to an abrupt halt.

"Wait here," he commanded marching off to the main house with the man in glasses.

Roger Boudon stood and stretched his fingers, trying to ease the cramping that came from writing too much. André considered the irony: here he was, an academic, engaged in "manly" endeavors, and there was Roger, a habitué of the outdoor physical life, spending most of his time chained to a desk and a mound of papers.

"So how did it go?" the chief asked. Jacques deferred to André who told his tale. "In other words," the chief concluded for him, "they're spies."

Warily André said, "So it seems. But there's no guarantee."

"They don't belong here!" the chief exploded. "They're not *from* here and they're certainly not here to grow their own food no matter how much they insist. That radio transmitter bears out the intelligence we received. What other conclusion could a reasonable man reach?"

"Agreed," André said grimly.

"I'm positive too," Jacques put in.

Roger sat back down to address his paperwork. "Bring the spies to me."

Jacques left. André felt foolish and agitated just standing there.

Roger came out from behind his desk to shake André's hand and pat his shoulder. "Good job," he said. "Thanks." He hesitated. "Do you want to be here for this?" André shook his head no. "That's fine. You've done what we needed. We can take care of the rest."

The chief went back behind his desk. Going out André ran into the spies who looked pale and shaken. The fat one almost had to be carried in by the Maquisard guards who held each of his arms. The thinner man gave André a look that, quick as it was, he would never forget: the cold glare of a man who has looked into his grave and accepted he'll soon lie at the bottom of it.

André hastened away, not wanting to see or hear more or to think about what would happen next. It was a great relief to see his brother coming toward him. Alin would understand.

Although he had already heard all about André's mission Alin still asked if he'd been successful, for his brother's opinion was the only one that mattered to him.

"Successful?" André seemed puzzled by the word. "If you mean successful in finding the men we were sent for—yes we succeeded."

"Then they aren't..."

"Yes they are. I'm sure they were sent to spy on the Resistance."

Having wandered behind the big barn, the brothers stopped side by side to study the sunset, so stark and luminous in the clear cold air of the Cévennes.

"It's good to have found them out," Alin said flatly. "They're a danger to us all including our loved ones. And when I think of our family—well I don't care a rap about what happens to anyone who puts their lives in jeopardy."

"I know," André said, weary and sad. "This war is a tragedy—all war is." He shaded his eyes against the bright glare of a corona caused by a passing cloud. "I know we must do what we have to. But when I look deeply into the faces of people who in other times and circumstances might have been as good as anyone else—selfish perhaps, possibly foolish and probably with opinions quite different from yours and mine, yet on the whole *decent*—then I despise this war, not just for what it is, but for what it's doing to us all." André put the butt of his rifle down on the ground, leaned the barrel up against his leg, and rubbed his shoulder where the strap had cut into his trim frame's flesh. "I don't think I can ever watch another killing no matter how necessary. And I could never do the deed myself—point the gun and pull the trigger."

"Not even if someone was shooting at you or me or Denise?" Alin loved his brother, but was tired of this endless repetitive argument. When would André reconcile himself to the way people actually behaved? Given all that they had already seen and experienced, how could André still cling to his pacifistic notions? The world had never worked the way either of them wished and it never would. "Believe me André, not everyone's as good as you are. I would far rather take the lives of those who would take ours than lose our own." André stared off into the distance. Alin feared he had gone too far. "Of course it helps if the enemy's far away. When you've never met the people you must kill, it must be easier."

"I still wouldn't want to do it." André shook his head pitifully. "Near or far."

A considerable commotion made them turn toward the big house. The door was open and Jacques stood on the top step. When he spotted the Severins he hurried their way.

"You want to come with us?" he asked André excitedly. "Having gotten all he can out of them the chief has decided to keep them from making their report—ever." Jacques grinned but sensing André's mood faltered. "You can come or not. That's up to you."

Two more Maquisards emerged from the house followed closely by the spies who were followed in turn by the three young men who had accompanied Jacques and André on their mission. The chief came out last. All headed toward the back of the barn.

The thinner spy walked past André without giving him a glance, eyes fixed on the last of the setting sun. But the fatter one—shoulders sagging, large belly seeming to hang more pathetically over his belt with each step—stopped within inches, staring at André with watery pleading eyes.

A young Maquisard leering maliciously, prodded the fat man from behind, forcing out of him a cracked voice that formed one word: "Please!"

The parade passed by. Jacques gave André a quick salute and a little wave. André kept his eyes on the fat man, the back of his head rising and falling as he trod the rough path, his folds of fat compressing and stretching as he bobbed along struggling to keep pace.

Alin kept his eyes on his brother.

"You can go in my place if you like," André told him weakly.

"I wouldn't take your place," Alin replied softly. "No one could."

The two brothers stood together silently, watching and waiting as the procession crossed the field and went down into a small ravine. All was quiet and eerily peaceful.

The camp's residents had wordlessly gathered near the brothers. Neither seemed to have noticed the massing of this silent crowd.

Suddenly rifle fire crackled. Two distinct pistol shots followed.

Roger emerged from the ravine with the rest of the resistants.

"You three," he said pointing to men next to the Severins. "Get shovels and get to work. Executioners shouldn't have to bury the results of their own efforts." The deputed gravediggers raced to obey. The chief turned to André and Alin. "Had to be done," he said coldly.

He returned to his office and the other Maquisards dispersed. But the Severins remained motionless. Alin listened closely to the bite of shovels plunged into the earth, staying faithfully by his brother's side.

André stared into the sky until it was too dark to see anything at all.

Chapter Fifteen

THE WEHRMACHT

March 20, 1944

S pring 1944 finally came to the high mountains of the Cévennes—an enormous relief to Irene Bastide. She always felt isolated in her remote hamlet but never more than when shut in by the deep snows of winter.

On the bright side, the forces of nature also prevented unwanted visitors—a great blessing during the snow of winter since, Hitler had ordered the occupation of unoccupied France. With the façade of Pétain's power shattered once and for all, even this obscure region no longer felt safe from search and seizure.

But with the softer weather, everyone went out almost every day. Irene found herself longing to attend Easter services in Vialas, as unusual as this was for her. A staunch member of the Religious Society of Friends, Irene's practice of faith centered on Bible reading and direct personal communing with the highest power—the opposite of an Easter pageant. But what appealed to her now was the chance to spend time in the company of other Cévenols whose belief in God had helped them make it through yet another rough winter.

Nor would Irene mind being bathed in a minister's words for a change, reassured in the midst of tumult by the steadiness of his Christian message. And Irene wanted to show her support, not for Pastor Burnand's interpretation of Christian principles so much as his embodiment of Christianity in his Resistance work.

"I can stay with some members of the congregation," she assured her troubled mother.

"If anyone asks meddlesome questions along the way," Ernestine said somberly, "say as little as possible."

"Oh it's safe enough now," Irene said lightly, bussing her mother on the cheek, "from what the mailman says—the tide is finally turning against the Germans."

"That's what makes them dangerous," Ernestine cautioned, "like cornered beasts."

"Mother. They're sticking to big cities like Mende, Nîmes, and Alès. They're hardly ever seen in Génolhac anymore, let alone Vialas or the little places I'll pass through along the way."

"What does the mailman say about the Milice eh?" the elderly woman asked fretfully.

"Thanks to the Resistance, it may be less safe here for the Milice than the rest of us!"

On Saturday, April 8, Irene put on her heavy coat and tied on a scarf to protect her hair from breezes blowing off the mountain.

"Come here little one," she called in the special gentle voice she reserved for Cristian as he manfully demonstrated his mastery of walking by striding back and forth in front of the stove. Sweeping him up into her arms as he squealed with delight, she gave him a great big kiss on the cheek. "Now don't you fall down and cause your mother concern while I'm not here."

She cuddled him close and set him down again, making sure he regained his balance before loosening her grip. Then she squeezed Denise's hand before giving her mother's hands an even bigger squeeze, picked up the little sack with her comb and changes of clothes, called good-bye to Ida and Christel playing upstairs, gave a short final wave, and stepped out briskly into the bright day and fresh spring air.

Her cares fell away as she marched toward the Route des Crêtes marveling at the renewed face of the world as it awoke from its long winter sleep. The bushes were just beginning to show a little color as new buds emerged from the brown branches springing back to life.

Irene knew this ground well and felt utterly safe. Her neighbors were perfectly aware of her houseguests and in complete sympathy with her efforts to keep them safe.

She hiked with joyful anticipation for an hour, but as she approached Vialas sensed something odd. Then she heard the rumbling of distant motors. That gave her pause since gasoline was only available to Germans, Vichy government functionaries, and the Milice.

Coming within sight of the town she saw trucks rolling slowly up the road from Génolhac, rounding the bends, hewing closely to the thinly covered sides of the mountain slopes. Her heart started pounding. Her breath grew short and shallow. She felt cold then hot then cold again. Her tightly clenched hands became moist with sweat.

Now she could clearly discern the German cross on the side door of the small open car facing her—the lead vehicle speeding ahead of two loud trucks. The little convoy left a faint trail of smoke in its wake, heading straight for the center of town.

Irene's heart thumped more heavily as she forced her fists open to stop her fingernails from biting into her palms. Should she turn tail and run or continue on into the belly of the beast? Disgusted with herself for hesitating, she went on.

After traversing the stone bridge across a stream, she stayed close to the stone walls bordering the path. The temple of gray stone rose straight and true before her and somehow gave her strength. The temple's small belfry enclosed the single bell that rang Sunday mornings to call the worshippers together and at other times to announce important news such as France's surrender to the Germans—or as now, that the Germans were driving into town.

A group of old men shuffled down side streets to the town square. Women wrapped tightly against the cold came too, but stood back to acknowledge this was man's business and to keep as far as possible from the Germans without losing sight of what was really going on.

Irene joined these other women as the German command car rolled to a screeching halt in the heart of the square. The German officer in the open front seat stood up and an accompanying soldier jumped from the rear, ran around, and opened the door for him.

As the officer stepped down onto the plaza's cobblestones and looked about imperiously, the mayor rushed along one side of the square having raced down from his home on the outskirts when he heard the temple bell. German troops jumped from the backs of the trucks that lurched to a stop opposite.

The German officer watched the mayor run right into the small city hall. Less than a minute later, the mayor reappeared with a blue, white, and red sash—the official badge of his office—tied around his waist. He pulled himself up to his full middling height, made his way around his townspeople, and stood at attention to confront the representatives of the German war machine with a dignified silence.

The German officer looked vaguely bored. Nearby soldiers formed ranks behind him. On the far side, others unloaded a large machine gun and set it up with unnerving efficiency.

Irene felt the women around her tense. All had heard stories of indiscriminate German cruelty—the needless and pointless machine-gunning of whole towns' citizenries. No one could deny their fear.

Having settled a good distance from the command car, Irene hadn't anticipated ending up a few feet from uniformed men with rifles or a machine gun. As if against her will she watched the machine gunners unload ammunition from the truck and place the long ribbons of bullets alongside the fearsome weapon.

She stumbled back a step and a soldier swiveled his eyes her way—brown eyes that looked almost black beneath his helmet's rim. Was his soul that black? He stared at Irene for an agonizingly long time making her heart race so quickly she thought she might be having a heart attack.

The soldier didn't avert his gaze until the officer placed one booted foot slightly ahead of the other and announced aggressively, "We are here to keep order." His formal stilted French had a stiff studied accent utterly devoid of the soft warmth of the Cévenol. "We will not tolerate the slightest deviation from the orders of your government. Do you understand?" He didn't wait for an answer, but finished off his effort to intimidate by bearing down upon the mayor.

Nervously adjusting his sash, then bravely jutting out his chin and stepping forward a couple of paces, the mayor swallowed hard and proclaimed, "The people of Vialas are well aware of orders sir."

"But are you aware it is necessary to *follow* those orders?"

"We are good Frenchmen."

"And a good Frenchman does as he's told eh?" Towering over the hapless mayor the German officer raised his voice enough to ensure that even the women standing at the farthest edge of the crowd could hear his threat. "If there is any disobedience at all or if there are any further attacks on authorities or government property I will take hostages. Innocent or not they will pay the ultimate price." The officer jerked his thumb toward the armed soldiers ranged in a phalanx behind him. The machine gun rolled forward for additional emphasis. "You in this village and throughout this area will comply." The officer glared at the mayor and grinned maliciously. "From now on, I expect the mayor to set a proper example you all will follow. If not, we can always *make* someone an example." He turned to the lower-ranked officer by his side. "Deploy the men. House them where you will." Then he turned back to the mayor. "You will work with my sergeant to find appropriate housing for my men. And no stinting. Treat them with the honor due soldiers of the Third Reich."

"For how long sir?" the mayor asked hoarsely.

"For as long as it takes every one of your fine citizens to realize their responsibilities and to cease any further support of those damned Maquisards."

The townspeople dispersed rapidly and Irene escaped into the temple. Others had already gathered there—a small group discussing what had happened in voices hushed as if the walls might give them away.

"Vialas is so much more dangerous now."

"It used to be easy to get rid of collaborators in the wrong place at the wrong time. But as of today…"

"A whole troop of Germans. This is new."

"Where do you think the mayor stands?"

"I hear he's part of the Resistance."

"No. He cooperates with those fools in Vichy and with the Milice. We can't trust him."

"Of course we can. He only pretends to work with Vichy. That's what protects him."

Pastor Burnand entered the chapel from his study. Had he watched the incident in the square from the assumed safety of the temple? Not that anyone imagined the Nazis respected such niceties as the sanctity and sanctuary of the church.

All fell silent. Many of the women reflexively sat down. Most of the men stayed standing near the door to the street as if to protect the rest from any evil that might enter.

"Easter services will go on as always," the pastor announced steadily, levelly, comfortingly. "We will hold our Holy Saturday service this evening as usual and tomorrow we will celebrate the Resurrection." He clasped his hands and held them out in front of him. "The rebirth of Jesus is our faith in the past and our hope for the future. Let us abide in this knowledge and understanding. Let the mayor settle this business with the Germans. In the meantime, please go home. We shall gather this evening to worship in the proper way as our persecuted forebears did for centuries preceding us and as our descendants will do for centuries to come."

Some parishioners left immediately. Others peppered the pastor with questions. Was the faith of the congregants as great as that of the pastor? Irene determined to take her strength from him.

Within moments, everyone except the pastor and Irene had departed. Deep in thought, Pastor Burnand turned and hurried back toward his office without noticing her. Was he anxious to inform his network of resistants of the latest? Irene didn't wish to delay his good and important work, but she had need of him and felt certain the word was already spreading rapidly.

"Pastor," she said feebly at his door.

"Ah Madame Bastide. What a pleasant surprise to see you. How fare the Severins and that precious precocious Ida. I wish you'd brought her with you."

Irene made a short report then placed her hand gently on the pastor's wrist.

"Father do you think there's a bed in which I can spend the night?"

"Always," Pastor Burnand replied with reassuring speed. "Unfortunately, we will have fewer available beds than usual this evening." He pressed his free hand on top of hers. "But come. We will find you one, and welcome."

Easter Sunday broke bright and clear as Pastor Burnand hoped it would. This day was important, not just because of its place in the theological calendar, but for the town's ability to survive and thrive despite the present assault. To resurrect itself.

The previous night's service had been sparsely attended, but now the faithful arrived full force. Even churchgoers with two-hour walks through the mountains had come.

With enormous satisfaction and gratitude the pastor thought, *This is still a tightly knit community in which each looks out for all the others.*

Then he saw Irene. Even this poor woman, forced to suffer by two great wars, and who now risked her life for others, had found the requisite strength.

She had braided her hair and carefully folded it on top of her head like a crown not of thorns but of pigtails.

For her and all the others like her, the pastor began the sanctified service using all the familiar consoling Bible readings for Easter—the sorrowful story of the last days of Jesus from his journey to Jerusalem to his trial, crucifixion, and resurrection. Pastor Burnand wasn't saying anything the congregants couldn't have repeated in their sleep as easily as he; yet he was immediately rewarded by their fervent attention and participation. He had worried his flock would fear the soldiers listening just a short distance away, but their singing was more strong, bell-toned, and joyous than he had ever heard it.

Inspired, the pastor spoke a fervent sermon on the long-enduring painfully tested faith of the Protestants of the Lozère. Though he couched his message in strictly religious and historical terms, the good citizens of Vialas needed no key to decode his true subject. Obviously it wasn't the ancient Romans who oppressed his people now or even the French Catholics of comparatively more recent times. The oppressors of the present were the Nazis who had insinuated themselves into his parishioners' own homes, bringing the threat and reality of arrest, torture, brutality, and death—a hateful and ignorant disregard of commonly held truths and the revealed word of a just God.

Irene listened, sang, and gained courage and strength. Filled with this worshipful congregation's festive determined spirit, she knew she would hide and protect the Severins no matter what.

Reentering the town square she saw the machine gun manned, loaded and pointing straight at the mayor's office window. Unintimidated, she strode straight ahead.

Then she saw a German patrol come around the corner of the temple. Turning in the opposite direction she felt an almost uncontrollable impulse to run back inside. But she knew that would be a mistake.

Hastening down one strange corner after another, she finally found her way. Reaching the outskirts of town she was startled to realize she was still wearing her lovely embroidered white blouse. It would get soiled as she hiked back to Le Salson, but she decided not to change it, even though the stone walls bordering the path hid her from view. The blouse had become a talisman. Superstitiously she believed it gave her direct access to the inspiration with which this visit to Vialas had rewarded her, despite the fearsome dispiriting things she had seen.

The higher up the mountain she climbed the more easily she breathed. But she looked over her shoulder reflexively every now and again, because each time she saw that no one was following her, she felt relieved of an overpowering presence.

At last, her fears drifted off and faded away like the last shadowy images of a very bad dream.

In late afternoon, Irene marched down the path to her home. How familiar and comforting the very gravel felt beneath her feet.

But when she opened her door she realized she was exhausted. Still everything was all right. There before her, Denise was peeling smoked chestnuts and Ernestine stirring broth.

"Oh," Denise exclaimed. "You're back!"

"Thank God," Ernestine sighed.

Denise rushed to wrap her arms around Irene. Ernestine kissed her daughter warmly on each cheek. And before Irene could sit, little Cristian ran to her, stumbling over an invisible obstacle and crashing against her knees.

"Did you miss your Tata?" she teased hugging him too tightly for him to answer. Then she told her mother and Denise about her journey and the Germans taking up residence in Vialas.

"Since when?" Denise asked shocked. "And for how long?"

"Do they mean to stay?" Ernestine inquired fearfully. "Will they come farther?"

Even if Irene could have answered, she would have held her tongue. Ida and Christel appeared at the foot of the stairs and she wanted to spare the little ones news they did not need to know.

Denise slept badly that night tormented by terrible dreams of the Nazis capturing André and Alin. When she awoke she didn't feel right. Ordinarily she had a positive attitude and outlook. But not today. Oh she fully understood how unlikely it was that any enemies would come all the way to Le Salson to hunt down a few Severins. But the Germans were already so close...

Lying in bed listening to the Bastides start the fire, eat breakfast, and head out to tend to the animals, she couldn't stop thinking about her eldest daughter. Late the previous fall Irene had suggested they could pretend Ida was her cousin from the city so she could go to school in the little village of Vimbouches at the base of the mountain opposite Le Salson. It was an hour's walk through the woods and across a stream on a two-log bridge but Ida loved to learn and would brave any difficulty to do so—even an arduous round-trip journey in wooden shoes.

But this morning, Denise decided to keep Ida home. She wouldn't tell the real reason: semi-irrational fear. Instead, she would claim she wanted to put aside responsibilities for once and spend some special time with her children.

The morning went well. Denise and the children had great fun playing hide-and-seek and tag and telling each other stories. The children were in such good humor they didn't even mind when their mother had to take a break to prepare the midday meal.

Looking out the kitchen window while stirring the pot, Denise watched the goats and sheep scrambling about a small pasture penned in by a rough rail fence. She also saw Tata Irene and Mamé—as they had all taken to calling Ernestine at her insistence—loosening the garden dirt in preparation for mixing in the winter's accumulation of manure.

Soon they were all eating, if not enjoying, bajana. But the silence in which this soup was usually consumed was broken by a persistent scrambling sound outside. It got louder and louder, closer and closer. Someone was running up the path.

"Hurry! Hurry!" a hoarse voice cried out.

Irene turning pale raised her large self laboriously out of her seat to look out the window. Denise got up too to peer over Irene's shoulder.

Both were surprised and alarmed to see Léon Guin not only because he hadn't come to Le Salson since the Severins' arrival, but because his appearance made his hurry plain. The hair he never much bothered with stood straight up on his head. As he puffed, panted and hobbled his way to the house his face was flushed, his eyes were popped open wide and his coat was on lopsided since he had buttoned the buttons in the wrong holes. In fact he made such a spectacle neighbors in the only two inhabited houses close by stepped out to see what could possibly be happening.

"The Germans are coming!" Léon huffed and rasped as Irene opened her door.

"But they're in Vialas," the big woman protested in both confusion and denial.

"No they've left Vialas," Léon said, "and they're coming here." He turned and pointed up to the Route des Crêtes. "They're already there." Then he swung his arm around in a half-circle as if to indicate that they might come into Le Salson from any direction.

"But why?" Irene demanded.

Crankily Léon told her he had no idea why the Germans did anything. But now they were doing this and André and Alin had asked him to warn them.

"So you've seen André?" Denise asked at Irene's shoulder, perplexed. She hadn't seen André for a long while, but had assumed he was staying in one of the Resistance camps.

"Seen him?" Léon retorted. "He and Alin are staying with me only to help with the planting."

"Then why didn't they come for us themselves?"

"Please Madame Severin don't ask so many questions. There's very little time and—believe me—André and Alin have more immediate concerns."

"What do they want us to do?" Denise asked deliberately becoming focused and purposeful.

"Hide of course," Léon shouted. "Scatter."

He pointed down into the valley and then more slowly up the other side toward Vimbouches. No vehicle could cross from here to there because there was only a well-worn footpath through the woods.

"Get Cristian into his coat please," Denise asked of Irene. "It's still a little cold out."

"And will only get colder after the sun goes down," Irene agreed.

"I'll take care of the girls," Denise said.

"I'll put some food into a sack," Ernestine offered.

"I'll keep moving," Léon growled. "You're not the only ones I've got to warn."

"Go on then," Ernestine growled back. "And thank you."

As Denise helped her girls into their heavy socks, wooden shoes and coats, Christel quailed. "I don't want to see Germans! We don't *like* the Germans do we Maman?"

"We don't like *these* Germans."

"Will we be gone long?" the little girl asked.

"Let's hope not," Denise said hurrying into her own heavy coat and wooden shoes. "Now button up. And tie your sweaters around your waists."

"Will we stay out after dark?" Ida asked as they went downstairs.

"Possibly," Denise replied.

"Probably," Irene said brushing by with Cristian in her arms. The boy was all bundled up and wriggling frantically to free himself from his heavy outerwear.

"But we never stay out after dark," Ida mewed uncharacteristically.

"Be a brave girl now," her mother pleaded.

"Let's go," Ernestine demanded opening the door and hurrying everyone out.

The women and children marched down the garden terraces toward the bottom of the valley with child-length strides because Cristian insisted on walking. Other local residents preceded them on the single path across the rock ledges. All moved a little more quickly when the path, primarily dirt instead of stone, angled across the fields. They slowed once more when entering the woods, the stream burbling just beyond. Rocks and pebbles tumbled and crashed, washed along by water plunging and coursing over and around all obstacles in its way.

"Try to keep pace," Irene said leading.

"I can't," little Christel whined. "I have a stone in my shoe."

"We need to keep moving," her mother said gently.

"It's okay for us to rest a minute," Ernestine called from the rear.

Irene sighed. "At least we're hidden by these trees."

Everyone except Christel leaned against a low stone wall built to hold back the soil on the uphill side of the path. The little girl sat carefully on a small flat rock, pulled off her wooden shoe and, after feeling all around, held up the offending stone with a great grin of success.

"Let's go," Ernestine said straightening up, "while there's still sun to light our way."

"Follow me, everybody," Ida cried out excitedly. "Christel hold my hand."

The energetic children dashed away laughing delightedly. Denise picked up Cristian, now too tired to resist.

On the other side of the stream, the path wound up gently between trees, rock walls and open fields dotted with chestnut trees. The modest slope was a relief but everyone mounting it was fully exposed to any watching eyes on the far side of the valley.

When Vimbouches hove into view above them, daylight was fading. In the steadily increasing gloom, small groups gathered in the village cemetery. Two dozen people crouched on raised mounds of earth or perched on some of the gravestones toppled over through the years. Trees that had grown up around the stonewall helped hide them all.

The graveyard hummed with a low steady murmur. Tata Irene and Mamé greeted their neighbors, mostly women and children. A few elderly gentlemen sat silently lost in thought.

The Severin children were respectfully quiet. Even Cristian didn't make a fuss having fallen asleep in his mother's arms.

As the sun dipped still lower behind the encompassing mountains, dusk bathed the ancient graveyard in misty shades of gray. The temperature dropped. Shadows stretched and blended into dark hollows. Only the highest mountaintops continued to glow with a pale light, silhouetted against the early evening sky.

Venus appeared on the horizon. Leaning against the old stonewall and marveling at the splendors of the heavens above, Denise noticed other adults looking nervously over the wall. Following their eyes she saw lights blazing above Le Salson on the Route des Crêtes—the headlights of a line of halted German trucks. Then searchlights surged, circling the fields, wooded copses and rock outcroppings of the valley, casting harsh disturbing shadows.

Denise ducked down heart pounding painfully. The abrupt falling motion roused Cristian who began to wail. Denise clapped a hand over his mouth loosely enough for him to breathe but the boy was startled into silence and stared at his mother with wide shocked eyes. She rocked him soothingly.

"Maman, what are those people doing?" Christel asked appearing and speaking as if out of nowhere, standing on tiptoe and staring over the wall. "What are all those lights?"

Without thought Denise grabbed her hand and yanked her down with unintended force. The poor girl landed on the ground with a thump and cried out in pain but Denise suspected her pride had been hurt more than her rear.

"I'm sorry darling," Denise apologized. "It's the Germans. They mustn't see us."

"Will they come *here*?" Christel fretted snuggling up to her mother. "I'm scared."

"It's all right." Denise stroked her brow. "It will all be all right."

Looking up toward the Route des Crêtes she tried to make out any movement. Would the troops go into Le Salson and make free with the houses there? How awful it would be to return to a home Nazis had eaten and slept in.

Ida came over and silently sank into a huddle with her family. They all found emotional relief in being so close at this moment of peril.

The constant circling of searchlights added to the surreal scene. Outlined by the powerful lights, dozens of German soldiers stood alert and at the ready in an uneven line, rifles pressed against their shoulders pointing menacingly at unseen enemies. Though hardened by war these young men suspected the Maquisards might attack from vantage points only they knew. Realizing this made Denise worry for André and Alin wherever they were.

"Are the bad men going to come over here?' Christel asked filling with fear again.

"I'm sure they won't," Denise said. "I doubt they know we're here."

"But what if they do?" Ida asked anxiously.

Denise answered quietly, "We'll have plenty of time to move into the woods. I'm sure the good people here know the right places to hide. I promise we'll be all right."

She encircled Ida and Christel with her free arm and drew them closer still. Then she offered wordless prayers that her promise be fulfilled.

German soldiers' voices floated across the valley. They kept turning their trucks on and off for no apparent reason. The generators powering their searchlights also made loud unsettling sounds.

"Maman I'm hungry," Christel said trying not to whine.

Mamé reached into her sack. "Here my precious one. A little bit of bread and cheese for you. You too Ida."

The children thanked her and gobbled down their snacks. As other families began to eat too, the cemetery took on an oddly festive air.

After a while Christel said, "Maman I need to stretch my legs."

Tata Irene said, "I think it's all right if she walks around a bit."

"All right," Denise agreed. "But be careful and come back quickly."

Christel proudly strolled about the graveyard on her own. It helped that many people were there. She was careful not to trip over anyone.

The lights went around and around overhead. It kept getting quieter and quieter. Suddenly Christel noticed two men who seemed much younger than the others. They carried rifles as they walked from one group to another. Though frightened by the rifles she trailed behind them at what she judged a safe distance, drawing close enough to catch snatches of what they said:

"Have you seen...?"

"Do you know Madame Roux or her daughter Irene?"

With a squeal Christel recognized the voices: "Papy! Oncle Alin!"

Lifting Christel into the air André felt a rush of joy and relief. For one moment he stopped worrying about the Germans with whom he and Alin had been playing a deadly game of hide-and-seek all day. He felt certain that the cemetery was well-enough hidden by wall, trees and dark to make Christel's wail of excitement an inconsequential lapse rather than a serious breach of security.

Back on the ground Christel led him and Alin away. A wave of anticipation swept over André as they approached huddled children and adults.

"Over here," Denise called in a loud whisper.

It was a wonderful reunion.

"Papy!" Cristian called excitedly

André could have cried as he lifted the boy into his arms and kissed him. It was the first time he had ever heard Cristian speak.

When Ida and Christel hugged their father tightly Denise called hoarsely, "Children, remember we need to stay low."

"Well we're here," Alin said sitting down beside the others, his back against the wall like theirs, his rifle balanced carefully across his knees. "But it wasn't easy."

Without prompting, he reported how he and André had been standing in a field at Le Tronc drinking mugs of ersatz coffee when Léon spotted the Nazi convoy up on the Crest and told the brothers to go inform their compatriots while he warned the family. Careful to keep under cover, the brothers laboriously made their way to their most recent Resistance camp in Vimbouches.

"Vimbouches?" Denise interrupted. "I thought you'd been staying at Les Bouzedes!"

"We changed camps in February," André explained, "after Les Bouzedes was betrayed by a colloborateur."

"Of course the Maquisards at Vimbouches already knew about the latest German movements," Alin resumed.

"They were about to send someone out to warn *us*," André added.

"Eventually we heard people were hiding here and came looking for you."

Then all caught up on their doings over the winter. André and Alin had spent much of it going back and forth between Resistance camps serving as messengers—which kept them from their families. They had only gone back to Le Tronc quite recently, hoping and expecting to see everyone again soon.

"Have you heard anything of Geneviève?" Alin asked Denise abruptly.

"Not a word," Denise responded softly. "But I'm sure she and the children are fine."

"I miss her so," Alin said thickly.

All subsided into silence. André mused that despite the lurking German troops, this was the most peaceful moment he had experienced in memory, and the longest stretch he had been able to spend with his family since leaving La Font more than a year before.

All at once Christel cried out, "What's that?"

Alin leapt to his feet rifle in hand, certain Christel must have spied a German soldier. Instead, the little girl pointed to a nearby grave and the strange blue vapor rising from it and curling up into the sky. Other similarly odd blue, green, white, and rose-colored apparitions appeared throughout the graveyard swirling, twisting and disappearing into the night.

"I don't like it," Christel whispered into mother's ear.

"Are they ghosts?" Ida asked her father, unable to conceal her terror yet transfixed by the extraordinary sight.

André said quietly but dramatically, "It's just the spirits of the dead escaping."

"Papy!" Ida chided giving him a little push. "What is it really?"

André was reluctant to convey the details of the chemical breakdown of a corpse—especially one buried in the simplest of wooden coffins and covered with just enough dirt to make a proper grave in the rocky hillside. Instead he said, "It's the kind of thing you'd see if you spent most every day in a cemetery. Nothing to worry about though it's eerie."

Alin sat back down and gave a little shiver. "I suppose there aren't many of us who've spent a whole night in a cemetery before. It's nothing I ever aspired to."

"I still don't like it," Christel said sullenly.

"Why don't you girls close your eyes and try to get some sleep?" Denise counseled.

"But the Germans are over there," Christel complained. "I want to stay awake so I'm ready to run!"

"Me too," Ida echoed, not to be outdone in bravery by her baby sister. "I'm not tired."

"Why don't you all get some sleep?" André recommended, passing his already sleeping son back to his wife. "Alin and I will stay up and keep watch."

"You want anything to eat?" Ernestine asked thoughtfully. "We only brought a little, but you're welcome to it."

"Thank you no," André said gingerly pushing the proffered sack back toward its owner. "You keep it. In the morning when we can see better and determine precisely where the Germans are, we'll go out to get food for everyone."

The brothers patrolled the perimeter. Soon all the villagers had drifted off to sleep. Though Christel had nodded off briefly, she awoke again and whispered to her passing father, "If the Germans come up here will you and Oncle Alin shoot them?"

"Don't worry," André said caressing her. "We'll protect you. You'll be safe."

After a few minutes, Christel was once again drawing the deep even breaths of sleep. If only André's concerns could be allayed half so easily.

About four o'clock in the morning, to judge by the moon's position in the sky, Denise awoke, uncertain how long she had slept. How oddly peaceful the cemetery seemed with almost everyone asleep and dreaming. In the dead of night, would the dead protect her? The thought gave her chills.

"Hello," André whispered crouching by her feet, pointing his rifle away. "Alin thought one of us should get some sleep. Me."

"I'm glad," Denise said "But be careful not to wake the children."

André gingerly positioned himself to one side of Christel. "This is a most peculiar way to spend the night together."

"You must be hungry. We still have a little bread in that sack."

André broke off a piece, popped it into his mouth, and chewed thoughtfully. "Homemade. A treat. Ever since New Year's, the bread in the camps has been adulterated with sawdust, inedible hard grains, and just plain dirt. Even so it's precious."

Denise asked whether he ever ran into Max Maurel anymore.

"Our paths haven't crossed in weeks. He's in great demand because of his medical training and travels between camps even more than Alin and I."

"It's funny that they use outsiders like you as messengers."

"I thought that too. But so many resistants know even less of the Cévennes than we do. And since we're older and well-traveled men with a certain sophistication, the camp commanders trust us to handle unusual, sometimes delicate situations."

"And you both blend in now."

André laughed lightly. "After three long years we almost pass for natives." Then he grew serious again. "I think you should get your identity cards reauthorized. Max had us do that some time ago."

"Funny," Denise said. "We had ours stamped again last July."

André nodded and then became even more thoughtful than usual. "Would you and the girls sometimes be willing to carry messages for us?"

"André!" Denise was plainly shocked. "The children?"

"They wouldn't be the first. And I think the girls are big enough now to carry hidden slips of paper from one camp near Le Salson to another not far away. Why, Ida walks greater distances to and from school every day. And Christel would enjoy tagging along. It would be a great way for them to feel they're fighting back against everything they fear."

"André," Denise said severely, "you're acting as if the Nazis aren't right across the valley camped out on the Route des Crêtes."

"This really is an anomalous situation," he replied soothingly. "For all intents and purposes we're practically liberated already."

"I'm sitting in a cemetery with searchlights circling over my head. I don't feel liberated in the slightest."

"Because you don't get around as much as I do. Because you haven't had access to the information I've been privy to these last few months."

"Such as?"

"At the end of last year Churchill, Roosevelt, and Stalin met in Tehran to coordinate operations against Germany and to plan an Allied invasion of France. It's coming soon. They've placed all the Allied Expeditionary Forces under American General Eisenhower. They sound quite confident."

"I'm sure that's very nice but..."

"Listen my dear. Things really are going our way. Since the beginning of this year, air warfare over Europe has been dominated by the Allies. We're wreaking untold damage and destruction on German cities, transportation systems, and all the industries that produce war machinery throughout Germany and German-held territories. Even Hitler's Chancellery was mostly destroyed after a direct hit during an RAF raid on Berlin."

"Francis!" Denise gasped. "I worry about my brother every day."

"Then relax. The Americans have taken over most big bombing raids. They've even begun attacking German positions in northern France to soften them up for the invasion."

"You sound so convinced I almost believe you."

"Believe me Denise. De Gaulle has consolidated power over the Free French forces and the Resistance grows bolder every day. Just last week we sabotaged and halted production at a ball-bearing factory and at an aircraft components plant near Paris. It's all coming together."

Denise could barely breathe. "So you really think this nightmare's finally going to end?"

"Of course. But not quite yet. Terrible things still keep happening. I'm afraid I've heard Belgian Jews are in great danger now of being arrested by the Brownshirts."

"Oh André. Our family!"

"I know. But you must believe we've got the Germans on the run."

Denise shivered. "Irene was in Vialas when they entered the town square."

"Right after we derailed that train outside of Génolhac." Denise gasped. "Don't worry, we got all the French passengers off at the station. Then when the train reached the tunnel north of town, we set off explosives on the tracks, putting that line out of commission for some time to come."

"You and Alin were involved?" Denise asked fearfully.

André chuckled. "I use the term 'we' very loosely."

Having gone this far, Denise asked, "That rifle. Can you use it?"

"I've only fired at targets," André said huskily. "Never a person."

"Would you?" Denise breathed.

"I hope not."

"I hope not too. Because I hope you never have to."

André pulled her close and kissed her lovingly. Then he leaned back and closed his eyes.

As André drifted into a light doze, his steady breathing helped steady hers. The sky was beginning to lighten faintly, but Denise still couldn't see her husband's face clearly. Even so, in that dark moment, she thought she could feel him smiling.

With the coming of dawn, the small crowd stirred and grew restless. Alin was glad of the company. All night he'd been distracted, amazed, and mildly disturbed by the occasional methane flares, their multihued luminescence dancing in the dark. Had Alin, like his brother, been of a more metaphysical turn of mind he might have been seduced into speculating about an afterlife. Were he not so exhausted and on edge, he doubted he would have given such nonsense even passing consideration.

Every now and again children cried. Together with the final hoots of a night owl perched in an overhanging branch, they served as a wake-up call for the few remaining sleepers.

Christel jerked awake and grabbed for her mother instinctively. Then Ida returned to consciousness shivering and looking frightened as the searchlights swung down and around from the Crest. Denise's eyes popped open wide and André's body startled. Only blanket clutching, finger-sucking Cristian snoozed on.

André stood up slowly, stiff after a couple of hours huddled against the wall and on ground that had grown more damp and cold throughout the night.

"All right?" he asked joining his brother.

"All right."

The moon had run its course and the first edge of the rising sun peeped over the farthest mountains. German trucks started up one after another, engines sputtering and catching, churning out a steady growling beat. The searchlights were extinguished. Then the trucks began to roll, slowly heading up toward the pass at Saint-Maurice-de-Ventalon—away from Vimbouches.

Everyone gathered to stare in hopeful fascination at the curious procession.

"They're leaving?" Denise asked carrying the still-drowsy Cristian.

"Looks that way," Alin said flatly.

"It looks like a retreat," André agreed.

Alin snarled, "My guess is the Nazis never meant to come after any of us and certainly didn't wish to stay the night. One of their trucks must have broken down. Unfortunately for us, it took them this long to make repairs."

"I bet they were as afraid as we were," André concurred. "Which explains why they kept their searchlights circling all night—not to locate us but to keep the Resistance away."

"Where do you think they're going now?" Denise asked.

"No way to know," Alin spat. "Let's just hope its miles and miles from here."

"And that they never come back," André sighed.

The crowd stared for what seemed hours. But the great blinding ball of the sun was still only half-visible over the mountaintops by the time the German trucks finally disappeared definitively among the trees lining the valley to the west. Then even the rattling of their engines faded away.

The pall lifted all at once from the involuntary cemetery guests. Suddenly, it felt like the morning after a slumber party. Everyone began chattering loudly at once, their voices betraying relief. Then the bigger children started running around like dogs let off the leash, playing tag and hide-and-seek amidst the headstones. One of the infants set up a wail of hunger in her mother's arms and the mother didn't bother to hush her.

"What now?" Ernestine asked gruffly, startling Alin.

André grinned. "As promised, Alin and I will go get food."

"Hurry up then," Mamé grumped. "I'm famished."

Chapter Sixteen

INVISIBLE INK

May 11, 1944

For the next several weeks, the Severin brothers labored steadily and contentedly on the Guins' farm and visited their families in Le Salson and L'Herm. But one evening, as the two sat listlessly in the barn, André obsessed about the fact that it was now more than four years since he had peered out of his top-floor apartment in Ixelles to see German dive-bombers bearing down on him. He wondered what could be causing the delay in the Allied invasion of France.

All signs suggested the war was going well for the Allies and for the Resistance. He and Alin hadn't been called on by the Maquisard for quite some time.

Even as he thought this, a sharp knock on the door made the Severins scramble for their rifles. But they relaxed when they saw a young familiar Maquisard who apologized for disturbing them after dark.

The chief wanted to see André the next day. At another new camp: Champdomergue.

In the predawn gloom of Friday, May 12, André stopped by the farmhouse to inform Léon and Yvonne that he would be going away again.

"But you'll be back?" Léon asked querulously.

"Let's hope so," Yvonne said kindly.

"Soon I trust," André agreed.

Starting off along the familiar trail, he soon diverted himself to a little-used pathway following directions to the recently installed camp.

Approaching the new facility he was startled then relaxed seeing Max Maurel sitting on the side of the road waving happily to him.

"Morning André."

"Max. What are you doing here?"

"I could ask the same of you."

"I have no idea," André answered shaking his head. "The chief always wants me to come to him before I know what I'm in for." They laughed and André asked, "What have you been hearing? We have plenty to eat at the Guins' but we're starved for information."

"Still expecting the Allied invasion any day," Max replied, "but it's impossible to say when that day may be. Bombing runs continue against German sites in the north: the coastal batteries in Normandy, marshaling yards and railway workshops in Juvisy-sur-Orge, Noisy-le-Sec, Rouen, Tergnier... Rumors had swirled for months that Hitler was either dead or in an insane asylum since he hadn't been seen in public for a time. Then he showed up at a funeral in Munich, but didn't speak. Maybe something's seriously wrong with him—besides mental and moral degeneracy I mean." Then Max asked, "What did Denise say about her stay at Villaret with Madame Guibal and Simone?"

The question struck André as odd since Max had delivered André's family into the care of Georgette Guibal. "I know Denise was grateful and fond of them," he said. "But she certainly prefers Le Salson. More freedom of movement."

Max poked at the dirt and stones around his feet with a long stick. "Yes but at Villaret…did she feel safe?"

Was Max embarrassed? His manner seemed so strange.

"Denise felt she and the children were as safe at Villaret as they could be," André told him. "Why do you ask?"

Hesitantly Max said, "I'm thinking about moving Fela there. She's been happy with Françoise at La Planche, but it seems the worse things get for our enemies, the farther afield the Milice and Gestapo go."

"As we have seen," André agreed. "But why would La Planche be less safe than Villaret? Has anything happened?"

"Perhaps." Max drew a straight line in front of his boots then stabbed at it several times. "At the end of April, twenty Maquisards escaped from the prison in Nîmes. The Germans had four or five hundred soldiers, police, and Milice fan out all the way to Vialas to control the populace and search for resistants."

"Again?"

"This was a bigger show of force than at Easter. Now they're gone, but I can't help feeling it would be best to get Fela out of there. A neighbor of Madame Guibal's—Fernande Velle—will gladly take her in."

"Sounds like you've decided."

"I've also received discouraging word from the same sources that tipped us off about you."

"Then you must move her. When?"

"This evening." Max got up and clapped André on the back. "But you'd better go. You know how the chief hates to wait."

Roger was glad to see André. Seated at his table with several associates, including two from a camp north of the mountains with whom he'd been discussing a variety of needs over several days, Roger depended entirely on the man he now rose to greet to solve a vexing and perplexing problem.

"Thanks for coming," the chief said rising and shaking André's hand heartily. "This is André," he told the others, not naming them. "The chemistry professor."

The others rose now too, each one exclaiming, "Ah."

Roger pulled out a chair for André and told him, "We Maquisard face a difficulty we hope you can help us with. We need to send messages to and from other camps, some on the far side of the mountains."

"I've done this for you many times," André quickly put in, "and I'm happy to help again. Usually you send me with my brother."

"This time we don't need your legs. We need your mind. You see we need a way to write down things that can only be seen by those in the know—a new kind of invisible ink that only we know how to make reappear. That way even if one of our messengers gets stopped by an enemy patrol he won't be able to betray or be betrayed by potentially dangerous secrets. With the Free French and the Resistance working more and more closely together, it's harder and harder for the leadership truly to know each and every one, and trust them fully. We've been getting more and more German Army deserters, mostly from the troops stationed in Mende. Ethnically, they tend to be Armenians who have felt the tug of turning tides. But could one or another of these fresh recruits be a spy? Wouldn't it be better all around if messengers did not personally know and could not detect the contents of an important message? Besides the information we need to exchange has become much more technical and complex. Perhaps a highly educated man such as yourself could be relied on to understand, remember, and transmit such messages faultlessly. But seriously André, we have very few like you."

Roger didn't say that camp commanders had been experimenting with shortwave radio communications for months or that the Gestapo had caught on almost immediately and were becoming more successful daily at blocking such transmissions. More dangerously, they listened in as the otherwise inexplicable betrayal of some secret operations proved.

André sank deeply into thought. One of the men from over the mountains soon demanded snappishly, "Well can you do it?"

"I'll need a supply of particular chemicals," André said distantly, still pondering.

"You give me a list," the chief said firmly and gratefully, "and we'll get you what you need. We know of a pharmacist in Génolhac."

The lieutenant handed André a pen and paper. Everyone watched intently as monsieur le professeur began to write.

He took his time with the list, thinking through every element repeatedly because retrieving chemicals entailed great danger. It could prove disastrous if a raid needed to be restaged because André left off even one significant compound.

Finished, he took his leave. Though it was only late morning he felt exhausted. Finding a free space in one of the outbuildings, he drifted heavily into sleep.

Deep in the afternoon he startled awake in a sweat realizing he might have made a dreadful mistake—not by leaving something off the list but by neglecting to consider that some of the chemicals he needed would likely be labeled under different names in a pharmacy than in a laboratory. Besides, there were potentially significant differences in nomenclature between Belgium and France.

Hurrying back to the chief's office he interrupted yet another meeting to say, "I've got to go with you on the raid."

Roger laughed pleasantly. "I can't run the risk of losing you now." André explained his concern but Roger was adamant. "Your accent might give you away."

"I won't say a word."

"Your glasses..."

"I'll take them off until you've led me into the pharmacy."

Roger stroked the stubble on his jaw. "It's dangerous, but I've put you in danger before." Pointing to a young man he said, "You were raised in Génolhac yes? You'll stick with the professor. He's yours to protect."

The young Maquisard brought André a crust of bread with a piece of cheese and some sausage sliced onto it first thing in the morning. The chief, impressed because the young Maquisards ordinarily showed such deference only to him, had rewarded the youth with one of his own pistols to take on the mission.

Bouncing around well past Vialas, the truck that the chief, André, André's bodyguard, two other young men, and one of Roger's lieutenants traveled in joined cargo-laden carts and bicycles also heading toward the market of Génolhac. It still was quite early when the men from Champdomergue reached the outskirts of town.

"There," Roger told the lieutenant behind the wheel, pointing out a bridge.

The lieutenant stopped the truck, applied the handbrake, carefully took hold of a small package on the front seat, and slipped out of the cab.

"What's going on?" André asked through the small opening between front and back.

"We want to create a little diversion," Roger answered easily. "With explosives."

"Explosives?"

"The charge isn't great enough to create real damage," the chief assured the chemist. "Just enough noise and smoke to distract any lurking police from our primary mission."

The lieutenant leapt back into the driver's seat, gunned the engine, and roared off.

"Slow down," Roger commanded. "This is supposed to be an unthreatening rattle-trap."

The lieutenant reduced speed. Several minutes later, they heard a muffled blast. Then they saw the police race past.

Entering town, they eased onto a side street from which they could see the pharmacy, distinguished by a green-cross sign. The elderly pharmacist unlocked the front door and turned on the lights. The Maquisards were in within seconds.

The pharmacist understood immediately. White-haired, with the ruddy face and jelly-like jowls of someone long accustomed to eating well and drinking too much, he whined about losing money, but one look at Roger's implacable face silenced him. Why risk health as well as wealth?

André slipped his glasses back on and went right to the shelves in the rear, as if he knew just where to find what he was looking for. Examining labels with professional assiduity, he handed the bottles he wanted to his young protector who placed them carefully into a produce carton.

When a customer came in Roger slid behind the counter and whispered heatedly to the pharmacist, "Tell her to come back later." Flustered the pharmacist hesitated. "Tell her now. And make it sound normal," Roger hissed pushing the terrified pharmacist forward.

As the customer drifted back out André grabbed one last bottle from a high shelf.

"Okay," he announced. "I've got everything."

"I hope so," Roger said. "I don't think we'll be shopping here again."

Back in the truck, André began to sweat. "It all went by in a flash," he said wiping his brow with both hands. "I didn't have time to feel nervous. But I sure feel nervous now."

Everyone laughed sympathetically knowing just how he felt.

As the squad hiked back into camp, the good news spread quickly. Tired and depleted, but also encouraged and enthused André was immediately conducted to a room in one of the outbuildings that had been cleared out except for a large counter—boards set on sawhorses—a short bench, a couple of chairs, and several lit candles. Unusually, the room had been swept, making the dust still clinging to cobwebs in the corners of beams overhead stand out.

Weary as well, the chief told André, "Keep me informed." Then he was gone.

The burden weighed on André, but as he sorted through the pharmacy booty, his excitement returned and his energy rose. Though he had no prior experience with anything analogous to this task, his record of successful experimentation encouraged him. Still he wished he had a chemistry textbook ready in hand—something to refer to besides memory.

No matter, he would have to proceed by trial and error—almost the definition of scientific endeavor. But given the limitations of time and materials, each error would be costly and possibly his last.

As he began manipulating chemicals, he found himself amused and intellectually engaged. He had never given invisible ink a prior thought. If he really could figure this out...this was no academic exercise, but potentially a significant contribution to the cause.

He labored deep into the night measuring and mixing, writing down a word or two once in a while, taking note of every chemical effect produced and ways they might be improved.

On other paper, he tested his "ink." The first efforts discouraged him. Sometimes the writing simply wouldn't disappear. Another time it became invisible and stayed that way.

He adjusted the quantities of chemicals repeatedly. Then he had a sudden inspiration: the bottle he had grabbed at the last moment. A fortuitous discovery: André added it to the mix and the word he wrote next became mostly invisible. Unfortunately the pressure of his pen's steel point left an impression that with concerted effort could still be discerned. Perhaps if Resistance camp commanders were instructed to press lightly...

Somewhat encouraged, André held up the slip of paper allowing it to dry thoroughly. Then he blew on it to make every last vestige of the word fade away.

Success!

Stunned, André sat back heavily on a chair almost afraid to try to restore the writing. He was running out of ideas. If this didn't work...

Choosing a candle that burned steadily, producing wispy black smoke, he held his prayed-over piece of paper above the flame, wafting it gently back and forth through the heat. After ten seconds he pulled it away. The smoke left a smudge, but hadn't adhered to the shape of the letters—which was good. Neither had the letters reappeared—which was bad.

André wasn't about to give up. He held the paper still closer to the candle. This time it smudged the paper with more soot—and the word began to come through in a deep legible brown.

Promising, promising...

André rubbed his finger across the word. The soot smeared—bad. But the word stayed firm—excellent! He brought the paper extremely close to his face, peering at it as a mostly blind man might. He even took off his glasses to explore the results more minutely.

It worked, he thought, allowing himself a small sense of satisfaction while guarding against exhilaration. Yes, he had done it—once. But no experiment could be deemed a true success until the results had been replicated. After all if his new "invention" was to be useful he couldn't be the only one capable of whipping up a batch.

He tried making more of the potent brew from scratch and again met with success. Now however when exhilaration was warranted, he felt totally spent. And he had a pounding headache—the inevitable outcome of his intense concentration and the strain.

But before he could rest, he had one last task to accomplish. On another piece of paper he wrote a comparatively long sentence: *Let this be the path for words that must remain secret.*

Watching the ink dry and the sentence fade away letter by letter he smiled with profound satisfaction. He had been extremely careful not to apply much pressure and that had worked too. The paper looked entirely blank—very important since he didn't want anyone even to suspect any writing was there. Only with the application of heat from a small candle or a stick of burning wood plucked cautiously from a fireplace...

Exhausted, he strode toward the great barn and pushed open the door to the chief's office. Roger's secretary sat at his desk writing, not even stopping when he glanced up at André with an expectant lift of an eyebrow.

"Yes?"

"Would you please give this to the chief?"

André handed the secretary the happy results of his concerted efforts. Peering at the slip the secretary looked puzzled, even annoyed. "You want me to disturb the chief at this time of night with a blank piece of paper? After the day he's had?"

"It's a message only he can understand," André said wearily. "I promise he'll be glad."

André went right back to the bed in which he had tried to sleep the previous night. The other occupants of the room snored with deep breaths, but André was too tired to be troubled by a little noise. Still, his shoulders and back ached and his eyes burned from all the careful measuring and the constant exposure to fumes released by the burning of soft wax and tallow candles.

A knock on the door startled him from his stupefied state. The others woke too, grumbling as one of the chief's lieutenants burst in and marched straight to André's rack.

"The chief needs to see you. Now."

It would have been better had the chief been allowed to sleep. At an hour like this, Roger was foul-tempered. And he was not alone: in addition to his secretary the two Resistance fighters from the north were there.

The chief's eyes kept flitting over the frustrating piece of paper in his hand as if they would suddenly discover whatever if anything André had inscribed on it. Roger had been so excited when his secretary had delivered it into his hands he hadn't even glanced at it before ordering him to rouse the visitors from the north. Now Roger feared he had been made to look a fool however he knew André wasn't one to play childish games.

There was a short rap on Roger's chamber door. The lieutenant entered with André.

"André," the chief bellowed rising to his full height. He waved André's paper in the air and jabbed at it repeatedly with his forefinger. "Is there a message on it or is there not?"

André smiled. "Oh it's there."

"Okay then," the chief insisted, turning confidently to the doubting northerners and then back to the professor. "So how do we read it?"

"Goodness," André said sorrowfully. "I was so tired I forgot to explain. Just hold it above heat briefly and the ink will appear like magic."

Roger snapped his fingers at his secretary who reached toward the fire, drew out a taper and held it for the chief. Roger waved the paper over it watching intently.

Nothing appeared. The chief tried to be patient, but forbearance wasn't his strong suit. Unable to help himself, he cast a dubious glance at André. But monsieur le professeur didn't wither or cower.

"Try again," the Belgian professor suggested gently.

This time the chief passed the paper over the small flame more slowly and a little more closely. Much to his surprise what looked like brown ink began to appear and darken. Letters became discernible then formed themselves into words: *Let this be the path...*

"You've done it!" the chief crowed in wonder and admiration, waving off the secretary and his taper, clapping André on the back. He turned to the northerners. "Satisfied?"

"Of course," they replied.

"Then for God's sake let's all get some rest. In the morning we can use André's miraculous ink to write out a message you can bring to your commander with a bit more safety than before—for you, for me, for all of us."

Everyone moved to leave but the chief gestured André to stay. Then Max Maurel appeared at the door. Roger waved him in.

"What's this I hear?" Max asked André as if floating on air. "You've done something new to thwart the Germans?"

Confused, André said, "I seem to have lost track of time. Did you...?"

"Yes," Max replied.

"And all...?"

"Went very, very well."

Roger had no idea what these two were talking about—and couldn't have cared less. "Your friend here," he told Max, "has developed an invisible ink for our messages."

"Merveilleux."

Max couldn't stop smiling. Roger wondered what could have put him into such a good humor at such an ungodly hour and demanded to know.

"It's my particular friend Fela," Max explained blushing. "She's safely tucked away in a new place. Which makes me feel much better." Trying to cover his embarrassment Max asked, "Any medical problems since I left?"

"Happily no. When you go away the men know not to get sick." More quietly he told Max feelingly, "I'm glad you've taken care of your Fela."

The young man blushed again. Suddenly the chief found himself thinking of his own wife and child back in Mende. But even in this newly convivial atmosphere, he knew it would do no one any good for him to reveal his inner turmoil. Besides, this was a hopeful moment. Thanks to André so much more seemed possible and within reach than just a few hours before.

"Let's celebrate," Roger suggested reaching into a small cabinet and pulling out a bottle of wine from which he poured three glasses. He raised his in a toast. "To André. I couldn't be happier about what this fine man has done tonight." Then turning to the younger resister he added, "And to Max who was good enough to bring André to us."

Denise had been feeling optimistic since the night in Vimbouches. André's certainty that the war was almost over had worked its way into her breast. Though still unconvinced the girls should serve as messengers, Denise felt emboldened to bring them with her to Champdomergue. Having taken to cleaning and mending clothes that the Maquisard sometimes brought her, she had decided this morning to return the bundle herself.

The children were thrilled, then terrified. But the day was beautiful. Denise sang all the way.

The camp was a bit of a shock. "Primitive" was too generous a description. The mostly young men looked ragged and unclean. Some carried rifles.

The girls marveled as Denise recovered and began greeting and chatting pleasantly with the Maquisards. She told Ida and Christel that they were just frightened kids themselves.

But one slightly older man started talking to the girls and petting their heads, which really scared them, especially since he spoke a foreign language. After he smiled and left, Denise explained he was a deserter from the German Army, probably starved for affection. That only confused the girls more. If he was German, wasn't he the enemy?

Sadly, André and Alin weren't there, having gone back to the Guins for a bit. Denise and the girls had so looked forward to surprising them.

A few days later Cristian celebrated his second birthday with a little noontime party Tata Irene and Mamé made for him. They wouldn't say where they had gotten the ingredients to bake a chocolate cake—or how they had kept it secret from the Severins.

Just after the *fête*, several young strangers appeared at the door asking for Denise. André had sent them to see if she wouldn't let Ida carry a message to Vimbouches.

Whether because she felt hopeful, because Vimbouches was so familiar to Ida, or because of the young people's pleasant faces, Denise no longer objected. She would leave the decision to Ida herself.

Privately she explained to her eldest child that she didn't have to do anything she didn't want to, but that if she thought she could do this it would be a great help to the war effort. She also said that she was now big enough to take on the responsibility.

The thought of carrying a secret message excited and scared Ida equally. But since her father had recommended her for the mission she said yes. Wouldn't he be proud of her?

Ida slipped the message into her school bag. She doubted she would run into anyone along the way, but if she did she could always say she was returning to school after lunch. No one would know that her mother had let her take from off school for Cristian's birthday.

Curiously, she was to deliver the message to her principal. Nobody had even suspected he was part of the Resistance.

He startled when she knocked at his office door and asked if she could speak to him alone as she had been instructed to do.

"You know what this is?" he asked after reading the communiqué.

Ida told him she didn't because her mother had told her not to look. So he explained that General Eisenhower had sent messages just like it to resisters all over Europe encouraging them to redouble their efforts in the fight for victory.

"Is that good?" Ida asked, not really understanding.

"Very good little one," the principal replied laughing heartily. "It means we'll end the war soon. Thank you for doing your part."

Shyly Ida asked, "Can I go home now? It's my little brother's birthday."

"Of course," the principal said laughing again. "You've had your lesson for the day."

Chapter Seventeen

FIGHTING AT LA RIVIERE

May 31, 1944

The pace was picking up. At the end of May, Alin and André were called from Le Tronc to Champdomergue. Léon grunted when the brothers headed out again, but the planting was done and the workload would be light until harvest time.

Alin hadn't stayed in a Resistance camp for months. Training had taken on a far more serious tone. The sense of anticipation was tremendous. Everyone knew the Allied invasion was days away because a BBC broadcast from London on the night of June first included a coded message to that effect, intended for Resistance fighters.

But what if the Germans had broken the code? That was the older resistants' concern. The young men, who shared a feeling of invincibility—the prerogative and bane of youth—had no qualms or doubts about the outcome.

They also shared rumors, such as the one about a new German rocket, the V-2, crash-landing near the Bug River east of Warsaw. Polish Resistance fighters supposedly recovered and hid the missile's remains before German forces could arrive to gather evidence that could help their scientists learn from the failure. To the youthful Maquisards, such stories constituted proof that Resistance forces scattered around the world were strong, confident, and ready to finish off the Third Reich.

Charles de Gaulle seemed to share youth's expectations. The day of the coded broadcast from London, the French Committee of National Liberation based in Algiers proclaimed itself the Provisional Government of the French Republic.

Sometimes, the Severin brothers thought the young people were on to something. After all, the Resistance pretty much possessed the mountains of the Cévennes. Collaborators were being eliminated systematically. The Germans and the Milice did control the principal roads, but nothing else. Maintaining power over those highly visible roadways left them exposed to the Maquisard, who bided their time with less and less patience.

On Sunday, June 4—one day before the longed-for offensive—something went very wrong. Reports trickled into Champdomergue about coordinated efforts by the Milice to arrest the mayor of La Rivière because they had uncovered one of the best-kept secrets in the Lozère: La Rivière's mayor was in charge of all of the region's Resistance forces.

When the Milice arrived, the mayor was nowhere to be found. Neither were any of the villagers able or willing to suggest reliably where he might be. Some said one place, others said another, and still more pretended they didn't know what mayor the Milice were talking about. The enraged Milice heatedly announced their intention to return that afternoon. If the mayor did not come back to turn himself over to them, they would burn down the village.

The inhabitants quickly devised a simple plan for self-preservation. All the women and children prepared and left immediately, carrying precious possessions on their backs and driving their flocks of goats and sheep ahead of them to the Crest where they could hide in isolated abandoned buildings. Meanwhile, the town's farmers mobilized to fight and sent word to Vimbouches and Champdomergue seeking reinforcements.

By noon, the camp commander ordered a full-scale mobilization. Every available Maquisard including the Severins loaded up with weapons and ammunition and marched off to the nearby village of La Rivière. Three trucks of Milice and Wehrmacht soldiers had been dispatched to capture the mayor.

The progress of enemy trucks was monitored meter by meter since a train happened to be running along the same route. An alert train conductor—by a stroke of luck, one of many who worked with the Resistance—had caught sight of the caravan and intuited its destination. At each station stop, he called in to report the trucks' progress. At one stop, he deputized children he knew as liaisons and messengers to bring word of the coming trouble to the mayor.

Marching along, the Severin brothers realized they might soon become engaged in an actual firefight. Alin could barely contain his excitement. André still wondered what he would do.

When the Maquisards of Vimbouches and Champdomergue converged on the outskirts of La Rivière, the farmers cheered. Gathered at the entrance to the village—where the road made an abrupt turn to avoid a massive boulder considered the town's founding stone—several farmers chopped at trees hoping to fell them and block the road entirely. At Roger Boudon's command, Alin and several of the younger Maquisards joined them.

Then the farmers and Resistance fighters posted themselves on the upper side of the road, taking cover behind chestnut trees and rocks. Alin and André positioned themselves side-by-side in back of a hedge.

The wait seemed interminable. Alin was anxious finally to take action against the hated Milice and their Wehrmacht compatriots.

After a long nervous time everyone heard the distant sound of engines approaching. Tensing as they raised their weapons and sighted along the road, the Resistance fighters knew to hold their fire until the chief whistled. But did the farmers know the signal? And how likely were they to maintain discipline when they saw their hometown invaded?

Alin's heart rate rose and a bead of sweat trickled down his brow when he spotted the first truck. At that moment, a single shot rang out—from where? There was no way to know and no time to care.

That first round struck home, hitting the driver just as the truck started into the big turn. The driver slumped and the truck veered wildly, crashing forcefully into the founding stone.

The driver of the second truck spun its steering wheel desperately to avoid a pileup. He succeeded, but ran up onto the edge of the road, pitching the truck violently on its side and tossing out all its passengers.

Trying to avoid his predecessors' fate, the third truck's driver slammed on the brakes. Their great shriek was drowned out by a massive fusillade.

Before the Milice and the German soldiers inside the last truck could figure out what was happening, a hail of bullets rained death down upon them. Had the chief whistled? Alin hadn't heard it, but the time to hesitate had passed. Like all the others, he rose to advance on the enemy. This was the most thrilling moment of his life.

But where was André?

For André, it all unfolded like a dream. He felt the rifle in his hands. Bullets exploded and whistled furiously through the air, penetrating the third truck's side as if it were made of paper. André heard screaming, saw raggedly dressed men racing, and uniformed men escaping. Their faces were contorted with terror.

Some bloodied and some with broken limbs, the escapees stomped and stumbled over fallen comrades—the dead and those too seriously wounded to flee. Trying to outrun their doom, they raced toward the bushes along the river followed hotly by outraged Maquisards and farmers—and more slowly by dazed André who watched in time-lapse horror as one after another of the enemy was gunned down before his unblinking eyes. Then André watched the long high arc of a well-aimed hand grenade fly as if in slow motion and explode fearsomely amidst the last few Milice, putting a loud smoke-filled end to them and their feeble return fire.

That couldn't have lasted more than a minute, André thought helplessly, struggling through the sulfurous atmosphere, snapped back into real time by a coughing fit.

Everything had gone well—if killing several dozen men could be called good. Unable to see Alin, André vacillated between feelings of anger, pride, and self-recrimination as he tried to comprehend his participation in this action. Though his finger had hardly touched let alone twitched his rifle's trigger, he felt fully implicated.

As the smoke began to clear André saw villagers and Maquisards laboring mightily to eliminate all signs of battle. However unsettled, he realized he needed to lend a hand.

Slinging his unused rifle over his shoulder, he didn't know why they needed to make it seem this dreadful event had never occurred. The Allied invasion would begin in a matter of hours so how likely was the German commandant at Florac to bother sending out a reconnaissance group for this missing convoy? He would be preoccupied and might not even find out about it before he and his men were engulfed in far more urgent matters.

But the road needed to be cleared no matter what. And the dead needed to be buried.

The overturned truck was righted and all three vehicles were loaded with corpses. By André's count there were thirty-eight Milice and German soldier dead and—mercifully—only one Maquisard.

The bullet-riddled third truck was used to pull the other two to a cul-de-sac off of the forest road. A trench was dug quickly and the enemy bodies were dumped into a common grave. The young resistant was afforded his own resting place in tribute.

André hadn't known him well but had admired him—a Pole drafted into the German Army against his will as he had insisted frequently and angrily. When the chance presented itself, he had deserted to fight with the Resistance. Now André offered up an unvoiced prayer for the poor boy's soul.

Walking back from the burial, site André found the celebratory shouts and cheers of the victors gross and unseemly. He still could not reconcile his beliefs with what he had done. He understood that this had been an instance of "kill or be killed," but what could such easy self-justification mean to a man with a vision of a world far better than this one and the will—no the need—to help make it? Yet, he was aware that he lived on Earth and not in heaven. Accommodations were required to make the best of an unfortunate lot.

With every step, he felt not better but more resigned and more resolved. Those who would perpetrate heinous and violent acts against the innocent must be stopped. There was honor as well as shame in taking up arms against outrageous fortune.

All too soon, he returned to the scene of the firefight where the triumphant hastened to erase the last traces—the terrible burn marks on the boulder. He found Alin again, scrubbing and scraping at the massive stained rock. André joined in. The two brothers worked and sweated together until the job was done.

They said not a word; but a great deal was communicated between them. Both had been alternately exhilarated and deeply saddened by this baptism by blood.

Denise was folding Maquisard laundry when the mailman arrived unexpectedly. On Monday, he had appeared with the unhappy news that the invasion hadn't begun as planned. But on Wednesday the news was so good he made a special trip to let Denise, Irene, and Ernestine know Operation Overlord had commenced at last the day before.

Details swirled in Denise's mind as she and the girls hiked back to Champdomergue with resistants' clothes. On Sunday—the day Rome had fallen to the Allies after the bloody battles of Monte Cassino and Anzio— Expeditionary Force convoys already bound for Normandy were called back due to rough seas and bad weather over the Channel. But Tuesday...Sword, Juno, Gold, Omaha, Utah...British, American, Canadian, Polish, and Free French forces...Thousands of ships and planes...Fifteen thousand aerial sorties...More than one hundred fifty thousand men...

Entering the Resistance camp, Denise felt jubilant. Understanding something good was happening, Ida and Christel skipped, danced and laughed. But it didn't take long to realize how somberly the Maquisards returned their greetings.

The girls spotted their father and raced to him gleefully. André embraced them and Denise. Then Alin joined them and took his nieces to play so husband and wife could talk quietly.

Denise was puzzled by André's air of despondency. Wasn't he pleased that the liberation of France had begun? Yes, but he was haunted by La Rivière.

Partway through André's explanation, Denise started trembling uncontrollably. Her mouth went dry and her spirit filled with terrible foreboding. "André. Did you shoot anyone?"

"No," he said sorrowfully, as if he regretted it. "No I did not."

Denise wrapped her arms around him. How strange and disturbing that André seemed mortally distressed not to have violated his principles.

But that wasn't what had upset him. "During the confusion and madness of the firefight," he explained, "no one noticed that two of the Milice from the overturned truck not only managed to survive, but to escape into the bramble. They must have run down along the river until they reached the train station when they telephoned their regiment. On Monday, Milice and German soldiers returned to La Rivière in force. Our men spotted them, but all they could do was send a messenger racing ahead—a teenager on a motorcycle. When the Nazis entered the village, every man, woman, child, and animal was gone and could not be found, though the enemy searched for miles around. But they did find the messenger, whose motorcycle had stalled outside the next town. They shot him dead. Then they went back to La Rivière, discovered the damaged trucks and the unmarked grave, and ransacked the town before burning it to the ground with the aid of an incendiary grenade. By dawn Tuesday, La Rivière was nothing but smoking ruins. That's when we got news of the Americans landing in Normandy—almost simultaneous misery and exaltation. But it could have been worse. We learned the Milice intended to search for the citizens of La Rivière again yesterday. Thankfully the Allied invasion put an end to that. And yesterday afternoon the villagers returned. Many of us went to help. Like diligent ants we cleaned up the aftermath and began rebuilding their homes."

Denise remained silent for more than a minute then said, "It's a terrible story. But it speaks volumes about the courage and indomitability of the people of La Rivière."

André shook his head regretfully. "While I looked at the remains of what had so recently been a lovely village—a strong people's home—I couldn't help thinking of a passage in the Stevenson book about the Catholics' assaults on the land of the Huguenots and Camisards, the devastation of the High Cévennes, when some four hundred sixty villages and hamlets were destroyed by fire and pickax. I don't know why this phrase stayed in my mind: 'A man standing on this eminence would have looked forth upon a silent, smokeless, and despoiled land.' Luckily I remembered this too: 'Time and man's activity have now repaired these ruins.'"

"André. You sound as if you blame yourself for this destruction."

"No," André sighed. "But I sorely wish I could have done more to stop it."

Holding her daughters' hands, Denise left the camp a short time later, heartsick for her troubled husband. Her final glimpse of him and Alin—shouldering their rifles and marching off to train with the other Maquisards—distressed her profoundly and left her possessed by irreducible fear.

Events proceeded quickly, but they couldn't move fast enough for Alin, who felt penned up at Champdomergue where there was little to do besides follow reports of action elsewhere, attend to the dull daily requirements of life in a Resistance camp, and train incessantly. The only part he liked was target practice.

Rightly or wrongly, Alin couldn't wait for another chance to use his rifle against the enemy, having gotten a taste of fighting at La Rivière. He couldn't say for sure whether any of his shots had struck any German, but he was ready for the next fight. Let André answer to his own beliefs.

Enormous rapid progress was made in the Normandy campaign, but Alin felt so stagnant that he almost wished he were back at Le Tronc. At least there, he could do something. The only advantage to camp life was ongoing reports from elsewhere in France due to the resumption of shortwave radio use. The Resistance no longer felt so threatened by local Fascist forces. No more need for invisible ink.

More than three hundred thousand Allied troops on French soil had linked up across the established beachheads creating a fifty-mile-wide front secure enough to allow separate visits by Britain's King George VI and General Charles de Gaulle. Emboldened by what he saw, the Free French leader began taking steps to restore civilian government in the retaken territory. The RAF launched raids from French airfields for the first time since 1940.

But the retreating German military still did terrible things. Some six hundred fifty inhabitants of the small village of Oradour-sur-Glane near Limoges had been ruthlessly killed. All had been locked inside a church and burned to death. The few who somehow managed to escape were gunned down mercilessly.

Meanwhile, more young men poured into the Maquisard camps emboldened by Allied advances and Nazi panic. Hoping to help complete the defeat of their oppressors, the new recruits were more anxious for battle than the elders recently rotated into Vimbouches and Champdomergue from other locations, including men who had seen fighting in the Spanish Civil War and on the Eastern Front in the early days of this World War. Their tales of wounding, maiming, and death could not deter youthful enthusiasts from wishing to enter the fray.

Despite his years, Alin felt more like the would-be warriors than the experienced and dismayed. And it seemed they might soon get their wish. The mayor of La Rivière had quickly reestablished Resistance operations in a rebuilt outpost and broadcast to his scattered underground forces, "They're pulling some units out of Nîmes."

"You think they'll come through here?" young Maquisards asked each other.

"Let's set up barricades on all the roads leading north."

"We've already blown up all the bridges."

"And we've wrecked trains in their tunnels and removed and hidden the rails."

"I understand the Germans lost a full convoy carrying away their guns and tanks."

Strolling by and overhearing the young ones speak boastfully of what they would do in firefights they hoped and prayed for, the chief told them, "Easy men. The leadership makes those decisions. That's why we've been so effective."

One young man piped up, "I hear a lone gunman shot at a German convoy and stopped it for a whole day by himself."

"And killed a lot of Nazi scum," another put in gleefully.

"When can we conduct another ambush?" a young farmer who had left the fields for a different kind of harvest wanted to know. "I'm busting to do something."

"You'll have your chance," Roger assured them. "Most Germans near here are heading up the Rhône Valley, but a whole group may soon leave Alès for Mende by way of Florac. If so, you won't have to wait much longer."

The young men and Alin were cheered by this news, but when the chief left, André, listening from a short distance away, ambled over.

"Don't be so anxious," he suggested taking off his glasses and rubbing his eyes. "I know it may not seem so to you, but war is a bad business no matter what."

"We need to kill Germans," the young farmer declared. His friends clapped and cheered.

"I understand," André said worrying his forehead. "But don't forget they also want to kill you. And I'm not sure you realize how terrible it is to be shot or to watch someone on either side bleed and moan and die. That doesn't leave you feeling triumphant. It leaves you feeling dead inside." The youngsters jeered, but André persisted. "It may be necessary to fight," he insisted, feeling the full toll taken by the last four years, "but there is no glory unless you're the one to survive."

Alin and the young men went off to distract themselves and blow off nervous energy with a game of pétanque. Walking by himself, André was surprised and delighted to bump into Max Maurel, who had just arrived.

"Have you heard the latest?" Max asked suddenly darkening after warmly greeting his old friend. "About the roundup of Resistance workers in Alès? The Milice turned them over to the Gestapo who tortured them for information and then shot them all." André bowed his head and shook it slowly. "They were betrayed by collaborateurs and killed as an example. Their bodies were thrown down a flooded mineshaft at Celas, about a dozen kilometers north of the city."

André breathed evenly, his eyes sad and sunken. "It's cruel. Beastly. Barbaric."

"The few who weren't betrayed know who did it," Max said heavily. "After our liberty is attained, the responsible parties will be called to account. As will many more."

"Good to see you Max," Roger said when the young man checked in at his office. "I may have need of you."

"Expecting injuries?" Max asked fearfully, never sure of his limited medical knowledge. How he regretted having not completed his education and training.

"Not immediately, no. But there's an action you can help with."

The chief sent for André with whom Max exchanged a quizzical look.

"Time for another raid," Roger explained closing his office door. "This time for money. We can't ask the farmers for more food—they've already given us as much as they can, and more than they should. But we still need to eat—and for that we need cash."

"How will we get it?" Max asked.

"We'll take it. From the government."

André and Max looked at one another again more puzzled than before.

"You know the office of the mining company at La Grand-Combe?" Roger asked.

Max was shocked. "Where they threw the bodies?"

Roger's eyes narrowed. "It's the last place they'll expect us now, even though other raids have been staged there for shoes, clothes, gasoline, even food from the storage sheds. But this time...The government owns the mine. So we won't be stealing from a person, though it will be a bit like picking Pétain's pocket." Roger snorted derisively. "The central office of *La Compagnie des Mines de La Grand-Combe* handles the payroll for five thousand miners. They pay out twice a month. *Friends* have told us the sum for the first two weeks of June—which is considerable—will be brought in today. Once we grab it, this section of the Maquisard should be able to subsist on the proceeds until our liberation."

"Those coal mine warehouses are heavily guarded," Max objected. "We'd have to go in with guns, maybe take and even kill hostages. Why would you want André or me for this mission?"

Roger turned to André. "You're the cover. Since you don't look like the typical Maquisard your very presence will help deflect suspicion." Then he addressed Max. "You know the area and the mine office. You're intelligent and quick. I don't want any shooting particularly since we're going in broad daylight—and I know you won't be in a hurry to pull the trigger."

"Those miners are going to be awfully upset when they don't get paid," Max pointed out.

"Their distress is just a side benefit." The chief grinned with satisfaction. "We all know who they really work for. They're no innocents. Many are full-fledged collaborators, so be glad for this chance to stick it to them."

"Are you going with us?" André asked.

"This time Émile's in charge. He'll give you all the details tomorrow."

"Chief," André said politely. "Could Alin come with us? He gets upset when he's left out."

Kindly but unshakably Roger said, "No. Frankly this scheme is a bit dangerous and except in cases like the attack on La Rivière when I absolutely need every available hand, I won't run the risk of losing both the Severin family's men at once."

This time the resistants traveled as a small brigade in three light trucks and two cars. Things really had changed since the invasion of Normandy. There was little chance of being stopped along the way, what with the Vichy government on the verge of collapse and the Milice and the Gestapo rarely moving about anymore without a reason.

As the Maquisards headed south, several trucks showed up on the road ahead of them—old cranky vehicles sputtering and fuming—just farmers bringing produce to market. When the towers of the mine works finally appeared, Max led the way, turning off the main road, rounding a small hill, and heading for the main office. The trucks stayed behind blocking the entrance.

Soon Émile, André, and Max were inside anxiously watching over several clerks. Three other resistants were in the back room with another clerk retrieving the money.

The clerks out front seemed calmer than the Maquisards. They sat quietly at their desks as if being robbed were an everyday occurrence and if they just waited patiently, this little drama would end quickly and well.

Only the men in the trucks were armed. The chief's prohibition against weapons in the office had seemed a sensible precaution back at the camp, but Émile realized now that he and the others had no way to defend themselves if anything untoward happened, except with their fists. That's why he kept his hands in his pants: if someone with evil intent came in suddenly, he would point his concealed index fingers pretending he had a pistol in each pocket.

After what seemed an eternity, but was only three minutes, the back-room door swung open with a bang. The mild-mannered clerk came out first followed by Émile's deputies.

"Here," the last man called to Émile jovially, holding up a large cloth sack stuffed to bursting. "Every franc we were told to expect."

"Let's go then," Émile ordered, annoyed that his deputy had spoken carelessly, thoughtlessly disclosing the fact that the resistants had an informant. "Hurry."

"Wait!" the clerk who had been forced into the back room shouted. "That's the workers' wages! They need to be paid!"

Émile sneered, suspecting the clerk was truly concerned only with his own pay packet. "Don't worry. You'll all get what's coming to you soon enough." Émile motioned his men to get out. When they were gone, he turned back to the clerks. "No funny business now. No running for help. Not that it matters. By the time you find someone we'll be far away."

"We're not going anywhere," the youngest clerk assured him from behind the farthest, neatest desk. The other clerks glowered at him until his face turned red. "What?" he grumbled shrugging his shoulders. "There's nothing we can do about this. It's not our responsibility and it's not our money either."

"You got that right," Émile said leaving happily.

Back in a car with André, Max pressed down on the accelerator, employing greater speed going out than coming in. Passing a telephone pole neither had noticed before, both were surprised to see wires dangling uselessly to the ground.

"I guess Émile and his crew cut them to prevent a call to the authorities," Max surmised.

"I still don't understand why we never ran into any guards," André said.

"They're probably all over at the warehouses," Max speculated. "Too late now."

Departing the grounds of La Compagnie des Mines, André and Max felt relaxed, even elated. When they reached the outskirts of La Grand-Combe they saw a German troop transport rumbling north. Too bad. A little more time to celebrate the successful heist would have been lovely before being forced to face grim reality again.

They proceeded with more caution and less speed. Fortunately, they didn't see any further evidence of reinforcements or the various police forces that could have stopped and challenged them.

The roads were considerably more trafficked than at daybreak, mostly with pedestrians and bicyclists. And why not? The sun was high in the sky. It was the kind of extraordinarily fine day that reminded Max why he loved the Cévennes so. Though much better traveled, André was equally enthusiastic.

"Any idea where the chief got his information?" André asked after a while. "How could he know how much money there was right down to the franc?"

Max laughed. "It was one of the clerks."

"No!"

"That's what the chief told me this morning."

A short time later André was perplexed again. "This doesn't look right," he said. "Is this the way back to the camp?"

"No," Max said beaming. "We're going to Le Tronc for a little break. The chief suggested it as a gesture of thanks for a job well done, assuming we would pull it off. And we did."

Yvonne Guin was glad to go inside her farmhouse for lunch, not just because she was hungry, but because she was physically exhausted from the heat. Her black dress was not well suited for work in the fields, but all her dresses were black. It might have been better had she put her long hair up in a chignon as intended, but she simply hadn't had time that morning what with

Léon yelling at her to hurry, hurry, hurry—and for what? The weeds would wait. But Yvonne always did her best to keep her husband's temper in check, if only to protect herself from further verbal abuse. Pulling her hair back into a ponytail was the best she could manage.

Thankfully, it was cool and dark in the house. Yvonne had left the shutters closed not out of habit, but because Léon had rushed her to get out and get to work. Now she was glad he had been so intemperate.

Opening one set of shutters to let a little light into the otherwise gloomy interior—what a shock! Where had André and Max come from and what were they doing standing out in the bright sunshine, grinning impishly, especially at a time of day when anyone happening by could see them large as life?

"Don't just stand out there dripping in the midday sun," she admonished, ushering the two men into the kitchen, arranging extra chairs about the round table and setting out milk, cheese, and chestnuts.

The guests launched into the tale of their daring raid, laughing as if it had been a farce and not a bold dangerous action. Yvonne impressed, laughed along.

"Serves them right," she said offering her visitors mugs of tea. Then she gave them an earful about the way her religious faith and the Communist ideology she shared with Léon made it possible for her to view their exploit at the mine offices as a justified act of righteous retribution rather than simple thievery.

In turn, André and Max told her how brave they thought she was to take them into her home without the slightest hesitation—wanted men, who might be being hunted at that very moment by the Milice and the Gestapo. Taking the situation more seriously, they assured her they had stashed their car in the barn and shut the doors. As long as they remained indoors, they were unlikely to be much of a threat to the Guins' security.

"As if we care," Yvonne hooted. "We're every bit as crazy as our Huguenot forebears. They didn't worry about taking risks for what they believed and neither do we."

"Who are we sticking our necks on the chopping block for this time?" Léon growled coming in. Seeing who was there, he smiled crookedly. "Good. Extra hands."

"Now Léon," Yvonne clucked. "These two have done yeoman service for the cause. They need and deserve some rest so you just let them rest."

For once Léon gave his wife no back talk.

Chapter Eighteen

INVASION

August 15, 1944

D uring the third week of June, a British officer parachuted into the Cévennes. Toward the end of July, the Captain, sequestered with Roger Boudon in his office at Champdomergue while he waited for someone the chief had recommended to him, talked about local conditions. The heat was oppressive, 1944 being one of the hottest summers ever in the Lozère. But worse than the heat was the cutback in rations for the adult population. All French citizens between twenty-two and seventy were now restricted to seventeen hundred calories a day—potentially beneficial for the severely overweight, but not for the typically wiry inhabitants of the Cévennes.

The Captain described what he knew of the complex operations with which the Allies captured Cherbourg in a week. He spoke about the longer, harder-fought action to take Saint-Lô in Lower Normandy, which forced a German withdrawal toward the Seine. On July 17, German Field Marshal Rommel, riding in a staff car on a country road outside of Livarot, had come under an airborne strafing attack that killed his driver, causing the car to spin out of control and hurl Rommel into a ditch, resulting in head injuries, hospitalization, and a return to Germany for further recuperation. Then an attempt had been made on the Führer's life at his command post on the Eastern Front.

Earlier in July, Charles de Gaulle had gone to Washington to talk about the Free French forces' need for aid. The United States had formally recognized de Gaulle's London-based administration as the de facto government of France.

"That's all well and good," the chief interrupted, "but what about southern France? When can we hope to see these mythical Americans?"

The Captain smiled knowingly. "I can't tell you specifically about Champdomergue, but another invasion has been scheduled for August fifteenth."

A knock on the door made them both jump in their seats and stop talking. But Roger relaxed as the door swung open. "This is the young fellow I was telling you about," he told the Captain, bringing Max Maurel to him. "He's okay."

"And he can keep his lips sealed?" the Brit asked with concern.

"Max has been with the Maquisard from the beginning. We can share anything with him."

As Max offered the Captain his hand, his eyes moved slowly from the Captain's face to his own commander's and back again.

"Without getting too specific," Roger told Max, "an Allied invasion of the south is coming soon, and we need to be ready." The chief sat down at his desk, took a map of the region out of his briefcase, and smoothed it out. "American,

British, and Free French forces will be involved and when they come here we need to be ready with a hospital at La Tour du Viala.

Walking back toward his quarters showing the British officer the layout of the camp, they passed men sitting outside, chatting, and enjoying the gentle refreshing breezes of a late July afternoon in the Cévennes.

"We'll teach the Germans a thing or two."

"They really do need a good lesson."

"Why don't we launch a sneak attack, catch them off-guard?"

"We have the guns and ammunition now."

"We're trained and ready to go."

"And the Germans are scared."

"So are the gendarmes."

"And the Milice, damn them."

"Hey Doc," one of the newer Maquisards called to Max. "Are we going to fight or what?"

Max stopped to look at his questioner who was much younger than himself—really a boy. "Soon," Max told him and then repeated with a touch of melancholy, "Soon."

One thing troubled Max as they met up with André and explained the plans during the anticipated invasion. "Our only transportation is our small truck. Once fighting begins, we need another way to quickly get around."

After a long pained silence, André said, "I know where we can get a car." He explained about the big black Buick sedan stashed in the Brignands' barn. "It could be just what we need assuming it still runs after sitting idle for almost four years. If it's still where we hid it!"

Max smiled gratefully. "Let's find out."

André had found his brother at Le Tronc, rhythmically wielding a scythe and sweating profusely. Quickly apprised about the potential invasion and the need for the Buick, Alin was happy to help. Not that he looked forward to a vehicle stained with blood from any fighting. But given the cause…

Finally reaching Soleyrols on foot—feeling both strange and encouraged to be so close to the place they had so long called home—they considered stopping at the Brignands' café.

"Is that wise?" Alin asked. "To risk making our presence known? I know you're tired, but surely you're not anxious for a cup of foul coffee."

"I wasn't thinking about coffee or a rest," André replied, "just that we should warn the Brignands of what we're doing. If someone sees us go into their barn unannounced we don't want them coming after us with guns."

Albertine grabbed the Severin brothers' hands and raced them into the back room, quickly shutting the door though there were no customers to see or overhear them. André and Alin politely declined her efforts to ply them with food and drink, explaining their haste.

They caught up on each other's family members and were delighted to learn everyone was reasonably well. Albertine lamented how much she missed the little Severins then couldn't help blurting our Yvette's news. "She's getting married! And at such a time as this. Life goes on eh? Maybe it's important to show those Nazi bastards they can't stop us from living our lives. But one thing breaks my heart. Hard as it is to find a fine handsome man in these dark days it's harder to find a good dress! I know that sounds trivial but for a once-in-a-lifetime occasion…We can't even come up with material to make one from scratch. My wedding gown's so moth-eaten there's not even enough to fashion a flower girl's outfit."

"Now, now," André consoled. "It might work out yet. When is the wedding?"

"In just a few weeks."

Alin looked thoughtful, but said nothing.

"No one can be sure," André continued, "but the Allies might be here by then."

"Oh," Albertine gasped. "From your lips to God's ears!"

At the old barn, the brothers made their way stealthily through the door jammed by weeds, its hinges rusted from years of disuse and rough weather. They kicked up dust from dried hay as they moved to the rear of the barn's lower level. Small farm implements and boards of wood they had stacked to help hide the canvas-covered car appeared undisturbed, as fortunately did the Buick.

They pulled aside rakes, hoes, and pieces of lumber and pushed several mounds of old desiccated hay into a corner. Then they lifted the canvas. The Buick's dark paint showed through thick layers of dust.

After they rolled the canvas over the roof and off the hood, the car looked just as they remembered it apart from the dust. Its condition was excellent. The inside was almost pristine.

"Shall we see if it runs?" Alin asked already imagining driving back to Belgium.

André climbed the rickety steps leading to the loft. Alin watched him reach here and there until his hands described the familiar shape of the battery. Next to it, André found the precious jar into which they had drained the fluid in the fall of 1940.

"Got it," André called down excitedly.

"What about the gas?"

While André fished around for the gas can Alin opened the car's hood. Together the brothers poured in the acid to fill and replenish the dry battery cells. Then Alin dropped the battery into its housing and connected the cables. André added gas to the tank.

They agreed to leave the car on its blocks until they determined whether or not the engine would turn over. André pulled open the driver's side door and felt under the mat for the key.

"Just where we left it."

He climbed in gingerly, inserted the key into the ignition and, after hesitating nervously, turned it to the start position. Slowly, gently, he depressed the starter button. Both men let out unconsciously held breaths as the engine responded fitfully.

"Stop it and try it again," Alin suggested. "It would be very bad if after we got out onto the road the car stalled and we couldn't get it started."

"The oil is congealed," André theorized. "It'll be sluggish as it works lose. Warming up it will liquefy again and spread along the cylinder walls." The test was run and the engine turned over much more rapidly, as if it had regained familiarity with what it was supposed to do. "Amazing," André called out relieved and exhilarated.

They listened to the strong steady thrum of the engine as if they couldn't hear enough of that wonderful sound. Almost regretfully, André shut it off again.

Working the jack was a slow process. They took turns, finally settling the car onto each of its tires. The tires clearly needed air but remarkably they had retained enough tire pressure to drive.

They left the trailer behind because, with it attached, it would be impossible to maneuver the Buick through narrow mountain passes. André found the sensation of driving again peculiar but enjoyable.

"I hope you have your driver's license with you," Alin joked.

"Worse than that," André said laughing and playing along. "The car's registration has expired."

The second week of August went very slowly. For Max Maurel in the temporary hospital at La Tour Viala, the wait was unbearable; the boredom was getting to everyone. How many times could they clean the premises, review the supplies, and test their equipment?

On the fifteenth of August, the wait came to an abrupt and overwhelming end. Operation Dragoon landed three American divisions at beaches code-named Alpha, Delta, and Camel along the Côte d'Azur. French General de

Lattre de Tassigny brought his forces ashore in southern France, five thousand French troops were airlifted to Le Muy and there was a seaborne landing on the Île du Levant, between Toulon and Saint-Tropez. The Allies encountered strikingly little resistance, swiftly conquering six towns and taking more than two thousand Germans prisoners.

Suddenly energized after what felt like an enormously long sleep, the Maquisard struck numerous German positions, derailed more trains, blew up more bridges, blocked roads, downed telephone and telegraph lines, and damaged factories. The German Army struggled to protect its garrisons and to preserve every available means of retreat.

The numberless young men who had come into the Resistance camps after D-Day were finally granted their wish to take the conflict to the enemy. Descending from scattered camps onto roads throughout the Lozère and into towns where the Wehrmacht had bivouacked, they assaulted Germans joyfully and viciously. Skirmishes ballooned into full-fledged fights and sustained battles. The Maquisard fired down from hills and from behind stone walls, but the German Army possessed superior armaments. Nazi machine guns replied with an intensity that overpowered the lightly armed Maquisards, who retreated into the woods and forests from which they had barely emerged.

The next ten days were extraordinary. Events moved swiftly. The rapid collapse of France in 1940 seemed mirrored by the German pullback now.

Though inundated and beleaguered, the hospital staff managed to acquire a radio—someone was always listening. News also reached them as new patients came in. Every day brought encouragement from the north and the south: the citadel at Saint-Malo surrendered to the Allies, and Orléans and Châteaudun were freed from their German captors. Hitler ordered his troops out of the south of France. Marshal Pétain refused to move to an area dominated by the Wehrmacht, causing the Führer to give direct orders for him and his staff to be arrested and interned at Belfort. The entire Vichy government resigned.

In Paris, Resistance fighters began rebelling openly. American General Patton's armored division crossed the Seine thirty miles northwest of the capital. The Germans petitioned for a short-lived truce allowing some of their cornered troops to withdraw.

With stunning rapidity, French Resistance forces claimed control of eight départements representing ten percent of the country. And in the south, Allied forces stretched from Cannes to Marseille and from Toulon to Arles, only seventy-five kilometers from Alès. Widespread rumors placed General de Gaulle on French soil. Then in the last week of August, General Choltitz, commander of the German garrison in Paris, disobeyed orders that the city be razed and instead surrendered. Despite the last few German snipers, de

Gaulle joined a ceremonial parade proclaiming the liberation of Paris and the establishment of a new Republic.

Still, the enemy fought on from widely scattered positions. After the Allies captured Avignon, most of the German Army in the region began withdrawing northward along the Rhône. Fighting in the eastern Cévennes became even more intense. Great numbers of Maquisards marched north behind the Germans, making their retreat miserable and often fatal.

When the irregular but dedicated Resistance troops finally reached and joined the more conventional Army of de Lattre de Tassigny, the real war was just beginning for them.

The news spread quickly and the radio confirmed it: town-by-town, city-by-city, control was being ceded to the Free French. Even when Alès was liberated, the idea that the Lozère was already rid of Germans was too shocking to comprehend fully.

"How does it feel?" an excited Max asked André who had come to La Tour Du Viala.

"I'm relieved," André answered weakly, "but emotionally and physically exhausted. More than anything, I regret I can't be with my family to share this moment. But I know they're enjoying their freedom. Just to step outside unafraid…" André smiled ironically. "It's funny. We've waited, worked, and prayed for this day; and now that it's here, I feel like I've stepped into a vacuum. Because I don't know where I should be: Belgium? France? I'm not a man of two countries, rather none. France clearly isn't mine and I can't go back to Brussels yet because Belgium has not been liberated. I'm not sure I'm ready to go anyway. After all this, I feel unprepared to be free. Everything I've struggled for these last four years has been accomplished, so now what do I do? My family and I can be together again without interference and nothing could be more wonderful than that. But we don't belong—*I* don't belong—anywhere."

André stared out across the valley toward the mountain ridge and La Font. Was *that* where he should go?

"You belong," Max told him earnestly. "You're part of the Cévennes now, part of *us*. You and your family have given so generously of yourselves—that's why you were accepted by the Cévenols, protected by us. And that's why you should feel warm, welcome, and comfortable here. Now that we're all free you can finally see how we truly behave, unafraid of getting shipped off to Germany." He reached out a hand to André's shoulder hoping his touch would convey more strongly than words what he wanted to say: *You can stay.*

André's tumultuous confusion cleared. He felt great calm and comfort—a fuller, more gratifying sense of release than any news had ever brought him. He knew now that he was among true friends, even more than he would be in his beloved Brussels. The more he thought of it—and he had been thinking about it since arriving in this rugged, isolated, stunningly beautiful land—the more he realized it had never mattered whether the natives had known the Severins only as "that family from Belgium" or "the people on the farm at La Font." Their openness, thoughtfulness, and generosity had been the same as if they'd been on a first-name basis.

The simple faith practiced here, in easy ways, now seemed improbably complex to André. *Will it all pass as if it was a dream—cruel sometimes, but also glorious?*

Unanswerable questions assailed him. Will the next generation ever know or understand what has happened here? Is life worth all this or has the war made life's value even greater? What happens when the armies have gone and civilian rule is reestablished? Will the winners be able to forgive the losers? Will those who supported the Vichy government and even actively aided the Nazis accept the new order—which may feel like the old order restored?

Max wore a bemused expression on his sweet face. "Any thoughts you'd care to share?"

André sighed. Sitting atop a mountain in the Lozère, he felt almost as if he were in the laboratory of the department of chemistry at God's own university.

Let the experiment proceed. The truth will become evident. Then we shall know.

Focusing on Max, he answered earnestly, "I feel the people of the Cévennes possess depth of character, constancy, and a commitment to a greater truth than we are readily able to see. Recent events have troubled, confused, and frightened me. Will liberation change the Cévenols for me, shine a different light on what seems to me to be these people's timeless values? I can barely express myself as I ponder all that has happened and all that may be. But I hope with a greater fervor than I knew myself capable of, that I have not been deceived in my perception of these people. That what has been offered to me and my family is not an illusion. That when this dream ends, as it seems to be doing, it will prove to have been no dream at all, but my first true experience of the deepest reality."

Max smiled the open, innocent smile of unfettered, unconquerable youth. Was this the way he smiled before the complicated, conflicted life necessitated by the Nazis?

"You need not fear," Max reassured him staunchly. "These people are real, steadfast, solid, and sincere. Their beliefs are transcendent: beyond the visible, outside of time. And they possess the endless joy that comes from knowing without doubt that there is a greater truth to guide and uphold us than is evidenced by the earthly ways of man."

André closed his eyes. He knew Max held no greater belief in God than Alin did. Yet he knew them both to be deeply spiritual people whether or not they accepted or acknowledged it. Oh, how true it was that even the agnostic can be possessed of the highest faith—greater than any mere mortal's conception of the deity.

The last German soldiers at Toulon and Marseille surrendered. The French Provisional Government was firmly established in Paris. On the first of September, General Eisenhower set up headquarters in France. Mopping-up operations continued throughout the newly reestablished nation and it became possible for U.S., British, and Canadian forces to turn their attention elsewhere—as the Soviet Army had done on the Eastern Front, sweeping through the Baltic states, eastern Poland, Byelorussia, Ukraine, and Romania.

On Monday, the second of September, the Allies crossed into Belgium. The British liberated Brussels the next day.

"I must write Professor Pinkus right away," André exclaimed when Max brought him the news. "I must find out how he and all our colleagues have fared, and discover whether he knows when we can expect the Free University of Brussels to reopen."

Max shared André's excitement, but it also made him sad. He had long been painfully aware that the days of André and the other Severins were numbered in France. But he had been too busy for this realization to have its full impact. Now...

Now the liberation of Belgium was as spotty as that of France. It still wasn't safe for anyone to return. But as more Belgian cities were liberated by the Allies—Antwerp, Ghent, Lille, Louvain, Malines, Courtrai, Liège—and after U.S. troops crossed the Albert Canal, the Meuse River ,and the Moselle, it was only natural for André's mind to turn more strongly toward family and home just as Max's turned to Fela and Alès. All of which made it hard for Max, at the end of the first week of September, to tell André what he needed to say until André gave him an opening.

Softly André asked, "How much longer do you think I'll be useful here? I'd dearly love to go to Le Salson to be with Denise and our little ones. It's been such a long time since we've been together without fear."

"And it may be a little longer yet," Max finally said as gently as he could, "for I need you for one more mission."

André eyed him warily. "Just one?"

"Yes. And for not much longer than a week. But it's important I assure you. And I need you to do it. I wouldn't ask otherwise. After this, I promise you can return to your family."

"Max if you believe I am absolutely necessary..."

"I can't force you," Max said somberly. "We are free in this region at last, but we still aren't free of the shame some have brought upon us."

Considering, André asked heavily, "When do we go?"

"Don't you want to know what it's about?"

"I know you need me. Knowing more might make it harder for me to agree."

Chapter Nineteen

RETRIBUTION

September 8, 1944

D r. Jean Bataille climbed into the backseat of the Buick with one of her orderlies. Max sat in the front passenger seat as André, surprised, started to drive. Max hadn't told him anyone else would be joining them. André still didn't know where they were headed and suspected he still didn't want to know.

Wending their way toward Alès, Dr. Bataille remarked on the "awakening" of the villages they passed through. The differences from even a few months earlier were striking. Formerly depopulated, at all hours the centers of these towns were now crowded with people moving freely, festively engaged in animated conversation, catching up with their neighbors.

"Wonderful," André declared.

Max agreed in part. "The threat has passed for anyone associated with the Resistance. But for those who collaborated…"

"I bet most of them have fled," the orderly suggested, "hoping to start fresh where no one knows them."

"The rest keep out of sight," Max said, "hoping to be forgotten."

"Fat chance," the orderly sneered. "One way or another, every one of them will pay."

As that last comment sank in, André decided he had to ask about this mission.

Max cleared his throat, but spoke so softly everyone strained to hear him. "We're going to Celas to satisfy some French families—to give comfort where possible, to provide closure to those who seek it, and doubtless to renew the bitterness of those who will never forgive." Dr. Bataille cleared her throat. André slowed the car involuntarily. Max cautiously choose his next words. "Between June and July, the Germans, aided by the Milice, shot and killed a number of Maquisards. Then they threw the bodies down an abandoned mineshaft in Celas."

"We're to recover and identify the bodies then determine incontrovertibly what happened," added Jean Bataille.

André gasped, swallowed hard and spluttered, "Why me? I have no expertise required for this mission."

"You keep good records," Max replied flatly. "We need to ensure accuracy for credibility."

"But you know how squeamish I am," André quailed. "And I don't know all the terms you'll use."

"The medical results aren't in question," Dr. Bataille said sorrowfully. "They're all dead." After a brief silence she added, "It's hard for us doctors too.

What could be more terrible for a doctor than to work on what used to be a person after the body has begun to decay?"

"Please," André said weakly. "I don't want to hear about this, or worse, look."

"You won't have to look," Dr. Bataille assured him. "Just write down what we say."

"It's not going to be fun," the orderly said glumly.

Driving through Alès, they passed a familiar-looking corner. André wished they could stop for a quick visit with their mothers, but that was not to be.

"It's curious how few cars are on the streets," Max said, "after the liberation."

"There's still not much gasoline," the orderly noted.

"Look," Dr. Bataille called out as they passed the city hall, pointing at a couple of drab green French Army trucks easily identified by the Cross of Lorraine painted on their sides. "I thought all our forces had gone north to pursue the Germans."

"Most have," Max said. "But a few must stick around to provide support and an example for the gendarmes and the new civil authorities."

André gazed intently at the uniformed soldiers, rifles slung over their shoulders, at once both nonchalant and self-important. How little different they seemed from Wehrmacht soldiers, apart from the color of their uniforms.

The orderly sniped sarcastically.

"How quickly the functionaries of Pétain's Vichy government have been transformed into the bureaucrats of de Gaulle's provisional government," he reflected.

"Some," Max agreed. "But many who collaborated with the Gestapo have been removed from office and placed in the same prisons that held our captured Resistance brethren."

"The Maquisards who weren't put to death you mean," the orderly spat.

Anxious to change the subject André asked, "How much longer to Celas?"

"Five or six kilometers east along decent roads."

Emerging from the city, André turned the car toward the still-rising sun. André filled with trepidation when he saw the mineshaft ahead rising twelve meters above the flat surrounding fields. As the car drew closer, he saw several buildings nearby. The setting reminded him of a public park except for the two ambulances lined up alongside several Army vehicles and the clusters of two or three dozen people standing near the exposed shaft.

"That's Laurent Spadale, the *sous-prefect* of Alès," Max said as the car came to a stop.

"Ah," Dr. Bataille responded. "He's the one who called for this inquiry."

A gendarme opened the rear door for Dr. Bataille who was greeted by two men.

"Those are Doctors Mosnier and Chametier," Max explained stepping out into the warm fresh air. "I recognize them from my student days."

The three doctors moved toward the clusters of people, with Max, André, and the orderly following. As they passed close by the mineshaft, André looked at the opening in the ground surrounded by a concrete-and-metal casing. He shuddered.

"Max," Dr. Bataille called, "please help set up our table for the bodies. André," she said pointing, "there's a table you can use for recording our comments." André flushed. "Goodness you've turned green." Dr. Bataille felt his forehead and took his pulse. "You'll be all right. Just keep your back to us if you like." She pointed out two men dressed as if to descend into caves. "That's Robert de Joly, the eminent speleologist. The other is a Resistance lieutenant, Réné 'Ulysse' Soustelle. They're the ones with the really hard job," Dr. Bataille continued. "They'll be going down into the mineshaft."

The sous-prefect called Dr. Bataille aside for a private consultation.

Max looked at the perspiration on André's forehead. "You all right?"

"I hope so."

Max stepped away to organize the medical equipment. André went to his table where he overheard Robert de Joly and Ulysse Soustelle.

"No problem," de Joly insisted. "This is straight down. I've gone into caves where the opening twisted and turned. Now *that's* complicated."

"We'll rappel down," Soustelle said, "in tandem."

"Ready gentlemen?" Sous-Prefect Spadale asked solemnly.

The two "divers" nodded then stepped to the lip of the mineshaft. In the great silence that followed, André realized he was holding his breath again..

Slowly the brave men began their descent.

As the men descended, Laurent Spadale signaled to a gendarme who had witnessed the original atrocity. The policeman saluted, turned to open the door of one of the mineshaft's outbuildings and ordered those inside to come out.

A dozen prisoners emerged: Milice and collaborator detainees being held against the discovery of definitive evidence of their treachery. The policeman made them sit on the ground not far from the great hole itself—the receptacle of their dirty deeds.

Everyone focused on two strong ropes—one end of each lashed securely to the iron bars of the mineshaft structure, the other to the spelunkers themselves—as they slowly slid down the shaft. The ropes were clearly marked and when the two investigators had descended one hundred ten meters the rope lines stopped moving then visibly jerked.

"They're signaling for the body basket," Dr. Mosnier cried out.

Max brought the basket forward and helped attach it to yet another rope. Two of the larger gendarmes gradually paid out the line.

The tension was evident on every aboveground face. Waves of anger, hatred, and disgust were directed at the prisoners seated on the ground, facing one another in a tight circle, most dressed in the despised blue and black of the Milice. Their belts had been removed though no one would have objected had they done themselves harm. They also had been stripped of the berets they, until recently, had worn at an arrogant angle as a mark of power. Bareheaded though they were, they hardly seemed humbled or repentant.

When de Joly and Soustelle emerged from the mineshaft, one prisoner said "Shit" and spat in the dirt—whether reacting to the spelunkers' solemn expressions, the dreadful smell coming off of them, or what he knew they had found at the bottom of the shaft. The nearest guard kicked his back viciously. He nursed his new bruise with bound hands.

Clear of the mineshaft, de Joly and Soustelle turned off the lamps atop their helmets. Half a dozen meters away observers gagged from the stench of decayed and rotting flesh.

Dr. Bataille hurried over. Right behind her Spadale called out, "What did you find?"

De Joly spoke about the glacial cold engulfing them as they descended and of the humidity that oozed from walls stained with blood.

"It's as we suspected only worse," Soustelle reported. "We could see bits of clothing and even skin hanging from the hooks cemented into the walls of the shaft. The hooks must have torn at the falling bodies as they bumped down."

"Then it got very dark," de Joly stated. "Even when we turned on our lamps we saw nothing. But by the hundred-meter mark the piercing stink of decomposing cadavers almost suffocated us."

"Below us very plainly," Soustelle continued, "we could see a white surface. But it wasn't until we were one hundred ten meters down that our horrified eyes could discern the awful spectacle."

"Bodies intertwined..."

"All mixed up..."

"Yes, well," Dr. Chametier said after forcefully clearing his throat several times, "that is what you'd expect of bodies submerged in water for three months."

For a long while no one said another word. Even the prisoners were shocked by what they had heard. How much worse it would be when the bodies were brought up.

Pulling off his rubber boots and pants de Joly said, "We had to take the greatest precaution trying to release any individuals from the layered mass." Taking off his rubber gloves last, he spread out all his gear carefully for one of the gendarmes to hose down with clean water. "Come on," Soustelle said cutting off de Joly while he stripped down as well. After waiting a decorous moment, de Joly concluded, "It took forever but we finally got one mostly whole body into the basket. If you're ready bring it up. But be careful. Any more disintegration will make identification even more difficult."

Spadale and his male colleagues stood slack-jawed so Dr. Bataille issued the order. Then she walked over to Max, put on her white smock and a face mask, and pulled on her gloves as several of the larger gendarmes and Maquisards pulled steadily on the line attached to the basket.

To everyone's horror and dismay the line stopped—snagged. The men had to lower it again to loosen it then jostle it around before they were able to pull on it steadily again.

Time slowed. The heat of the day increased as the sun reached its apex.

Finally, what remained of a man appeared.

Everyone standing took a step back reflexively except Max who stood his ground and motioned to two orderlies. "Let's get that basket and bring it over here."

The three doctors lifted the remains gingerly from the basket and placed them carefully on the metal examining table.

André stared at the body peculiarly. Then with a sudden lurch, he turned away, doubled over, and threw up on the ground next to his makeshift desk. His stomach heaved several more times before he slumped down onto his chair.

Captain Lucien, a French Army officer, marched over and asked, "Will you be able to identify anyone in such a...condition?"

"It won't be easy," Dr. Bataille snapped.

The police chief approached and suggested, "With information from families about missing loved ones, the scraps of clothing we can still see and some dental records..."

The sous-prefect wasn't prepared to wait. "I'm sure this is one of the men the Milice were reported to have executed in June."

"We warned the Resistance to wait for us," Captain Lucien said shaking his head dolefully. "They were no match for the Germans." He passed a hand over his moistened brow, straightened up, and squared his shoulders. "Poor brave men. Foolish perhaps. But brave."

"Bring those prisoners over here," Sous-Prefect Spadale ordered.

"Get up!" a Maquisard barked at the former Milice members and collaborateurs. Grudgingly, listlessly, the prisoners got to their feet. Their outraged captors shoved them forward with rifle butts.

The French Army was in charge technically, but its leader seemed inclined to leave this affair to local authorities. The gendarmes represented the restored civilian government, but preferred deferring to the Resistance in crimes committed against its members. The sous-prefect could only hope to unite these disparate factions.

As the prisoners approached, fear mixed with an ill-concealed hatred on their faces. Spadale told the gendarmes, "Send them into the mineshaft two at a time. Let *them* bring up the bodies."

The accused looked shocked. Their reluctance to confront the remains of men they hadn't hesitated to kill was richly satisfying.

The gendarmes dragged two resisting Milice to the mineshaft opening, untied their hands, placed helmets on their heads and lashed them tightly with support ropes.

"Into the shaft," a gendarme growled. Then he and his partners put the two men over the side of the hole and gave them a little push.

"Let them down slowly," the sous-prefect commanded. Then he leaned over the side of the shaft, and shouted to the prisoners, "Take care. No more damage to anybody."

The other prisoners slumped to the ground. One actually had tears in his eyes.

"Don't you worry," one of the Maquisards snarled, crouching down to leer into those teary eyes. "You'll get your chance."

This is awful, Max thought. Each day seemed worse than the one before. How many more bodies could possibly be down there and how much longer would it take to get all of them out?

Every morning, as Max and André emerged from the home of a victim's family that local authorities had arranged for them in which to stay, he saw more and more people gathered at the site: friends, relatives, curiosity seekers, reporters. Throughout each day, everyone waited for a visible tug on a rope line. Then big men pulled until the submerged pair of prisoners came back into sight followed—inevitably, unbearably—by another body or as much of a body as was found and fit into the basket. As the remains were taken to a metal table the onlookers gasped, gagged, keened, and wept. Meanwhile two more of the accused were outfitted and deposited into the mineshaft.

The stench hung over the open field, like a fog that never lifted. André kept moving his makeshift desk farther and farther from the doctors performing the autopsies. By Saturday, September 16, it was surprising he could hear anything the doctors said. Dr. Bataille asked de Joly if he thought the recovery phase was almost over.

"I hope so," he said fervently. With another tug on the rope lines, the gruesome process began again. "That's got to be the last."

He was right. In all, thirty-one bodies had been brought up from the dark depths of the mineshaft into the harsh light of day. Remarkably, every one of them had been identified. Twenty-eight belonged to members of the Resistance and accounted for all reported missing from Alès. The surprise was the other three: collaborators who had also been reported missing, but whom no one knew had suffered the same fate. The assumption had been that they had run away to escape Maquisard retribution. Now it was conjectured that they had been killed by members of the Milice or the Gestapo trying to keep the terrible murders secret.

Standing beside Sous-Prefect Spadale, Lieutenant Soustelle announced, "Now that we have all the evidence, justice needs to be done."

André, his features distorted as much by disgust as rage, went to Max and said, "I've done my duty."

"Yes," Max responded feelingly. "Now we have our proof."

They both fell silent studying the somber faces all around them.

"It could have been you or me down there," André whispered hoarsely. "You or me."

What Sous-Prefect Spadale feared most wasn't summary judgment—that had already been rendered—but summary *justice*. He could feel the desire for retribution and the expectation of its imminent arrival and wondered, *Will this settle the score when the score is too great to be settled? Will it give us back our sanity or degrade our humanity? Restore our civilization or reduce us, as these prisoners reeking of death have been reduced, to mere animals?*

Soustelle told him softly, "We need to settle this. Now."

Spadale looked to Captain Lucien who had, after the last body was identified, conducted the brief military trial establishing the guilt of the accused. His silence insinuated his belief that this was now a local matter. And the several gendarmes present, dressed in fresh crisp uniforms, weren't about to prevent the Resistance fighters from doing as they wished either.

Soustelle's Maquisards stood straight and tall beside their leader, rifles either over their shoulders, resting on the ground, or cradled in their arms. No one would get in their way.

"The convicted need to pay," Soustelle insisted coldly. "The military panel has determined their guilt. And if anyone doubts them the proof lies there," he pointed dramatically to a row of pine coffins, "and there," he pointed to the families of the dead. "We have all the proof we need in their loved ones' eyes.

Besides," Soustelle said directly to the sous-prefect, "you knew the facts before we got here, thanks to the testimony of two gendarmes forced to participate in these bestial acts." He took a step forward. "Now we must cleanse our town. It is our duty to serve justice, to bring an end to this cruel episode in our long history, and to restore our people and our beloved region to the path of righteousness."

Soustelle stopped speaking. He could take no pleasure in what was about to happen but he took comfort in its justification.

He nodded to his men. Several moved forward to grab the condemned men underneath the arms and drag them one by one to a short concrete wall beside the mineshaft.

Spadale sighed and muttered to himself, "Let this end here."

André could hardly believe his eyes. The Milice and their collaborators— a dozen now after a very few had been released for lack of evidence—were lined up in front of the mineshaft facing a Maquisard firing squad. Did he really have to see this through to the bitter end?

"No!" cried a Milice in his mid-twenties, his whiskers unshaved and his eyes rimmed red. "They made me do it!" he shouted as his knees buckled. Then he sobbed openly.

The man standing next to him recited either a prayer or a confession repeatedly with a sub vocalized droning sound. The rest of the condemned men looked defiant, staring murderously at the sous-prefect, the Army captain, the Resistance lieutenant, and the would-be executioners. They had known their fate all along.

The crowd of onlookers instinctively backed off, except for several children who pressed forward excitedly. Their mothers quickly drew them back and forcibly turned them away.

Despite his natural inclination, André could not avert his eyes even as this mantra played and replayed in his mind: *The heat of battle is one thing. Murder is another. The heat of battle is one thing. Murder is…*

As if reading André's mind, Max leaned close and whispered, "Execution is not murder."

"They're both cold-blooded," André argued.

"This is simply necessary," Max insisted.

"Is it?" André demanded.

"I'm sure the widows think so."

"And who are they to judge?"

"Who else should?"

"Only God."

"Where was your God when these men committed murder?" Max admonished him gently. "And where is He now?"

"I don't know," André said sadly. "But if these men are shot dead like this, I'll know He's not here."

Max nodded toward the people of Celas. "I bet they believe that only when these men are dead will God return to this town and this region."

"Then He will come too late."

It was already too late. As Soustelle lifted his hand, the praying Milice grew louder but no more comprehensible. Little gasps and cries went up from the small crowd of observers.

"No!" the groveling young man shrieked as Soustelle lowered his hand and shots rang out—an initial furious barrage followed by a few scattered firings and one last final shot to each.

The bodies slumped and fell flat, some backward; some face down in the dirt. Blood poured from their bodies, pooled on, and seeped into the ground. Amidst the horrifying scene, André's eyes traveled swiftly to the face of the man who had died praying. His body was splayed out on its back, eyes and mouth open wide, as if offering up one final plea to a God who had failed him long before this day of death.

"I suppose we need to bury them," the sous-prefect said civilly, unemotionally.

"That's too good for the leader," Soustelle spat. "Down the mineshaft is where he belongs."

His men carried out this order immediately. Neither Free French forces nor gendarmes interfered as the newly dead body was heaved over the lip.

André could not see, but could all too easily visualize what he thought he heard: flesh and bone thumping against the walls, shredding on hooks and, after what seemed an eternity, splashing down into an eternal watery grave.

"A fitting end," Lieutenant Soustelle said gladly.

"Justice is often cruel especially in war," Captain Lucien pronounced haughtily.

"May peace now return to our town," Sous-Prefect Spadale prayed.

"Let's go home," Max suggested to André who was confused about what "home" might mean: Le Tronc? Le Salson? La Font? Brussels? "We can finally see our mothers, yes?"

"Yes," André managed to say before turning away.

Chapter Twenty

LIBERATION

September 18, 1944

A ndré, Denise, and their children had a reunion as fulfilling as André hoped and dreamed. Better still, Alin and his family joined them at Le Salson, staying in a barn owned by the absent Hugons. Being together again was especially wonderful for Ida and Katie. But there was no greater joy than Philippe's return to the bosom of his family. Now an impressive five-year-old Philippe was fussed over and indulged even more than in Brussels.

Only Rose's presence could have made the Severins happier. André had spent some time with her and the Maurels in Alès after Celas. She was in remarkable shape and spirits for a widow of her age and wartime experience. But André had thought it best that she remain where she was pending an exact determination of the family's living conditions.

Mamé and Tata Irene's little cottage was incredibly crowded. The Severins briefly considered returning to La Font for which all had strong warm feelings. But André wasn't anxious to resume the incredibly hard work of farming.

Not that he could avoid it altogether. Delighted to be surrounded by so much life, the Bastides could now keep their crops for themselves, but needed extra hands for the myriad chores in their newly expanded household.

Each day and night, the children delighted. The grown-ups reveled in watching them play so well together. Philippe was thrilled to discover in Cristian a male Severin with whom he could pal around.

In some ways, little Christel—a great big six-year-old—had developed most in hiding. Geneviève began teaching her again—an education too long interrupted. The most-changed Severin was Geneviève. Her haughtiness and self-regard had so diminished throughout the family's exile that she no longer felt removed from or superior to the less-educated poorer rural folks with whom she had lived so long. Nor did possessions hold the meaning and importance they once had, as evidenced by what she had given away after Alin had brought word of Yvette Brignand's bridal plight. Geneviève had immediately sent her husband back to Soleyrols to tell Yvette to go into her trunk in the rafters of the Brignands' barn, and pick out and tailor as necessary whichever dress she wished for her wedding.

Even more startlingly, as a gesture of thanks for taking good care of Philippe, Geneviève had given her big diamond engagement ring to Edouard Ours' fiancée. And Alin approved. The gesture impressed him.

Mostly encouraging news reached the Severins easily now, but the war continued. Recently named "Reich Plenipotentiary for Total War" Joseph

Goebbels exhorted all Germans to fight with the utmost fanaticism, symbolized by a new "flying bomb" campaign.

When would the exiles be able to go home? Impossible to say. But they took heart after learning that the Belgian Parliament had met in a formal session in Brussels on the nineteenth of September—for the first time since May 1940.

Freedom brought out many emotions in the French. One local farmer—always a bit crazy—appeared under the windows of the Bastides' little house to sing, "When you shit, you're alive!" Whenever the Severins saw him coming down the path, they hid in the Hugon barn until he left.

Tata Irene suffered frequent fits of deep personal sorrow despite the many distractions. As the war wound down throughout France, she realized she might never know where her husband was, whether or not he was alive, or if she would ever see him again.

Sunday, September 24, André and Ida once again joined Irene in a nearby meeting of the Society of Friends. André's quest for peace not only in the world, but also in himself, had been sorely tried by recent events, causing him to enter the meeting's humble abode tremulously.

A dozen people were already seated quietly in a circle. André was impressed by the traveling pastor's short introductory speech, expressing gratitude for restoration of French autonomy and the end of immediate suffering. After reading several brief Bible passages aloud, the gentle pastor announced a period of silent worship.

This Quaker practice intrigued André the most and, in the event, had the most significant impact on him. Though he had meditated on God in the past, no previous experience compared with the power he felt in this group's shared deep concentration.

Before falling silent, the pastor had encouraged everyone to speak freely if and as the spirit moved them. André listened intently as others spoke without volition as if but simple vessels God used to communicate the underlying unity of humankind and the universe's quest for harmony, compassion, and generosity. Then the spirit spoke directly in the silence to André.

This is it, he thought involuntarily. *We want the ability to think for ourselves, to worship as we will—to learn directly from the Lord, not always and only from a priest who reads his sermon or Bible passage as if it contained instructions for the week ahead. We must join together with those who also know there is no one path for faith, but who seek to learn perpetually...*

He had always hoped to find himself a ready receptacle for "inner light." Seated amidst these humble thoughtful devotees, he believed that what he thought he had lost on that miserable morning of May 10, 1940 was finally within reach.

Back at Le Salson, he tried to explain his experience to Denise and daringly Alin, who was unsurprisingly skeptical. Remarkably though, his brother wasn't entirely dismissive.

"We'll see," Alin said quietly. "We'll see."

André still hadn't heard back from the Free University. More worryingly, Denise had written to many relatives in Belgium and received no response of any sort.

Nonetheless, Wednesday, September 27, was a day of celebration: Ida's tenth birthday. Sadly, Rose couldn't be there. Unexpectedly though, Max and Fela drove up on Max's motorcycle and brought a big surprise: news that they would wed in October when Max hoped to get a three-day pass from the Army.

That Max had joined the Army was also news. After Celas, he decided he couldn't rest until the last Nazis were out of France. Soon he would leave the Cévennes to meet up with de Lattre de Tassigny's Army to serve in the medical corps.

The next day, the mailman paid a rare extra visit, as what he had in hand seemed so important that he had gone out of his way to bring it before his next scheduled delivery.

"A letter for you," he called out gaily to André, waving it in the air. "It's from Brussels, Belgium, for a Professor Severin. Such an official looking envelope. All typed-up."

André's eyes opened wide when he saw the return address. He read over the letter quickly and smiled with deep satisfaction.

With a nod, a wave, and one last wink the mailman said, "Good luck Professor."

Denise watched André carefully until he finally called out joyfully, "The Free University of Brussels is ready to reopen. They want me back!"

"When?" Denise asked encouragingly though she worried about the danger.

"As soon as I can return," André declared beaming. "Classes resume in mid-October."

"Who tells you this? Alexandre Pinkus?"

"No not Pinkus. The faculty secretary." André's face fell. "I hope he's all right. The letter's quite explicit that with German rockets falling Brussels still isn't one hundred percent safe. What do you think?"

"I'm thinking of the children," Denise said anxiously. "Should we stay on here while you go back? Oh, I would hate to be separated from you so soon again." Denise threw her arms around him. "I would hate to be separated from you *ever* again!"

"I know, I know," André said feelingly.

"How will Christel react to a place she doesn't remember? How will Cristian respond to a place he's never been?"

"One step at a time," André counseled calmly. "We'll talk. We'll think."

The adult Severins returned to Soleyrols and reunited with the Brignands in a flurry of hugs and kisses. Yvette showed her wedding dress, almost unrecognizable to Geneviève after the adjustments for Yvette's slighter frame.

"Beautiful," Albertine remarked repeatedly, caressing the dress. "So beautiful."

"Yvette chose well," Geneviève said smiling.

Albertine insisted that after making a few repairs she would return it. But Geneviève wanted the Brignands to keep it.

"It has far more meaning for you than it ever had for me. Besides, I only wore it to parties and teas. I no longer think about such frivolities."

Albertine pressed a meal upon the Severins. Afterward, she accompanied them to the cemetery in Vialas to see Louis' grave.

Everyone remarked on how well the grounds were kept. The Severins were overwhelmed with emotion and stunned to see a plain marble marker embedded in the ground where Louis had been laid four years before.

"We felt we must do something," Albertine explained wiping a tear from the corner of her eye. "Quite a few of us contributed from both Soleyrols and Vialas."

Standing side by side, sighing and misty-eyed, arms around each other's waists for support, André, Denise, Alin, and Geneviève read the simple moving inscription:

Louis Severin
1869-1940.
Rest in peace here in this hospitable land

Visiting his father's grave shook André and summed up his experience in the Cévennes: great losses in the midst of untold kindness. Was this what God intended for His children?

Day after day reports from the front sounded optimistic. "Americans attack the Siegfried Line." "RAF bombers destroy dikes in Holland, flooding German defenses." "Allies sink German mini-submarines off the coast of the Scheldt."

"Heavy day and night raids rain death and destruction on Berlin." Still, there were many reverses and it was discouraging to hear similar reports repeatedly. How often could the Allied Expeditionary Forces break out of Belgium into the Netherlands and the northern plains of Germany?

One afternoon while the adults sat inside and the children played outside, a shriek stopped all hearts, froze all thoughts.

"Christel!" Denise cried racing out. Everyone followed in her wake.

The accident resulted from Ida and Christel's desire to help. André had offhandedly remarked in their presence that a large part of the ground near the spot the spring emerged from underground was perpetually wet, slippery, dangerous. Without telling anyone the little sisters had gone off to find a large stone to plop into the mud so the spring water would run down onto it instead of flowing into the ground. Locating the perfect stone, they had excitedly lifted it together. But while being awkwardly maneuvered into place it had slipped, dropping onto bent-over Christel's thumb with a sickening thud, surprising and then frightening her with pain.

The bone was badly broken. Nothing could be done but to wash the finger and wrap it in a cloth to heal—a sad reminder that war wasn't the only danger the family faced.

More German soldiers deserted to join the Resistance. Somehow having heard what had happened to Christel, one stopped by to cheer her up. A very nice man—caring, courteous, and circumspect—he frightened the Severin children simply by having been in the Wehrmacht. Despite his concern for Christel's thumb, the children were mean to him. Embarrassed by their children's reaction, Denise and Geneviève apologized to the poor perplexed young man.

Reminded of the terrible early days of May 1940 when Katie and Ida had been terrified by the attentions of rifle-toting Belgian soldiers on the beach in Le Coq, the mothers explained to the younger Severins that this soldier had probably only been thinking of his own sons or daughters back home. Though the children were not mollified by this, at least the German had so upset Christel that she forgot about her thumb.

When André and Denise decided to return to Brussels, their offspring were very excited. Ida claimed she remembered everything about the city and tried to lord that over Christel. But Christel didn't believe Ida remembered the land of their birth any better than she did. Whenever she asked for details Ida spoke vaguely about flowers and a big park.

"So?" Christel challenged. "There are plenty of flowers right here. And now that we can go out into it the whole valley; seems like a great big park to me."

Did Brussels have real mountains like the Cévennes? Denise told Christel, no, but it did have streetcars and buildings as many as five stories high.

The children became upset when they realized Katie and Philippe weren't leaving too. Alin and Geneviève had decided not to run the risk of returning home until the Germans surrendered and the war was truly over. Meantime they hoped to find a place smaller than La Font to farm, but large enough for Rose to live in with them.

One night Christel complained to Ida, "I thought the war was over."

"Hitler isn't dead yet," Ida explained, "and not enough Nazis have been killed. I guess they still haven't had enough of the destruction of their own country."

On the day of departure, André walked back to the house from the Hugons' barn where he had delivered his few books to Alin. Finding his wife upstairs in the midst of their half-filled suitcases he said, "Better hurry and change."

"And you?" Denise teased. "What about those pants?"

André glanced down at the woolen pants that had served him well, but had seen better days. "I'm going to miss these sturdy pants."

"Can't we take several pairs?" Denise suggested. "You might be a professeur, but isn't it better—even in Brussels—to be a warm rustic professor than a cold fancy one?" Beginning to get dressed she added, "There's a lot I'll miss about this region starting with the people."

"I'll miss them too," André agreed doing likewise. "Still it will be good to be back where I can do what I was trained for. Besides life is easier in a city—or at least it used to be."

The imminent departure of André and his family was making Alin more than grumpy and dour. He was depressed, though he tried not to show it, attempting to alleviate and mask his feelings by throwing himself into helping André carry three packed duffle bags up to the road along the crest of the mountain. There in the lee of a small group of sheltering trees Denise, Ida, Christel, and Cristian waited with Geneviève, Katie, and Philippe who meant to keep them company until the last possible second. Farewells had already been said to Mamé and Tata Irene.

The homeward-bound Severins also carried a fair quantity of food given them by the many Cévenol friends, concerned about them starving on the trip back to Belgium. Though the travelers wouldn't spend too long on the bus, there was no telling how many hours the train trip would take since there were places where tracks had been wrecked, tunnels blocked, and bridges blown up and had not yet been repaired. And there might not be any food decent or otherwise available onboard. Nor could they expect working toilets.

Alin didn't feel like idle chit-chat, and André seemed more self-absorbed than usual. Geneviève and Denise didn't say much either—just clung to each other, tears streaming down Geneviève's cheeks as Denise tried with intermittent success to keep from crying too.

But the children chattered and gamboled. Impressively two-and-a-half-year-old Cristian participated fully. Having grown fond of the little tyke, Alin worried about how Cristian would fit in in Brussels with his soft sibilant Cévenol accent. How long before he would understand, let alone speak, the tongue he had rarely heard: Flemish?

The old red bus came around the far bend. Suddenly family members frantically hugged, kissed, wept, and called out, "Take care!" "I love you!" "See you soon!"

André and Alin shook hands solemnly then gave each other the traditional embrace of the Cévennes, simultaneously kissing each other on opposite cheeks then a third kiss—once more than in Brussels. Finally, with a general clattering and commotion, the Severins clambered aboard the bus. When Ida, Christel, and Cristian reached their seats they leaned out a window waving and calling good-bye.

On the side of the road, Alin gathered his family into a protective embrace. They waved encouragement and regret to those they would miss terribly. Alin silently wished those leaving the Lozère a safe journey home and inwardly determined to follow when circumstances allowed.

Denise felt her heart would break. She was excited to return to Brussels, but also afraid. And to be torn so soon again from her beloved Geneviève...

How strange after four and a half years to watch all the familiar houses and terraced slopes of her host country pass from view. In her mind, Denise bid adieu to every meter. Here again was Soleyrols: the Brignands' café, the house in which Louis and Rose had lived and, at the top of the hill, La Font...

Entering Vialas, Denise was surprised by the strength of her reaction. She hadn't spent much time there, but as the bus stopped to let passengers off and on, she relived Louis' funeral and pictured the horrible Easter-time scene of German soldiers and machine guns Tata Irene had described so vividly...

Denise's mind snapped back to the present when she heard André cry, "Fela! Max! What are you two doing here?"

"Going with you as far as Génolhac," Max explained laughing as he and Fela offered hugs all around.

"You can't leave the Cévennes without a proper farewell," Fela said sweetly.

"I was among the first to meet you in our part of the world," Max offered seriously. "I need to complete the cycle by being the last."

Fela enjoyed the company. She'd spent so long in hiding that as much she loved Suzanne, Rose, Françoise, and Fernande Velle she had felt isolated.

But now, this interlude too was coming to an end. When Génolhac hove into view, sorrow welled up within her. Soon the bus pulled up behind the dreary station.

As she and Max assisted the Severins off the bus and into the terminal, Fela noticed paper littering every corner of the waiting room and small piles of dry leaves that shifted and grew with the wind and passing trains. No fresh paint had been applied to the peeling ceiling since before the war. The walls were covered with posters and graffiti first applied by Pétain's Vichy officials, then by the Germans and finally by Americans and the Free French—each set of "rulers" supplying different, often diametrically opposed visions of the future. None had proved trustworthy, not even the latest, for there were still unresolved conflicts between the victors. The Communists who had the greatest influence in the local Resistance now competed with the Maquisard, who were supported by de Gaulle...

After purchasing tickets, the Severins went outside to await their train on a bench on the one platform. Max and Fela stood close by.

"It's strange," André remarked perplexedly, "not to have to look around for collaborators. But I keep scrutinizing faces anyway out of nervous habit."

Denise grasped her husband's hand. "I'm sure we will all take time to adjust."

Fela wondered whether the Severin children felt the new spirit in the land. They didn't seem sufficiently confident of their safety to separate themselves from their parents by even a few meters.

"It's coming!" Christel cried hearing the chug-chug of a train and racing to the edge of the platform.

Puffs of smoke—steam and soot—shot up into the sky as the old engine rolled into view, pulling several aged passenger cars and three small boxcars in its wake. When it squealed to a halt, few people got off. Everyone was heading to Paris.

A flurry of activity ensued as everyone tried to kiss, hug, and say good-bye one last time. Afraid the train would depart without them, André helped Denise up the stairs to the first car and pushed the girls on after her. With Max's help, he lifted the baggage and bags of food into the vestibule. Then he took Cristian from Fela, and handed him up into his mother's outstretched arms.

Impatient passengers crowded and pushed from behind. Fela looked through the car windows and could just make out André and Denise squeezing down into seats and gathering their children onto their laps. The Severins looked out and waved.

Max waved back with one hand while sliding his other arm lovingly, easefully, comfortingly around Fela's shoulders. Then the train started up.

How strange it must be for them, Fela thought, *to be going home after all this time.*

Everything was strange for Fela too. As the train disappeared from view, she realized as never before that nothing would ever be the same for her. She knew she would never go home to Poland. France was her home now—with Max whom she loved beyond all measure.

Chapter Twenty One

PARIS

October 8, 1944

D enise explained to her overexcited children that they would only be in Paris long enough to sleep before catching the early morning train for Brussels. The six hundred twenty-five kilometer journey would take far longer than before the war since everyone would have to get off periodically to go by Army truck around bombed-out bridges and such.

André guessed it would take twelve hours or more. The children were horrified. *Twelve hours on a train?*

Once again, Ida was interfered with—abused by a grown man. Even she could never explain how it happened with her family nearby. But when they were all taken around a blocked tunnel on a crowded truck she somehow ended up sitting on the man's lap...Fortunately, it only lasted seconds. Ida didn't like it and the man seemed disappointed. She couldn't believe he got right onto the train that met them on the other side as if nothing had happened. She thought about telling someone, but doubted even her parents would take the word of a ten-year-old girl over a full-grown man's.

How good to have ham, sausage, bread, cheese, butter, and honey. There was even a bottle of wine for André and Denise. No one could abide the chestnuts though. They thought about giving them away but who would take them? Everyone from that part of the world had already had more than his or her fair share.

Dusk came on. Amazing colors shone through the windows: pink, orange, purple, and then gray.

Drawing close to Paris, they could see more and more lights. But it still seemed a long way away with no means to relieve themselves.

The monotonous rocking of the train lulled them to sleep. Sometimes the brakes, the uneven roadbed, or the train whistle woke them slightly, but they drifted right off again.

When the engineer slowed the train for the signals and control blocks near the end of the line they couldn't sleep. There was a violent braking until the engineer eased off so the train could glide the rest of the way with very little power.

Ida felt strange, as if something was dripping onto her forehead. Reaching up to brush back whatever it was she felt, her hand came away sticky and sweet-smelling, and she sat bolt upright.

It was honey. The last of the food had been put in a sack on the rack overhead. All the jolting must have opened the container above Ida's head. The honey leaked into her hair.

"Maman!" she shrieked panicking.

"Oh my dear," Denise cried shaking still-slumbering André's arm to wake him. She settled Cristian onto her seat, reached up to the sack, and pulled out the leaking jar. Honey had gotten all over the rest of their food. Even the cheese was coated with the stuff. There was a thin line running down the side of the compartment.

"I don't like it," Ida wailed between sobs. "I can't put my head anyplace!"

"I'm not sure what to do," Denise told André. "We have so little water. How can I clean her up before we reach the station?"

Then Christel piped up, "Just stick a piece of bread on her head!"

The train pulled into Paris after midnight. Even at that hour, the station was crowded. With all their possessions, Christel half asleep, and Cristian asleep entirely, the Severins struggled to get off.

Denise piloted her brood to the restrooms. Everyone had to go badly. And there was Ida's honey mess. The attendant in the ladies' room helped Denise with Ida's hair for a few francs. Despite concerted efforts, Ida still smelled of honey. Anxious to see to accommodations and to make certain of the morning train schedule, André first carried all their bags and then took Cristian to the men's room.

The war had taken its toll on the great station where time seemed simply to have stopped in May 1940. Numerous light bulbs had burned out and not been replaced, making the terminal poorly illuminated.

André led his little family through streams of people on the grand concourse, surrounded by still-open shops and cafés. He longed for a cup of real coffee and Denise urged him to indulge himself. Unfortunately, the "coffee" was mostly chicory—a step up from soybeans, but too small a step for André to bother with it. He hoped for better luck in Brussels the next day.

Pushing on toward the hotel information booth, André disappeared into a shoving throng clamoring for rooms—any room if cheap enough, though most would pay whatever it took. On the outer edge of the crowd, surrounded by children and luggage, Denise could tell by André's puzzled, discouraged expression that finding lodging would be difficult. The city was full up since refugees from fighting in the east sought safety in the capital and many French citizens were returning home via the hub of Paris.

When André, squeezed left and right by others and got to the counter, the woman in charge smiled wanly in a resigned matter-of-fact manner. Bored by constant demands from the never-ending slew of new arrivals and resentful of being blamed for the lack of available rooms, the housing agent followed André's despairing eyes to his dead-tired family. Shrugging she spoke and pointed. André nodded and hurried back through the crowd.

"This way," he said. "The YMCA may have something."

As André lifted all three suitcases and began marching toward the Y's waiting area Denise said, "This is as crazy as when we arrived in Millau."

André gazed woefully at the lone, tired person working the desk and asked, "Do you have a room for us? Just for tonight?"

"There are no rooms," she said regretfully, eyes rimmed with exhaustion. "The best I can offer you is space right here—a bench, a table, some chairs." She pointed to the small waiting area for passengers caught between trains. "I won't ask you to leave."

Denise looked at the dull dusty partitions of stained wood that set the area apart from the main concourse. They would provide no privacy.

"There's nothing else to do," André said reading the struggle in his wife's features.

Abruptly Denise sat down on a chair next to a bench thinking, *We've slept in the car. We've slept beside a canal. We've slept in confined quarters in hiding. We've even slept in a graveyard. We've survived so much for so long we can manage this minor inconvenience.*

"Come girls," she said quietly, motioning gently. "Lie down on this bench."

"But it's not comfortable," Christel complained, instantly popping back up again.

"It will just have to do," Denise said bunching her scarf into a small pillow for Christel.

Ida climbed up beside her sister. "I don't like it," she said unable to hide how upset she felt. "My scalp is still sticky."

"But we won't be able to wash it thoroughly until we're back in Brussels."

Noticing tossed-aside newspapers, Denise retrieved them and spread them out for Ida to lie down on them. Even black ink would be less messy than the worn dirty bench.

Upright on a chair at one end of the bench, across from the chair in which Denise slept with Cristian in her arms, André kept nodding off. He meant to stay awake since he suspected Paris was full of dark dangerous characters ready to take advantage of anyone. The black market continued to flourish and the train station was rife with dubious dealers of questionable merchandise.

"Cigarettes Monsieur?" an unshaven man asked softly, happening by in the middle of the night, his long topcoat covering, but not concealing bulges alongside his legs.

André jerked around. Now completely awake and unusually alert, he appraised the intentions of this disheveled disreputable-looking man who gave him a gray, dirty smile, his upper lip peeled back in a disturbing curl that revealed a missing front tooth. The man opened his coat slightly displaying cartons of American-made Lucky Strikes.

"Good price. Quick. Name your own."

"I don't smoke," André protested. It wasn't entirely true, but it had acquired real resonance during the years of deprivation in the Cévennes. André wasn't willing to renounce the soothing habit of smoking altogether, but this didn't seem the moment to start up again. Besides, he doubted he should part with any of the small sum of cash he had left. He and his family might need every franc to ensure their safe passage home.

"With an offer like this," the man said letting his coat flap close dramatically, "you should become a smoker now. Maybe you don't know how scarce these really are."

"Then how do you happen to have them?"

"American soldiers. They had what I wanted and I had what they wanted." The unpleasant man winked and gave André a truly disgusting leer. "Okay so you don't smoke," he said shifting gears. "Do you need stockings? Chocolate? Cognac?"

"Maybe no one's told you there's a war on," André spat.

"It's over or hadn't you heard?" The illicit salesman kicked up a quick soft shoe. "I don't know about you, but I plan on living again starting now." He gave his coat a twirl and turned around swiftly. His scarf went flying out behind him as he all but skipped away.

A pigeon fluttered against the dirty windows up high. It gave a glass pane a thump before flying off and finding a way out of the terminal—only to be replaced by another lost confused pigeon.

Somehow André found himself thinking of his last train ride from Brussels to Le Coq on that fateful May night four years before. How unnerving and unpleasant that had been. At least on this strange mirror journey he would have his family with him.

Denise startled awake stiffly, and quickly realized Cristian was sound asleep in her arms. She sat very still while trying to remember where she was. The train station! Of course! Dreary. Grim. But even at a very early hour on Monday morning, increasing human activity gave life to the sterile vaulted concourse.

André appeared and placed a hand over the hands clutching Cristian. "The train leaves in two hours," he said. "We need to line up early if we hope to find seats together."

Denise glanced up. "It will be so good to get home."

"To our *new* home," he reminded her, thinking of the apartment the university had arranged for them. "I'll wake the girls."

Cranky, Ida, and Christel sat up slowly and lazily dangled their legs over the side of the bench.

"I'm hungry," Cristian said before his mother realized he was awake.

"Soon," Denise said looking to André imploringly. "We'll eat soon."

"Let me see what I can find," André suggested, marching away.

Denise reached into their small sack of food. "Here little one," she said breaking off a piece of honey-covered cheese, which was all that was left, hoping Cristian would not notice or care.

Cristian didn't mind the unusual mix of flavors. That encouraged Christel to ask if she could have some cheese too. But Ida didn't want any. She had had enough of honey.

Looking about for André, Denise spotted men in baker's outfits making deliveries to small stands and cafés. Pastries? Morning breads? How comforting a simple slice would be.

Croissants! That's what Denise smelled! So different from the coarse brown butter-free bread the Severins had lived on for years.

Then Denise saw British and American soldiers walking about. Were they waiting to be sent to the front? Some looked so young it would have to be their first taste of combat.

"Look!" Ida cried out pointing.

André pushed through the growing mass of flesh. His expression was glum until he saw them. Then he smiled triumphantly and held up his precious catch: a baguette.

The train was late, but it was the only one going to Brussels that morning. There still was fighting in the east. Ida kept huffing because of the honey in her hair. Denise suggested that the children run around a little since André estimated that the three hundred kilometers to Brussels would take six hours or more.

It might only be half as long as the previous day's train trip. But that would still be an awfully long time for little ones to stay cooped up.

Chapter Twenty Two

BRUSSELS

October 9, 1944

A ndré, Denise, and Cristian were excited. Ida was agitated. Christel seemed nervous.

As the train rolled along André kept looking through the dirty windows, pointing out factories destroyed by the war, villages with whole sections turned to rubble, and roads and bridges blown up, not yet repaired. The Germans had done this in retreat trying to delay the destruction of Germany by destroying France first.

"That's mean," Christel said. "We're supposed to take care of each other aren't we? That's what I learned in the Cévennes."

Denise sighed. "I hope it's nothing like this in Brussels."

Approaching the border, André explained they would have to show their papers to government officials on both sides. But their papers were in order so there was no need to worry. "Just smile and be polite," he said. "Leave the talking to me and your Maman." The train stopped, but kept wheezing and shaking while they waited for French customs officials to make their way through the cars. "They must be glad to once again be guarding a frontier that only recently wasn't theirs to guard. See the pride they take in following form? That helps restore their confidence."

When the next officials came through the children were excited to see real Belgians who weren't family.

"So officious," Denise said watching how they handled others.

"They've gone back to their old habits," André agreed, "as though the Germans had never been here."

"Look how worn their uniforms are," Denise clucked.

"And the insignia are tarnished."

"Papers please." The words were polite, but the official sounded stern.

The children hugged their mother anxiously as André showed the man their passports and Cristian's birth certificate from Aubenas. The official studied Denise's British passport carefully, asked a couple of questions, then handed the passports back.

"This is from French authorities in the south," André said volunteering a document signed by the notary in Vialas and countersigned by the mayor, proclaiming the diamonds in the Severins' possession legitimately theirs. André was glad he had thought to get it.

"Why did you leave Belgium?" the customs man asked.

"To save my family."

The official shrugged. "I need to inspect. Let me see your bags." André got them down from the overhead rack. The man poked his hands in and felt around. "This paper says you have diamonds. Let me see them."

"Why?" André asked growing hot. "Our papers are in order."

"I still have to see them. Will I have to search your wife or perhaps put you and the children off the train right now?"

The children buried their faces in their mother's dress.

"That won't be necessary," André sighed reaching into his pocket and pulling out the small velvet pouch.

The official took the bag, opened it, poured out the diamonds, and counted. "The same number listed. Good."

He handed the document back to André, but put the pouch and diamonds into his pocket.

"What are you doing? Even you admit our papers say those diamonds are ours!"

"Procedure," the official said opening a little book with an official-looking stamp on the cover. "Don't worry. I'll give you a receipt." André tried to control himself while the customs officer wrote in pencil, pressing down hard to make a carbon copy. "If all really is in order you may claim your diamonds from the customs office in Brussels."

Red-faced, André accepted the receipt and suppressed his rage. Within minutes, the train crossed the border into Belgium.

The train finally pulled into the old gray south station, so familiar and yet so different than before. Gone were the lively colorful crowds. The flower shop stood empty. The candy stores appeared to have closed long before. Only the shoe repair shop remained open—busier than ever since nothing new had been obtainable for years and old cracked leather had to be sewn and patched time and again unless the entire population of Brussels were to go barefoot or wear the wooden clogs of the Cévennes.

Firmly leading his family into the early autumn evening, André recognized buildings, but not the spirit of the city. His children were energetic and enthusiastic, but André couldn't pay proper attention or answer their barrage of questions until he figured out how to get them to the small two-bedroom apartment near the university's chemistry department.

The few slow-moving taxis were loaded with passengers. After several frustrating minutes, André wondered about boarding a streetcar. He thought he knew the right one.

While they waited, Ida kept looking about trying to take in and remember everything. Christel stared fixedly at the olive-brown Army trucks rumbling and growling past, exhaust spewing from their tailpipes. She'd never seen so many different types of vehicle before.

The Army was completely in control. Every civilian vehicle automatically gave way before military transports.

Far down the street in a great space between two buildings, rubble was piled high where an apartment house had once stood. André was carried back to the initial bombing of Brussels: the building with its façade torn away by a bomb blast and the dead man he had seen perched in an easy chair...

Though most fighting had bypassed Brussels for the strategically vital port of Antwerp, V-1 and V-2 rockets occasionally dropped silently and exploded loudly on the capital. How safe would they truly be with a resentful Germany continuing to try to claw its way back from a steady series of defeats? Nazi rocket launchers in the Netherlands had been captured, but there were still firings from the other side of the Rhine.

Other would-be streetcar passengers gathered behind the Severins. André and Denise felt pangs of hurt, regret, and anger as they stared at the lovely trees lining the great boulevards. Bare of leaves, their desolation seemed to speak of present-day Brussels, as did the cracked and chipped shop and street signs, their colors showing up faded in the failing light of day.

A crowded streetcar finally arrived, and the Severins squeezed onto it with everyone else. As returning refugees they thought their emotional difference would announce their presence if their strange clothes didn't. But no one took the slightest notice of them, too deeply involved in their own concerns to perceive the cares of others.

Once André would have been affronted, had he, as a member of the Free University's faculty, not been accorded some small deference. But he expected none now. In the Brussels of October 1944, even a repatriated professor was of little moment and hardly any interest at all.

They found the address and climbed the single flight of stairs. Denise kept reminding herself that they really were back even if this place didn't feel like home in the slightest.

Taking a great collective breath, they opened the door and stepped into the small, cold, barely furnished space they would inhabit for some time to come. Christel looked up at her mother imploringly. Denise couldn't think of a thing to say.

"It's been a long time," André offered, forcing a smile for the children's sake. "But here we are."

Denise put Cristian on the floor, certain he could not get lost in a place so small. Then she took her husband's hand, realizing André could use some reassurance too. "It's lovely to be back," she said. "Different of course. But we're together, in Brussels!"

"I was never sure we'd see it again," André said hoarsely.

Denise kissed and released his hand then began to poke about the kitchen fitted out with a small stove and a few cabinets. The little dining table was covered with dust and crumbles of plaster shaken loose from the ceiling by the explosions of bombs and rockets and the firings of heavy guns. Tiny time-worn wooden chairs with rush seating surrounded the table. The one easy chair in the front room was more substantial, but its leather was cracked and its arms were burnished by countless resting elbows. A single hanging lamp cast a bare glare across the room and spilled into the back.

"I thought we would have more space in Brussels," Ida said petulantly, returning from the one bedroom. "This is smaller than where we lived before the war." She scrunched up her face. "It's even smaller than the space we shared with Mamé and Tata Irene."

"Ah, but we're lucky to have it," Denise said as soothingly as she could, considering her own uncertainty and distress.

"Will we have to stay here long?" Christel asked matching her older sister's petulant tone and scrunched-up face. "It's not very nice."

Slowly, deliberately, André said, "This is our home now. And look, we have our own bathroom. You never had *that* in the Cévennes."

At that moment, they realized Cristian had already found his way to the bathroom since he had somehow reached up and pulled on the chain to the tank. The gurgle and rush of water announced his whereabouts to them and the chain's function to him.

Laughing, Cristian returned with water splashed all over the front of his clothes. "That's fun!" he declared having never experienced an overhead water tank before.

"Well don't waste water," Denise said gently, struggling vainly to suppress her own laughter. "Only pull the chain after you use the toilet."

"You mean we don't have to carry our chamber pots outside anymore?" Cristian asked in stark amazement.

"No silly," Christel said showing off the superior knowledge she pretended to have. "You don't use a chamber pot when you live in a big city like Brussels."

Denise suddenly realized she must go out to obtain food for her family no matter how tired she was. She might have guessed food would still be scarce and sold mainly in the black market at prices she was in no position to pay. But with a little effort, she found and bought enough to make sure her family didn't starve that night and would have something nourishing with which to start the next day. Unfortunately, she couldn't find coffee. Oh, how she had hoped to surprise André with the real thing first thing in the morning.

Even as she trudged back up the stairs to their new home, hoping her family would be pleased with what she brought them, she knew what André would say when she apologized for her coffee failure: "Not to worry my dear. Someday…"

Cristian, who slept in a special blanket-bed his mother had made for him on the floor, woke up first and looked out the window. He marveled at the difference between Brussels and Le Salson. But his new home was gray and misty. Frightened he crawled into bed with his parents.

"I have to get ready," André said, opening his eyes, kissing his wife, and carrying his son with him into the front room. He told the boy to be quiet and not to wake his sisters.

"That's not fair," Cristian complained in a sibilant whisper. "I want to tickle them!"

The little boy put his hands over his eyes and watched between his fingers as André, for the first time in Cristian's life, put on a suit and a big dark tie.

"You look like a professor again," Denise said happily, entering the room. "Let me straighten your lapels."

"It's a funny feeling," André admitted, while Denise also straightened his tie.

"Maman," Christel called sitting up in bed and rubbing her eyes. "Can we go out to play?"

"Later," Denise said. "First we have to get your papy off to the university."

"What about breakfast?" Ida asked not even lifting her head. "I'm hungry Maman."

They all sat down to breakfast, which was meager. But the bread was very good.

"I plan to visit Tante Anna and her family on the way home," André said wiping his lips with a napkin and standing up. "To see how the family is."

"Oh, it will be so wonderful to be with them again," Denise declared. Then she asked Ida, "Do you remember your great Tante Anna and her daughters?"

"A little," Ida answered. "Wasn't she just like Bonnemama?"

"A little younger," Denise said smiling, "but very much like your Bonnemama Rose."

André gave each child two kisses on each cheek in turn.

"Not a third one?" Christel asked perplexed.

Denise explained the difference between the south of France and Belgium again.

"But for you," André said leaning down to Christel. "Well we haven't been away from the Lozère so long that we've forgotten already!"

Then he gave each of the children another set of kisses.

At least money wasn't going to be an issue. Upon André's return to the Free University he was surprised and relieved to discover that what would have been his pay for the last four years had been saved and then given to him in a great lump sum.

The university also gave him the day off to get his affairs in order. He immediately presented himself at the customs office. The agent on the train had been quite right: Jack Freedman's diamonds were returned speedily with sincere repeated apologies.

Then he took his money and diamonds to his old bank where the tellers he had known still continued to work. Fortunately, those tellers had been on duty when the Germans had arrived. They had made them open many safes for pilfering, including the safe with the Severins' valuables. The tellers had cleverly told the Germans that the Severins' sterling silver wasn't truly valuable—that it was only silver-plated, not worth the trouble of carting off.

André was less lucky in Le Coq where he went to see about the family's other belongings. Remarkably, Juli their maid still lived in the cottage. But André was incensed that she had married a Nazi. Juli professed happiness in seeing André again and learning that Denise and the children were well, but denied that anything in the villa belonged to the Severins.

André wasn't ready to deal with her then. But he warned he would return soon to reclaim everything he could identify—including the bed linen, which he would strip off in front of her face if he had to.

By the time he got back to Brussels, it was almost dinnertime, but he still had to go see the relatives.

André climbed the stairs to his new apartment with Anna Severin following slowly. She longed to see her family and was especially anxious to discover for herself how much Ida and Christel had grown. She had never even seen a picture of Cristian.

Finally, Anna stood at the threshold, tears filling her eyes and obscuring her vision. The children weren't there just then, but Denise took her by the hand and gave her a gentle insistent hug, and said, "It's good to see you again."

Looking up into Denise's sweet face Anna burst out crying and leaned her head against her chest. She felt distraught, bitter, angry, torn to pieces, and lost in her memories.

Right behind, supporting her, André took her shoulders in his hands. When Denise looked around at him, he appeared somber and pale. His gray-green eyes seemed sunken into his head.

"What is it?" Denise asked sensing something terribly wrong.

Anna could not let Denise go nor speak. The recitation had to be left to André.

"They took the girls," he said simply but thickly.

Denise gasped and clutched a hand to her chest. "The Germans?"

"In 1941. The Gestapo rounded up almost all the Jews. Male and female."

"They only left old women like me," Anna wailed. "Took all the rest!"

Denise gently led Anna to the easy chair. Anna tried to catch her breath, but that was hard to do between sobs.

Persistently questioned, Anna tried to clarify what had happened to the Jews in Belgium. When the Nazis had come to look for them initially they had been nearly impossible to identify since public records revealed nothing and few citizens of any persuasion wanted to assist the Nazis, particularly since so many still had terrible memories of the occupation during the Great War. Encouraged by the Belgian government-in-exile in London and by the Catholic Church at home, many did what they could to help the Jews. Christian families took in and hid Jewish children at great risk to their own safety. An active Resistance emerged with both Jewish and non-Jewish participants. The Committee for Jewish Defense published and distributed informational pamphlets and propaganda materials and did everything from sequestering Jews to fighting as partisans, forging identification papers and ration coupons, raising money and establishing escape routes and networks.

All together, these efforts had kept down the death toll, but they ultimately could not fend off the Nazis and their collaborators. Of the nearly hundred thousand Jews living in Belgium when the war began, some seventy thousand had been deported and more than twenty-five thousand had been killed outright.

"Some say government officials were complicit," André fretted. "I don't see how so many Belgian Jews could have been destroyed if that wasn't true."

Fewer than five thousand Jews continued to live in Belgium. Anna was one.

"But I don't understand why they came for the girls," Denise said miserably. "Were they members of the Resistance?"

"No!" Anna keened.

"None of Anna's family participated in Resistance activities," André said softly.

"There was no reason to take anyone!" Anna howled. "Except that they were Jews!"

Denise knelt beside Anna, took her hands, and asked, "Why didn't they take you?"

"They did!" Anna shrieked. "I was already on the truck with my poor girls. My babies!"

André explained, "The Queen of the Belgians intervened. She had little power, but demanded that women over sixty-five be spared. Anna was saved at the last minute."

"To outlive my children and all the others! To live out my years in endless tears!"

Denise turned green, released Anna, and begged of her husband, "All the others? What does she mean?"

André took a deep breath, got down onto his knees next to his wife, and took her hands. "Tante Anna says none of our family is left in Brussels or Antwerp. The only survivors besides her are those who like us left before the war."

"Rose," Anna muttered weeping. "When can I see my sister, Rose?"

Very quietly, André told Denise, "We've lost sixty-five members of our extended family, mostly in Auschwitz. When I think that some of them mocked us when they learned of our plans to leave Brussels..."

"Where are the children?" Anna asked hopefully, drying her eyes with the backs of her hands. "I so need to see them."

"Playing outside," Denise breathed huskily. "They'll be back soon I'm sure."

"They're all I have left," Anna said smiling as best she could.

"What about the university, your colleagues?" Denise finally thought to ask her husband.

André shuddered. "Alexandre Pinkus was arrested as a professor and a Jew. He also died in Auschwitz." André lowered his head. "At least the members of Le Cercle du Libre Examen, which I founded, formed the core of the Resistance. I can be proud of that." When he looked up again he said, "They've made me head of the chemistry department at the University. Temporarily."

In a hushed voice Denise said, "You hoped for that position someday."

"Not this way."

The door opened and the children rushed in. Christel and Cristian began playing with their delighted great aunt immediately. Ida drew her parents into the bedroom.

"We heard a rocket pass overhead. We were so scared! Then some American soldiers came by. One gave each of us a lemon."

"Aren't the Americans nice," Denise intoned pulling her daughter close and wrapping her in her arms. Then she looked at her husband imploringly, eyes full of fear.

"We survived," André told her compassionately, prayerfully. "With all we have survived."

The End

IN THIS HOSPITABLE LAND

Epilogue

André Severin returned in October of 1944 to resume teaching at the Free University of Brussels as a full professor and chair of the Chemistry Department in place of his mentor, Alexandre Pinkus, who had remained in Brussels and subsequently perished at Auschwitz. Alin Severin, returning to Brussels at the war's end in May 1945, resumed pursuit of his business as an expert philatelist. In 1950, the family immigrated to the United States, André as a Fulbright exchange professor at The University of Pennsylvania in Philadelphia, in large part because of the Quaker heritage of the city. When Denise died in 1952 André determined to remain permanently in the U.S., resigned his position at the Free University of Brussels, only the second tenured professor at the university to do so since its founding in 1834. He was acclaimed Professeur Honoraire of the University.

MAX MAUREL'S REMARKS FOR THE DEDICATION OF THE GRANITE BENCH IN VIALAS, FRANCE OCTOBER 2003

Vialas welcomes today the children of the family of André Severin who have come here from the United States with the desire to show their attachment to this community where they spent four years during World War II. They are offering to the community, in a gesture of gratefulness, a granite bench, which hopefully will decorate our public area.

In 1940, the Severin family escaped Belgium and arrived here in the south with the flow of the refugees. How and why did they come to here in Vialas? Probably they chose this region of the Cévennes for geographic and historic reasons, then also the minister of Millau where they were living advised them to settle in this area, since they lost all hope to go back to occupied Belgium.

This choice revealed itself to be a good one, and for the last 60 years, the children have kept these memories alive, and every time these children travel in Europe they try to come back to Vialas to see the region and many of the friends that they knew at the period of their lives.

Having arrived in 1940, the family settled in the farm "La Font" which they rented in Soleyrols. The family is a city family, ignoring the realities of the countryside and the rugged terrain. Yet, from the first year on the farm and with the help of their neighbors, they are self sufficient with their harvest of their farming, due to their willpower and courage, which attracted the respect and admiration of their neighbors. André said one time after he had worked at hard labor on the farm, "I never knew that my body had so many muscles and tonight the pains are teaching me this!"

In 1943, when the Milice made several attempts to arrest refugees and those families who were protecting them, the family gets dispersed, and André moves to be close to the Maquis while other members of the family are placed into several families who live in the community of Saint Frezal.

Yet for them, the memories of those years remain with them alive, Vialas where they left one of their family in the cemetery, where one of their children was born, where their children went to school, where friendships were made and where the names of the different farms, households, roads, the paths still remain familiar...

In this region of the Cévennes, which has seen so many refugees during those dark years, there are very few examples such as this family has done, by coming from so far and from all over the world to share with us, thus the work and the philosophy of the Cévenoles.

I did know well André and Denise his spouse. Allow me to say that their relationship with those who knew them...(allow me to mention some of their names like the Brignand, Guibal, Benoit, Velay, Bonijols, Le Pasteur Burnand...) it was really a relationship of the spirit acting in a symbiotic manner with the others by their willpower, their energy, and their hope, surmounting any difficulties of daily life, and this same spirit shines in their children.

FIN

ADDITIONAL SOURCES AND ACKNOWLEDGMENTS

Quand le Gard Résistait
1940-1944

Pierre Mazier
Aimé Vielzeuf
LACOUR/COLPORTEUR

Cévennes
Terre de Refuge 1940-1944

Philippe Joutard
Jacques Ponjol
Patrick Cabanel
Presses Du Languedoc/Club Cevenol

Vichy France
Old Guard and New Order 1940-1944

Robert O. Paxton
Columbia University Press

Pétain

Nicholas Atkin
Longman

Made in the USA
Charleston, SC
25 March 2012